Powhatan:

The Story of a People

by

Saxon Wrenn

PublishAmerica
Baltimore

© 2006 by Saxon Wrenn.
All rights reserved. No part of this book may be reproduced, stored in a retrieval system or transmitted in any form or by any means without the prior written permission of the publishers, except by a reviewer who may quote brief passages in a review to be printed in a newspaper, magazine or journal.

First printing

This is a work of fiction set in a background of history. Public personages both living and dead may appear in the story under their right names. Scenes and dialogue involving them with fictitious characters are of course invented. Any other usage of real people's names is coincidental. Any resemblance of the imaginary characters to actual persons, living or dead, is entirely coincidental.

At the specific preference of the author, PublishAmerica allowed this work to remain exactly as the author intended, verbatim, without editorial input.

ISBN: 1-4241-4687-9
PUBLISHED BY PUBLISHAMERICA, LLLP
www.publishamerica.com
Baltimore

Printed in the United States of America

You are not wrong, who deem
That my days have been a dream;
Yet if hope has flown away
In a night, or in a day,
In a vision, or in none,
Is it therefore the less gone?
All that we see or seem
Is but a dream within a dream.

Edgar Allen Poe

Chapter 1

The worlds of past centuries are still with us. What was can be revisited through the journey of a single dream. Let go of your present surroundings. Leave your reality. Draw back the veil that is today and explore the past that lies underneath.

Enter the world of Pamasawu. It is immense, and full of unknowns. Few have discovered even a portion of its dominion. Only the mystics have explored its outer reaches through travels taken by their souls.

These mystics have learned that Pamasawu has two sides. On the one is an immeasurable land mass populated by creatures, plants, and those beings that are neither. On the other side is endless water where a variety of creatures live within its depths, but where nothing lives above. Look to where the two sides meet. The land extends like fingers into the water. Here is where creatures from the great land and the great water intermix.

In the bay swim the *patawok*. They are large air-breathing animals that have taken the shape of fish. Their dark brown bodies glisten as they pierce the boundary between air and water. Among the clouds are *koyakwus*. These balky white birds have grey wings and even greyer expressions upon their faces. They are a breed from the Before Time.

Nearing the beaches are the *tukupewuk*, with wings of solid flesh. Also from the Before Time, they soar through the currents as gracefully as their old friends glide upon the winds. Both begin their lives on the land where neither can move with any confidence.

There are five great rivers that flow into the bay. Migrating birds of various shapes and colors come to the marshes during their eternal pursuit of warm weather. Fish of just as many shapes and colors have claimed these waters as their home.

There are also life forms whose existence are predominantly on the land. They are located farther up the rivers. Follow the little brook that winds through the trees. Look closely for movement in the undergrowth. A pair of two-legged creatures are actively at play. With unclothed bodies and loose, shoulder-length hair cut short at the bangs, the brothers experience their world completely unhindered. They have found an *aposum*. As little boys do, they gleefully torment the furry white form. With sticks they prod the poor thing and roll it about. They search for the pocket at her stomach where her young would mature in warm safety. It is empty now. They stare at her conical face, waiting for the slightest movement of her eyelids. There is no hint of life what so ever.

Movement near the water diverts the attention of the older brother. Not to be left out of anything, the younger promptly abandons his play and follows. The boys do not venture too close to this creature. They recognize it to be an *awakun*. This ring-tailed beast is much more appealing to the eye. But the playful vagabond can turn vicious when conditions are appropriate. It is busy preparing a fish just plucked from the river. They quietly observe the dark form as it meticulously drenches the catch, pressing the body upon the stones until it is soft enough for eating. The process is much too long for the brothers. The elder nudges. It is time to go. They turn back to the trail home to find that the *aposum* is no longer there. The brothers smile at each other. She has fooled them both.

Twilight spreads along the trail. The two boys skip through the trees. Follow them as they assail the steep hill, making their way to the little village in the clearing that overlooks the great river called, Powhatan. The sky fills with the pink and violet hues of evening. The setting sun is deep saffron, as is the great fire in the community.

The town is named for the river. It is a collection of twenty round-roofed structures that are slender and long in shape—like cocoons in appearance. In some ways, that is their purpose. The frames of green saplings are covered with bark and mats woven from river reeds. A circular wall of posts, placed closely together in the ground, protects the two hundred inhabitants from outside dangers. Tonight, the population is twice that number with visiting dignitaries from neighboring tribes.

Men assemble near the dancing ground that surrounds the fire. Their drum is a wooden bowl, hollowed out from the base of an *asunomink* tree. It is filled with just the right amount of water to produce the correct swollen twang when the cover is struck. An *asiminz* is attached to each corner of the stretched skin covering so that the knot will hold firm at the bottom of the bowl.

The musicians are eight in number, but one in purpose. High-pitched wails tax the vocal cords to the point of collapse. Arm muscles swell with the strain of repeated motion. Sweat rolls as internal energy burns. And still, they play on in exact unison. Each accepts the challenge to quicken the very heart of the Mother.

Females align the dancing circle. They face the central fire in a posture of statuesque refinement. Long hair of silken black hang like mantles over bare skin. The feminine roundness of each head is finely decorated with bone pins and shell beads in strings of purple and of white. One by one, they begin. Knees bend just enough to allow the carriage to sway up and down in harmony. It is a liquid motion, portraying deity-like mannerism. Anklets of soft *matasun* cones electrify the air with a raspy jingle as the dancers progress inward and around to the tune of universal time.

The noise of celebration drifts through the river valley. A new era is about to begin with the emergence of a new leader. He is inside the great ceremonial hall preparing for his transformation into a half-god.

Darkness saturates the interior. The glow of the fire pit reveals three forms in this chamber. One man meditates before the embers as two others prepare him. He is entranced by the flame that is Life; that which is a ray from the sun. The seers could better explain this for they exist between the two worlds. They cover half their bodies with red *pokun*, from bloodroot, to represent the strength of life here in Pamasawu. The other half is smeared with black soot. This is the color that the spirit takes when in the other world. One murmurs an ancient prayer. His sunken eyes exemplifies the long life that he has seen, while his straightness of posture foretells the long life he is yet to experience. The attendants apply the yellow *pokun* of goldenseal along his solid shoulders. This is the color of the sun's power at dawn when life is new.

Gentle light escapes from the embers to rest upon the shaven heads of the two seers. Both have a bristled crest of hair along the front of their foreheads, stiffened with a red paste. Their short cloaks are the uniform of their position. Each garment consists of a number of tightly-braided *wikutis* pelts. Always, they tie one end at the right shoulder and allow the loose garment to hang down to the middle of the thighs.

One seer sprinkles the red down of an *ashowut* bird onto the man's frame where it clings to his painted skin. The *matahay* he wears is like an apron that covers the front and sides of his pelvis. The edges are decorated with fringe along the bottom and along the top over-flap that covers his leather belt.

The attendants adorn him with strings of *matasun* beads. More of this precious metal dangle in ringlets from his ears. His head is shaven on the right side. On the left hangs his long mane. A strand of *tsekoma* beads holds the hair knot in place just above the shoulder. Their hue is a light purple. They are almost translucent against his thick, black locks. The attendants stiffen his scalp comb all along the center of the head with red paste.

His father left behind great wealth. Tonight, the son will give all these riches to the visiting tribes in hopes of becoming a greater authority in the region. He is a striking form, with a broad face that projects an ambitious spirit and a daring disposition. He is the eldest of four brothers and two sisters. Their father was a victim of the drought that continues to plague the area. All living things upon the land are suffering from lack of water. But Okius continues to hold back the rains.

The new leader faces a great challenge. But his siblings know that he lives to the fullest in the face of calamity. They know the vigilance that empowers his thoughts. They know him. Look into his dark eyes. Discover the making of his persona. Then, you too may better predict who he shall become.

Find the first memory. People are moving about in the morning mist. A *huskina* is in progress. It is a great test of human endurance that lasts one rotation of the Moon. Notice how the community dances around the fire. All are in attendance. All are in their finest. They dance four abreast in two rings. The inner ring moves in one direction. The outer one takes the opposing course. The dance is solemn. Its purpose is to stop the heart beat of Time. All morning long, five seers police the dancers from the center to make sure that none lose step. At one point, the five break into mournful song and rush out. They stop at a sapling. With bare hands, they rip the little tree apart. A young life is thus sacrificed.

In the center of town, twelve youths are being prepared by the healers. Their bodies have been covered with white clay and their feet and hands are bound. All were selected due to their mental and physical fitness. Our subject is among them. His mother grieves at the edge of the woods, for she knows she is loosing her child.

The sun reaches the top of the sky. The dancing stops and the youths are taken to an old tree where their male parents guard over them. The rest of the men form a gauntlet that stretches over fifty paces. Six young men, covered in black, come to the tree. One by one, they carry the youths through the lane while the others flog them with bound reeds. The mothers cry from afar as they witness their children's symbolic flight into the world of the spirits.

His turn approaches. He realizes the bare feet clinching the ground, the scent of the forest, the sting of the reeds, the taste of sweat and clay upon his lips, the sound of heavy breathing from the one who carries him.

The boy is taken into the wilderness. They stop at a shallow dell. His conveyor dumps him onto the pile of bodies. Here, he will lie motionless during the long night.

When daylight finally returns, the twelve are moved to a cage. It is made of thin poles buried into the ground in a circular pattern and tied together at the top. Nimble branches are interwoven horizontally between these vertical poles. The seers feed their brood *wisokan*; a poison made from the roots of milkweed. This will be their primary food for the duration of the test.

The twelve continue their hallucinogenic coma. Each day, the dosage increases. The past becomes easier to forget. The boy no longer understands time. He no longer sees the solid world of reality. He does not hear life's sweet songs. He can no longer smell his surroundings or feel the air upon his skin. He knows only the flavor of *wisokan*.

One night, the boy perceives a visitor. Okius materializes from the evening fire and approaches the cage. Observance is his expression. The celestial hunter looks for the weakest in the group. In turn, the drowsy boy studies the apparition. The face is the color of *matasun*, but the chest and thighs are white. Long, midnight hair hangs down the left side of the black body to brush the ground. The eyes, the eyes contain the light of all the stars in the sky.

The specter slips into the cage. It leans over the chosen one and begins to suckle her left breast. Once the shell is empty, Okius reenters the fire and the seer on the night watch realizes his duty. The victim is thus brought out and handed over to the flames.

The dosage is lessened each day. The remaining eleven return to reality. Ten of them successfully forget their former lives. The one who failed will have to go through it again next year. The successful ones return to their town as new children. They no longer recognize their parents. The seers are now their true guardians. During the next eight months, the students will relearn everything. They will master the tools of language and religion. They will master the science of leadership and the art of warfare. Our subject will earn the stewardship of his mother's tribe.

Tonight, his reign expands beyond the walls of Powhatan. Tonight, the six tribes that were his father's responsibility become his own. He accepts the inheritance and the new name, Wahunsenakok. The gathering outside begins a song to honor their new leader. Expectation is in the collective voice. It is the sound of yearning to move beyond current discomforts. Anxiety is also in the collective mind. New beginnings can cause so much disruption in a life. It can bring about so much drudgery that would not be necessary if circumstances could simply remain constant and predictable. It is this unpredictability that can both frighten and encourage. It is the tension brought about when the spirit is willing to venture, but the body is not.

The seers finish their work. Wahunsenakok is ready.

CHAPTER 2

Katapewuk has arrived! It is first of the five seasons; a time when the land restores the vigor of life. Only one tree is in bloom thus far. Its flower clusters permeate the grey wilderness with refreshing dabs of white. This is Nature's signal that the *monawateyug* are beginning their pilgrimage inland to spawn.

Swift winds play among the trees. Budding branches dance with excited gyrations. Unpredictability is everywhere. Any occurrence that takes place in this season can set the course of an entire year. One such incident is about to begin. There, at the edge of the field. Look closely. Can you see? The dark woods are filled with faces. Each is covered with streaks, lines, or blotches of black soot, white clay, or red *pokun* to enhance the strong features or exaggerate the ugliness of the human male. There are six hundred of them. Malice is their shared expression.

All eyes are fixed toward the western end of the field. All ears listen for movement in the wilderness beyond. They wait in silence, as hunters do. But this is not a hunting party. Their purpose is to murder.

Wahunsenakok has brought them here. He stands motionless. A few tresses on his head reach out to touch fragments of wind that scatter through the forest. A human hand embellishes his hair knot. In his own hand is a bow as long as he is tall. He straightens his archer's guard of *wushakwun* hide that is wrapped around the left forearm. More of the same shields each leg from the prickly underbrush. A thick *mokasin* provides each foot with protection from the rugged ground. His breechcloth is a *nantam* pelt. A large *tsekoma* pearl is fixed into each eye socket while shell beads embroider the furry leg endings and tail.

Wahunsenakok is the example of his men. His dress is their dress. His thoughts are what each man emulates. And his intentions to make war with his enemy are their determination. It is a cultural hatred that has been nursed for generations.

The hated are called, Monakan. They speak an entirely different language. Compared to the rhythmic tone of Powhatan speech, it is harsh and choppy. These people are contradiction embodied. Monakan towns are much larger than any in Tsenakomako. And yet, the inhabitants will disperse more freely along smaller rivers during the leaner period of the year. Their cultivated fields are enormous. And still, they depend more on the gathering of meat than the harvest of food from the soil.

All these things explain how these people are. It is not who they were when they lived far to the west of the Blue Mountains. Long ago, their ancestors where part of a great civilization that lived along a river once called, Aligewi. They built great cities and surrounded them with walls of earth. They created small mountains from the flat land upon which to construct lavish temples and regal houses. Crops produced far more then needed. Back then, commerce was their lifestyle, and culture was their primary concern.

All of this came to an end. It occurred a thousand years earlier when the sky grew dark and the air became cold. Red rain poured down from clouds of ash. Night controlled time. A dim sun visited for only a moment each day. Such days lasted one entire year—and half of another. It rendered the land barren. The result was a general collapse of consumption at every level and of every form imaginable.

After long debates, the leaders of Aligewi admitted that there were too many living in one location. Some had to leave and find a fertile home elsewhere. People were chosen by lottery to journey eastward. The wanderers eventually came upon the great woodlands east of the Blue Mountains and created a new town. It still lies at the confluence of the Rasawik and Powhatan rivers. A pyramidal pile of stones is there as a monument to these ancestors whose bones rest in burial mounds that clutter the region. New tribes detached from the original band and spread throughout the vast woodlands to claim the entire piedmont. Eventually, they became the primary threat to Powhatan existence.

Those who remained along the Aligewi River evolved into a more simplistic society. They were slowly driven south by the Masawomik to the end of the mountain range. That is where their descendents now live. The Masawomik renamed the river, Ohio, and claim it their own to this day.

At least once a year, the Monakan raid the lands to the east. Their purpose is more for sport then for any need of spoils. Admittedly, the Monakan are

POWHATAN:
THE STORY OF A PEOPLE

better fighters. They always join together, while those in Tsenakomako are fiercely independent minded. Seldom are the Powhatan united for anything. The price is isolation and vulnerability.

Every year, as the *monawateyug* move west, the Monakan gather in their most eastern town of Machimko. The stone *nesakan* where laid across the river before memory. They have become a permanent feature of the river. Machimko lies a little over a day above the town of Powhatan. This season, the Monakan have secretly assembled in mass at Machimko. The spies of Wahunsenakok are everywhere. They discovered the meaning of this gathering before it had even begun.

The Monakan plan to make a great incursion eastward to embarrass the new leader of the joined Powhatan tribes. But the young chieftain knows old tricks. He has brought the fight westward in hopes of shaping his little nation into a larger, stronger league.

Along with warriors from the six tribes are twenty Weyanok mercenaries, paid with small treasures of *matasun*. One morning, the twenty adventurers filled their great war *akwintan* and set off from the north bank of the Powhatan river. Such watercrafts are merely tree trunks, without heartwood. But they are swift and maneuverable on any river.

They met up with their neighbors from the Apamatuk River that flows into the Powhatan. Five vehicles pushed up the curling water route, coming to the little town of Awohatek. This tribe provided willing fighters to fill two more *akwintan*. By the next morning, the flotilla was on its way again.

Wet paddles flashed in unison, sliding back into the liquid to push the vessels against the current. Stomachs tightened and shoulder blades stiffened from the labor. All were together in their work. All were a part of a greater purpose. Some broke out in timed melodies to keep in step. Others gave hardy shouts of exuberance. Still others withdrew into themselves to become the movement. By afternoon, they landed near the great hill on which Powhatan Town stands.

A little to the north, and well east of here is where the rivers of Yugtamund and Matapaniyund join to form the broad Pamunkey. It is also the location where the great Pamunkey tribe welcomed their neighbors from the two tributaries. After they were ferried across to the south bank, the column of four hundred men moved along the overland trail to Powhatan Town. Swift steps moved this procession. Breaths grew heavy. Legs became numb. Their voices where much more subdued. This was a collection of individuals. And yet, participants of this group developed a quiet mood of allegiance to one another.

The residents of Powhatan welcomed all their guests. Celebrations full of stimulation and camaraderie ran into the evening. Women provided food and inspiration to their protectors. They broke out in wonderful song, so that their sweet voices would please the spirits. The vitality of this night was enormous. But as a flame will slowly dissipate, so did the revelry. All eventually succumbed to a deep sleep.

The flame sparked again with the coming of the morning sun. Wahunsenakok rekindled their passions with this oration:

"Beyond the mountains, far to the west, is Popogusu. It is the place for the damned! We now go west and meet those who came across the mountains to plague our lives. I look around and I no longer see the faces of many I once knew. They have gone with my father to Monshakwatu to live their spirit lives in bliss. But how can we live happily when those people are among us? They have caused us much suffering. Must we allow them to go unpunished?

"*Taws! Taws!* Let us unite as one. Let us go and meet our *maskapow*. Together, we can drive them back to where they belong. Let us quench Okius with blood so that he might end the drought. It is a new year! Let it not be another of hunger and sickness and dread."

A great thunder of human cries echoed in the river valley. Wahunsenakok motioned to the temple, "Bring out Okius! He will witness our fight."

Four seers appeared from the temple with an idol upon their limber. The crowd gathered around the image. All tried to make eye contact so that they could reach the divine. Impassioned words issued from quivering mouths. Pleas for success and requests for glory flooded the air. Warriors reached out for blessing as the idol wound through the crowd. Wahunsenakok led his force to the entrance of the walled village. "Tonight, we will sleep in the wilderness with Okius, for we are not afraid. Tomorrow, we will die for his pleasure. Let us stand firm against those cursed people and drive them back across the mountains!"

They have waited the better part of the morning. Wahunsenakok sent his youngest brother, Opechankano, with a small company to give advance warning. Nothing has been heard from them.

The sounds of the forest are all around. Insects compete with the birds, but the wind seems to have the most noticeable voice today. The sun has broken free from the grasp of the eastern trees. Echoes come from the wilderness beyond. The distant sound of panting men keeps in rhythm with their heavy steps. Opechankano and his group emerge from the woods on the other side of the field.

They come closer toward their waiting friends. Blank faces brighten. Their collective nod signals that the *maskapow* is on the move.

They wait. They listen. A soft, low noise is in the woods. Hearts beat wildly, almost breaking free from their chests. Breathing becomes difficult. For the first time, these young men are going to look right into the eyes of their nightmares.

Shadows move among the trees. Ghostly forms slowly solidify as they near the edge of the field. Sunlight touches flesh. They come into the open ground. Their bodies are covered in black. Their hair is fixed with feathers from various birds of prey. They are ready for a fight. They are true warriors.

The mass grows in the clearing. Wahunsenakok looks about his group. Does he have enough? Are they going to run from this reality now that it is upon them? They have journeyed far from home. If his men are not up to the fight, few will be left to agonize over their end. He examines each expression. That look is just not there. That look of a killer is just not there. All that he sees is a silent, confused panic.

The idol catches his eye. He meditates on the grim expression that is carved into the wooden head. This is only a material thing; a solid form of that which is formless. The torso is held upright with the aid of shaped branches. Each appendage of *wushakwun* skin is stuffed with moss. All proportions and dimensions are modeled from the human form and painted black with white chest and thighs. A large, round *matasun* plate, with a hole in its center, hangs against the chest. Separately, the construction is meaningless. And separately is how these materials are stored. But when the parts are assembled, it creates a solid vessel for all that is Okius.

The young leader softly whispers, "You are among us. Long ago, you blessed me and let me keep my life. That boon will protect me now."

With a broadening smile, the one who has brought these men to this field stands up and walks into the clearing.

The sun feels good upon his skin. He spreads his arms to embrace the nourishment of the light. A cry comes from the Monakan hoard. The line widens in front of the lone man. The second most dreadful thing humans can do to each other is about to happen.

Wahunsenakok yells out, "Dirt diggers, hear my words! We have tolerated you long enough! The tribes of Tsenakomako will no longer put up with you! We are many, and shall grow! Today we are men! Kill us, and we shall become legends! Feel our power! Feel our power!"

Men strut into the field. Eyes glaze over with inspiration. Hearts pound with unstoppable momentum. The ranks are buzzing.

The Monakan flock tightly together at the opposite end. They see six separate rows before them. Each line is one hundred men long. Small gaps are between them. The Powhatan lines move closer until they are only two hundred strides away. The Monakan caw back with scorn. Brave men on both sides begin to boast and taunt. Individual heroes try to be noticed above the crowds. This battle of high words continue as both sides work up their courage and delay the inevitable for just a little longer.

Wahunsenakok embraces the moment. With closed eyes and open lips, he draws back his bow. The arrow takes flight. All follow his example. A swarm of projectiles prick the ranks of the stunned Monakan. The battle begins before reality has even a chance to join.

Action and reaction takes control of minds. One line after the other rushes forward to let loose their arrows, then falls back to reload.

Projectiles disappear in the sunlight, then reappear among the Monakan defenders. The Powhatan lines switch positions at a constant pace as one cloud after another comes across the field. The western people sing out, "The Powhatan are not fighting fairly! These cowards are not allowing us to fight back! We can not stand against this. They are getting closer. Return to the trees. Find safety among the trees!"

The defenders flee into the shadows of the forest. The Powhatan ranks quicken their advance. Encouragement moves them only forward. The six lines join into one as they surge toward the woods. A few Monakan projectiles peck at the line, bringing down a few unfortunates. The middle of the line begins to crawl low on the ground as the two ends make their way into the woods.

The Monakan try to move deeper into the forest, only to find the enemy on three sides. The warriors of Tsenakomako pass by their wounded foe near the tree line. With nervous excitement, one wields his *monahak* in a taunting fashion before striking a deathblow to the head of his dejected victim.

"They are only mortals!" he cries out.

The Monakan try to get around one end of the opposing line, but the Powhatan are too spread out among the trees and too intoxicated from the nectar of Triumph.

POWHATAN:
THE STORY OF A PEOPLE

"Let us not loose the fourth side to them," the defenders sing out to one another, "If their ends join, we will be surrounded!"

Slowly, the Monakan force their way through the area of escape and head back to the safety of their town. The Powhatan roar with enthusiasm. They actually have their *maskapow* on the run.

The combatants continue toward Machimko, leaving the field in silence. The seers bring the idol to the middle of the clearing so that Okius can consume the expelled souls. Healers fan out, searching for those in need. One healer finds a man with an arrow in his upper leg. The stone point is just visible in the skin. "There is only one thing to do, my boy."

The patient nods understandingly. The healer slowly pushes the point through. He snaps off the back end of the rod and pulls the point until the rest is completely out. With a few words of remedy, he sticks the point in a fresh fire to heat the stone. One moment for the sake of hesitation is observed. The patient grimaces as the hot stone melts the flesh shut. The healer finishes the last verse. To help ease the pain, he chews on some *wisokan* and spits the juice onto the wound.

Once the victory song is complete, the seers go forth to bless their fallen heroes and mutilate the bodies of their foe.

One comes across a soul barely clinging to its body. The seer takes out a scalping reed from his bag. He places the shoulders of the victim against his knees and bends back the head. The scalp lock is finely decorated with three feathers bound to a lock of hair by a strand of shell beads and colored stones that are shaped into distinct animal forms.

"You will be remembered," the old man murmurs as he places the sharp edge of his reed at the top of the forehead. Carefully, he makes an incision. The life-liquid wells in the gash as a slight vapor escapes from the opening. With a few verses in the language of the ancients, the seer peels the skin back until he can get two fingers firmly underneath. One steady breath, one quick pull, and the scalp cleanly rips off.

The combatants reach Machimko. The invaders gather along the high bluffs that overlook the town across the river. Buildings are scattered far and wide in the floodplain that stretches a comfortable distance along the south bank. The defenders line the bank. The invaders search for an easy descent, but they find none among the steep cliffs. The floodplain along the north bank is much more narrow and thick with swamp. One would surely be trapped.

Powhatan archers begin an informal contest. Here and there, an arrow is sent from the bluffs. Of these, one or two make it to the other side of the river. Shouts are exchanged. They taunt. They threaten. They celebrate. And the Monakan can do nothing about it.

The tree tops in the west have taken hold of the sun. A group sneaks down to the *nesakan* that stretches across the river. They manage to steal away a fish or two. They pack each fish in mud and place it upon an open fire where the Monakan can see them. As the mud hardens into a dry shell of dirt, it is taken out of the fire and cracked open. The revelers feast and celebrate the moment. It is a moment of which their people could only dream. They could never expect it would actually come.

Wahunsenakok sits along the bluff in counsel with his brother. "I want to see that cursed town, and all within it, smolder." A silence comes over him. His focus is distracted by the darkening sky. One star, then another, emerges from the depths of dusk. Thoughts change. "But, is that one task too many? Should I test our fortune with one more risk?"

Opechankano bows in thought. "You know, brother, I will do anything you say. If you have a plan, we will all follow."

"No," the elder brother admits. "What plan could I have? You have proven yourselves enough. I will not risk the gains of this day any further."

The brothers concentrate on the river's constant flow. Its brown shadows warm them. The green highlights of the soft, rippling liquid calms their nerves.

"Patience...yes. Patience is stronger then Desire." Wahunsenakok rises. "The moment is not right. I can wait for that moment. We are far from home and the night will bring danger to us if we stay. Take your group back now for the dead and wounded. I will gather the rest and be close behind you."

Slowly, the invaders disappear into the dark wilderness. They eventually distance themselves from Machimko. Upon returning to the battleground, their leader assembles his men for a quick rest.

A silhouette sings out in the cool night air, "We have fought bravely! We have hurt our *maskapow*. We have surprised and frightened them. We made them hide like children! You will talk of this day for years. Our people will celebrate it forever! Now we are safe. But we must continue our journey home. The dirt diggers will expect us to sleep tonight. They will look for us with the sun. We can not stay here. We shall sleep good tomorrow night in Powhatan."

Chapter 3

On the Lower Peninsula, atop a prominent hill that overlooks the wide Pamunkey River, is the town of Chiskiyak. Distinguished figures have gathered in the council house for an afternoon of deliberation.

Pakikino stands to brief his audience, "I have seen many worlds during the past nine years. Now, I have finally returned."

The crowd warmly acknowledges him. He begins his story, "It was during the second season of *Kohatayo*. I was only seventeen then. My father and I had traveled to the end of the peninsula to visit our neighbors, the Kekotan. We were exchanging gifts when someone entered the town with word of a sighting upon the water.

"There were two *musawusuk*. One had come close to shore. A crowd had already gathered upon the beach. We'd only had such sightings a few times before…and those were years between each other. This time, the strangers had come right up to us, asking to trade.

"My father and I joined those rowing out. We came along side and climbed to the roof of the floating house. Men with beards greeted us. Some wore clothes of *osawas* that shined like water in the sun. They had wonderful tools and unique jewelry. They were willing to trade all of that for our simple supplies of food and fur pelts. We were robbing them blind!

"Their leader was called, Pedro Menendez de Aviles. He liked me and gestured that I should go to his land. That's right. These people do not live on their *musawusuk* all their lives. And the great water to the east is not boundless. I can tell you confidently that there is another world behind the horizon."

The crowd is aghast. Some wish not to listen to such mysteries. But most know a good story. They urge Pakikino to continue.

"This man promised me wealth in knowledge and material. My heart felt good. Since I had several brothers, my father agreed to leave me in their care. The Kekotan also provided one of their own. The two of us set off on an adventure to rival any ever imagined.

"The strangers dropped the cloth mats from their tree limbs and we moved by the power of the winds. We soon joined the other *musawusuk* in the bay. Together, we journeyed out to where none of us have ever been. It was like flying atop a liquid sky. We broke from the cruel waters near the last remaining islands and surrounded ourselves with the Great Blue.

"For two moons, the horizon encircled us. There was nothing but sky and water all around. But we were always moving. The winds pushed us ever forward. These people know how to keep busy so that madness does not take them during such long journeys. I also kept busy by learning their language and customs. They were astonished on how quickly I could learn.

"Their world comprises of two enormous islands. The size of each is larger then all of Pamasawu! Their territory is on the end of a great peninsula on the largest island. At its tip is a city called, Cadiz. Like Kekotan, this city has been there since the beginning of time. It sits along a narrow island that forms a bay, just like the Eastern Peninsula forms our own. And like Kekotan, this city is the most important coastal settlement in their domain. Everywhere are perfect blocks of stone in which they live. The walls reflect every variation of white. A large stone wall encircles everything.

"We journeyed to another city called, Sevilla. It stretches beyond the length of sight along the eastern bank of a river they call, Guadalquivir. The buildings are tall and close together and teeming with people and strange animals that they control. It was the most magnificent dream I have ever had. All the colors, all the materials and shapes created by the hands of these people.

"The entrance of this walled city is an impressive structure in itself. They call it, Torre del Oro. It is where they store a yellow metal that is as precious to them as our *matasun* is to us. I also saw a building where they prepare their *upook*. It is much sweeter than ours. There is also an impressive temple there. It was built on the same sight of former temples. The present one is a combination of new and old, with a decorative tower that is like no other. They built this temple with framework as we build our structures. But their stone frames are both inside and outside to support the heavy walls and hold up the extraordinarily high ceiling, which is built separately.

POWHATAN:
THE STORY OF A PEOPLE

"Sevilla became my new home. They put me with a group of seers to learn from them. The ruler of their land wanted to meet me. He is known as, Phillip. His father had taught him the best ways to govern people. He was a man of physical and mental health. He had a strong face, thick hair that he threw back, a long nose, tight lips that he knew how to control, and a beard that framed his strong jaw. I was greatly impressed by him. He was equally impressed with me.

"They call our land, Bai de Santa Maria. I told them that we know it simply as, *Ahakan*. They asked me about a river that could take them to the other side of the Blue Mountains. I told them the Powhatan is the longest, but the Patawomik River is the one that flows from a northwesterly direction...and is the quickest way through.

"I learned their religion thoroughly. Their *manitow* are first common people who usually die horribly. Their most important *manitow* is called, Jesucristo. His mother was a human who mated with the supreme being. Their son suffered a torturous death at an early age. Until then, he walked among humans as one of their finest speakers of sacred knowledge.

"I first returned from their world to the land of the Mesheeka, which is far south of here. They were once the most powerful nation in either world. Their primary city was a place on an island in the middle of a lake. But they had a prophecy that their *manitow* would come and conquer them. That *manitow* turned out to be Jesucristo.

"The old city was torn down and the lake was filled with dirt. And then, a new city was built on top of it all. And it was renamed, Ciudad de Mexico. People there are now full servants to Jesucristo. He holds great power and his followers surrender fully to him. Because of it, they are the richest, most powerful people on both sides of the Great Blue.

"While there, we became very ill. None of their healers could help my companion. But I was strong. I soon recovered. I decided it was the Mother, Maria, who had given me the disease. By giving myself to her, I recovered. They performed a ritual, called bautismo, on me. With that, I was renamed, Don Luis.

"My popularity grew. They entrusted me with guiding them back here. Unfortunately, we couldn't find the bay. They travel so far from the coast because the waters are so dangerous closer in. It is so difficult to discern a break in the land from so far off. We turned around but got caught in a storm and were forced back into the Great Blue. My return was not yet to be."

The ending of this story is thus delayed right at the point when it seemed obtainable. The crowd's interest is firmly in the palm of this fine story teller. Pakikino continues the next episode, "We returned to their world. They placed me with another group of seers who cared for me for three years. I learned more of their religion and how to communicate on leaves. It is a fascinating way to keep thoughts forever without having to commit them to memory. True, our seers bite symbols into bark to remember ideas and thoughts. But these people use a special paint to make symbols for each sound of their speech and can break down an entire thought word by word.

"After learning all their knowledge, I was granted another chance to return home. This time, the journey was successful. We landed on one island, and then another. And then we found the entrance to the bay. We passed Kekotan and entered the Powhatan River. Memories rained heavily upon me as I saw one familiar sight after another. Old feelings, I thought I had lost, found me. And the path home to you, I rediscovered.

"My eight friends are here to help all of you live better. They are led by Father Juan Baptista de Segura. He has brought four seers and two younger attendants with him. The boy, Alonso de Los Olmos, is here to learn of your ways. Be assured that their intentions are guided by Religion. Be willing to accept the wisdom they possess. It will improve all your lives here, and in the afterworld."

The orator counts those he has won over. It is the majority of the audience. The time for his conclusion has come. "That is the great purpose for which these people have returned me. They request only good living quarters with room for a temple to their powerful *manitow*. And I, I simply wish to be their servant and share this good news to all of you."

Celebration reverberates through the smoky hall. It soon grows quiet when the old mystic stands up. With eyes closed and head bent, he comes to the middle of the crowd.

He waits until the moment is just right. "The One, the All—that which tells the sun, the moon, and the stars what to do—allowed each *manitow* to create a being to live in Pamasawu."

All have heard this story before and have recited it verbatim many times. But it is the duty of the seers to retell these stories—lest they are lost to all memory. They listen carefully, for they know he is about to make a point.

He proceeds, "Some of those creatures still live. Some are no more. Then, Woman was created. She saw the other animals living simply and dying simply. She realized that her children might also go the way of the others. She grew afraid.

"She convinced the *manitow* that created her to also mate with her. The two made Humankind. That is why humans are far different to all other things in this world.

"The parents were very proud of what they had done. They asked Manibuzo, the great *wikutis*, to protect these precious forms of life. He placed all into a large bag and kept it in his home that is located at the point of the rising sun.

"One day, the four winds came to the home of Manibuzo in the form of giants. They sought to eat the humans. They thought by doing such, they would make themselves stronger. But Manibuzo was able to run them off.

"The great *wikutis* realized he could not protect the people forever. He took a man and a woman from the bag. He placed such a pair in every location he could find throughout Pamasawu. We grew from these pairings. That is why we are so many different clans today. That is why there are so many different tribes."

The old mystic looks at the light coming down from the smoke hole. "We all thought that everyone had been taken out of the bag long ago. Now, we must face the fact that such a thought is wrong. These people from the rising sun are newer in this world than we. But they are still humans. They, however, are children of the winds. That is what controls their method of travel. They are lesser examples of our kind. They will only bring danger of the winds to us."

He looks at Pakikino. "It is good to see you again. You are finally returned to us, where you belong. We worried for you and thought you dead. Now, you have returned. That is good.

"But you bring us fantastic stories. You have also brought these others here. What good is it to have them here? I am certain that their ways are wonderful because they are new to us. But those ways can not work on this side of the world. They are opposite.

"Look at them! They are seers. Yet, they can not take care of themselves. Nor do they expect to. They do not know how to survive without our help, of which we have none to provide. Since you left, Okius has punished the land with drought. That is what took your own father and elder brother from this world. It now threatens your younger brother with sickness. The drought has continued to this day. It is not yet the end of the year and many have already dispersed into smaller families to get through the final season of, *Popano*.

These people have little with them. They can not expect us to share what little we have. Their metal tools are wonders. But we have so little food to trade for them. Food, now, is worth so much more.

"If there are those among us who wish to help the Wind Children to build shelter, it is good. But they can not demand us to work for them simply because they give away their own *netshetsun* to a greedy *manitow*. We are not the Mesheeka! Our *manitow* are powerful too…and they are real. The Wind Children have come to mistaken their heroes for something more. They should go back from where they came.

"And you, Pakikino, wish not to lead your people after they have requested? That is shameful! Will you at least counsel your youngest brother? Reacquaint yourself with the ways of your people and relearn who you are."

All in the council lodge agrees with the wisdom of the old mystic. Perhaps not so much Pakikino. But he will, eventually.

Pakikino sees the Wind Children less each day, until he abandons them all together. The strangers become lost without him. They run out of food. They run out of trade goods for food. Father Luis and the two attendants are chosen to retrieve their lost ambassador. Long wanderings bring them to the land of the Chikahominy. This is the most prestigious nation on the Lower Peninsula. Their river almost cuts the narrow land in half. From the mouth that flows into the Powhatan to the upper reaches where it turns to swamp are almost twenty towns sprinkled along either bank. More than fifteen hundred people live here. Their equitable society is what gives them influence in the region. They are a shelter to those who deviate from the growing tumor that is the Powhatan Chiefdom.

"How did they find me?" Pakikino wonders as he peers out of his uncle's residence. The three dark visitors stand in silence as the crowd around them grows. There is a familiar face in the crowd who appears a bit proud of himself. "He must have brought them. Why?"

His uncle takes a quick peek. "Oh, he never did like you. You didn't know that?"

Pakikino is overcome. He is so popular. Every man begs his company, and he can have any woman he sees. How could someone not like him?

"What can I do, uncle? I don't want to see them any more. Those people are helpless on this side of the world. They haven't even tried to make it on their own."

POWHATAN:
THE STORY OF A PEOPLE

The elder dismisses them, "It's as if they want to suffer. They haven't made any one else happy for these past five moons. They don't hunt or fish on their own, but wait for handouts. They aren't even trying."

The younger explains, "They are waiting for their *manitow* to provide for them."

The elder rejects, "The spirits have given up on them. See how they've deteriorated?"

The two study the strangers. Their faces are gaunt and pallid from deprivation. They shiver in their ragged robes. They speak to no one. They stare at each other and occasionally at the crowd. Everyone in this barren scene exchange only their vaporous breaths. All wait in the cold for Pakikino.

"What can I do about them uncle?"

The elder purses his lips. "What you should do."

Pakikino takes a few long breaths before quietly stepping outside. They begin their strange language. The crowd watches more then listens. Such talk sounds like a flock of exited birds to them. It seems happy talk. Pakikino beams with pleasant smiles. He humbles himself in an air of charity for his visitors. The melancholy trio appear content from what they have heard. They nod and press their hands together. Pakikino points to the most direct trail back to the mission and bids them goodbye.

There are only a few in the town of Chiskiyak. The only house that rustles with activity is that of the young leader who entertains his elder brother. Pakikino sits with his group from Chikahominy. The boy from the mission occupies a dark corner of the hall.

Pakikino recalls the afternoon's episode, "I told them their three companions will be back tomorrow with the baskets of *opominz* I was gathering for them. That was my excuse for originally deserting them. They believed me without question. They gave us every *tomahak* they had, so that we could start building a new mission house tomorrow."

The brother queries, "So you have taken every possible weapon from them?"

Pakikino looks at his prized cutlass. It was presented to him by King Phillip. "I didn't see any other. They had so little left. Only the wooden box that is covered in leather. They just keep their sacred articles in that. Besides, they are seers. They don't use weapons to defend themselves…At least not these kind."

The brother advises, "Then tonight you should prepare yourselves against their other weapons."

Pakikino disagrees, "I see no need. The other three were easy to bring down. Our arrows covered them before they were an earshot out of town. Their bodies burned as easily as any other."

"Still," the brother councils, "these seers have their box of talismans."

Pakikino nods in agreement. The black drink is passed around. Each fills a *tsekoma* with the sacred formula. The presiding healer sprinkles a pinch of *upook* into the liquid.

Pakikino notices movement in the corner. "We must kill all of them, including the boy. We'll need to hide everything from sight, so that when their people return, they won't find a trace."

His brother disagrees, "No. Boys must live to replace the men who are lost. Besides, we owe a life to our friends in Kekotan for their son who went with you and died. He shall go to them."

The chosen ones imbibe the drink. It quickly takes effect. Soon, all are purging their systems, stimulating their bodies, inspiring their thoughts for the morning task.

The morning comes with solemn prayers in the mission house. It is still a poor hovel in the middle of a fallow field. It is a simple cube of logs, with a small apartment attached on one side. Those within are excited about the expected reunions of the day. Don Luis and his crew arrive first.

The young man enters. The strangers draw close to welcome their flock. While in conversation, Pakikino grasps the handle of his cutlass. He slides the blade out of the sheath. He takes time to admire this object of both power and beauty. It is more a work of art than a tool of death. He looks up at his people. "Well, that's it."

The desperate eyes of Father Segura lock onto Pakikino as he forces the long knife into his mentor's head. The blade slices down the face. The others have to wait only a moment before they too feel cold metal inside their fragile bodies.

The skull slides down off the blade. Pakikino proclaims, "Their seers have no power here. None of them do! They will stay on their side of the world."

The victors finish looting and set fire to the mission and the mutilated bodies therein. Souvenirs of clothing and equipment are passed out to both Chikahominy and Chiskiyak accomplices. And the sacred box is brought back to the quiet little town that sits atop a hill that overlooks the broad Pamunkey River.

POWHATAN:
THE STORY OF A PEOPLE

People all along the Chikahominy are in shock. They are afraid and confused. Every *kawkawas* arrives in the principal town of Mamanahunt. They hide in the council house. They try to explain away the problem. One stands to speak. "So what must we do? They have twelve of our brave young men. They have the boy. Now, they want Pakikino. What demand will they make of us next?"

"It is simple," an angry father of one of the captured stands up, "Pakikino is the cause of all this. He is the reason why so many have died. To end his life will be to end this impasse. Let us deliver him to the strangers!"

A voice echoes in the dark hall, "He is Chiskiyak, not Chikahominy!"

The angry man spits back, "He is not Chiskiyak! His mother's brother was Chikahominy." Approval resounds in the room. All understand that the ties with family and clan come before any tribal affiliation.

The voice in the dark continues, "Listen, my brothers. His uncle was one of our finest leaders. We can not tarnish his memory. Yes, his mother was Chikahominy. Pakikino is from her womb. He is therefore from ours. Wahunsenakok has settled on the Pamunkey River, across from Chiskiyak. His influence is strong. If we surrender Pakikino to those barbarous Wind Children, we will lose our friendship with the Chiskiyak!"

The hall thunders with the clamor of confusion. The speaker continues, "We are being surrounded by the Powhatan tribes. All we have left are our immediate neighbors. The end of Pakikino would be the end of us!"

The new chief *kawkawas* blurts out, "But what has really happened? Why do we now sit here like scared children? Why have these strangers come to terrorize us? We can not think of that evil man across the Pamunkey. What must we do to make those strangers go away for good? What must we do?"

"The *musawusuk*..." another *kawkawas* interjects, "It is an evil island that moves upon the water. We of the land have no defense from such an instrument. I was there when it came to our river six days ago. It started innocently enough. A wide *akwintan* stopped in the middle of the river to trade. I was one of the first to row over to the strangers. We received wonderful gifts for our simple supply of food and furs. We were treated to their cakes made with a sweet juice that is produced by an insect in their world.

"As we returned, our great leader, Pakikino's beloved uncle and new father, went to the strangers. We saw from the shore how that miserable trap was sprung upon him. A large mass of their warriors ascended from under the roof of their vessel with long sticks that blew smoke from the ends. I then heard the sharp crackle of our people's bones. That is how we came to this point. That is how we lost him and over twenty of our brethren. And that is how twelve of our sons are in captivity as ransom for Pakikino."

The chief *kawkawas* further interrogates, "But what did you do for them?"

The narrator tries to explain, "We released our arrows from shore and took to our *akwintan*. The strangers made more of the thunder. We were prepared to sacrifice all. But the strangers were not. They dropped their cloth and the winds blew their vessel away from us. We lost them to cowards who ran away."

Another question is asked, "But why did they attack the second group and not yours?"

The answer is given, "I noticed one member of the second group had a metal tray from the dead seers. He was wearing it as a breastplate. Is that not how they acted a year ago, when they first came looking for their lost friends?"

One in the crowd answers, "Yes. It is true. I and my group wore some clothes of the dead seers…and some of their trinkets. They let us come aboard to trade. That was our reason for wearing them. It is true that Pakikino wanted all evidence destroyed. He knew best how the strangers would react. But by wearing the clothes, we thought it would show that we knew the seers…and that they were still alive.

"We exchanged presents. All went well, until they sent that broad leaf of word art to their seers. Such a thing could not be answered. The strangers grew impatient. We were ready to fight them. But we waited too long. Old blood was spotted on the clothes. The strangers attacked first. I and the others could only jump into the water and swim to the safety of land. But in the fight…two of our own were captured.

"We also gathered our great warriors and rowed out to reclaim our captive brothers. The strangers used their weapons that sound like the hollow echo of braking branches in an ice storm. Soon after, they empowered the winds to carry them away.

"These people may live on a great island, but they truly are masters of the water. I felt that we had seen the last of them. They had taken revenge for their lost seers.

"The prisoners must have told about the seers and about their boy whom we gave to the Kekotan. Of the two captives, one ended his life on the open waters by jumping off their vessel. They brainwashed the other, as they had done to Pakikino. He is now their guide. He is rendered without possession of

POWHATAN:
THE STORY OF A PEOPLE

his own life. That is what our negotiators found out three days ago. These people have come back a year later, taken more revenge for their seers, and hold our twelve sons in ransom for the boy and Pakikino."

Another adds, "Our good friends at Kekotan have returned the boy to the strangers. If we convince Pakikino to go to them, the strangers may see an end to their cause. We may not have the right to force him, but he should understand that it must be done. The strangers just want what belongs to them."

"But brothers," the speaker steps from the darkness, "Pakikino does not belong to them. He is of our world. In two days, the strangers will kill their hostages. We have that much time to prepare our families for the loss." He looks into the darkened eyes of the father. "It is a terrible thing I ask. But we must not comply to every wish of the strangers. That will only encourage them to stay longer...to demand more from us. The strangers must go away. They must realize that they can not threaten us. We are Chikahominy! We must stand strong against such people. We must stand up to the strangers if we are to retain any respect from our neighbors. We must prove to Wahunsenakok that we still control the Lower Peninsula. We must sacrifice to survive. The drought is ending! The seers have told us so. The influence Wahunsenakok has over the starved tribes will end with it. The land will soon flourish anew...and so will independent hearts. The Wind Children will see that, too. And they will eventually become a memory."

The father observes, "Perhaps you do not love your son who is now a prisoner. Perhaps that helps you think of the tribe before the family. Well then, consider this. There are twelve—no, thirteen Chikahominy lives in jeopardy. Are not their lives more important than the one miserable waist of life that we know as, Pakikino?"

The chief *kawkawas* rises. "Let us decide on how we can end this nightmare. We will put the question to a vote." He begins the process. "Place your vote in the gourd as I pass it around. A kernel of *poketawas* if we should give Pakikino to the strangers. A *pekatas* if we should refuse their demands."

The voters reach into their leather purses. One after the other takes the gourd and drops his choice into the small opening. The decision is thus tallied.

Chapter 4

Takwitok is the fourth season. It brings a refreshing coolness to the air. It fills the trees with brilliant color and ripens important foods. This year's harvest of *poketawas*, *makak*, and *askutaskwash* is tremendous. The principal town of every tribe hosts its own festival. But none can compare to what is seen at Weyowakomako. It is an extravagant city that aligns a cove along the Pamunkey River. The land has various incisions of little creeks and even smaller brooks. They create a level plain on which to toil and recreate, rolling highland on which to dwell, and low marshes in which to hunt and fish. A strong fence of timber bounds the city in a half-circle.

Most houses have a good view of the waterfront. Each is a separate family estate. All are bursting with visiting relatives during the four-day celebration. Sand has been generously sprinkled on the pathways throughout the city. A large fire is ready to burn strong tonight at the dancing circle. Mothers chatter as they prepare food to end the fast while hordes of children run free of care and clothing. The young, and the young at heart, call upon each other for leisurely pursuits. The serious males congregate in the men's section of the homes to plan for raids and community hunts.

Beside the largest creek within the city is a field. A crowd assembles there. People align both sides of the arena that is one hundred strides long and half that wide. At each end are two tall posts with colorful streamers fluttering from the tops and at both ends of the cross bars.

The old players are talked out of their stories of past games and are ready for new memories. Young women step into a dance full of vibrancy. Their glossy skin reflects the bright sun as limbs flow in smooth rhythm. Tattooed breasts surge. Smiles reveal the joy of physical movement. Their forms motivate the male players as they parade onto the field. Both teams are

POWHATAN:
THE STORY OF A PEOPLE

welcomed with clapping and cheers or slapping and jeers. The spectators succumb to the aura of Sport. Emotion grows into a state of passion.

One team wears the *utakaway* breechcloths of their clan. Pokinz leads the host team. He is a tall, well-proportioned young man with a swimmer's lungs and a runner's physique. His charismatic appeal is the same as that of his father, Wahunsenakok.

The players' oiled forms shine in manly strength. All raise their rackets above their heads in pre-determined triumph. Each racket is a straight *pakohikowo* branch, ringed at one end. Tightly-twisted strips of *masanek* skin make the netting.

Three healers meet at the center of the field. They voice a prayer for blessing from each direction. The crowd quiets down.

An old man brings forth the ball to open the game. The leather orb fits well in his hand. He rubs the stitching with his thumb. It feels so familiar. Many in the crowd can still recognize his robust form of yesteryear through the worn body of the present. Team leaders are at the center of the field with their best players not far behind. The rest are scattered toward each goal where they will wait for the game to come to them. In the interest of time and physical wellbeing, the teams agree to set the game at twelve points. The old veteran hurls the ball up and the opponents rush into a melee.

Back and forth. The ball is tossed from one net pocket to another. Bodies collide. A runner zigzags through the swarm of opponents before slinging the ball to an open teammate. The prized orb is run through one set of goal posts. Later, it is tossed over the cross bar of the other. The players sweat. They bruise and bleed. Fatigued participants make for the creek to cool off. But the game does not stop.

Hopes, promises, wealth, dreams—all of these ride on the outcome. Pokinz rallies his men throughout to keep the game close. At times, they look invincible. At other times, their opponents seem unstoppable. The game goes on to entertain and inspire everyone in the clearing.

The seers are also busy in the quiet darkness of the temple. They are about to renew the perpetual flame. It is an annual task that causes a great strain on their bodies. One leans down to pick out the primary coal while another carefully brushes away the old fire. Two more participants methodically place fresh fuel into the pit. They breathe heavily, yet they know that such breath can extinguish the flame—and such a mistake could threaten their lives. If the flame ceases to exist for even a blink of an eye, it could cause unspeakable ill to the entire land.

With intense concentration, the chief seer holds up the last remnant of the old fire. The small flame dances on the end of its crumbling coal. He exhales the appropriate hymn with quick delivery. The face of another seer—half red, half black, and full of apprehension—comes close to the coal. He raises a shaving beside the shrinking flame. All wait at this point of eternity. The flame gyrates on the coal. It pulls free from the old fuel. It jumps! It latches onto the new perch.

The four wait. They watch as the blaze slides down the tender strip of wood. The holder gently lowers it onto the pile of fresh kindling. The flame spreads. It fully engulfs the sacred hearth. Each seer falls back in elated exhaustion. "Well," exhales the chief seer, "we are safe for another year. Our duties are almost done. Tomorrow, we will prepare for the last day's funeral procession and prayer dance. Then, then all these retched festivities will be over." The others moan in agreement.

The crowd from the ball field is making its way back to the town center. For Pokinz, the competition did not end as desired. But, that is Life. From time to time, one group falls short in the face of another. And the victor strives onward, until losing as well. He consoles his shame with the fact that the season is young. There is still plenty of time to improve.

Everyone comes to feast. Those who have committed crimes sit beside victims who are willing to forgive them. The youth stand coyly in the dancing circle to expose their intentions of courtship. Individuals form into groups. Groups split and reform into other groups. All will mingle throughout the night in the great exercise of socializing.

But this is not the only assemblage in the city. Less than three hundred strides inland, along the edge of the hill that separates the flood plain from the interior is the residence of Wahunsenakok. There are three large buildings situated within a maze of walls. Successful entrance to the interior courtyard is only achieved by a patient and alert journey along a narrow path between the inner and outer fences, and through their correct openings. Each of the three long buildings is partitioned into chambers. Within the central building is a large assembly hall where representatives of the Powhatan Nation have gathered to impress one another with their gifts of oratory.

Three fires produce a striking orange glow in the great hall. The benches that align the length of both sides are filled with lavishly adorned members of the highest society. Wahunsenakok listens on the platform at the end of the hall. Flanking him are his two favorite wives—at present. The one to his right is called, Oposumokwonusk. Robust of countenance, she possesses that quality of transforming from a grim façade into a comely pose by way of a simple smile. Her presence is protective. The affection she gives is bright and dangerous. On the opposite side sits a woman of almost opposing nature. She is a long, sleek woman with a delicate face and thin hair that falls down her back. She has a searching spirit, overflowing of individuality. She is a person of both physical and social grace. Her love is soft, like a long swim downstream.

All the guests have a wooden bowl of boiled *askutaskwash* in *asiminz* milk, as well as a generous helping of *moninag* meat to stretch their bellies and send their minds into a drowsy state of bliss. Even the Chikahominy are among the guests. The sacrifice they made during their most trying moment has preserved the affection of the neighbors. Never the less, their significance in the region has eroded. They have evolved into a silent stance of independence, hidden behind a shield of diplomacy.

A newcomer is also in the crowd. The *weyowanz* of Akomak has made the trip from the Eastern Peninsula. He waits patiently as the speaker from Tapahanok concludes, "I tell you, good people of Powhatan, we are much interested in your fellowship. With your help in defending us from our enemies to the north and to the west, you may yet create a strong bond with us." The crowd roars. Some slap at the ground with joy, while others shake their rattle gourds in excited approval.

The speaker sits and Wahunsenakok rises. "The people of the Upper Peninsula are not of the original ones, as we. They came from lands farther north. The mystics know that their arrival occurred many generations ago when they were pushed aside by stronger foes. They have stayed together and grown into healthy numbers all along their neck of land. These people share a connection with us. In distant time, we were all one. Unlike the Monakan, the people of the Upper Peninsula hold blood ties with us. Their enemies are ours! I wish to embrace these distant cousins and strengthen the bond we share!" He asks above the roar, "Will you help me? Will you help me?"

The host looks at the man from Akomak. "What do you say to this, my good friend from across the bay?"

His turn has finally come. Kiktopeyak slowly rises and walks to the center of the hall. The crowd hushes. He takes a hidden breath and begins the speech of his life, "I am overjoyed to stand among such noble people. My heart flutters like a young bird just beginning to fly. My journey began three days ago. I departed my humble tribe whose home lies on the tip of the Eastern Peninsula. They were generous to supply me with the meager tribute my three *akwintan* were able to carry to this gathering of great people. I feel as a lost child who has been taken in by a gracious and strong family."

He looks at Wahunsenakok. The crowd notices. "You, good leader of these people, have been the best of hosts. Without question, you invite me into your warm *ahakan*. This experience has almost allowed me to forget the great trouble that I left behind."

Heads rise. Eyes widen in wonder to what he refers. The speaker resumes, "It has been months since the occurrence. It came from the Great Blue. We have always looked to the watery East with reverence, for it is the shining abode of Manibuzo. But while we looked eastward, they slipped into the bay from the south, and blew into us by the west wind.

"They stole two of our happy young men!" The crowd sighs, but not in confusion nor disbelief. No, they all understand what this means. The new Chiskiyak leader, Otahotin, sinks low into his place. The two Chikahominy representatives hang their heads. They sit in silence, remembering their own seven men who were kept to pay for their people's defiance—those who were not released, but were hung by the neck from the tree branches of the *musawusuk*. Starved of breath, the bodies danced in the air until their souls abandoned them.

Kiktopeyak continues, "Yes, my friends, we hear the stories of these strangers from the water. We have heard of their visits and have had sightings of them for years. Never did my people feel that such things would happen to us, for we rejoice every day to gaze with love at the eastern horizon. But now, we are also victims of the Wind Children. The body of one of our boys washed up on shore weeks after the incident. The other...

"I had a chance to visit your great seers. They have all agreed that we will not see the other boy ever again. How can we expect kind treatment from the Wind Children? How can we ever defend ourselves from such evil?"

He turns again. "Wahunsenakok, we are alone in our land to the east. We are helpless against these people of the waters. Across the mouth of the bay from us are the Chesapeak. They are a strong nation and claim not to be afraid. But we once said the same. They are one nation, while you are many. That is why I present you with my homage of *poketawas*. Say you will guide my people, Wahunsenakok!"

The intensity of human voice vibrates against the compound fencing. The speaker giggles at the positive reception. Wahunsenakok rises. The two embrace. Topping this speech will be a task.

POWHATAN:
THE STORY OF A PEOPLE

A woman stands in the crowd. Dripping with pearls and *matasun* beads, she sparkles brighter then the fire pits. The crowd regains their composure. The extravagant *weyowanskwa* from the tribe of Kwiyokohanok sways toward the platform. Her *kawasow* of dark *moninag* feathers sweeps the smoky air from her path. She was temporarily married to Wahunsenakok, and has a child by him. She is the youngest sibling in her family and aquired her tribal leadership naturally.

Ohalas gives that sly, side glance of hers before she begins, "My good man, Wahunsenakok, I have also traveled far to visit you in this wonderful spot.

"My people feel safe under your guidance. To you, Kiktopeyak, I say your decision is good." The audience voices their agreement. She silences the crowd with one raised hand. "I have also come to bring you news from my part of the world. Our good Weyanok neighbors were kind enough to escort a few of my people to trade with the southern tribes." The Weyanok representative in the crowd smiles and nods.

She changes the tone, "Sadly, however, I fear my neighbors, the Nansemund, feel burdened by their proximity to the Chesapeak, who have recently sheltered those strangers from the Sekotan Territory. The good people of Nansemund are torn between choosing them or us. The Chesapeak live beside them. Their cronies, the Kekotan, live just across the river at the end of the Lower Peninsula. Those two tribes have become upstarts in the region. They have reduced our freedom to come and go in the bay as we choose. The Kekotan are especially mean, and act as stubbornly as their aging *weyowanz*.

"But do not forget the Chesapeak. They are the most danger to us all. Those that came and committed such horrible atrocities to our friends on the Eastern Peninsula were obviously looking for the strangers that the Chesapeak now harbor.

"The good tribes in the south finally killed off those who settled amongst them. But who will do the same to those in Chesapeak? As long as they live, so lives the threat that more dangers will come. This is unacceptable."

Agreement sounds throughout. She decides to end on a high and returns to her place. The host rises once more. "As many of you know, I visited the site where the effort to annihilate the strangers was made. I heard of seven who survived. They somehow escaped to the sheltering arms of the Chowanok people. They also refuse to give up those people, for they are of great service to them. They produce wonderful things out of that tribe's high-quality *matasun*. They build square houses with a room on top of another. They have created things that delight and mesmerize even the healers. The Chowanok are happy with them. I say that the Chesapeak have also grown fond of their dependants."

"Why were these people abandoned? Why have they become slaves to the Chesapeak and the Chowanok? Why would the Wind Children be fearful of leaving them among us? The fear is that they can be of great use to us! The Wind Children have tried for so long to establish themselves here. But they are not suited for Pamasawu. We should not be afraid of the abandoned ones, but of those who seek them. The Chesapeak are a rich and powerful tribe. Their allies, the Kekotan, are also powerful. Neither has influence in this region. But both are still revered by those to the south. The Nansemund are unsure. With a little coaxing, they can favor a path with us. Let us strive to isolate the Chesapeak! We all feel pain caused by the Kekotan. But listen. Their *weyowanz* is an old man. He can not live forever!" The framing quakes from the supportive echo in the hall. The host concludes, "We will live forever! We will live forever! Let us dispense with our worries. Go now and celebrate with our people."

The protectress leads the crowd outside. The pet stays behind in quiet humor. Wahunsenakok glides his hand down her long waist. His palm tingles from her warm flesh. The back of his hand tickles from her cool locks. He playfully clenches her fleshy base. She presses her shoulder into his armpit with a slight nudge. "Careful where you touch," she whispers, "there is someone inside me now."

The sun shines cleanly on the *muskiminz* tree that stands in the inner courtyard. The cradleboard hangs from a branch on the short trunk. Safely bound within fur swaddling is a baby girl. Her mother is busy working with damp *poketawas* leaves on the ground. She first tears off a piece from one husk and rolls it into a ball. She folds the rest around and twists it tight. She pulls a husk from the bowl of water, rolls it lengthways, and flattens the ends to look like out-stretched hands. She wraps it around to fasten under the head. Splitting a third husk down its length, she folds each half over either shoulder. The final leaf is wrapped around the midsection of the doll to form a waist that will hold it all together. Her work complete, she holds it up for her child's approval.

But the baby is too busy to take notice. She has managed to get one arm free again. She waives it, watching her little fat hand sway like the broad

POWHATAN:
THE STORY OF A PEOPLE

leaves of the tree. Some leaves are still intact. Others have been devoured by the little worms that make the tree their home. Rows of them march all about. It is an important tree, for its fruit is satisfying and its milky sap is pleasing. The bark can be stripped and woven into good apparel. The roots can cleanse the blood and clear the bowels. Most importantly, it shades the little baby from the afternoon sun. Her attention is transfixed on the dazzling interplay of light and shade. The little arm sways like the branches. Her skin is light and soft and fully greased so that it will not turn dark or grow tuff prematurely.

Father's deep voice vibrates in her ear, "My little Pokahantas is ready to be free of her cradleboard."

Mother tilts her head to one side as she studies her newest creation. "Yes, I can't keep her bound up anymore." She looks up at him. "Hang this in front of her."

Wahunsenakok looks into his daughter's shinning eyes. "Are you ready to run with me?"

Her mother warns, "Watch out, she'll have you running about 'till you drop. She's nothing but energy."

"She's nothing but happiness," he grins.

Pokahantas grips his finger with all the power she can muster. She squeals in victory.

"Let me go," Father pleads. But the baby just grips that much harder as she coos. Father plays with her for a little while. He has no place to go until his brother, Kekwatog, arrives to announce, "The sweat lodge is ready for us."

The two walk toward the creek. A small domed structure is near the low bank. Opichapan is waiting there. The eldest brother murmurs, "So he is not better on such a good day?"

The other replies, "He is really hurting. He can hardly make a step without feeling the soreness in his legs. The healer thought it best if all four of us were together."

Opechankano arrives. The four brothers gather at the entrance. The healer accepts his payment, motions them in, and seals up the opening.

They take their positions around the oven pit. Four large stones, fresh from the fire, lie inside. Covering them is a layer of inner bark from a *powamink* tree. The surface is pounded smooth so that it will not burn.

"Well," Opechankano mumbles, "this heat is what I need, too."

"Did the fight wear you out?" Wahunsenakok muses.

"This is not the body that used to be." Opechankano remembers the recent episode. He and two hundred warriors hid in the forest as the young sportsman, Pokinz, led his small band into the walled city of Kekotan. The visiting group hid their true intentions behind a show of sympathy for the tribe who had just lost their venerable old leader. They danced for their hosts with wonderful display. They gifted the son with prizes suitable for a new leader, as if the two had never shared animosity. The young leader proved his inexperience by allowing his guests to keep their weapons and be lodged privately together. Before the sun rose again, the small band broke the defenses so that the attackers could rush in without obstruction.

Opechankano relaxes. "Pokinz did well. He is a fine warrior...a fine leader."

"He is my son," Wahunsenakok beams.

"They are wiped out?" Kekwatog questions.

The youngest answers, "Yes, oh yes. The young *weyowanz* is ours, along with his pretty women and healthy children." He gazes at the glowing red stones. "So many scalps." He turns to his eldest brother. "They are a son's, and a brother's present to you."

The entrance flap loosens. The healer pokes his gnarled nose inside. The time is right. He climbs in and pours water upon the stones and sprinkles the flesh of each brother for some relief. All four wince at the steam as the stones crackle under the pressure. The opening is sealed again. The cleansing torment resumes.

"And what of the Chesapeak?" Wahunsenakok wonders.

Opechankano closes his eyes. "They did nothing. We taunted them as they watched from far across the river...like helpless mothers do when a predator devours their young in front of them."

Kekwatog concludes, "Then they are alone. Not even the southern tribes will have respect for them."

White teeth sparkle in the dim chamber. The four sit in silence as their bodies broil in a membrane of sweat. Heat reaches deep into the bodies. Internal organs strain to function. Each mind escapes the reality of the suffering by retreating into itself. Wahunsenakok meditates on the future that the past has granted. He utters heavily, "The bay is now our heart. All the wealth of food and pearls that are in the waters...the best pearls in all of Pamasawu are now ours."

Once again, the healer visits his customers. The four may be ageing, but they can still take a sweat to the limit of endurance. He leaves them alone.

The proud father plans aloud, "Pokinz will begin a new Kekotan. They will be from our own tribes. The survivors of the old will come here, to

Weyowakomako. Their young *weyowanz* can learn from me. I owe his father that much."

Kekwatog interjects, "You hated the old man."

"I respected him, as well," Wahunsenakok explains. "Why do you think I waited for his death before I acted?"

Opichapan finally says something, "I want to get out. Now!"

Arms burst through the entrance. The brothers lurch toward the creek. Frightened birds scatter in frenzy as the four plummet into the soothing liquid. Heart rates calm. Bodies cool. The men sit in the shallow water.

Wahunsenakok gazes at the clouds. "Yes, my family is good. My family is strong." He splashes his brothers. "We are now greater then any in this land!"

CHAPTER 5

Time summons a new generation to prominence in Tsenakomako. New concerns come. Old issues go. Pokinz builds a new Kekotan while his brother, Pawahunt, continues to watch the western region from Powhatan Town. Pawahunt is as strong of body and mind as his father. But he tends to be socially distant. He simply relies on his actions to speak for him. That is how he handles his stewardship of the same tribe that was his father's.

One day, he quietly joins a group of raiders who travel southward to resume the ongoing war with the Mowatuk Nation. Last year's combat resulted in the loss of three Powhatan lives, while another was irreparably injured.

The children of Tsenakomako travel down the Yapiya River which designates their southwestern boundary. It is a shallow, lazy stream. The water is blackened by *mowok* and *powamink* swamps that feed into it.

Over one hundred men of varying ages move steadily through the frontier. They travel light so that they can range far. Where it is possible, they ride the waterway in eight small *akwintan*. Where they must, they pull and push them along. Scouts explore ahead of the main column and guard both its flanks. To their right is Monakan territory. To their left is the great swamp that lies in the center of the Southern Peninsula. It is a dismal region, claimed by no one.

Below it is the complex world of the southern nations. A variety of cultures live here in peaceful coexistence. They govern themselves as the Chikahominy, where many voices speak for the community. They also organize as the Monakan, where nations consist of a collection of large tribes that live in expansive towns with no walls.

Along the eastern coast are those that speak as the Powhatan. In the western hinterlands live distant relatives of the Masawomik. They are a collection of almost twenty independent tribes. They go by many names. But

POWHATAN:
THE STORY OF A PEOPLE

the Powhatan call them, Mowatuk, after the main river that courses through the heart of their country. Each tribe holds close ties with the others. They also enjoy close friendships with their neighbors.

The raiders travel to where the stream joins the peaceful Chowanok River. There are two more tributaries nearby. The travelers bypass one of them and head west through the country to cross the other. It is a flat landscape, thick with coniferous and deciduous growth. Soft hills provide some distinction. However, it is generally a bland locality where everything looks the same.

Opechankano is at the head of the column. The raid is his responsibility. Most of his retinue are from Apamatuk, Weyanok, and Nansemund. They embarked from the Kwiyokohanok territory. The stunning Ohalas provided the *akwintan*. She filled their food pouches with her own dried *poketawas*. She conscripted members of her tribe to help fill the ranks. But most importantly, she supplied her eldest son, Pepiskunima, to accompany them. Debonair in both manner and posture, he possesses a good mind and a thoughtful outlook. These traits become useful when the travelers reach a Mowatuk hunting village.

Many in the village are from the Notaway tribe. Their corner of the world is a unique spot. They communicate with the Monakan to their west and interact with the Powhatan to their north. They are good friends of the Chowanok to their east and protective of their Mowatuk confederates to their south. They refuse the raiders any further advance. Instead, they convene a grand council in the village square to solve matters.

The members assemble in grand fashion. Each wears his finest *machkow*—lavishly embroidered with shell and *matasun* beads, and lined with various furs. Each is tied at the left shoulder so that the right arm can move for effect during oration.

The speakers perform in diverse languages and dialects, but all are clear in their delivery. Pepiskunima orchestrates a fine diplomatic harangue concerning the three Powhatan traders who where recently killed by those from the town of Hokomawonank. The defendants explain away the incident as a simple lack of recognizing familiar *peak* in the hands of unfamiliar traders. They naturally took the *peak* as they had use for it. They had no use for the three corpses. Those were left in the wilderness.

Pepiskunima guides the conference to an acceptable agreement. Although the guilty will not be punished by the Powhatan, the stolen *peak* will be replaced with the *pokiyu* skins that were originally sought for trade. Additionally, any personal effects of the victims that are still in human possession will be returned with condolences and blood payments. The gathering concludes. The Powhatan separate from the hunting village to set up their own camp along the trail home.

This respite gives Pawahunt an opportunity to invite the venerable Chowanok leader, Menatonon, to stop by their camp and receive a special gift. The request is sent. The response is positive.

The cripple sits quietly on a sturdy platform which four strong men carry. Withering leaves flash their colors of orange and red and yellow in the sunlight that coats the timber. Dry leaves twist in the cool breeze. The weakest let go of their branches and scatter upon the trail. This is a path that has been smoothed from centuries of use by both two- and four-legged creatures. Leaves crunch underfoot. The pace is steady but the movements are quiet. Human activity is detected ahead. The entourage announces their arrival with a pair of high-pitched shouts.

The Powhatan camp takes up a small clearing along the western side of the trail. Menatonon motions to be placed in an open spot on the opposite side. His grace shields his failing health. The old Chowanok is revered by all his neighbors. He has weathered many trials of nature. He has even outlasted the Wind Children who once terrorized the southern lands. They captured his town and then took his favorite son hostage. Now, he owns a handful of their survivors.

The host appears from a small hut. Menatonon can see this is a son of Wahunsenakok, as he shares many features with his father. He looks about the camp. The people of Tsenakomako are different. Their motions are less quiet. The eyes are less gentle in their gaze. Their hair is not fashioned with cropped sides and a stiff comb along the scalp. Instead, the comb is flanked by one side that is clean of hair while the other is thick with long tresses.

The Powhatan members mingle with the visitors. Menatonon anticipates the gift that Pawahunt has promised him. He has also brought a sizeable amount of his *matasun* for possible trade. His people had long exchanged their precious metal for the fine *peak* and prefect pearls of Kekotan. Their former leader was a dear friend. That relationship is no more.

A smile grows upon the face of Pawahunt. He approaches the platform with both arms outstretched.

Menatonon directs the conversation, "You show greatness in forgiving this old man."

Pawahunt leans in to embrace the elderly figure. As he brings his lips to the wrinkled ear, Pawahunt whispers, "Never think that, wife stealer." A bow string slips around Menatonon's neck. It constricts. Pawahunt shows his delight. One Chowanok hero answers the crisis. He rushes toward his beloved leader. Salvation is instantly halted by a blow to the head. Lethal *monahak* are swung at scattering men. The Chowanok abandon the scene.

Pawahunt pulls tighter. The cord cuts into the soft throat. He seethes, "No woman of Powhatan will be held hostage, by you or anyone, ever again." Pawahunt heaves the carcass to the ground. "Death is my gift to you!"

Word of this crime reaches the hunting village. The Notaway are hushed in their humiliation. They have allowed the death of someone they loved. What love they had for their northern neighbors has also expired with old Menatonon.

A large watercraft comes up the Pamunkey River. The curious follow it along the wooded shoreline. A group of friendly women and men gather at the outer landing of Weyowakomako. The Wind Children fill a smaller craft and approach the shore.

Pokahantas stands at the forefront of the welcoming party on the bank. She is with her father and her uncle, Opichapan. Prosperity has weakened the predacious mindset of her father. It has also softened his paranoia. He has no hidden agenda with these visitors, nor does he feel any uneasiness of their intentions. But curiosity does occupy his mind.

Pokahantas is also curious of these people. She has heard about them throughout the decade of her life. Nimble and erect, she reaches almost to her father's chest. Her eyes are always searching. She always wears a smile that warms the heart of any onlooker.

Father gives her a slight nudge. Distracted only for a moment, the girl remembers her job and steps forward with a small basket she has filled with assorted nuts. The stranger is a towering fellow with eyes of layered blue, like the sky. It is this complexity in their hue that both allures and dismays the little observer. They seem to cut right into her.

She hears her father's warm greeting. The tall one puts out his right leg and bends slightly forward, while taking off his hat in a circular movement. In confusion, she does the only thing a little girl can do. She warmly reacts with a bashful giggle and an energetic shrug of the shoulders. Placing the basket upon the ground, she struts back to her father's protective hands.

The strangers speak to one another in a strange language. They bring forth their gifts. Wahunsenakok nods in acceptance of the metal tools and pots.

"Not much," Opichapan hums.

"They are evidently just passing through," Wahunsenakok guesses. His brother motions for the proper exchange of food and fresh water.

Mats are laid out by the women. The two parties take their places fronting each other. The women go into an *ahakan* nearby while the armed men of both parties gather in small groups in the background.

The opposing colleagues talk quietly among themselves until the women reappear with large plates of food. Wahunsenakok rises with the proper etiquette of a host. "See what our wonderful women have. They bring *poketawas* in various recipes to satisfy your hunger. This food was brought to us by Manibuzo long ago. It is half of what we eat. It is all that we are." He points out various dishes,

"Good *wokohomin*, from crushing the kernels." He points to a pile of flat disks, "That is *apetapon*, prepared with a wonderful taste." He picks up another bread, "This *apon* has *pitukwu* roots mixed into the dough and is baked in *pakohikowo* ash for a fine flavor. We call it, *takahowapon*. Take. It will bring back a healthy color in your skin."

The eyes of the strangers widen in acceptance. What they cannot understand, they can at least realize. All the participants feast in universal revelry.

The women bring out gourds of water to clean the hands after the meal. Opichapan pulls out a pipe and grabs a glowing twig from the fire. The thin line of smoke rises slowly. His eyes fixate on the ethereal strand that links this world to the next. He offers the pipe to his guest who gives the instrument a careful try. Wahunsenakok accepts the pipe and replies with a slow, thoughtful smoke.

Things get a little quiet. Opichapan again whispers, "Shouldn't you make a speech, or something?"

His elder brother thinks for a moment and then hands over the pipe. "Why bother, they wouldn't understand it anyway. Just smile at them and enjoy the *upook*."

Wahunsenakok discerns that his guest wishes to put forward a query. He tries to say something, but keeps repeating, "Mace? Mace?" Wahunsenakok wonders if they are searching for the last *musawusuk* that came into the bay about two years ago.

A party came ashore on the Eastern Peninsula looking for food and water and wood. Kiktopeyak ambushed the trespassers and did a fine job of running them off. Their leader was killed with four of his men. The Akomak are no longer afraid.

POWHATAN:
THE STORY OF A PEOPLE

Opichapan suggests, "I think his name is such. He keeps poking his chest when he says that word."

Wahunsenakok nods with a smile to the man, but he is not about to play such a childish game of primitive verbal intercourse. Opichapan motions for the gifts to be handed over to the strangers. They take the goods back to their wide *akwintan*.

Wahunsenakok reaches to interlock first fingers with the man. Instead, the palm of his hand is grasped. The old statesman smiles as he blurts out to his brother, "Must be the way they do it." Both nod continuously as the strangers launch into the water.

Opichapan turns to his brother once more, "Well, that was a good visit."

Wahunsenakok agrees, "It went well."

The *musawusuk* does not leave Tsenakomako. It goes north around the middle peninsula and up the Tapahanok river. It stops at the principle town of the Tapahanok tribe. Their *weyowanz* also greets the strangers at the river bank. As soon as the gifts are placed down, one becomes greedy. He goes over to the pile of glittering wonders. He reaches for an item that charges his temptation. One of the guests halts this action. A struggle breaks out. Smoke. A clap of thunder when there is not a cloud in the sky. The *weyowanz* falls to the ground as the rest scatter in confused anguish. The strangers grab hold of a few young men and drag them into their wide *akwintan*. By the time the warriors return with their weapons, the *musawusuk* begins to move down the big river.

The chase is given up. Instead, a messenger runs to Weyowakomako. Wahunsenakok ponders, "It is murder and thievery of the highest offence!"

He tries to put the pieces together from the description of the incident. But he is still at a loss for understanding.

What can this mean? The sightings are increasing. The contacts are growing more harmful. But why? Who are they? What is their purpose, their motive? When will they strike again? How long will this continue? And where will it lead? Such questions can only be answered at the most sacred of sites in Pamasawu.

The couple pushes up the Yugtamund River toward home. Their little *akwintan* slowly turns a sharp bend. The three secondary temples at Utamusak come into view. They are just visible on the wooded hill to the couple's right. As they pass, the wife whispers a small prayer and sprinkles a few of her *wowanok* into the water.

All three buildings are the same in size; six paces wide and twelve strides long. The western third of each structure is filled with the mummified remains of past leaders. They now sleep on platform shelves. Thick mat walls divide the tombs from the main halls where blackened likenesses gaze toward the departed. Stuffed bodies of wild canines and scavenger birds hang from the curved rafters to guard over the store of riches. These are the houses of the nation's wealth and the living quarters of the seven high priests.

But no one is home. They have all gathered in the main temple. Go along the sanded path. Touch the *pokowanz* stone that rests atop a low pile of rocks. It is a solid crystal, the size of an infant in fetal slumber. The main temple can be seen from here. It is much larger, being eight strides by thirty three. Wooden statues stand at each corner of the building. They represent a *ketasku*, an *amonsokwat*, an *utakaway*, and a human giant.

The ossuary holds the mummies of the most important leaders of old. It is a physical map of lineage and lore. Completed epochs sleep in the tuff skin. The faces of past personalities are now expressionless. They are so still that one can imagine a hint of movement which is not there.

The main hall is the repository of the greatest wealth in sacred material and bark writings. All the known history, all the proven philosophies are preserved in strands of symbols bitten across the bark. Only the seven can bring full meaning to each thought as they alone have put in the years of learning. The perpetual fire is directly in the center of the building. It cracks and hisses in the wet wood. It is enough light for only the immediate surroundings.

The seven have gathered near the eastern entrance. Twilight lingers just outside the covered threshold. Four men find a spot at each cardinal direction. They sit around the marked circle. Their power of sight grows internal. The ability to comprehend has advanced into pure intuition. One recites a prayer in the language of the ancients. Following each stanza, the three others exhale, "*Hwow*." They verbalize in unison to best send the words to spirit ears.

The volunteer for this journey lies with limbs stretched outward and head toward the East. Two others attend him. They administer the divine liquid in a steady dosage. He drifts from his wakened state. The soul begins to seek an exit from the flesh. The body reacts. The two hold him down, but one arm escapes and rises to touch the next dimension. His mouth widens.

Breath becomes speech. Syllables are deciphered into meaning by the two listeners as they hunch over the body. One interprets aloud:

POWHATAN:
THE STORY OF A PEOPLE

"Pamasawu."
"Pamasawu...a hollow shell."
"Nightfall, emptiness, hollow entrapment."
"The, the sun sets, east."
"Great city. Pull down the sun."
"A city, glowing. Rings. It is a shell."
"Land melts into the bay."
"All dissolves in water."
"Sand, in changing currents."
The second attendant whispers into the receptacle, "Why? Tell us!"
The interpreter continues, "The shell is strong. The sands rush against it once. A second great struggle."
"Helplessness, defeat. Ruin."
"It grows...moves west. It opens."
"The sand. It closes."
"The, mouth, tight. A creature. Trapped."
"Sand rolls. The spirit...is lost."
"Knowledge lost."
"No one. No more."
"Solid, all things inside the pearl."
"Abandon. Forget."
"The shell is tight."
"No one to open."
"A pearl...no light upon it."
"Piles. The one sinks lower...out of sight."
"In the darkness. In eternity."
The body turns onto one side and curls into a ball. Silence is all he has left to give.

The hall is engulfed in confusion. Each strains to interpret this message from beyond. Debate turns into discord. Passion takes over reason.

Finally, the head priest calms his associates, "It is simple! The Chesapeak, they are a danger that will only grow. If they are not dealt with, they will eventually overpower us all. We will lose everything we are. That is what lies in the future."

The chorus sounds, "We can not allow it!"

"We have no choice!" an individual speaks up, "How can we begin to fight them when that will be the first step in the cycle toward our doom?"

Another contributes, "We can not let them be! We can not make it easy for them! The Wind Children. Some are with them. Their blood is mixed!"

"No, no!" the head priest mediates, "We will not let them be. We can not be passive. We must act. But we will not fight them."

"What then can we do?"

"We will just kill them…all."

And so, the oracle is delivered to Wahunsenakok. He assembles his hunters and chooses one thousand of them. The half-god taps each on the shoulder in blessing. Opechankano leads them to the southern peninsula.

Humans regress into their bestial state. Predators fall upon their surprised quarry. No gestures of compassion are performed. No remorse is felt. No spoils are gathered. And as the day ends, all that was a shining civilization in the east is consumed in the flames of eradication.

Chapter 6

Five days now. Nothing but the grime and sweat that hardens the shirt. Nothing but the stars and the salt sea in every direction. It has been five days since the storm blew the fleet into oblivion. Christopher Newport looks for two lanterns in the darkness. Both are there. Distance can be discerned from the size and location of the lights. Faint silhouettes are distinguished on the rolling black surface. Captain Ratcliffe almost took the Discovery home, but he managed to regain his bearings. All three vessels are still together.

Good Captain Newport sniffs twice. There is a hearty strain of sweetness in the air. It is a sweetness of berries and flowers. It dispels the stale sea brine which has filled the nostrils for far too long. Sightings of insects are becoming more constant. Just yesterday, someone swore that he heard the clatter of sea birds. Christopher believes in himself. He believes in the stars that guide him. Land is out there. The bay they seek is near. It has to be.

Another night is almost done. The gentle luminescence of morning reveals an uneven horizon in the west. The deliverance of those simple words returns his confidence. "Land ho!"

Eyes open below deck. Passengers stir. Mariners clamor. It has been one hundred and twenty days on the barren sea. Today is the only one that will be remembered. The waiting that rusts one's mettle now dissipates. Land ho! Land ho!

The Susan Constant leads the fleet in. This must be the bay. Captain Gosnold shouts out a confirmation from the God Speed. He would know best where they are. He has explored the American coast extensively.

Cheers burst out on every deck. They have not been taken too far north after all. Instead, they have come right to the fabled bay they call, Chesapeake—that lagoon of giants that is so well hidden by its eastern peninsula.

Christopher beams. Smiling faces look upon him. Their faith in his abilities is revived. He participated in Drake's famous raid into the harbor of Cadiz. He helped capture the biggest prize of the Spanish treasure fleet. Now, this accomplishment is added to the list. Captain Newport has made the Caribbean his nautical play ground. America is a part of him, and he is a part of it. After all, he left an arm on this side of the ocean while fighting the Spanish. The good captain has not stumbled. Their hero has delivered them to their destiny.

Slowly they move through the narrow opening. Methodically, a sounder swings the weight forward into the water. It hits bottom. By the time the hull crosses over, the colored leather ties inform him of the depth.

Patawok swim along side the three large bodies. *Koyakwus* glide in close to get a good look. The better sort on the list of passengers is allowed above deck. Their faces warm in the sunshine. Their eyes consume the glorious sight of pines and sandy earth which make up the low-lying shore. Their ears fill with the squawks of escorting birds. Their noses inflate with the sweet breeze. Their mouths open to taste the flavors of fruits and foliage that thicken the air. They have arrived! Salvation is this place.

Good Captain Newport chooses twenty soldiers and gentlemen to accompany him for landfall. Oars push the longboat to match the waves. As the hull runs aground, boots splash the light surf. Soft dunes and tuff beach grass are witness to this moment. The newcomers play out their parts for droves of scampering *monahamsha*. They strut and fret for an hour upon the sand before entering the wooded interior.

The wanderers are beside themselves as they stumble through this unfamiliar world. The trees are towers. They appear to hold up the very sky. Strait, proud trees—nothing the like in England. These are healthy growths—virgins, with long lives and unblemished trunks.

Small freshwater creeks meander through the woods. Meadows are blanketed with wild flowers. Brilliant red fruits, with their seeds latched upon the skin, are large enough to fill the palm. Everything is larger here. The ancient earth controls this paradise. It is not overrun by the pollution of humanity that so easily stunts the growth of natural life.

The sun grows weary. It slides down the sky as the explorers trek back to the beach. They begin to sense a difference in the land around them. Shadows slink about the trees. The feeling that frightens all sun-loving creatures sinks into the stomach.

POWHATAN:
THE STORY OF A PEOPLE

A few of them reach the longboat as it happens. A swarm of short rods glide through the darkness. Two arrows hit their mark in the body of a mariner. The surprised crowd reacts. A few run to the longboat. They see objects creeping toward them on all fours. Their gestures are neither human nor animal. Poor Gabriel Archer throws up his arms in self-defense. An arrowhead cuts through both his hands. At least his face does not feel the sharp stone.

Closer they come, with bows clenched tightly in their mouths. They rush the landing party. Captain Newport fires a shot at the darkness. Others do the same, yet they hear nothing but the hollow echo of wasted lead. It is swallowed up by the eerie cries that only men can make in fits of rage. Howls slowly fade into the woods. Their point is clear. The Indigenies do not accept this arrival.

A moment of stillness, the length indeterminate. Pokinz waits for an occurrence that has not yet been scheduled by time. He knows they are coming. Today feels as good as any.

He meditates. They've wandered about for so long. They must be searching for their people at Chesapeak. But those were rubbed out almost two years ago. The earth has covered all. It is a forsaken place. The Nansemund hardly go there. Even ghosts don't dwell there.

Toes clench the sandy ground. Pokinz studies the grains that jostle between the slender digits. He has always had pretty feet. They are perfect in proportion, agile, with good muscle tone. His are the only pair of feet at the river bank. Everyone else waits back in town. They have not the usual toils today. The fishing equipment goes without repair. The crops go untended. All concentration is on the preparation for a grand welcoming, which none can guarantee will even happen today.

A fire rages under the square grilling rack that is filled with *tatamoho*. Spits, holding *kupotun*, lean against the rack to dry for long storage. The great cooking pot simmers in its nest of hot coals. A stew of *tutaskuk* meat and *pakohikowo* ash boils within. Another pot overflows with *misikwatash* while *apetapon* cakes sizzle on a heated slab beside it. The delectable aroma perfumes the whole town.

Pokinz wonders about the five men he sent to the tribe's hunting island. He worries about their progress in catching the stranger's attention.

He continues to sort through the many thoughts in his mind. Where did that fourth one come from? They came in three large *musawusuk*. Then, on the third day, a fourth one appeared. It's much smaller then the others. One of the others must have been pregnant. A grin spreads across his face. Fingers stretch to feel a soft wind. The air is warming. It is a good day. It is too good for dealing with those people.

Pokinz remembers the last report of how the strangers sailed right to an old Chesapeak city as if they knew where it was. They must be searching for their lost people. The attack was very thorough. The only thing the intruders found were *muskeskiminz*.

At least the strangers did nothing to the *akwintan* they had found. So much time goes into making a good one. All the slow burning of the trunk and chipping away of the charred wood with stone awls until the log is hollowed out...It is such time-consuming and exacting work to strip the bark and tighten the wood properly so that it will resist water.

Pokinz nurses a personal oath. The strangers will not come unannounced to Kekotan. They will not intrude as they had done the second day. A frightened group of Nansemund had to hide in the forest until those trespassers finally left. A whole morning's work of gathering had been ruined. Just when the fire was perfect, and the *kaway* began to open, those thieves showed up and took the pearls.

The playful gurgle of water soothes his reasoning.

"Symbols..." Pokinz utters.

Concepts parade through his mind. What is that symbol they planted like a tree on the beach? It had a bare trunk and a branch on either side of its top portion. What does it mean to them? What is the meaning behind their very existence? What is their purpose here? They must come today.

One of the five lookouts splash up the near bank. He calls out, "The strangers saw us. Their leader has one arm. He held it first up to the sky in challenge, but then covered his heart in respect. They are coming."

"Let us welcome them!" Pokinz trumpets. Decorated warriors assemble at the river's edge. Activity increases in the town. Guides swim ahead of the little vessel as it makes its way upstream. The water is like polished silver. Its dancing surface intensifies the brightness of the day. Rays of sunlight cut through every available opening along the shaded beach, creating a broken haze of fanciful beauty.

Pokinz can see them clearly. Such hairy faces. So many garments. What kind of material is it? It is not *tsehaho*, or *wikiyopis*, or any tree bark. So many things made from material that is not of this world. How different is their world?

POWHATAN:
THE STORY OF A PEOPLE

He fakes a smile. Two men slowly hop out from either side and pull the craft firmly aground. Appropriate hand gestures are made. All step upon the sandy soil. The Kekotan bow before their company and scratch the ground to show that they, the children of the land, greet those from the waters and pray that the earth will bless them, and hold them upon her bosom with loving care.

The host makes the customary speech, knowing that the words can not be understood. He hopes the strangers may be able to comprehend the hospitable tone in his voice. "I, Pokinz, father to this tribe, son of the great father of this land, welcome you. Come. Eat to strengthen your bodies and rest to refresh your minds. I hear you have been busy exploring our world." He gestures with both hands in a beckoning motion, "Follow. I will guide you to where we can all sit together as one." He straightens the *kawasow* upon his shoulders and proceeds up the slope to the reception that awaits them in town.

The strangers are slower in feasting as the food is unfamiliar to them. But the flavor quickens their pace until all jaws are busy. Tongues roll in delight. Eyes glitter with the warm sensation of consumption.

As the food disappears, the women return to collect the plates. Everyone sits in the afterglow of digestion. Pokinz presents a new pipe of dried clay, embellished with bits of *matasun*. One hand holds the long, slender shaft as the other carefully empties the chopped leaves into the narrow bowl. Smoke rushes out of the bowl that is angled away from the face. Pokinz relaxes his expression. Shoulders drop slightly. "This gift of the spirits...I share with you. We all are kindred spirits, even though our bodies are different."

He passes the pipe to his guest who gently takes hold of its stem with his one hand. The stranger gently handles it in the proper position and imbibes the smoke. There is a familiarity that each of the strangers show in this pleasure. But they are not yet experienced with the herb. They suck on the pipe, as if drinking the smoke for simple consumption rather then for spiritual communion.

The dance show begins. An elderly instructor keeps in time by clapping his hands in a steady beat. His high-pitched voice rings out above the jingling anklets and rattling instruments of the dancers. It is another legend of ancient times when heroes hunted monsters and dangers of this world were created more often by beings from the beyond. Some dancers become wild-faced, as if possessed by the very characters they play. Feet scorch the ground in a mesmerizing blaze as the audience looses itself in bewildering imagination. The basic story is interpreted by the mixed audience, but only some of them can understand the important lessons learned by the protagonist.

Pokinz studies his guest from the corner of his eye. If the dance fascinates them, they will want to learn. They will stay and they will become willing to share. But how long will they want to stay? How much will they be willing to share?

The one-armed man turns to his host. Pokinz gently smiles. The left hand pulls out a few blue beads to thank the dancers. Pokinz acknowledges the stranger's generosity, "These beads are as precious as pearls. You have much of them. We have heard of your interest in our pearls. Our pearls are valued far and wide. Even the Masawomik trade for them. With trade comes the sharing of more. May our two worlds come together with such beads. It is good for us both."

Pepiskunima sits at the edge of the high ground that overlooks the Powhatan River. He is now a grown man who governs the town of Chawopo for his mother, Ohalas. But he still listens to his mother. That is why he sits alone this night with all his attention on the river island across from him.

It is a familiar scene with unfamiliar components. Three *musawusuk* are tethered to shoreline trees at the western end of the Paspaheg hunting island. They had been at the mouth of the river for days. Slowly, the flotilla maneuvered through the tight channel, avoiding thick shoals of *kaway* and *tsekoma* beds that clog the banks. They had first looked at the back water channel that leads to Chiskiyak—the place where all those past misfortunes began. But these are not the same people as the ones Pakikino had brought. Their physical features are more unique. The skin is lighter, like that of a newborn. Their hair and eyes have much more variety of colors.

"What interest would they have there?" Pepiskunima examines aloud, "I was not even born when that happened. Pakikino is long dead. Few bother telling his story anymore."

He works out the puzzle in his mind. Why have they moved so slowly and stayed so long? That island is nothing but swamp and vines. Food can not grow there. The river at this point becomes undrinkable as the year warms.

Bobbing in the water beside the largest vessel is the *kekwiyos*. It is the same one that the Paspaheg welcomed a few days ago. Word of this visit reached Ohalas. She immediately sent her tactful son amongst those staunch allies of the Chikahominy to coax the strangers away. He managed to entice them for a visit to his own town.

The warming rays of that morning found Pepiskunima and his entourage in grand style. Men glimmered in translucent yellow or red *pokun*; the

POWHATAN:
THE STORY OF A PEOPLE

common emollient of *amonsokwat* fat and herbal dye that protects the skin and enhances the appearance as any clothing. They had ceremonial weapons—not made to withstand battle but simply worn to impress.

The women were embellished with tattoos. They displayed elaborate designs under their high cheeks, on the balls of their chins, and across their short foreheads. Limbs were wrapped with lively images of snakes and geometric patterns. The tattoos portrayed an array of pretty flowers and fruits and animals in cartoon form. Such is stained in black, red and other warm hues from permanent dyes rubbed inside punctured flesh.

As the strangers landed, their hosts descended the high embankment to greet them. Pepiskunima played a song on his reed flute. He then sat down upon his mat and lit his pipe. As he calmly smoked, the wind children studied him. With his crown of *wushakwun* hair, it was easy for the strangers to surmise that this was a man of high status. The long locks at his left were knotted in the shape of a flower, while his shaved side was covered by a soft *matasun* plate that molded the skull. Two long feathers were attached to the scalp comb that spiked through the opening of his crown. His body was covered in red with a chain of *wowanok* beads harnessing his neck and pearl bracelets bounding his wrists. His face was coated in blue with grains of *machkwon* that sparkled like the night sky. And hanging from each lobe was a bird claw, set in *matasun*.

The welcoming party stood around their leader. Their display had a spectral quality that would lead anyone to question the true position of humans in the cosmic arrangement. They were a part of—as well as apart from—the natural world in which they existed.

Pepiskunima also studied the small group that stood before him. Their garments were too bizarre to fathom. Their tools looked so unworldly. The man with one arm...was he born that way? The reports from Kekotan suggested that he was their leader. The gaunt man who stood beside him was also mentioned. His skin was so pallid. The way he carried himself was with frailty. The eyes were framed in sunken weariness, and yet they burned with a youthful thrill.

At the proper moment, Pepiskunima rose from his spot and beckoned all to follow. The motley group assailed the steep hill. They ventured along the path through emerald trees and by silver brooks until they reached freshly-planted fields. Hanging from poles that aligned the gardens were large gourds. They were hollow containers with one hole in the side, just large enough for *mowakus* birds to slip through. They are welcomed tenants for their hunger keeps insects from the maturing crops.

The parade wound past the flat baking stones covered with *apon* cakes that dried by the heat of the sun. The dough had been fully pounded into a paste and soaked in boiling water. The strangers liked this gritty bread. They liked the way its sharp, spicy taste lingered in their mouths and how it filled their stomachs with a satisfying heaviness. They enjoyed the hospitality and the entertainment. The festivities were no different than any other. All the usual dancing shows and long, intense speeches that drain the orators to near collapse were performed on cue.

Trouble occurred later when the *kekwiyos* entered the Apamatuk River. After some time, they spotted the thin white smoke of habitation streaming up along the west bank. Warriors appeared at the water's edge, fully armed with bows in their hands. A *monahak* was slung across every back.

Without a hint of fear, the black-faced leader crossed his legs to sit before them. His speech of inquisition and defiance was thunderous. A distinct ingredient of anger rang in his clear delivery. He then held out his bow with one arm and his pipe with the other, demanding from the intruders which they meant to choose. They chose peace and were allowed to land.

The comparative events of that day still linger in the thin man's memory. He stands in the cool night air above deck. Long, spindly fingers dance upon the railing. His concentration slowly drowns in the river.

This man does have a name. It is, George Percy. This is a name that is larger then his appearance may hint. It is a name that, only two hundred years earlier, was on the cusp of royalty. But its prominence was lost in battle. It is his old, blue blood that emaciates him, and causes a chill from his company.

Percy gazes across the water to the black high ground along the opposite bank. The esquire may feel the presence of Pepiskunima, but does not see him there. All that Pepiskunima can see are listless shadows that occupy the floating lodges. There is a steady yellow glow at the back of each. It is reminiscent of the insects that come to illuminate the night when the year is older.

Pepiskunima knows the strangers mean to take that island for their own. That is what happened in the southern country. People like them took over an island and explored the rivers. They are trying to learn something about this world, which takes a while.

He listens to the pleasant songs that resonate from within the vessels. The sound is a bit melancholy. They expose a soft yearning. Pepiskunima

POWHATAN:
THE STORY OF A PEOPLE

whispers to the stars above him. "These people still came from the same bag that Manibuzo had kept for the first woman. Not one is among them. They are without feminine support. Every man needs the harmony of womanhood to help him get through life." He accepts this as he bids goodnight to the great *amonsokwat* that twinkles in the sky beyond.

Chapter 7

A father sprinkles *upook* in a thin ring upon the ground. He sits in the middle and performs a prayer of gratitude to Ahon for bringing another beautiful day. The river swells with bathers. They playfully submerge into the liquid that purifies their bodies and revitalizes their souls. And when this day is done, the same routine will take place again.

These are the people of Paspaheg. The main township lies along a flat plain on the low north bank of the Powhatan River, near the mouth of the Chikahominy. Their *weyowanz* is at home with his wife.

Wowinchopunk is quiet. The stress of decisions to make for his people clouds the mind. The wife does not want to calmly wait for him to speak. "Men just can't think and talk at the same time." She sighs.

"And women just talk without thinking," he returns.

She stiffens. "Well, that kind of talk won't help."

Gentle fingers caress his face.

"Hum," she muses, "time you had another plucking. We've let your right side grow out. Kohatayo is already here. It's too warm now for so much hair. Maybe it will help you feel better."

"No," he moans, "I feel enough pain as it is."

She pays him no mind and searches the basket beside her, pulling out two shells of matching size. "These should do." She feels the sharp edges carefully.

He pleads with her, "I don't need much."

"Oh yes you do," she sings back.

Slowly, she scrapes the skin with one shell until it collects a few hairs. Then, she clamps down with the other, trapping them in between. With a swift jerk, she pulls the hairs out by their roots. He grimaces quietly.

POWHATAN:
THE STORY OF A PEOPLE

The wife probes, "You don't want to look like those strangers. All that nasty body hair. Just think of the dirt and insects they have trapped in those beards, and how uncomfortable their skin must be, chafing all day long."

He shrugs, "I don't want to think about them."

"But that is all you think about. Tell me," she pursues.

"What can I do?" Wowinchopunk mulls over the situation, "They have forced their way onto the island. They are clearing the land. They are resistant when we meet them. They show no manners toward me or our people. I sent two councilmen with open arms…They just stared at them and gave them nothing."

"What happened yesterday, when you went there?" She glares when he hesitates.

Wowinchopunk purses his lips to formulate an answer. "It was a disgrace. It was a…disgrace."

She moves to his chest. Wowinchopunk gazes into his wife's eyes. He can not resist those searching eyes. "I sent for our neighbors to join me. I had one hundred fighting men to show them. The strangers showed me terrible things. They had all their things unloaded. They were cutting down the trees and slicing them up with a variety of strange knives. Half of them were guarding the other half, forcing them to work. They had placed their hunting camp in the middle of a dirt clearing. Their lodges were tubular huts, made of cloth. They had lean-twos and conical hovels of wasted timber and driftwood. It was a dirty camp. Only the simplest of people would live in such conditions."

She pulls back the shells. "What happened?"

Wowinchopunk continues, "We were an impressive sight. We matched them in number. We excelled them in courage!

"I signed out my threats to them. I signed out my willingness to accept their pleas for forgiveness. I received nothing. They refused my demand to lay their weapons aside. They refused to communicate their intentions. They refused friendship."

"What did you do?"

"It happened without me." He explains, "One of my people ventured too close. His eye caught site of a *tomahak*. He went for it. That is how it began.

"One of their people grabbed it from him and struck him on the arm. One of my men came at them with a raised *monahak* to defend his friend. I was not in control. Events were taking control of themselves. It didn't feel right. It didn't feel right at all.

"But we were ready. We would have shown our worth. Still, it would not have been war, but mindless killing on both sides. How could our ancestors look favorably upon us? We couldn't have won.

"I lead my men away. I was filled with anger. Should I have made such a sacrifice to rid this world of those people?"

His wife looks away for a moment. "Just yesterday, a very gangly man found the trail that follows the river from Kekotan all the way to the foot hills of the Blue Mountains. He had three others with him. Just imagine the wonders they saw, like an *ayosapanik*—its cheeks bloating with *chikikwaminz* and *picheminz*. I can just see the little thing guiding the explorers from above, stretching its little legs wide as it jumps from a perch high in the canopy of *mowok* trees. The air inflates the folds of skin along both its sides. And the little thing glides a nice distance, before landing on another branch. I admire their life. Their whole world is between solid earth and ethereal sky.

"Anyway, that gangly man—I think they call him, Percy—he and his partners enjoyed all the wildflowers in the underbrush. So many cheerful colors. They couldn't help but keep walking, just to see more.

"And when they came to the first community, well, that was our most eastern village, just down the river from here. All the people welcomed those unexpected guests. They had come to us, with nothing in their arms and nothing on their backs. They were simply exploring the trail that has been used by so many for so long. All they wanted to do that day was travel.

"Our men were all out hunting. So the women did a wonderful job in hosting their guests. They filled them with *muskeskiminz* and other delightful things. Percy was quite happy. His friends were too. Of course, the messenger that came to tell us of their arrival startled them when he left there. They spook easily, it seems. Just think if they had not been disturbed, they might have kept going up the trail. They could have dropped by to see us, personally. They might even have made it to Awohatek by now, just walking along, simply following the trail to see where it would take them next."

Wowinchopunk rolls his eyes, but does not interrupt. She scrapes his chest smooth and verbalizes her thoughts further, "Well, they did turn back. But then, they ran across one of our healers. You know. The real old one? He was so kind to them by showing his garden with all its flowering berries and fruits and herbs. He didn't tell them anything. Healers are so secretive of their medicines. But he did offer each a sample of *upook*. Just think what joy it brought those strangers. I hear they were all so thankful for his generosity.

POWHATAN:
THE STORY OF A PEOPLE

"Well, the day was about up. They got back to their people. And here we are...You still haven't given them the *wushakwun* you promised."

"Perhaps another chance at kindness?" Wowinchopunk gently tugs at her earring. The strand of tiny shell beads only looks fragile. Purple and white nestle together in a circle, expressing a universal beauty.

He concludes, "It would be a good test to see what those people are really about. Perhaps they deserve that much before we can make a final judgment of them."

She slaps his legs with affection. "Let's get you glistening like a fish." She applies *asiminz* oil along her husband's shapely arms and shoulders, and all over his solid chest and upper back. The skin is soft. She likes it that way.

He caresses her forearms. "Looks like you also need a bit of plucking." The wife looks up with anxiety. She knows he is right.

Nawiwan studies the water beside him. It is light brown. It is a shade that is both warm in nurturing quality and soothingly cool to the skin. Farther off, the liquid is green. Farther still are strips of silver ripples that appear and disappear upon a fluctuating blue plain. He knows the river has many complexities. It possesses a personality, as any living thing, with an array of characteristics strung together along its course.

Nawiwan brings seven bowmen with him. Word had traveled upriver from Weyanok that the strangers where in the area. The single *akwintan* winds around the island bend where the *moninag* flourish. These birds have inhabited the place since—always.

Nawiwan is outwardly calm, although his heart beats uncontrollably. His eyes move all around to realize everything. The strangers are twenty four in number and about the same in appearance. Distinctions hide behind the veil of unfamiliarity. One of the strangers, a stout little man with a beard the color of burning coals, calls out repeatedly, "Wingapow!" One bowman murmurs in relief, "Well, they are learning."

Paddles slice into the water to push the little craft along. The two parties meet at the bank and communicate with hand signals. Nawiwan surmises that the strangers mean to explore up river. One gets his attention. His hands show the scars of some recent mishap, but they move well and must be healing. These hands smooth out a thin, broad leaf upon a soft patch of ground. He draws on it like the seers do when recording on skins.

Nawiwan gives it a try. He glides the staining stick along, picturing the river as best he knows. He begins where it feeds the bay and continues to the great curls where they are now. He designates Awohatek and Powhatan, then far beyond to the source of the river in the mountainous land that is Kwiwank. The strangers talk among themselves in their peculiar language. Exuberance grows.

Two groups detach. The strangers travel up river while Nawiwan heads for another landing site to exchange all but one of his bowmen for his two sisters and their baskets full of smoked *tsekoma*. They can not keep up with the *kekwiyos* which has the advantage of catching the winds in its open cloth. Both vessels maneuver through the great winding course. Once past the curls, the strangers finally stop at a landing where a few onlookers have gathered. Nawiwan catches up with them here.

The females are so happy with their gifts of metal bells and blue beads. They flutter in delight over the decorative hair needles. A tall, intensely thin man notices the captive boy from the south. The blond hair gives him away. The *kekwiyos* people treat the matter as an abnormality and dismiss it before uneasy questions are sounded.

The travelers enter the hilly country. Eventually, they come to a familiar landing site. Nawiwan spots his brother-in-law sitting on a reed mat. His name is, Ashuwakwid. He is the *weyowanz* of the Awohatek people.

Another mat fronting the leader is soon filled by the one called, Newport.

"One Arm," Ashuwakwid announces, "I give you my headpiece, as we are brothers." The man smiles in acceptance as he grasps the crown of *wushakwun* hair, stiffened with red *pokun*.

The feast is interrupted by a messenger. Quickly, the Awohatek form a welcoming gauntlet and raise a shout as someone strides through. The *kekwiyos* people do not know what to do in this circumstance. And so, they remain seated and silent.

Pawahunt sits beside his co-guest. Christopher hands out gifts to both tribal leaders. Nawiwan draws the map again to everyone's satisfaction and is granted responsibility to be the official guide.

The party is relocated to Powhatan town. This time, Nawiwan sits with Newport who faces the two tribal leaders and a senior spiritual adviser.

Pawahunt motions as best he can the words he voices. "I am the end of Tsenakomako. The beginning is at the great bay. All that lies between is my father's possession. We are all his children."

The one with the bruised hands performs a tale of hate and friendship, of visits that did, and did not go well. The trio works in tandem to interpret the story. They have heard of the sour reception at old Chesapeak, where they

POWHATAN:
THE STORY OF A PEOPLE

first landed, and how most of the other tribes welcomed them. The news has been fully reported throughout

Tsenakomako. They even know of the problems with Paspaheg who see the Wind Children as trespassers.

Pawahunt tries to console them. "Your people camp in a wasteland. Why should they care if someone finds use of such a place? If you do not cause any discomfort to any one, or harm to the land itself, then camp there. Children of Powhatan will welcome you and protect your people."

Christopher understands enough. He moves toward Pawahunt and places his own cloth *kawasow* upon the man's shoulders. The left hand presses against the oiled chest. With a firm voice, he utters, "Wingapow. Cham." A hand print is left.

One of the travelers stays for the night with Pawahunt while Nawiwan goes with his charges to scout the area of the *pakwachonk* before the sun leaves them.

This is the place where the river is most active. Water rushes over smooth boulders. It crashes against them, boring holes into the stone over lengths of time that can not be witnessed by only one life span. It can release rocks from the earth, and it can bury them forever.

The explorers decide that the waters are too harsh for their vessel to get through. They return to the landing at Powhatan for the night. Nawiwan settles in among his new friends on board. The water rocks them to sleep and the sounds of hungry birds wake them for another day.

The one who stayed the night in Powhatan Town returns to his comrades. He tells of all the mats provided him for sleeping and all the night-time snacks. Even a woman came to him. But when she found that he had nothing of value to give her, she lost interest and left.

Pawahunt is treated to their food. They have a fine meat, called pork. It is light, and plentiful of flavor. Their bread, however, is hard and tasteless. Their water is an irony in itself. How a liquid can burn like fire in the mouth is beyond reason. Ashuwakwid has a few helpings of the liquid to see if its horrid taste gets any better. Somehow, it does.

The strangers mention a minor thievery of two bags. Pawahunt is able to retrieve them, along with other items the travelers did not even know were missing. Captain Newport expresses an interest of the land beyond the *pakwachonk*. Pawahunt interprets the hand gesturing, "How long to Kwiwank?"

Pawahunt tries to explain, "That is days from here…through dangerous wilderness. My people never go there."

The left hand scratches out a map in the dirt. Pawahunt studies it. "And who is beyond?" He decides to delay an answer. The gathering separates with the Awohatek returning for home, Pawahunt moving overland, and Nawiwan guiding his guests upriver once again.

The strangers find Pawahunt at the edge of the rolling waters. He stands at the bank, viewing the rocky stretch of the river. Tree carcasses, ripped from the banks as far away as Kwiwank, litter the area. Every islet and sandbar is thick with crowds of resting *koyakwus* and other fish-eating birds. The roar of the water is so great here that one can actually feel the noise. After a long moment of reflection, Pawahunt explains, "Along the main trail, skirting the river for a day and a half, you would come to Machimko. They are our *maskapow*." He studies Captain Newport's reaction, not continuing until he is sure that what he has tried to relay has been fully understood. "There is another town after that, and then another where the river splits in two. You would be in dark wilderness. Then, you reach the ruff country of Kwiwank. It is too far. My people can not help you there. You should not try."

The captain responds with an idea. It is understood to be an offer of military help. Five hundred Wind Children would be at Pawahunt's disposal. Together, they could easily bring down Machimko. All the captives would be his. It is a very tempting idea.

Pawahunt adds, "Every year, at the falling of the leaves, when all settle down, is when the Monakan raid our towns. That is the time we look to the west with blood in our eyes. That is the best time for such a war.

Captain Newport seems to understand. Pawahunt departs, leaving his new allies to enjoy the *pakwachonk* by themselves. They scrutinize the large rocks and small islands that lie in the wake of the rapids. The largest island is at the extreme of their visual range. Across the center of this low plain is a tall mount of solid rock that breaks through a thin coating of earth. Trees latch on by their roots to every available nook. Nawiwan has been there many times. The flat slabs of stone that spread across the water from the island make for good platforms from which to lay *nesakan*. There have been fishing camps on that island since—always.

Nawiwan draws his attention back to his friends. They have dug a hole on one of the islets nearby. They hoist up a post that looks like a tree with only two branches near its top. They carve symbols on the trunk between the branches. All gather around it with clasped hands and bowed heads.

POWHATAN:
THE STORY OF A PEOPLE

Nawiwan watches them in silence, waiting to see what comes next. It is a great shout with right arms hurled into the air. He looks about for a new arrival, but sees no one. "They must be shouting at this tree they just planted." He whispers.

The good captain tries to explain how each of the two branches represents Newport and Pawahunt. The carving proclaims the joining of the two. Such is this sturdy tree that now stands for all to witness, forever and ever more.

The *kekwiyos* finally returns to Awohatek late in the night. Poor Ashuwakwid gingerly sees to his guests. He does not stay with them for long, being too ill from the effects of that hot drink. The feeling of exhaustion is similar to that of taking *winak* drink at the beginning of every year. That drink also creates a violent period of vomiting. But at least it energizes the body and cleans the blood, and does not leave the head pounding.

By the next day, Ashuwakwid feels well enough to see the visitors off with a good celebratory meal. Another thief is caught and beaten to everyone's satisfaction before the usual revelry fills the rest of the morning.

Ashuwakwid expresses curiosity of his guest's weaponry. After a moment of coaxing, a demonstration is performed. The audience sits attentively as the shooter strikes metal against a black rock. A small spark ignites a thick string that is fastened to the weapon. They watch as he brings the long stick up to his face. Fingers pull at a lever. Another lever drops the hissing coil into a pan. A moment is ripped from reality in a violent seizure that shakes the very ground. The weak take flight. The weakest cower with screeching cries. Christopher immediately rises. He moves to Ashuwakwid, pealing off his red sleeveless garment to give to the troubled man. The good Captain makes an oath never to use such a weapon upon friends.

Another day brings the explorers back to the great curls. Nawiwan guides them past the *moninag* colony.

The group goes ashore just above the Apamatuk confluence. Nawiwan escorts them over the low plain. The trail passes a large field, freshly seeded with *poketawas*. As the group ascends a gentle hill, the world around them transforms completely in its feel. An open meadow welcomes them. It is peaceful here. There is a warm breeze that exhilarates the senses. The ground is speckled with the various colors of wildflowers. Some distance away is a collection of females in the shade of an illustrious *muskiminz* tree. It is the court of Oposumokwonusk. She governs her people with the help of her brother, Kokwowasum. He has already encountered these *kekwiyos* people. Now, it is her turn.

Her long raven hair falls unbound to the reed mat upon which she sits. She covers her robust figure with only a *matahay,* buffed white and accentuated with purple shell beading all along the fringed edges. Her face is solid and handsome under a coronet of *matasun* that is beset with tiny white bones. More of this precious metal dangles from each ear and wraps six times around her neck, framing her face in a saffron aura.

The maidens are at an appropriate distance behind her. Their hair is uniform, with short sides and bangs while braided tresses tumble down their backs. They provide *apon* and smiles. The *weyowanskwa* offers *upook*. She requests a demonstration of the *pakusak*. As expected, the woman hardly flinches when it is discharged.

The *kekwiyos* crosses the great river to Weyanok. From a sandy landing area, they trek up a slight depression in the riverbank. The town lies in a large swath of cleared land that begins near a deep crevice where a tiny creek hides within. It skirts the riverside to the edge of a great marsh and pushes the trees far inland toward higher ground. Large gardens surround the various buildings that make up this community. Activity is everywhere. But no movement is hurried. Enjoyment of the day is what seems most important.

Kekwatog is also visiting. He meets the one-armed man with his own offering of *upook*. He hears how impressive Oposumokwonusk had been. His attempt to better her falls well short. Nawiwan repeats the oaths of friendship and retells the stories of the tour.

Kekwatog and Captain Newport eventually send their respective followers away for a while to go on a private walk along the riverside. The two enjoy the quietness of the river. A constant breeze sends small waves crashing against the bank below them. Newport studies the ring of soft *matasun* in both of the old man's ears and the chain of pearls that is rapped three times around his neck. He is not an official man, but plain, quiet, genuine by nature. He is more an observer than a participant in anything that happens in his world. Kekwatog does not study the Captain. Impressions are what he collects. He can sense the concern that the outsider nurses. It is a quiet fear of rejection by those of Pamasawu. He knows the strangers have uneasy relations with the Paspaheg. The Weyanok also have bad blood with that tribe. The Weyanok are loyal to his brother.

In town, the strangers meet the old seer who came with Kekwatog. His frame is slight, but not frail. He is as limber and energetic as the next. The sunken eyes even retain a faint luster of youth. His thin beard glows pure white. The hair on his arms is greyer. Nawiwan picks up a branch. With each plucked leaf, he counts: "nekut, ning, nus, yog, pawan, komoting, topawos, nuswasto, kekata, kask."

The last leaf falls to the ground. He drops ten more leaves, and then announces, "That is the age of this man. He is our past. He is our wisdom."

The travelers fidget. Each knows the main camp is near. They are uneasy and want to conclude their adventure. Nawiwan has harvested many memories. Sadly, he too knows the time for departure has come. He may never share his presence with these people again—at least in this lifetime.

Two hundred mercenaries from Chikahominy, Paspaheg, and Chiskiyak move stealthily through the woods. Arrows enter the stranger's camp. Many fall at the start. The defenders have not their weapons at the ready. Little resistance quickly turns into no resistance at all. Some gather along their eastern trench to fight with what ever they can. Hovels within the camp are ripped open by the waves of arrows. The attackers rush in and retreat at will. A thunder roars out from the riverbank. Wrenching echoes bounce off every tree. Storm clouds hover at the water's edge. Hot metal balls crash through the trees. Branches split apart. Showers of deadly splinters strip the flesh of screaming men.

Momentum evaporates. The attack is lost within the confusion. Now comes the moment when some yearn to pull back time for second chances and second guessing. That, of course, can never be.

None of this will be forgotten. When the year is at an end, an elderly seer at Utamusak will carefully unfold a *wushakwun* skin. He will position in front of him the next empty space of the volume. And on that space he will paint a *wopusok* with wings full of wind. It will float upon water, breathing fire and snorting smoke. This will be remembered as the year when the English came.

CHAPTER 8

The heat of *Nepino* lies thick on the land. Everyone stays quiet, waiting for the nights to bring cooler weather.

At Weyowakomako, mat walls are rolled up on every building. Pokahantas sits under the *muskiminz* tree with a pile of sticks. Her sister, Matachana, sits across from her with eyes blinking in anticipation.

"All right, which hand has, less?" Pokahantas grabs at the pile with both hands, raising them up to either side of her face. Matachana stops blinking. She immediately points to the left hand. Pokahantas is a little discouraged as her sister snatches a stick from the pile, giggling in victory.

Pokahantas continues, "All right, which pile is, even?"

The hands swoop down. Matachana quickly pats the left again.

Pokahantas opens the hand, "Wrong, ha!"

Her sister pulls back in sour defeat.

Pokahantas drops the odd stick into her pile of points. "Now it's even."

The play continues. "All right, how many in, this hand?"

Matachana hesitates.

"Come on, hurry!" Pokahantas shakes the bundle at her little sister.

"Oh, seven. No, eight."

Pokahantas studies the hand, "Six."

Matachana leans back in disgust.

Pokahantas drops another stick onto her pile. "You better get the rest of these or I'm going to win this round."

The girls keep one ear toward the conversations emanating from within the great *ahakan*. It is the usual spirited chatter of mature females, mixed with a steady low hum from the far end of the building where their father and three uncles have gathered. Even though a house is women's property, there is this small sanctuary within where a man can be among his own.

POWHATAN:
THE STORY OF A PEOPLE

The four brothers are near their final stage. All his life, Wahunsenakok has worked to create a society that he deems perfect. He is now eager to enjoy the fruits of his long labor in a gentler lifestyle where responsibilities are for others and prestige is all his own. But mortality forever calls on a soul's stamina. Old issues never end. They merely evolve into other forms.

Smoke from a shared pipe fills the space.

"The Pawankatank are showing dissension," Kekwatog mentions the tribe on the river just north of where he sits.

"They will conform or will not exist," Wahunsenakok retorts. It is not up for discussion.

Opechankano brings up a more important topic, "What will you do of Pepiskunima stealing my wife? She's been with him a few times. Now, he steals her from me. I want his life."

"He is not my son," Wahunsenakok refuses. "His mother is still a love to me. Your lost wife is a young one...with big eyes. You are simply too ugly. That one would make you poor trying to keep her happy."

"I will steel her back!" Opechankano challenges.

Wahunsenakok tries to calm him, "You do and she will likely kill you as you sleep. Let her go. People will look up to you more for your courage in letting it pass. She is a woman. You can not expect her obedience. If a woman is through with you...well, that's it. Just be grateful they have us around at all."

"The island people are resistant as well," Kekwatog mentions. "They have made things difficult for the Chikahominy and their neighbors. They want no part of anyone else."

Wahunsenakok concludes, "So be it. I know there will be revenge killings. That is our right. But tribal actions against the island people will end now. We promised them some of the harvest. If there are any of them left by then, we will abide by that promise. Opechankano, you have the most sway with the Chikahominy. Keep them peaceful. We must make the strangers part of Tsenakomako. With their technology and our strength, we could rival the Masawomik."

George Percy sits against a tree. The shade continues to move. He must follow it. Each movement brings exhaustion. The air is thick with moisture that blurs vision. Thoughts swim in his head. The heat has nearly taken him too. It is a dirty heat that makes one feel filthy all over.

"Oh, misery!" he releases in half voice, half breath. It is not just a thought, but a plea to that which consumes him.

There is no food available but a handful of old barley with more worms than grain. No liquids. The river has turned brackish. The well water has turned rancid. This land of enchantment; how could it have turned into such hell? The natives had promised food, but their crops are slow in ripening this year.

At least when the mariners where here, there was biscuit and what not to barter. Perhaps cruel they were to sell their stores for the men's possessions and the boys' persons.

Hollow eyes scan the fort. Originally, there was thought to leave the camp open to make it appear inviting for the neighbors. That idea was given up after the great attack. The wall of split logs creates a large triangular enclosure. It is a mere fence that towers above the cleared land. The longest side stretches parallel to the river, providing a defensive line against waterborne attack. The other two sides create a good right-left flank formation against any more land assaults. At each corner are elevated mounds, protected by circular walls, for the artillery pieces.

It has become a place of imprisonment. None can venture outside. Arrows from the forest edge will pick them off for mere sport. It is nothing more than a dirt pen inside. Some have managed to piece together small, conical hovels from old bark and other forest waist. What were tents are now mere bolts of tattered cloth.

None of the inmates can find the strength to move. Most simply lie on the ground, waiting for the elements to take them. They yearn for the cooler air of late night, which only leaves them with the chills by morning.

There are a pair of men dragging a corpse to the burial ground. George observes their slow struggle to complete this daily chore. They dump the body into a shallow hole beside the grave of poor Captain Gosnold. Nearly half the colony now lie with him in this garden of bones.

The shade has moved away. George follows it. His breath is heavy. His chest swells with hot, sticky air. As a gentleman of high standing, George should have been included in the Governing Council. He should at least be on board the Discovery with the more fortunate. But his brother, Henry, tried to kill the king and parliament. Another generation of his family failed to achieve royalty. George can only hope that time can wipe clean his family's reputation. But none of that matters now. The only thing he can do now is wait for relief to come—one way or another.

POWHATAN:
THE STORY OF A PEOPLE

It is quiet on the Chikahominy River. It is pleasant. It is cool. The days of deadly heat are no more. There is only one vessel on the water. It is filled with ten Wind Children who have nothing to do but explore. John Smith leads them. He is the most content of the group. Events have surely turned to his favor. John had come to the new world confined in the brig for rebellious posturing during the sojourn in the Canary Islands. Now, he is fully free and securely on the council. Captain Ratcliffe is now the President. His predecessor, Sir Wingfield, has lost all authority and faces charges of hoarding supplies for his own.

It was not really mutiny that John had instigated. It was merely an expression of opinion, of which he has much. If the others had been better leaders, he would not have found the urge to challenge them. Simply that.

Well, what they withheld, they were forced to return. John has become an important part of this venture. He can show his worth to those—gentlemen.

It has been his life's search to find a proper position in the world. It has been a journey by way of physical experience rather than intellectual training. John began as a protestant soldier on the old continent. But fighting Catholics became a bit too disturbing. He thus returned home to pursue social advancement in England and Scotland. A knighthood would have been satisfactory, but the best title this yeoman's son has been able to obtain is, Captain. He acquired this rank by selling his military expertise to the Austrian army against the Ottoman Empire. He found it much more comfortable to kill Turks whose sentiments were so different to his own.

There is a slight jut as the vessel scrapes bottom. The river is growing shallow. John tries to remember the right word. The Indigenies call this watercraft a "*kekwiyos*." There are so many words to learn. Many languages from Europe sleep in his memory. But as in all places, John knows just a handful of words from any language are all that is needed to get by. His recent expedition to Kekotan is proof. He remembers the journey. The people recognized this same *kekwiyos* that had visited them once before. They seemed disappointed by the absence of the one-armed man. They did not know Captain Smith as he was still in the brig when these two groups first met.

The first day of trade was such a poor showing. John presented the children with little gifts and laid out his assortment in an attractive display. But he received a minor return. He had given out the best trade goods all at once. They made him a fool. John knew he could not fail. His position would be taken, and with it, his freedom. He used the one thing that has always served him best: brute force. The next day, four men with firearms followed Captain Smith right into the walled town. The exchange rate gainfully improved. If only he had a score of soldiers, he could have cleaned out the whole town of goods and supplies.

Upon returning, John managed to make contact with the Wawaskoyak tribe. They live along the south bank of the Powhatan, just down river from the Kwiyokohanok people. Everyone else along the Powhatan had made contact with the strangers. The Wawaskoyak took full advantage of the opportunity so that they would not be overlooked any longer.

Those at the fort were impressed with the captain's results. Plans were thus made for a larger expedition to take the Discovery upriver. Important friendships needed to be reaffirmed with the Weyanok, the Awohatek, and the Powhatan. At first, Captain Smith grudgingly accepted the duty to secure food for the colony. But he soon realized that it provided him a chance to be away from the fort. While preparations were underway, he managed to slip across the river to Chawopo in hopes of meeting Pepiskunima who had been so hospitable to Captain Newport. Unfortunately, the young man was nowhere to be found. There were only panicky women and children in town who would only tell him that their men were all out hunting and that their leader was now someone else.

The expedition to Powhatan Town was of utmost importance in the eyes of many at the fort. And John sincerely intended to follow his instructions. But the Chikahominy people came to see the little *kekwiyos* that stopped over night in the mouth of their river. It just seemed understandable to take advantage of that situation first.

That evening, John accepted an invitation to the town nearby and even left one of his men there overnight. The next morning came with a hundred smiling faces to greet him. There were faces from the very small to the very wrinkled.

John learned his lesson from Kekotan. He laid out just enough trade goods at a time to gain the top rate of exchange.

They ventured upriver, deeper into the Chikahominy territory to visit more towns. The merry travelers came to Mamanahunt where two hundred and more were gathered for trade. It was a circus atmosphere. The little red-haired clown charmed the crowd with sing-song words from their own language. The games of trade enthralled the audience. The shiny tools and dazzling toys warmed all hearts. John returned to the fort late that night fully laden. He was relieved to find that the Discovery had run aground before even

POWHATAN:
THE STORY OF A PEOPLE

leaving the island. And so, the expedition, as it was originally planned, had been called off.

John returned to Mamanahunt as soon as he could. He liked the majestic town that spread across dry, flat land high above the blue waters. He liked the clean marshes that extended into the waters to shelter abundant populations of both fowl and fish. And he liked the various satellite towns that lie on every available spot in this district of large river bends.

People where already waiting with hundreds of baskets. Even the baskets where part of the deal. Such beautifully crafted containers, woven in complex designs of varying colors from varying plants. There were small hand baskets woven from different silk grasses and larger storage containers woven form strips of sturdy bark. The locals have a talent for pealing off the bark of a standing tree and working the strips into these baskets that lasts forever.

A large basket for a metal tool. A female's artwork for a handful of blue beads. A little basket for a toy. Captain Smith took them all, so long as they were filled with food. He held a demonstration of firearms for the audience. Everyone was fully entertained. That trip was his best.

The wait for a third visit was agonizingly long. Happenings at the fort finally culminated in George Kendal's execution for subversion. The plot was discovered and the councilman was found to be the mastermind. Kendal's background as a spy by profession and a Catholic by affiliation finalized the verdict. If circumstances had not improved for himself, it could well have been John facing the firing squad.

The third visit proved not to be worth the wait. John dropped by numerous towns but reaped in much less. He returned to the fort to find that the Discovery was no longer entrapped in the shallows. That Wingfield fellow was floating an idea to take the Discovery back to England for help. President Ratcliffe also wanted to be aboard. It was, after all, his vessel. The plan reeked of abandonment. To the relief of most, these plans were called off. Instead, they decided to leave the Discovery right where it was to be ready for any possible situation that called for the evacuation of the whole colony.

With the store house satisfactorily full, John was allowed to return up the Chikahominy once more to seek out its source. The river has seduced his adventurous heart. It has become an obsession far beyond reason. John has always been the wanderer. It began in his youth, just after his father died. He found comfort in the open countryside and in the jungles of cities. There was always more to find ahead. He found truth in the philosophy that genuine wealth is to be harvested by those on a tail.

By traveling to the source of the Chikahominy, John feels he will be able to stop by the town of Powhatan and satisfy those at the fort. Master Percy said there was a trail. It must be somewhere near the river.

Beyond Mamanahunt, the marshes turn to swamp banks. The river itself spills out into a lake atmosphere with many islands of various sizes. But it eventually shrinks into a narrow course. They pass by the last settlement. The village of Apokant is small and isolated. It is on low ground, quiet, almost vacant in appearance. The *kekwiyos* passes by without any loss of momentum. They enter a murky world. It is a scene of variable browns that mix into a general hue of dull decay; an environment full of lost phantoms and mistaken sounds.

The travelers continue deeper into the abyss where the forest thickens, the land sinks, and the muck covers all. Scattered on either side are large trunks that lie uprooted in the decaying forest. More timber lean precariously across the waterway ahead of them.

Some express concern of loosing the vessel in the swamps. Their captain reluctantly gives in and backtracks to Apokant. Luckily, they run into two men who are willing to furnish their *akwintan* and themselves. The rest of the day is used in regaining ground.

The next day, Captain Smith leaves his *kekwiyos* behind. He takes with him only two of his own and the pair of guides. Once again, John has to hear rumblings about broken promises because he does not allow the *kekwiyos* to go back to Apokant. Just for spite, he gives them strict orders to stay right where they are in the middle of the water and not to set foot on terra-firma until he returns.

The two guides row to where their client points—not giving advice when not asked nor instruction when not requested. They are the best subordinates John has had this whole journey. He feels these are good people. But there is hatred deep in their eyes, as if there is something deep in their past of which they can not let go.

John wonders how those at the fort will take all this. But what will it matter? There will probably be only a handful of survivors when Newport finally returns to re-supply them. Individual survival is all that matters now.

The journey is long. A suitable rest stop is taken, but John is still restless. He takes one of the guides for a walk across the windings. If there are not too many forges to make, they may be able to save time and distance. Upon leaving, the captain instructs Master Robbinson and Thomas Emry to light their fire locks and be ready for the slightest alarm.

POWHATAN:
THE STORY OF A PEOPLE

Captain Smith and his guide twist and turn along any hint of a trail through the patches of dark water and around the *powamink* trunks. This variety of swamp tree has a wrinkled bark and branches that hang wearily downward. Everything around John seems weary. It...

That sound. Human. The quick cry echoes in the distance. It is one of his own. Howling. Now, many voices ring out.

"I am betrayed!" John spits.

The guide stops. That is all the captain needs. He grabs the man from behind.

The guide is surprised, but mostly confused. The strange man's actions feel so undecided. Arms are constrained with a binding from the captor's clothing. Hot, excited breath whips against the captive's neck.

Shadows dance in the woods. They increase in number. An arrow buries into the fleshy part of John's right thigh. The captain spots the shooter who is checking to see how he did. Another is next to him, stretching his bow for a try.

The hostage is in the way. He makes it perfectly clear to the bowmen that he has little confidence in their marksmanship. John raises his French pistol and gives it a quick squeeze of the trigger in their direction. The forest echoes. The two bowmen retreat into the underbrush.

There are more figures dancing among the trees. They are closing in on all sides. The *nantam* heads that front the breech clothes hop among the underbrush as if alive. Human yelps ring out.

The hostage keeps squealing, "Weyowanz!"

John is surprised to see them lay down their bows. They demand him to do the same with his weapon. The numbers grow. They come closer. But none try for the kill.

John sloshes about. They are all around him. He can not load his pistol while holding on to his hostage. He pulls the young man closer. A step to the side. A step back. When he feels the ground giving out, it is too late. John lies on his back with his human shield squirming on top of him. Pushing him aside, John throws up his arms, bellowing his final cry, "Bloody pox on ye all!"

A man who had survived great wars on the Continent. A man who had overcome the hardships of confinement and humiliation in two worlds. For what? His final breath is about to be taken from him by these people in this place. What an unceremonious end for the life that is, John Smith.

CHAPTER 9

Smokey fires line the forest floor. Underbrush has been gathered for fuel. Between the walls of smoke are openings that lead into *wushakwun* traps. But nothing is happening. The two hundred men in this hunting party have already caught a prize. He stands at the center of those who tower over him. Tallest is the form of Opechankano. He studies the little pallid man with hair the color of hot coals.

The captor challenges, "How can you be a *weyowanz*? You are a fat little creature. You are a sight only to laugh at."

"I *weyowanz*. I *weyowanz*." The captive remembers another word, "*Wingapow!*" The little man takes out an object from his pocket and hands it to Opechankano. There is a needle displaying a zigzag emblem near its pointed tip. He makes a gesture with pressed palms and utters, "North…always."

Opechankano plays with it, twirling himself around in an almost dance-like mood. The needle really does point in one direction, always. "It seems a little off. North is just over, there. See where the sun is setting?" He makes an arching wave of his left arm to retrace the course of the falling sun.

John points at the instrument, "True North. North pole…This ball we live on."

"Ball?"

"Yes. Pamasawu is round…like Sun, moon?"

"Nonsense." Opechankano studies the instrument further. "This is a wonderful toy." He tries to figure out what the materials are and how it is put together. After a while, he takes some dried kernels out of his leather bag. It is a long, tube-like container that wraps half-way around the body. The ends are four long strips that are tied together at the shoulder. Each facing is decorated with a geometric pattern of shells. This is one of the better sort, due to the rank of its owner. "Take some. You are my guest. I will bring you to the hunting camp where we can rest."

They come across the *akwintan* where poor John Robbinson lies. Twenty and more arrows are in his body. His eyes are open, but no life shines through them. This body is now a material thing, with no more purpose.

"The other lies nearby," Opechankano mentions. "You may be a *weyowanz*, but you no longer lead."

The procession toward camp is in military fashion. Five men are spaced out across the front. Five more fan out along each side. All carefully scan the wilderness around them. Opechankano walks in the center with another rank of five behind him. Two bowmen escort the captive while the rest of the company files along the path behind. Group leaders jog from one flank to another while their aging general with hunched shoulders steadily brings one foot forward after the other.

Captain Smith is reminded of his days of military drill on the old continent. The discipline, the general personality created from one moving form of indistinguishable parts...

They reach a small clearing. Lighter, warmer colors of temporary arbors and cooking pits radiate in the grey surroundings. Excited children greet their fathers and uncles with squeals in perfect soprano and arms outstretched like birds do when drying their feathers. Wives and mothers gather around the children as their men move to the central fire in the communal ground. They encircle the fire and perform their dance of return to thank the spirits for the rewards of their successes and the education received from their failures.

The residents take a look at the prize. Camp dogs join in the festival of gawking. They are timid creatures, but without the dumb look of domestication. Their eyes are almond shaped, spread wide apart. The tawny color of their upper parts are the same as the skin of their owners. Their under portions are white. Everything about them is solid. Their ears, their snouts—both are long and pointed. They curl their tails upward, as wilderness canines do. They are a wild species with straight backs and hard pads for their small feet. It is a pure breed from ancient times. None can bark, but one or another howls at leisure for the rising moon. John barks a disgruntled command at them to dispense. They only cower close to the ground and study him all the more.

Respect? Smith can not expect such a reaction from animals or humans. He is simply not one to enjoy such treatment. When John was captured in battle and auctioned off at the Turkish slave market, did he go for much? He was sold for what he was instead of who he was. Did the princess, who owned him, even want him? She passed him over to her brother who had less love of living things. John was stripped naked and his head was shaven clean. His story became no more significant or unique than the thousands like him.

At least these women show John no sour faces and the children no callous grins. They are simply interested in the newness that he is. At least it will keep him safe for a while. One of the group leaders motions for John to follow. Upon reaching the small lodge, he quietly enters the bright interior where food and gentle treatment await.

The trio of serving girls have come and gone with their warm laughter and large wooden plates of food. He feels his belly stretch close to bursting. The bread was thick and the venison well-smoked. This confinement is a far cry from any other bondage he has experienced.

John reaches for the tablet and compass that was given back to him. The naturals show a sincere interest in John's experiences on the big blue ocean, of the lands he has seen, his view of the heavens, and of the god he knows. John even spoke of the defenses at the fort, like the mines planted in the fields around it and the big guns inside. He spoke of Newport. It seems that man is liked by everyone.

Opechankano allowed John to send a letter by three runners to the fort so that they could learn his situation—just in case they wanted to rescue him. Captain Smith seems to be important among these people. Perhaps that is what the religious men were about.

John thinks back on the incident. It lasted from mid-morning to the start of evening. Once John was placed on the mat and the central fire was ablaze, the guards left. Then, the one entered. He was a big man with a body coated in an admixture of charcoal dust and oil. His head was covered to the shoulders by a headpiece unlike any John had ever seen. It consisted of tassels made from *ketasku* skins that were stuffed with moss. All the tails were tied together at the crown which were fastened to a coronet of feathers. His presence was unworldly. His movements were un-human. His voice was not of the body, but of the spirit within.

He began an invocation. The dim hall swayed with the voice of the mystic. He circled the fire, forming a ring around it with bits of *apon*. To guide his utterances in the appropriate meter, he shook a rattle made of a *tuwupen* shell. Three more seers entered. Their bodies were half red, half black. Patches of white covered their eyes. Fine lines of red streaked across their black faces.

POWHATAN:
THE STORY OF A PEOPLE

Their expressions were beyond mortality. Their eyes could see through the flesh and examine that within. It was a power beyond color, beyond form, that could focus directly on the intangible essence of one's thoughts.

After the ring had been circumvented, another three seers entered. They were the same as the first trio, except that their eyes were patched with red and their cheeks lined with white. The chief seer sat before the fire with the two triads on either side. Quietly, they gathered strength to proceed through the rest of the exercise.

Upon rising, the seven moved in a circle, shaking their rattles in unison. Sweating profusely, straining every sinew in his arms and hands, the chief seer let forth an impassioned address. His colleagues validated each outcry with a harmonious, "*Hwow!*"

The chanting continued as they moved. A mantra was exhaled. *Poketawas* kernels fell from their hands. It continued until they had formed another half-circle of these small piles to bracket the inner ring. In the same manner, two more circles were created outside of this.

The leader placed small sticks between the little piles of *poketawas*. The others stepped deliberately with great exertion. *Wikutis* hair broke free of their garments to float in the chilled air as if to join in this phantom ballet. Then, it stopped. They quietly filed out of the lodge. When the entrance flap was pushed open, John could see that evening had come.

Shouting is just outside John's lodge. The eight men who guard him has halted an elder. He swings his *monahak* wildly. He eventually drops it and readies his bow to shoot the white face peering out of the entrance flap. But the old man is slow. The guards gingerly guide him away.

"What is happening?" John motions. None take notice of him.

Opechankano arrives. He explains, "Your weapon killed that man's son. He wanted your death in return. But you must live. You must travel to see others." John looks around the camp. Some have already begun rolling up mats.

The travelers move deep into the upper reaches of the Yugtamund and Matapaniyund rivers. They find lively greetings at every stop. All come to see this new version of a man. John is treated with a mix of awe, pity, and delight.

Everyone in the Matapaniyund town is festive. The men have just returned from their communal hunt. They ready themselves for an upcoming raid by reenacting an historic battle. It is the famous engagement between the old Monakan and the young Powhatan. John is the honored spectator. Two hundred players divide into two groups.

Old veterans from the original battle gather 'round. So much they recognize. Fifteen men make up each of the six columns. With songs and yells of bravado, the two sides close in on each other. Pointless arrows soar high into the air. Men rush enemy lines. The Powhatan are fearless. They beat their foes to the ground in hardy triumph.

John studies the maneuvers with his military eye. He takes note of the methods and strategies of these woodland soldiers.

Just as it was before, the Monakan ranks dwindle. The Powhatan reform into a half-circle in preparation for the death-blow. Just in time, the Monakan horde makes for the safety of the woods behind them. The victorious Powhatan warriors rejoice in the open field. They win again.

The re-enactment winds down. The spectators begin to stir. Old veterans nod to each other in nostalgic agreement. That was exactly how it was long ago when the great Wahunsenakok lead them to quell their *maskapow*. Yes, that was exactly how it happened.

As usual, John rises the next day to hit the trail. They snake along the wilderness path until coming upon a slight overlook. A different world reveals itself. It is an open landscape where broad swaths of marshland entwine with a silvery plain of high water. Long expanses of low woodland embrace this river valley. Just in the middle ground, but still far away, is the tip of a stretch of land that splits the wide Pamunkey River in two. This is the heartland of the Pamunkey nation where the Yugtamund and Matapaniyund rivers converge. As the Pamunkey are the blood of the Powhatan people, this location is the heart of their domain. All knowledge, all news, all wealth of Tsenakomako comes here.

John is taken across the water to the land within the narrow fork. He finds the urban areas in this territory enormous. And yet, each is isolated from the other. The territory itself is spacious. It is almost opposite to the intimate closeness of the Chikahominy boroughs that sit along the tighter curls of a smaller stream. Here, the ground is flat and almost level with the water. The naked trees are tall and straight with varying girth. Vines fall to sparse, low undergrowth.

John comes to the bare crop fields that skirt the principal city of Menapukunt. Over a hundred buildings surround a sandy rise where the five great houses of Opechankano are located. Each is thirty strides long. They are the most dominant landmarks of this municipality. The city is quiet. Only a

POWHATAN:
THE STORY OF A PEOPLE

few inhabitants rustle about. The broader population has disbursed into smaller camps so that they can make it through the latent season of *Popano*.

The regal dwellings enjoy a westward view of the rich low country that the Yugtamund River's crooked course maintains. It is a view of vast marshes that can swell with fish and fowl during much of the year. Just upriver is Utamusak. Thin strands of smoke rise from the thick, naked timber where the rolling hills of higher ground persist. Seldom is that place accessible to anyone. For most, it is only to be viewed from a distance.

Kekwatog comes to see the prisoner. He remembers seeing the little man at Weyanok. Kekwatog assembles a feast in John's honor. Every one begins to warm up to the stranger. Even his forty guards develop a friendship with him.

Word comes that another leader requests to see Captain Smith. He marches along frigid wilderness trails. He journeys over hill and through dell, across ice-coated springs and small meadows where the winds sting the face. Eventually, they reach the Tapahanok community. A crowd of serious people study the man. The young *weyowanz* looks about his flock of older followers who shake their heads. "No, the one who killed your uncle was a tall man. This one is a little *amonsokwat* that only barks out baby words in our language." John Smith is spared once again.

John is brought to a hunting camp deep in the woods. On the next day, he enters the seat of power for this world. The city of Weyowakomako existed long before it became a gathering site for the great leaders. Once an outpost for a much smaller confederacy of tribes, it is now the breath-source of a nation.

They pass through the outer palisade and move toward the central compound. Captain Smith examines the stronghold. It reminds him of a fortress keep. There are two squares, one within the other. Yet, the sides that face north are slightly convex. Such makes for a position that is more easily defensible. And where one wall is good, two are that much more impregnable.

The captain questions his escort, "How this made?"

Opechankano stops at the entrance to the double wall. He pauses to organize his reply. "Two great ditches were dug. Tall trees were placed on either side of each ditch. A log from one side was pulled in until its base dropped against the opposite corner of the ditch. Then, it was pulled and pushed upward. Then, a log from the opposite bank was pulled and pushed into place, crossing the first log near the top, there. They are lashed together with strong vines at the point where they intersect. As the walls went up, the ditches were covered again, but not fully."

He points downward, "You see? The ditch is shallow, but it is still there. No one can breach these defenses."

Opechankano leads his guest through the ramparts. They come to the council house at the center of the inner courtyard. The interior contains a saffron haze, born from the central fire. Four rows of important people fill the narrow chamber. Two inner rows of embroidered mats are occupied by men while their female companions sit along the long benches that align either wall behind them. Their collective expression is more of curiosity than any show of reception.

The composition of the interior directs John's view straight to the end of the hall where, atop a raised platform, is the *mamanatowik* of this land. He reclines upon a pile of mats. One woman is at his head and another at his feet. Chains of large pearls coil multiple times around his neck. A tall crown of *moninag* feathers, each one straight and narrow, extends from his leather headband that is lavishly adorned with *tsekoma* and *matasun* beadwork. His oiled countenance shimmers in benevolent splendor. It is the shape of a down-turned spade. Strong features restrain all the explosive intensity that flare in his eyes. Here is the one who has conquered a region, and still controls his conquest absolutely. The stories are true. This man does exist.

Opechankano begins the introduction, "My brother, I come with a guest from the squatters on the Paspaheg hunting island. He has seen much of our land and has learned many things of us. He is a *weyowanz*, deserving respect for his life. He is one who may speak for his people. He has told me much about his world."

Opechankano motions for John to come forward. The mantle that hangs on the back wall of the raised sanctum catches his attention. It reminds him of the tapestries that insulate an interior from the cold stone of castle walls. But this tapestry is not of threads. This is made of four *wushakwun* hides. Sewn onto the skin are shell beads. They exhibit a semblance of a man in the middle of two animals. They are surrounded by an array of spiral circles—as if the three creatures are celestials swimming in the starry sky.

Artistically, the spiraling disks are not unique objects, but the very symbols that recall a time and place before the great migrations of the ancestors. It is a design that can be found where ever civilization has rooted.

POWHATAN:
THE STORY OF A PEOPLE

It is an expressed understanding of that which lives on from the beginning of humanity and binds all generations that have been, are, and will be.

John's attention returns to the confines of his present by the voice of his host. "I welcome you. Many times your people have touched my life through stories heard and occurrences witnessed. You have seen much of Tsenakomako. Go now to the *ahakan* that I have reserved for you and regain your strength from all your travels."

On the next day, the two sit and slowly work out communication in voice and hand gesture. Wahunsenakok begins, "My brother has spoken of wonderful stories. Things that another once told me from when he was among your kind. Old memories have reawakened. I wish to hear more. Why have you come?"

John searches his imagination for a good reply, "It was a fight with the Spanish. They overpowered us. We went into an ocean storm to escape. We found shelter with the Kekotan who directed us upriver for fresh water. We only stay on our island to be with our damaged *musawusuk*. We are waiting for my father, Newport, to return and repair it."

"Newport?" Wahunsenakok interrupts, "He is your father? By blood or allegiance?"

John is unsure in the meaning and does not return a direct reply. Wahunsenakok looses himself in contemplation and does not listen further. Thoughts battle one another to gain clarity within the silent caverns of his mind. He recognizes the wrong moves made by his son, Pokinz, who directed them up the wrong river. The strangers are too close to the Chikahominy and too far from himself. He realizes something else. The Wind Children are not one people. Differences abound among them.

Questions begin to nag him. Why would such a little *musawusuk* need so many men to stay with it in a temporary camp that looks more permanent each day? And, if fresh water was what they needed, why do they sit at a place where fresh and salt water collide to bear nothing but a poisonous stew. And, why dig in the murky ground of that swamp patch of an island to pull out water when the springs of the mainland freely provide drinkable liquid?

Wahunsenakok recognizes that John has finished his little speech. The host renews the conversation, "I see, yes. Is it true you took the *kekwiyos* far inland, on many of our rivers?"

John replies, "Father Newport had a child who was slain...by the Monakan. He wishes revenge."

Wahunsenakok responds, "Of course. It is only right. Where is the one-armed man now?"

"To…Wowanok."

"To find more of your kind; those with the clothes you wear?"

"Yes."

The battle rages anew in the old leader's mind. It is strange that they still look for those people. Are these people as ruthless as they were? The earlier ones deserved what they got, due to their mistreatment of those whose lands they trespassed. Every time those strangers were desperate, they where gentle. Every time they were confident, they turned to barbaric ways.

"There are none left," Wahunsenakok utters. "They have not been for…over thirty years."

John argues, "We saw a small boy with hair the color of the sun near Weyanok."

His host is undaunted. "A gift to the *weyowanz* from the Chowanok. That tribe still has a few who were once part of the Wowanok group. The Chowanok are far to the south. They are not a good people. Why did we find you so far west?"

After a moment, John replies, "I was searching for the great water that we hear lies northwest of the mainland."

Wahunsenakok offers, "That is very far away…past the land of the Monakan. Since I could run, I have fought them. I have lost many family members to them and have taken the lives of many in revenge. If you wish to know what is farther west, I can tell you this much:

"There is a land where a great water lies. It is a violent water with waves that constantly slap its rocky shores. With every storm, it turns the head waters into a muddy soup.

"There is a mighty nation deep in the interior whom you should also beware. Some call them Suskwehanok. They eat men. They war with the Patawomik and other friends who live at the top of the bay. Just a year ago, they killed one hundred strong Patawomik warriors. One can recognize the monsters easily. They shave their crowns, but have long hair growing from their necks that they fix in a tight knot. Their war clubs are both sharp and weighted weapons.

"Beyond them is another great river where people with short coats and long sleeves, like yours, have been. The Masawomik control that land. They are great in their number, yet all live as one. My people are also one. I have made them such. Perhaps we are not as mighty as the Masawomik. But we do rival them. They treat us with caution.

"To the south are more tribes who will eventually be one with us. Do you know of such lands in your world?"

John affirms, "My land is on a great island. Many tribes have owned it. My great leader has brought all of them together. Those on an island beside our own are fearful of us. We have conquered them."

Wahunsenakok enjoys this. "I would like to meet your great leader. I would like to meet your father, Newport. When he returns from Wowanok, you must send him."

The old man rises. "I shall send you home. You may gather your people and bring them here. I will protect and care for you all. I have heard much of your people's creativity. They can make me things. Your people can live happily at a sight just downriver from here. Our lives will be one."

The calming effect of true authority has come this night to the little island fort in the Powhatan River. Captain Newport has returned with badly-needed supplies. Not only does he bring material but also more people to replenish the small group of survivors. The vessel that accompanied him was blown back into the vast waters and is most likely lost. But the good captain has proven his skill once more by reaching the colony.

Earlier in the day, Captain Smith managed to return with abundant gifts of food. But poor John did not receive a hero's welcome. Captain Archer led those who cast forth the angry words. His hands were well healed to point the finger of chastisement. All judged that Captain Smith had selfishly abandoned those for whom he was responsible. In effect, John had murdered them. What's more, he enjoyed comfort with the naturals while his own brethren suffered through a harsh, cold season within a decaying stockade.

Good Captain Newport's return could not have been better timed. He restores order to the colony and calms its leadership. He also acknowledges the position of importance that poor John has managed to secure by befriending the one who rules this land. Once again, Captain Smith has survived.

CHAPTER 10

It sounds like a raging river. A blaze lights up the island in bright yellow and orange and red. The thrashing of flames echo against the surrounding forest. The fort is fully engulfed. All the equipment, all the new supplies, and all the food are in flames.

Men scurry about in confusion. Some watch helplessly with defeated expressions melted onto their faces. Even Captain Newport can do nothing for them. The new supplies were unpacked. Nothing is left. Nothing.

Flames color the night. People from Paspaheg gather along the mainland to watch the fire dance among the tree tops. Others from Kwiyokohanok assemble across the Powhatan River. Those in the know proudly share criticism among themselves. They explain to one another how the strangers had cut the trees at the wrong time. The timber had lain rotting in the heat for far too long. The wood was not even smoked to seal the fibers. It dried out too quickly, making it nothing more than kindling.

Smaller lights bob on the river. Opportunists take full advantage of the water's illumination for night fishing. They hardly need the small fires in their *akwintan* to see into the depths. Spear points of jagged bone pluck into the water with a dancing lightness of thrust. Success is felt with heaviness in the return. Everyone on the river is in wonderful cheer.

On the island, flames stretch to the stars.

"What happened?" The cry is made.

It all happened so quickly. How could it have started? Why did it spread so rapidly?

Others voice, "What is there now to be done? What is left of us? Where should we go?"

POWHATAN:
THE STORY OF A PEOPLE

Pokahantas and her sister, Matachana, are busy with their clay. Both would much prefer being at the ball field with the other young ladies. But work does come before pleasure at their age. Still, to ignore the giggles and squeals from those at play is almost impossible.

What a wonderful game. They kick the little ball along, making sure it does not touch any other part of their bodies. All run and jump from one end to the other in hopes of sending it through the goal posts for a point.

The sisters drench their clay. They knead and whip it until the texture is entirely smooth. They form little cakes that have a very flexible softness—almost like pudding.

Another girl comes to them. She is a daughter of their uncle, Opechankano.

Pokahantas welcomes her cousin, "Well, well. Did you talk to the Wind Children?"

The cousin nods, "I tried my best to convince them to visit Menapukunt."

Matachana chimes in, "Who could resist feminine charm?"

The cousin answers, "The Wind Children. I tried every excuse. But nothing. Maybe they'll come. I want to wait 'till tomorrow to be sure."

The sisters get back to their task. Pokahantas gingerly takes hold of a cake. The clay is a sandy white with sprinkles of shell mixed into the recipe for strength. She rolls it into a long coil similar in length and girth of a small snake. She wets the stone slab and begins laying the coil down in a circular format.

Matachana is already on her second coil. She lays it down with precision atop the first. Carefully pressing the material together, she reinforces the crevasses with added clay. With a flat stick, she smoothes both the inner and outer surface.

Their cousin finds a comfortable place near them to watch.

Pokahantas uses her wrist to point at the bundle of blue beads fixed in her hair. "Johnsmith had them. My father paid much in *poketawas* for them. He got more from Newport the next day. But I got the first strand even before any of my aunties.

Matachana adds, "Trading is difficult with those people. But father has managed to get just about everything they have."

Pokahantas tries to give a narrative of the past events, "It was difficult. The whole visit has been difficult. First, Johnsmith came to make ready Newport's arrival. Our brother, Nakakwawis, waited at the main landing to greet them. But the Wind Children entered the wrong creek."

Matachana mentions, "Johnsmith brought twenty warriors with him. All had a *pakusak* and war garments of thick leather for protection. Nakakwawis and his greeting party were a little worried, since they didn't have any weapons."

Pokahantas re-enacts the dialog, "Nakakwawis asked, 'Where is your father, Newport?' And Johnsmith explained, 'We come first to prepare his arrival. Tomorrow, he will be here.' So our brother said, 'Walk with me. I will show you the way to where my father waits for you.' And off they went. Some took the *kekwiyos* around to the correct landing place, while the rest walked along the river trail. We mixed in with them until it was one group."

Matachana adds some flavor to the story, "It must have been a nice walk. The trees are greening again. Some wildflowers are in bloom…"

Pokahantas continues, "When they came to the bridge over the creek, over there…" Her hand lightly flutters toward the direction to which she refers. "Johnsmith refused to cross it."

Matachana elaborates, "Some how, the bridge just didn't suit Johnsmith at all. It is a perfectly good bridge. The four sets of cross-posts are firmly in the ground; one on either bank, and two in the creek itself. The bark strips that hold the posts together where they criss-cross near the top are firmly bound. All they had to do was walk across the string of poles placed along top and go down the other side. Any sure-footed person would have no trouble with it. But the Wind Children must not know about such…"

Pokahantas interrupts, "Well, Johnsmith demanded Nakakwawis to get an *akwintan* and ferry them over, a few at a time."

Matachana questions, "Why make such a simple crossing so complicated?"

Pokahantas moves on, "They finally made it to the city where a crowd of over three hundred had gathered to see them."

Matachana explains, "Most have returned from private camps, now that Popano is over."

Pokahantas resumes her story, "Nakakwawis cleared a path and they slowly made their way through the throng of people to reach the inner compound. We were in front of the council house to help bring in the forty platters of food."

Matachana includes, "That's when Johnsmith's twenty warriors met our father's forty. Our men looked much more impressive."

Pokahantas attempts to proceed, "Our brother escorted Johnsmith inside. All the chief councilors where there, fully adorned with pearls and wearing their *kawasow* and what not. And all our aunties too, with shiny red pokun covering their faces and shoulders, and bright white shell necklaces...Father wrapped himself in his great mantle—the one he usually hangs on the back wall—so that he could keep the chill in the air off his shoulders. No fire was lit because it would have made the place too hot. But all the smoke flaps above were open for light. Father lounged on his bed of mats and leather pillows. He made a place for Johnsmith to sit right beside him. Our new auntie from Apamatuk waited on him. First, she offered Johnsmith some *moninag* meat and some *apon*. Then, she provided him water to clean his hands and used her feather fan to blow them dry."

Matachana interrupts, "Father treated that man like a *weyowanz*. But Johnsmith didn't act like one at all."

Pokahantas snaps, "Hey, you're getting ahead of me!" She gets back on track. "Well, after the food was passed all around, and the speeches were made, our father talked to his honored guest. First, he said, 'It is good to see you again, Johnsmith. The memory of your face has almost faded from my mind. Why have you not come sooner? You know you are always welcome. The town I offered your people waits for you still.' And Johnsmith replied, 'The fire has kept me busy.' And father said, 'Never the less. You are here now. I look forward to the sun's return so that I can at last meet your good father, Newport.' Then, Johnsmith got his warriors to come in, two at a time, to meet father and get their handful of food, and show off their weapons, and so on."

Matachana adds, "He even asked if they would lay down their weapons and perform a friendly dance, or sing, or something. But Johnsmith said that they saw such things as things done between *maskapow!* They think so opposite to us, after all. Father also asked about the big *pakusak* that Johnsmith had promised to give him, but didn't. Johnsmith made up some excuse that he actually offered his escort, who returned him to his people, some smaller ones. But since that was not what they were told to get, they refused to take them. Something about the weapons being too heavy to carry anyway..."

Pokahantas returns to her narrative, "Johnsmith had other gifts with him on this trip. He gave father a cloak the color of an *ashowut* bird and a hat as black as the night. He also received an odd looking dog they call a greyhound. It's as starved as any poor creature could be. Johnsmith said that the poor dog was perfectly healthy and that they are that shape so that they can run very fast to hunt down escaping prey. They are closer to a bird than some heavy land animal. But they are no good for work animals, or for food.

"Well, our father graciously accepted the gifts. Johnsmith said that Newport would show his friendship by delivering our *maskapow* to us. Our father accepted this offer by proclaiming, 'This man is a *weyowanz*. His people are a proud and powerful tribe. He is our *cham*. We two are one. They are as we. And all that is Tsenakomako is for them, as it is for all of us.'

"That night, the strangers returned to their *kekwiyos*, only to find it grounded from the ebb of the river. It looked like it was going to rain. So the strangers were brought back to the warrior's lodge for the night. Our warriors hosted them very well. Everybody socialized well into the night before they finally separated and went to sleep."

The two girls work on their pots. Pokahantas fashions a round bottom for her vessel, angling the top to form a curving mouth. Matachana shapes hers into a tall, oblong container. Stooped over their creations with straight legs and straight backs—a posture only women can manage—each sister smoothes her piece and models the base so that it can stand perfectly balanced in nests of hot ash.

Matachana reaches for a woven piece of *wikiyopis*. The pattern is her favorite. It is an open weave with knots at each intersection. She applies it all along the middle. The impressions come out perfectly. She borders it with another thin pattern of closely-aligned knots. Pokahantas just picks up a used cob and rolls it along the top third of her pot. She then holds a stick between each finger of her fist and rakes the surface with varying diagonal hash marks. The two are energized from their creativity.

A look of boredom is frozen upon their cousin's face. Pokahantas tries to entertain her by resuming the story, "Well then, the morning sun found our father and Johnsmith at the *akwintan* park. He has many just as long as a *musawusuk*. My father told Johnsmith, 'I send them across the bay for the annual tribute owed me. They collect food, beads, *matasun*, and skins from all over Tsenakomako.'

"Suddenly, they spot a *musawusuk* far downriver. It is the same one that the island people have kept with them when the two larger ones went away…"

Matachana comments, "The same one Johnsmith said was broken."

Pokahantas continues, "Our father made his way back to the reception area while Johnsmith met his father. Newport made a grand entrance with blowing instruments and fluttering cloths and such.

POWHATAN:
THE STORY OF A PEOPLE

"Johnsmith interpreted for the two great men. Newport presented a boy of thirteen years and said, 'He is called, Tomsavage. Care for him. Teach him of your world so that he may teach us.' And father replied, 'You are a true and good man. And a trusting man. I will take good care of him. I give you these tokens of gratitude in return.' Out came a basket as large as the boy, woven of strong bark and filled with *pekatas*. Both agreed to start trade on the next day. And so, everyone met again on the beach the next morning."

Matachana inserts, "Once again, Johnsmith and his warriors showed up in full battle garb. Father was so mad."

Pokahantas includes, "But Newport immediately ordered them to stay at the landing and proceeded with Father to the trade site where mats and food and *upook* and so forth were already waiting."

Matachana clarifies, "They still needed Johnsmith to interpret, so he joined them and started trying to make the rules for trade. Father was so mad."

Pokahantas regains control, "Yes, Father said, 'My brother, I tend to this land like your great leader sees over his. We are not simple people meeting in the woods and exchanging simple gifts. You have wealth to show the greatness of your nation. I have the same of mine. Lay out all of what your people have, so that we can trade as great allies...'"

Matachana interrupts, "But Johnsmith muttered something else to his leader. Our father just knew from his tone that it was full of distrust."

Pokahantas jumps lightly as she tries to continue her story. "But Newport brushed the interpreter aside and called for one of his people to bring twelve large cooking pots from the *musawusuk*. Every one of these pots was made of solid *matasun*! Father ordered to place an opening sum of *poketawas* baskets beside it."

Matachana remarks, "And Newport either decided that the amount was agreeable, or he was too afraid to haggle, because he accepted it without hesitation."

Pokahantas grins, "Father set the amount in food for the number of *tomahak*. He managed to get a handful of these the last time one of those people came, just a few years ago. I was there too. Now, he has a full supply for a fraction of their true value."

Matachana explains, "A *tomahak* can make life so easy. They can cut and carve wood real quickly. Before, we would have to burn and chop away with some heavy *kunsenakwus* all day long. The metal head can butcher game and dig up the ground and kill more easily than any bone or stone tool. They practically last forever."

Pokahantas ties her story together, "Well, the strangers ran out of trade goods. But father was ready for more. He asked, 'Is this all your great nation has to offer? Perhaps the fire consumed much. I understand. I hope that the supply of food that I sent has helped you these past days. But do you have nothing else?' And that is when Johnsmith pulled out his handful of beads." She playfully brushes the bundle in her hair with one hand.

"Father called him over, and the two began to haggle. Johnsmith said, 'These are all I have. They are dear to me. Newport may have more on board the *musawusuk*.' Father couldn't resist. These are blue beads. Only the Wind Children have them. And only the most important people in Tsenakomako can afford them. They are more valuable then *wowanok* or *peak*!" Father commanded, 'Bring what ever more you have tomorrow and you will get full price for them.' And the Wind Children agreed."

Matachana picks up the story, "The next morning, Nakakwawis swam over to the *musawusuk* to collect the strangers. He told them that they should leave their weapons this time, because they were scaring the women and children." She looks over to her sister. "But did they?"

Pokahantas laughingly replies, "No!"

Matachana repeats, "No. That little Johnsmith snuck his warriors on shore all the same. He even carried his shield, *monahak,* and his little *pakusak*—the same one that he had with him when he was captured; the same one he said was broken when he was asked to demonstrate how it worked. You see? Those weapons can be fixed as easily as they are broken. That conniving Johnsmith is just like those who terrorized the South Country."

Pokahantas chimes in, "Our father was so mad."

Matachana agrees, "Father took a breath and a moment before he said, 'Johnsmith, why are you still in a fighting mind. Did I not prove these past days that you are protected? Do you see any of my own so laden in their fighting gear? Look around you. These are the same people who have always looked upon you with love.'

"But Johnsmith could only think up another version of the same excuse. He cried back, 'But going among you unarmed is how my brother was killed!' That didn't make any sense."

Pokahantas offers, "Newport was visibly tired of all this. He ordered them all to stay at the beach. He alone went to trade the blue beads, unarmed and unafraid, side by side with our father."

Matachana shakes her head. "That Johnsmith. After everything wound down, Newport took the food and most of his men with him in the *kekwiyos*

POWHATAN:
THE STORY OF A PEOPLE

and left Johnsmith and his warriors to find their own way back. Father was kind enough to give him two *akwintan*. But as soon as Johnsmith left shore, he got himself stuck in low water. How he can get an *akwintan* grounded is beyond me. Anyway, the other half of his men decided to try the deeper creek beyond. And do you know? They went right over that same bridge without even thinking about it. Well, these masters of the great waters could not handle simple wind and rain. So they landed again and made a shelter from the mats that were in their craft. But Johnsmith had no mats in his. He was getting soaked."

Pokahantas interjects, "Nakakwawis tried to come to his aide. Slowly, indifferent to his own wellbeing, he waded out through the rain, through the swampy cold liquid, to offer to carry that man ashore. Johnsmith refused him. He was worried they might drop him before reaching solid ground. So our brother waded back, gathered mats and firewood and food, and went back to make the strangers comfortable. Perhaps Johnsmith was embarrassed. He didn't give them any thanks, but paid them with small metal bells. They will be the most noticeable men at the dancing ground."

The game is almost over at the ball field. The two girls sit proudly as their pots dry and harden in the oven pit. Fire crackles in the hearth at the center of a low, square earthen wall. The heat bounces evenly for all the objects placed inside. When done, they will be a rusty orange in color and ready for many good stews. Even shattered or lost, these simple ceramic objects will out-last their creators and preserve their stories for all those still to come.

Captain Newport has given the order. The volley hurls toward the beach. It punctures human flesh. Young men scatter. Older men hurl back scornful words before following them into safer surroundings. But they refuse to give up the site entirely.

The Nansemund had provoked them. The tribe has not changed their sour view of the Wind Children. Christopher is disappointed, but not discouraged. Too many positive events have occurred during this stopover. Still, every moment has possessed a shade of tension. The visit to Pamunkey was the most pleasant. Christopher is happy that he changed his mind and took the Discovery upriver to meet Opechankano and his family.

The first stop was at the city called, Sinkwotek, which lies along the narrow land at the fork of the river. He reunited with Kekwatog and met the elder brother, Opichapan. Then, Opechankano and the loyal members of his family arrived. As always, the visitors were entertained and fed in the most lavish and abundant measure. *Misikwatash* was the most memorable dish served. It is an old recipe where *poketawas* and *pekatas* are boiled together. Long has it been a popular dish in this land.

The trail to Menapukunt was only a brief walk. But Captain Newport wanted to test the channel. He maneuvered the Discovery into the Yugtamund river and found a perfect site to moor near the city's *akwintan* park. The whole area around the fork could be made into a major commercial harbor. The naturals could be an unwavering obstacle. But they also tend to be gentle to those they like.

That same potential is present on the Nansemund river. Their attitude just needs improvement. Such can only come with honest diplomacy. When a bond of friendship is secured with the Indigenies, it tends to hold strong. Alliances. Yes, forming alliances works best. Christopher has already seeded the very alliance he needs with Wahunsenakok. The two men even held a war council together, as close allies would do.

The good captain recalls the meeting. It occurred after trade was completed. Wahunsenakok, with only a few of his most important councilors, sat in the great hall with Captain Newport and only his most important subordinates.

The old man presented his proposal, "Since war is on your mind, I will offer you this. I know how deeply you must feel about the loss of your son to the Monakan. I know them well. I can help you achieve revenge. I can send spies to determine their present strength and capability. This information I will freely give, along with two of my sons, my brother, Opechankano, and a hundred of my best fighting men. If you can send the same amount of your men up river (we can help you get your watercraft around the falls), the two columns can meet at Machimko. All the plunder in food and equipment you may deem useful to your own can weigh your watercraft. We would also want to put any wounded on board. I desire the women and young children that survive. This strategy, I know, will work."

Captain Newport agreed. He still agrees. What better way to create a bond between the two groups? He could then go farther into the hinterland for what riches he may find. Gold is what the company desires most. There is more than one rumor stating that gold is what hides in the interior.

The good captain must leave this search to the colonists. He must return to open waters. He must take his cargo of simple wood commodities and food stuffs homeward. On board are Master Wingfield and Captain Archer. Both are anxious to be rid of this place. Also on board is Namontak, the young man

POWHATAN:
THE STORY OF A PEOPLE

who has been placed into their care as a form of exchange for the boy, Thomas Savage. Namontak is also anxious—it is more in the nervous sense of the word.

The little *kekwiyos* bobs in the water nearby. It has led the departing vessel through the shoals that choke the Powhatan River. Captain Newport councils, "Captain Smith, ye must negotiate with these Naturals. All discord must end. The Nansemund, and this situation, may be of great import."

The vessel pushes into the Great Blue. There is so much Namontak must accept. But he was hand picked for this mission. He is trusted by Wahunsenakok to take this journey in stride and collect as many treasures of experience that await him on the opposite side of the world.

One day, he will explore the crowded streets of the strangers' primary city. On another, he will amuse himself in a park. Onlookers will be in awe of his exotic poise and natural charm. He will pose for the artists and display his archery skills for the sportsmen. All the ladies will swoon. Many will not know how to look upon him. Should it be with wonder, fear, lust, or repulsion? To them, he will be a man from a world much contrary to their own.

Chapter 11

There is a steady thump of a hewing axe among the subtle murmur of human voices. A man stands upon the fallen trunk with his feet apart. He swings the axe downward in front of him, striking the bark squarely. He strikes at a left angle, then a right, until he has cut halfway into the trunk. He turns around to start again. All his concentration is on the controlled swing—or else the blade may go into his leg.

Another man has stripped off the excess branches from the bottom upward. Yet another man takes the long iron rod with the perpendicular blade at its end to skin the tree of bark. He pushes along the length to peal off large strips at a time. This is actually the easiest duty. It goes to the most inexperienced.

Twine runs the length of both sides. With a quick jerk, the chalk coating leaves a perfect line on the wood. The man with the axe swings again. The blade burrows into the wood to the chalk line. With one step to the left, he repeats this action until he reaches the end. Returning down the log, he uses angled swats to create simple teeth for the man with a broad axe to chisel them off. With a square and fro and mallet he smoothes out the sides for a perfectly squared post.

The finished beam is ready for drying. This time, they know to take it into the shade and pile it between thin strips of wood. The product will lay here until the next supply fleet comes to take it home. It is not gold. But for England, good timber is wealth. It will have to do for now.

Others have propped a log on scaffolds that stand above a deep trench. A saw blade slices through the length. One man stands atop while another stands in the pit to work the saw in tandem. The boards that come from this work will go toward completing the walls of the new fort.

POWHATAN:
THE STORY OF A PEOPLE

More proper procedures have been taught by the ship's carpenter. This time, the harvest of building material is less straining for the men. Still, it is a taxing exercise, calling for brute strength and extreme endurance—two qualities that are difficult to have together. Exhaustion comes quickly. Breathing grows heavy. Arms shake from the vibration of repeated pounding and stern grips of the axe that dulls too quickly from extensive use. The abdomen knots from constantly pushing and pulling the saw. Hot sweat drips from every pore of the face and all along the arms and upper chest. Muscles feel as if on fire. Eyes burn from the salty sweat.

Cleared land on the little island is expanding. A few men sow seeds in the two large mounds that stand near the fort. It does not produce as well as native crops. Tensions between neighbors returned as soon as Captain Newport departed.

The days are warming. Paradise is leaving once again. The locals are getting testier by the day. The colonists can no longer expect to live off supplies brought in. They have to learn the basics of reaping from the land; those basics that still sleep in the core of their being. They are the same basics that their neighbors have developed into a culture more advanced then their own. John contemplates the situation. He can tell that relations between the two groups are turning sour. He remembers one event of a few days ago. As many of them do, one native came to the fort looking for any opportunity of payment or handout. Another just waited for the right moment to steal a tool. The stealing is getting worse. It is as if they feel they were not compensated enough for their land and provisions. They are not waiting any longer for what they feel is owed them.

Yesterday was a triumph. John caught a thief and placed him in the bilboes for the afternoon. He was…he was…that man, there!

There are three others with him. Each carries a *monahak*. Smith observes them in silence as the gang meander inside. They are definitely Paspaheg. Only those people are so brazenly combative. John finally has enough. He approaches them.

The four close in. Captain Smith lets his arms flutter while repeating, "Now, go. You go, now. No stay, no." The leader raises his *monahak* in a threatening gesture. John does not wait. Instincts of a soldier take hold. He brings a straight arm forcefully up into the other's face. The man staggers. More Englishmen gather 'round. The four men flee out of the closest gate with John leading half a dozen armed men after them. The chase comes to no avail as the trespassers wade across to the safety of the mainland.

The alarm sounds from the fort. All stop and look up. Scattered groups run to the walls. Each group attaches to another as they near the few openings. But as they near, the mood lightens to that of rejoicing.

The Phoenix is on the river. The vessel thought lost at sea has appeared in all its tattered glory. Within its hold are more needed supplies and more men to increase the general wellbeing of the colony.

The urge to explore comes out of hibernation. Plans are made for an expedition into the land of the Monakan. The men train. In six days they are a fighting force of over three score in number. Commanders bark and a thunderous crack of muskets take flight upon the winds. The sounds ride the air to Weyowakomako.

Wahunsenakok winces with every muffled echo of the *pakusak*. Children cry and mothers glare at him. The great *mamanatowik* knows he has to do something. Reports come to him. The strangers are very confident with their little army. They boast of a march beyond the *pakwachonk*. Wahunsenakok has not been invited to participate, even though it was his idea.

The lower peninsular is buzzing with speculation over the activity on the hunting island. The Paspaheg fret. The Chiskiyak fume. The Chikahominy meet in council. All agree that something must be done.

The slow screech of a falling tree is its final cry for help. It snaps apart at the wound and tumbles to the bed of decayed underbrush. Methodically, the strangers clear this grove of *mowok* trees. There are fifty men harvesting them. They have nothing else to do, now that the grand expedition has been cancelled. Captain Nelson promised to provide both his mariners and the Phoenix. At first, everyone was in agreement of the plan. That was before greed set in. Captain Nelson took back his offer, demanding payment for time and material. Confusion also developed over the ownership of any possible treasures. Naturally, anything and any land would be Newport's. None wished to waist themselves on an exercise where their own gains could not be realized. Eventually, John Martin decided that such a large scale march was just not feasible. He reduced the plan into a simple excursion for himself and six hand-picked followers. But now, no one is going.

President Ratcliff and Captain Martin busy the men with any chore possible. The pipe maker begins his production. The product is different from any of the native crafters. He shapes smaller bowls that are more at a ninety-degree angle from the stem. He does not bother with artistic embellishments.

POWHATAN:
THE STORY OF A PEOPLE

This is a mass-production item, no longer possessing the pride and detail of craftsmanship.

The apothecaries begin their studies of the native plants with the help of some of the locals who are willing to share such information. More sophisticated knowledge, however, is kept in close secrecy by the healers. The strangers also study the little worms in the *muskiminz* tree that create their cocoons of fine silk. Perhaps there can be enough silk for commercial proportion. All that is needed is the right number of trees.

Some of the laborers build a house for the president. Under his direction, they work on a design befitting the grandness of the position. Captain Martin barks commands and forces each worker into action. He makes the perfect strongman for his chief magistrate. President Ratcliff is still recovering from a misfire of his pistol which tore his hand apart between the thumb and index finger. Captain Martin has also been ill for many days, but is improving.

The six new tailors look over their crops of *tsehaho* and *wikiyopis*. Captain Smith is at the *poketawas* field with Master Shrivner. The new councilman has shown himself to be a faithful companion. He stood with John throughout the last visit to Weyowakomako and has shared much of the duties of handling the thieves.

Two visitors come to the fort. John notices them circumventing toward him. Sometimes, people can just have an appearance of trouble. Both are freshly painted and armed with a *monahak*. Their glances are searching in nature. John returns to the fort, meeting them at the gate. The two men approach him with uplifted hands. One relates his desire to enter and collect some of his people. John allows entrance, but continues to watch them.

Inside, the two spot poor Amokis. He is a Paspaheg who is a regular at the fort. He often stays over night. They approach the sitting man who stares at them like a caught animal. One challenges, "You. I must punish you."

John notices two more men in like appearance enter through another gate. As they near, John waives merrily at a friend who strolls up. They laugh and speak in their language for a moment, and then John gets back to the situation. The original four gather close to him. The leader quietly announces, "If you want to protect him, then you are the one to be beaten."

People mull about. The doors to the fort are closed and secured. The naturals notice that the Wind Children have armed themselves. The leader questions, "Why do you have weapons? What are you doing?"

John grins back, "Tell me."

The Wind Children search the interior, rounding up suspicious characters. The captives are pushed and prodded into a building where they are locked in. Men armed with pikes face every opening.

After a while, four men show up at the gates. They wait. They consult one another. They leave to tell their people what has happened.

But what were their intentions? What scheme was thwarted before it could take affect? Who are these twelve captives, and who has sent them?

A new sun burns the faces of two Paspaheg ambassadors who stand before the western gate. They patiently wait for the inhabitants who stir inside. The gate opens and Captain Smith walks toward them.

One of the ambassadors speaks up, "It is a good day. It is not good that twelve of our friends are unable to enjoy the day."

John complains, "It is not good that they came yesterday with bad thoughts."

One retorts, "I do not know their thoughts. I know they are human. And humans must be free."

John negotiates, "We will free them for a price. Your people have stolen many tools and weapons that belong to us. We know you have them. We must have these things back, or by the next sun, your friends will hang."

The ambassadors do not seem impressed. They merely look down their noses at John in silence. One inquires, "Johnsmith, you speak of material things. Such things can be replaced and discarded like the trees shed their leaves. We speak of people; lives that are dear. We miss our friends greatly. Do you not miss your own?"

"My own?" John is confused.

The ambassador explains, "We have two of your friends who were found in our woods. They had no business there. So, we kept them. Do you want to see your friends?"

John blinks twice but says not one word. He does not even try. The ambassador continues, "Perhaps we all should think further."

The moment the fort inhabitants see their cohort's silent, quick steps is the moment they realize that the upper hand they had thought to enjoy is non-existent. They must not act further in such ignorance.

The room is dark. The prisoners huddle together. The only sound they make is the rustling of their limbs in hopeless efforts to find some kind of comfort among each other. Some focus on the shadows of the guards outside. Others focus within themselves. They have been shuffled about all day. In the morning they were taken to prayers in the church where all could keep an eye on them. The same was repeated later in the day. It is a new church, rebuilt after the fire. It is no longer a simple structure. The sea carpenters combined their know-how with some farmers to create a combination barn and sea vessel. It is the best structure they've made yet.

The two Wind Children have been returned, but only one captive was freed. Another captive has been taken away. Nothing is known of his fate. A clamor at the door. It swings open. Guards enter. The lantern shines in the direction of the captives. Captain Smith studies the group for a moment until, "You."

The one chosen does not offer himself. Two guards force their way over and pluck him from the group. The door is shut and sealed as the chosen one is dragged to the Phoenix.

Captain Smith stands hunched over a small table where six *pakusak* lay. Rats scuffle about the shadows to find a good vantage point. Councilman Shrivner steps in and closes the little door with gentle care.

Captain Smith begins his interrogation, "The other one has already told me who you are, Makano. I tied him to that vary mast behind you and made him speak. You are a Paspaheg councilor, and you know what I want to find out. Tell me, or I will have you placed on a table with your hands and legs tied to the ends. I will stretch you until you speak, or until you snap in two. What will it be?"

He comes closer. "Why such thievery of our tools?"

Makano speaks up, "Why have you not given the twenty long knives that you owe Wahunsenakok? He gave Father Newport twenty *moninug* and you sent him the payment of twenty long knives. He then sent you, Johnsmith, the same for the same. He still waits for his."

"Your people do not follow Wahunsenakok," John argues.

Makano contradicts, "No, we are friendly with him. After all, the hunting party that caught you was hosted by the Chikahominy and included ourselves, the Yugtamund, Pamunkey, Matapaniyund, and the Chiskiyak. We are all *wingapow*. You are not. You trespass on our island. You cheat us. You lie."

The interrogator scoffs, "We have not lied."

"Yes. Tomsavage returned to you the box with the cloth mantle and hat that your father, Newport, had given him in friendship. Wahunsenakok felt that you ruined the friendship and wanted you to send new gifts to begin again. You sent Tomsavage back with hollow promises. You have not traded for a long time. You scare the women and children with your war practice.

"We sent Tomsavage back with our assurances that we intend no harm. You asked for a Weyanok guide to take you to Powhatan. But your plans were to go even farther west. We know that this *musawusuk* has re-supplied you. The Weyanok came, but none of your goods have been delivered. Tomsavage came again to ask you about the friendship. You have not returned the boy."

John explains, "The Weyanok left us. We wanted to find the site near Powhatan Town where we could dig for the black rock from which we make our metal."

Makano argues, "Can you blame the Weyanok? Can you really blame the distrust we, the Paspaheg and the Chikahominy, have of you?"

With that, councilmen Smith and Schrivner leave. They order a volley to ring out in the darkness, hoping it will cause those that might be listening to think the prisoners have been killed.

But everyone knows the captives are still alive. Everyone knows their *mamanatowik* will do something for them. It comes one day in the guise of a peculiar couple. They appear before the main gate of the fort. One is Wahunsenakok's chief messenger, Wawunt. He grows more deformed of body from age with each passing day. But he is still subtle and crafty of mind. The other is the youthful, feminine figure of Pokahantas. Aside from the noticeable overbite, her continence is regal and her spirit is infatuating. A strand of pearls and bits of copper tubing is wrapped thrice around her youthful neck, intertwined with a garland of wild flowers and young vines.

She stands proudly as the old man sings out his greeting. "We are here to relay that Wahunsenakok loves and respects you, Johnsmith. You should not doubt his kindness and his warm thoughts for you. Proof is in the one beside me. She is his favorite child. Proof is in the abundance of *wushakwun* and *apon* we have brought you. Will you not return the boy, Tomsavage? Wahunsenakok misses him. He loves him dearly. Nakakwawis was here the day of the capture and has told his father the distressing news. How should this go on?"

The two are welcomed into the fort and treated warmly. The little princess enjoys the attention of all the inhabitants. She is only thirteen years of age. Pretty, but not beautiful. Yet, she possesses the winsome charm that can woo any man. She delights in her reunion with her adopted brother, Tomsavage. They enjoy the fort together as she waits for a decision to be made of the captives.

Pokahantas continues to play the happy dignitary by melting the cold hearts of stubbornness. It is a skill that comes easy to her.

The prisoners are finally handed over to her. It happens in the church while she attends the afternoon prayers. Once the final sermon is concluded, the councilmen motion for the captives to exit with Pokahantas. They also present a long string of blue beads for her and a piece of *matasun* to give to her father. The sprightly youth leads her charges out of the fort.

Chapter 12

Storm clouds roll over Tsenakomako. Okius is restless, and so is Wahunsenakok. He sits in the council hall. Nakakwawis talks to him about the recent events on the Paspaheg Island, "Their *kekwiyos* was battered by the storms. The pole that holds the sail had been snapped in two. The sail was a patchwork of their shirts. Their food was wet and molding. One or two men had severe injuries and others were just plain sick. They say Johnsmith forced them to stay out in the great bay longer then they wanted."

"So this was the *kekwiyos* that disappeared after escorting their *musawusuk*, they call Phoenix, into the Great Blue." Wahunsenakok tries to understand the situation. "This was the one that carried back Johnsmith?"

"Yes. They carried him to shore…a pitiful sight."

"So, we got him."

"No, father." The two men look at each other. "His wound was from a stinging fish. One of the big brown ones. It got him on the wrist."

"Is that all?"

The son nods, "He thought he was done for. They even picked out an island near the mouth of the Tapahanok River to bury him. His arm swelled up like a dead fish on the beach."

Wahunsenakok ponders, "How did it happen?"

"He was spear fishing, with his long knife. He stabbed one good. But it got him back. They ended their journey and came home as quickly as possible."

Father inquires, "When they disappeared into the bay, where did they go?"

Once more, the two men look at the ground. Nakakwawis slowly answers, "They first went to Akomak where many tried to warn them away. But Johnsmith did not listen. Eventually, he won them over with gifts. In return, they received food and information about the eastern peninsula and the northern reaches of the bay. They went north and got caught up in the storms which blew them from one island to another, until they reached Wikokomiko. They filled their *kekwiyos* with furs.

"Their vessel was battered by the storms. But Johnsmith continued north until he reached the land of the Nantikok. He attacked them without thought. The defenders used up many arrows, but the Wind Children were not impressed. Their *pakusak* are far superior. The Nantikok also submitted to him.

"The strangers went farther up the bay. Then, they stopped. Then, they turned back."

Wahunsenakok remembers the story sent to him. "But they did reach the falls of the Patawomik…"

His son recalls the events, "Yes. They reached the falls at the swamp on the north bank, just above the town of Nakochant. The Patawomik attacked the Wind Children there."

Wahunsenakok interrupts, "The Patawomik were not successful?"

"No. They sent everyone they had to scare them off, but were scared off themselves. The strangers shot into the water, causing it to bubble. The Patawomik made peace with them and showed them their quarry where they collect the *machkwon* that they sell to us to sprinkle on our bodies. Johnsmith…got some."

Nakakwawis studies his father. He studies the lines that have deepened in his face which has grown long over the years. He studies the hair on his upper lip that has grown out thin and white. The body is weaker, but it continues to be sturdy. The fire is bright in the eyes and the strength is still clear in the voice. Nakakwawis wonders whether he will also look this way once time has handled him.

The son leaves his father to sit in quiet reflection. The large hall expands in the silence. Wahunsenakok wonders why Johnsmith would go north. He knew that he was traveling outside of Tsenakomako. He could never sneak away without the *mamanatowik* finding out. The Wind Children are ignoring Wahunsenakok. There can be no other explanation.

Rain beats in a fierce rhythm on the mat roof above. It is dim inside. It is calm. He is alone with the three small fires that dance softly in their shallow pits.

At the other end of the great hall enters his new favorite wife. Slowly, Winganusk makes her way toward the first fire. Rain water drips from the fringe of her cream-tinted *matahay*. She peels off her skin rap that has grown heavy from wetness.

Wahunsenakok murmurs just loud enough for her to hear, "I wish to be alone."

She looks up and smiles, then comes to the second fire. She is a woman. It matters not what he might want. Wahunsenakok watches her in silence. She slowly wipes off excess rain from her arms. Her hands gracefully press over her face and around her long neck. She touches her shoulders gently. They glide along her taut bosom. The old man counts the times he has touched her vibrant form in this same manner with hands wrinkled and worn.

Winganusk steps to the third fire which is closest to her man. Her body is elegantly lithe. It moves in a dainty sway. She snaps the mat. It floats to the ground. She lowers herself upon it. Winganusk is perfect in both appearance and action. She has always been this way. Stitching beads onto a leather bag, she works with an ease of motion that few can manage. Purposely, she does not acknowledge her man's presence. Winganusk strokes her long, pleated tresses in quiet diversion. Her attention is only on her work—so it would seem. She successfully makes Wahunsenakok the intruder, who stays on to watch her.

In the northern reaches of the great bay is a woodland paradise. It is where the water is a deep blue. It is where viridian foliage grows lush. Large, fortified towns dot the area. The people are more reserved. They are more firm in their attitude and more defensive of their livelihoods. As in the southern lands, they are a complicated mix of differing peoples.

One man joins a gathering in Wikokomiko. This is a walled town with dwellings layered in tree bark to protect against harsh, cold winds and harsh, cold-blooded attackers. The one of interest is a local. And yet he is a foreigner to the people here. He has made his way to this body of water from the distant north. His origins are from even farther away. He keeps a bushy, black beard with challenging pride. The season for storytelling has not yet come. But he can not wait any longer to share his tale.

"Come closer, people!" he announces. "Let me tell you of my time with Johnsmith. It was earlier this year that he and eleven of his followers came to this town.

"But I shall tell you the story of their second trip to this region. Close to the Tokwug people, at the uppermost reaches of the bay, did these warriors from another world meet up with our dreaded *maskapow*. There were eight

POWHATAN:
THE STORY OF A PEOPLE

akwintan full of Masawomik bowmen. Only half in the *kekwiyos* were well enough to fight. Without care, Johnsmith and his band fought the Masawomik and sent them running for safety. Those fearless demons at last know fear!

"The next act between these two forces was a talk of peace and a surrender of weapons. That is how the Tokwug people found the strangers. The *kekwiyos* was decorated with Masawomik shields! Johnsmith said that he came to them on the request of Tsenakomako. He told them he was sent north from Kekotan to fight the Masawomik who forever come to terrorize us.

"The Tokwug were very grateful. They welcomed and feasted their hero. How they showered him with eighteen *machkow* of various furs and long chains of white *wowanok*. How they weighted his shoulders with the painted *amonsokwat* mantel. At that moment, he transformed into a half-god. His eyes showed it! He influenced sixty Suskwehanok—those who grow much taller than any of us on the eastern peninsula; those who have pipes as long as arms—to come to Tokwug for peaceful trade. Five of their chief men came across the bay to pay their respects to Johnsmith.

"Johnsmith heard of the lands to the north. He heard how we get the metal tools from the others like him—those who are settling along the great river that runs across the northern borders of the Masawomik. They are the same people from whom I am made.

"When their great protector left the Tokwug, they were so unhappy to see him go. But he promised to return next year. He promised us in Wikokomiko the same thing. We now have access to the *tomahak* and other trinkets that the Suskwchanok get from those to the far north!

"I did not wish to wait a year. I journeyed to Mowatakunt and met Johnsmith there. I told the people of his greatness, and they welcomed him graciously.

"I served the strangers with water, wood, and helpers. I guided them into the hostile land of the Tapahanok. Of course, they attacked him. But Johnsmith and his men used their *pakusak* and rowed right through the ambush without care. They went farther upriver and received friendly greetings from all the tribes on the upper reaches of the Tapahanok River.

"And when the rocky falls stopped his water travel, I showed him through the land on foot. We met up with Manahowak warriors. We had a grand fight with these cousins of the Monakan. Those feared people of the big woods where the Tapahanok River forks also turned away in fear of Johnsmith! He killed and wounded many. I fought along side him, using most of the Masawomik arrows that he had given me.

"One of the wounded was Amowolek—the brother of the one who speaks for the people of Hasuwiga. We treated the wound to his knee. Johnsmith forced friendship with him. He forced him to guide us to his outpost town of Mahaskahod. Even the Manahowak, who fight so ferociously with the Masawomik that trespass from behind the Blue Mountains, begged Johnsmith for peace!

"We returned down river. Johnsmith boldly ended the war between the Mowatakunt and the Tapahanok by seizing the three Tapahanok women whom the Mowatakunt *weyowanz* had stolen. He allowed the Tapahanok *weyowanz* to take back only one of them. He gave the Mowatakunt *weyowanz* another. And I, I received the third, because I am now a big man! I am a *cham* to Johnsmith."

The audience is overwhelmed with the wonders that flood their ears. Yes, these Wind Children are a great people. All agree on that. Why worry of Wahunsenakok and his weak promises? The Masawomik still know the Powhatan only by name. Even the Pawankatank speak freely against that tired old *mamanatowik*.

A new *takwitok* dawns. Captain Newport returns aboard the Mary & Margaret. A few naturals loitering around the fort gather near the landing to observe. They find the supplies to be generally the same. The passengers, however, are more diverse. There is almost equal portions of gentlemen, tradesmen, and laborers. Among them are five men of varying ages from the old kingdom of Poland, where the production of glass items are well-known. In the Old Country, none of these men would be able to progress above the rank of an apprentice within any reasonable span of time. Each has succumbed to their impatience and made this arduous journey in a quest to become master craftsmen.

The same can be said of the three men from Central Europe where the Rhine River flows. They were nothing more than skilled help, with no fixed future. But as their feet tap the soil, Frances, Adam, and young Samuel instantly become experienced carpenters. They call themselves, "Deutsch" men. The best the English can pronounce is, "Dutch." And so, Dutchmen they are.

Another surprise comes ashore in the form of two women—real women from the opposite side of the world. They are delicate, always mindful of their beauty that can be tarnished rather than enhanced. So white. Hair that is on fire. One is attached to a gentleman who controls her completely. Powhatan women warn their men not to get any ideas. How could they control the will of a woman? Where can they gain strength from their women if they take that very thing out of them? The other female is in service to the first. She is not a second wife, but a type of slave. She is similar to captive young females in Pamasawu. She is instantly the focus of every bachelor in the colony. With two hundred men from which to choose, she should not be spouseless for long. Hers is the happiest face on the whole island.

Two new councilmen have come to replenish the leadership. Poor Captain Martin has already left on the Phoenix and poor Captain Ratcliff expresses his utmost desire to be aboard when the Mary & Margaret departs.

Of greatest significance is the arrival of Francis West. He is the brother to Sir Thomas West, one of the most important members of the Virginia Company.

Yes, gentle reader, the colony is shaping into an England in miniature. Now, the settlement will be twice its original size and will take on the challenges of creating a real business venture. The opportunistic hardihood of the English Renaissance will bloom in this new world.

Captain Newport has returned with the expectation of finding a settlement well-prepared for this new phase. Instead, he finds the same pitiful site. The fort has been redesigned into five walls. Only an army man like Captain Smith understands the strategic advantages of such a configuration. It is stronger, more compact, and easier to defend. But Christopher Newport sees no foundation for a growing settlement, no motivation for any productivity, no peace with the Indigenies. Worst of all, the presidency has fallen to John Smith; the man with all the answers, but no resolve.

One step at a time. John marches as he knows how. At Chiskiyak, his party can borrow an *akwintan* to ferry across the wide Pamunkey River to Weyowakomako. John returns to that place once again. He has been sent by that Newport fellow. The old lord of this land is to be coroneted! A primitive is to be royally recognized. John shakes his head at the thought.

John knows the future of this colony lies up the great bay where the forests are thicker, the furs more prevalent, and iron ore lies just at the fork of the Tapahanok River. There is even a good chance of finding gold in the region. John has already made contacts with prominent members in the north. He established a food supply that will begin to flow next year. All that Newport fellow can speak of is the Powhatan River. He still thinks there are plenty of mining opportunities near the *pakwachonk*. But John knows it matters not that food alliances had already been made with those along the Powhatan. Such would not be closer to the colony if the colony was not where it is. John is certain that they should abandon all that was originally established and seek a fresh start in new surroundings with new hosts.

Captain Newport can only speak of delay. Delay, delay, delay. He refuses to see any of the progress made. Yes, the Virginia Company expects the colony to be well-established by now. But things do take time—especially when real leadership was not demonstrated at the beginning. John is now the President. He should be informed. He should have a say in things. John should not have to take commands from such a…sea dog.

Namontak is with the group. He is so happy to be back and has so much to tell of his adventures on the great island of the Wind Children. Otahotin escorts the party across the wide water. He is not very happy with his charges, but the duties of a *weyowanz* overrule all personal feelings he might nurse.

Namontak receives a hero's welcome. He is a man who has braved the journey to the realm of Manibuzo. He carries back descriptions that have not been uttered in these parts for ages.

The guests parade into the city center. John recognizes their hostess. Pokahantas takes command for her father who is a day and a half away. Messengers have already been sent to collect him. In the meantime, she oversees the entertaining of the guests. They have come at an opportune moment. A dance performance is ready to be presented for the upcoming festivals. The topic is timely. It denotes the importance of the *wushakwun*. Soon, the forest floor will be ablaze with grand hunts for this creature.

The young lady directs the sitting arrangements. She then checks on the players. The field is alight with a strong fire. A circle of eight posts surround the excited flames. Each is topped with a carved head, possessing long flowing hair. All are human faces that look upon the fire with open mouths of wonderment. The dance troupe consists of the most agile and pretty young girls in town. They assemble offstage in the forest.

The pageant begins with a song coming from the trees. The audience is alarmed. They take arms. Pokahantas quickly calms them with smiles and calming words. The thirty women begin the dance. Some are painted white, others red, and still others black or multicolored. None is similar to the other. The lead dancer adorns her head with *wushakwun* horns. Around her pelvis is a *matahay* that still holds its hair secure in the skin. Holding different items,

POWHATAN:
THE STORY OF A PEOPLE

the rest move in and out of the trees shouting. After a while, they assemble in a ring around the stage. They scatter once more. The dance is long, as such dances are. It challenges the stamina of the young women. It tests their devotion to the story they portray. It is the legend of the first *wushakwun* and the four winds.

Once, so very long ago, the first *wushakwun* was the only *wushakwun*. Therefore, it was enormous. It was beautiful. It was adored by the world. The four winds were jealous of such popularity. From each of the four directions, the wind brothers closed in on it. They cornered the great *wushakwun* and killed it with their hunting lances. After dressing the meat and feasting upon it for days, each returned to their homes. Manibuzo was furious of this malicious act. He thought long on how he could turn this tragedy into something good for the humans he so loves. Carefully, he collected all the great hairs of the slain animal and cast them over the land. From the powerful word charms that were uttered, each hair became a *wushakwun* of the size they are today. Manibuzo then showed the first people how to hunt them. That is why the *wushakwun* is so important.

The dancers enact this legend well. All those who can see the story in the pageant agree. Those who are completely oblivious to such things are at least entertained. The guests are refreshed with fruits, fish, and flesh. They are escorted to their lodgings where some of the dancers offer themselves for another type of performance. After all, a dancer in any world must utilize her body in various ways for her means. Some of the guests accept. The business of physical delight is transacted.

Another sun rises. Wahunsenakok arrives and President Smith delivers the message that father Newport wishes the *mamanatowik* to visit him.

John walks past a tall post. He counts twenty four new scalps swaying in the breeze. They are Pawankatank. That is where Wahunsenakok has been. He had assembled all of their men in their own town. All thought they were joining a communal hunt with him. Instead, they found themselves to be the prey. The *weyowanz* and all the women and children have been brought to Weyowakomako. Any survivors who can not find asylum with clan members in other tribes will eventually have their scalps hanging with the rest.

The *weyowanz* of those who once where the original Kekotan tribe departs from the council lodge. He has just received permission to take the remnants of his tribe to resettle the Pawankatank territory.

Wahunsenakok is victorious. He is not in the mood to be diplomatic. "It is good to hear that your…king has sent gifts to me. Truly, he believes me also a king. This is my kingdom. I will not come to your settlement that lies in my land. I will stay here eight days to receive Newport. He should come to me with his gifts. It is good to hear your father has not forgotten his promise to fight the Monakan. He should no longer concern himself with that. I can avenge myself. As for the site of your slain brother, the trail there is not as you suppose it. You should forget the place. You should forget of the salt water you seek beyond Kwiwank. There is no such water. You are either ill-informed or have misinterpreted. You can find only the Masawomik in that place…And the great waters there are fresh."

Another day brings Captain Newport to Weyowakomako. Through Namontak, he presents greetings from King James, "With the greatest wish to recognize your rule over Virginia, he wants you to accept these gifts reserved for only such great men."

The cloak that had been returned is offered again with all the apparel of a royal gentleman. Captain Newport holds out a simple crown. Namontak assures his father that no harm is intended in the request to kneel. But the old man disagrees. "A king does not kneel to have his brains beaten out. They stand tall and proud. You should be on all fours to me."

The good captain gives in and places the crown atop the erect sovereign as ceremoniously possible. He gives the signal for the salute by *pakusak*. It startles Wahunsenakok, but only for a moment. Composure returns quickly. "This is all fine. It is a ceremony befitting any here in Pamasawu. You are truly a noble and good man, Newport. Your king is a good ruler of his people. I look forward to the stories of your land from Namontak. Thank you for his safe return. You kept your promise to care for him, and I have done the same for your son, Tomsavage…at least when he stayed with me. Long has he been kept away.

"These are good gifts. I show my thanks by asking you to send something of my own to your great king." Wahunsenakok pulls out a lavish pair of *mokasin*. He then takes down his favorite mantle that hangs on the back wall. He explains the three figures sewn into the skins, "These are the symbols of myself, my clan, and my personal spirit guide. Surrounding them are the stars of eternity. I hope the length of kindness between our worlds shall be as long."

Christopher broaches, "I wish to make a journey to Monakan, as we spoke of once before. I feel it a good idea."

POWHATAN:
THE STORY OF A PEOPLE

"Much time has passed, since then," Wahunsenakok returns. "I no longer feel the same of it. Johnsmith has learned how to journey all over our land without my aide...or blessings. You needn't worry of the Monakan. They will always be. I must concern myself with a future among them. I know of your desire for precious metals like the yellow dust. Again, you are misinformed. The Monakan are guardians of *matasun* quarries. They are dealers in the red stone from the people of the great waters that lie far west of Kwiwank. That is the only thing you may find in the land of the Monakan...besides death. If you still seek them, I will not deny Namontak to guide you. But be warned. The Monakan are animals. You shall find only misery in their country."

Activity is steady at the fort. George Percy observes all the happenings around him. The colony is finally a factory site. The Dutchmen have completed construction of the glass foundry. It stands just at the entrance of the thin isthmus that bridges James Island to the mainland when the river ebbs. The Poles are settling into their business. Others work in the swamp on the island to produce tar and pitch from its murk. At one corner of the island, men burn great piles of hardwood logs. Smoke billows wide and thick. Mounds of cooled wood slag are packed into barrels for soap ash.

The President has returned with his thirty woodsmen who cut and split clapboard for England. It was the only way he could leave the fort and all those who were watching him.

John shuffles through his papers. He gathers his notes and the map he has drawn. From the place names designated on the map, one can easily see who had been with him on the expedition. Included in this parcel is a blunt, scathing letter that lashes back at Captain Newport and the others who have given him nothing but discord. John also includes his thoughts on Newport's failures in the Monakan territory. Who better to chastise than the one man who could not go?

George thinks back on the trip up the Powhatan River. Orders and funds had been issued by the company. The grand march had to be made. Captain Newport took a hundred and twenty men with him.

A quartet of *kekwiyos* made their way to Powhatan Town. Travel was not as before. There were only fragmented glimpses of people along the wooded banks. At the *pakwachonk*, they disassembled the largest vessel and carried its four parts up the riverside trail along the north bank to bypass the thunderous rapids. They observed the small fishing party on the big river island. In turn, those fishing stopped their work of setting up their *nesakan* among the rocks to stare back.

The little army reached calm water. They reassembled their watercraft and packed it with the supplies. The channel grew distinct. The flood plains on both banks became more ensnared between towering bluffs. Generally, the river valley was narrow all the way to the town of Machimko. At that point, the land suddenly opened along the southern bank. A large habitation cluttered the area. The place was almost hidden behind a tall ridge to the east that lay perpendicular to the course of the river. Everything was open. There was no stockade, no clustering of buildings. The river was at peace. Its surface mirrored the trees that sparsely aligned the bank.

George will never forget the deafening sound of the frogs in the area. They have infested that place longer than any human. He is certain that the little creatures will be there forever.

Of the people, George saw nothing but droll faces under long hair and broad feathers. The Monakan people where not menacing. Neither where they friendly. They care little for the trinkets that so delight the Powhatan people. They had little of any worth to exchange. Their existence lies too deep in the natural world. And their interests are lost in the spiritual, as exemplified by the religious monument of red stones that rose chest-high in the city center.

One of their co-leaders finally agreed to guide the expedition upriver to the city of Masinakak. It was a larger, more permanent site, lying on the great north-south trading road. For hundreds of years, goods from the upper reaches of the Suskwehanok Territory have come through Masinakak on their way to where the descendants of Aligewi now live. George remembers the land was shallow, with expansive low hills. It is a place with beautiful vistas that the inhabitants enjoy. For the English, the landscape was as dull as the reception they encountered.

George learned that they could find gold near the foothills of Kwiwank. It is where the great *matasun* mines lie, and where the herds of wisent range. It is a land more hardy then any in Tsenakomako. But it is also a land much more difficult to traverse.

A bitter sense of danger grew in Captain Newport's mind. It was an uneasy feeling that was stronger than at any time during his numerous adventures. He listened to his instincts and turned back.

Everything was ventured. Yet, nothing was gained from this expedition. The travelers returned just before all their food and their strength were used up. In spite of alliances that were formed just two years previous, no one along the Powhatan River came to rescue poor Captain Newport. He made a journey deep into the land of their *maskapow*. He let not one drop of blood. Such actions and inactions can create an irreversible scorn from those in Tsenakomako.

CHAPTER 13

There is an unusual assemblage at the fringe of Weyowakomako. An *ahakan*, like the Wind Children have, is taking shape at the point overlooking the Pamunkey River. The water is the color of rust from recent rains.

There are five builders at the site. Two are English. The three Dutchmen hold the majority. President Smith promised Wahunsenakok a European style dwelling. He has sent Francis, Adam, and Samuel for the task. They feel at home in this river valley. The trees and the open sky remind them of the world they have left behind. The city is peaceful, friendly. There is a bounty of beautiful women. But most appealing is the fact that they are away from the English who think so little of them.

Francis looks over the building material. Posts and beams of native *powamink* have already been hewn. The bases of the four corner posts still retain their roundness. Each of the squared sides is a man's foot in width. All are strong and heavy. They are durable, with plenty of tannic acid in the fiber to protect against fungi and insects. Boards are straight and long, without knots as these trees raced for the sky in their growth and sprouted branches only near the top.

They have chosen a spot of visual prominence. It is the high ground along the eastern rim of the little bay at Weyowakomako. From here, one can see the city and far down the river. The design effects an atmosphere of permanence—one that can stand on its own well after its surroundings change and its builders depart this life. It is unlike any in the city.

A crowd gathers near the site for an afternoon's amusement. The smiling strangers invite some in the crowd to assist. They are indeed different from the English. Their speech is more gruff and sliced. Yet, their tone is soft, with a demeanor more at peace with itself. Their eyes smile coyly. These are people of the land, much more so then the islanders who have brought them

POWHATAN:
THE STORY OF A PEOPLE

here. They are close to the natural world rather than awash in social interaction which only advances an agitated demeanor.

The men dig six rectangular holes about a leg long and an arm wide. They line a perfectly-measured rectangle on the ground with knotted string and fancy toys. One by one, the Dutchmen slide each post into the length of a hole. The base goes down and against the far end of the rectangular cavity. Adam and Francis hold the post level as young Samuel packs in the fill dirt.

Talk of the new *ahakan* goes through the city as fast as a child's run. All can see the point from various parts of the community. It is a very slow show indeed. People check in on the progress from time to time while going about their own work.

One is not so pleased. Winganusk is threatened by this construction. She can not allow these strangers to take any attention away from her.

"It is an outrage!" she steams. "Who are these men to come here? They don't know how to build a real *ahakan*. That is woman's work! Who do they think they are?"

She stands. A group of unfortunates are halted by her glare. "My man will not approve of such a small thing. I will build him a real *ahakan* and he can use that other thing for a storage hut. We will gather at the meadow and begin today. All new material!"

Sullen heads nod. So many plans for the day are obliterated by one woman's inclination.

Now, the spectators have a real show. The meadow fills with activity as long green saplings are piled thick. The men search about the forest for trees with just the right dexterity and tender youth. Winganusk looks over the stack, choosing the ones that are good enough and sending the men back into the woods to harvest more.

Each man uses his new *tomahak*. They can cut hard wood in no time. With just three chops straight across and three chops downward at an angle, most of the work is done. After that, another gash is made on the opposite side of the trunk, just above the original cut. The trunk snaps apart with ease. Such a simple tool can change an entire way of life.

Women position long, straight saplings along the ground. They dig small holes, the size of a fist, at intervals along the outer edge of these marking poles. Each hole descends at an angle under the marking pole.

Men take one sapling after the next, inserting it securely into the ground. Male arms pull with all available strength to bow the sapling inward. A pole opposite to this is bent inward until the two ends meet. The ends are then twisted together and wrapped with wet strips of *asunomink* bark that will tighten as they dry. The result is an arch. Its strength is based on the natural outward pull of the saplings. The process continues until all the arches along the length are completed. They are augmented with poles lashed across the exterior horizontally. Each span is distanced evenly above the other. At each end of the structure, two poles are planted straight into the ground. Each is further braced with a horizontal pole lashed near the top.

The Wind Children work on their frame. The floor is raised above the ground for more permanence. The three carpenters carve out tenons on both ends of the sills and dig out mortis joints just above the rounded base of each post. The tenons slide perfectly in. The sills rest on the rounded ledges of the posts. They are further secured at each corner with down braces.

The Dutchmen lay joists across the width of this perimeter. Each end slips into a lap joint made in the sills. Mortise joints are also chiseled out along the top of the sills at measured intervals for the studs. Francis and Adam top their framework with long, flat plates. Once the joists are laid, and the rafters put up, the men have a solid box skeleton. They have tightened every important joint with trunnels, which are inserted at an angle so that everything will lock together as the wood ages.

Winganusk observes that the strangers take a long time in working with such large, balky pieces. They work with wood as if carving stone. True, the form is more solid and sturdy. But flexibility is the key to long life. Her design is held together by forces unexplainable. It is a testimony of conformity to natural laws. Her house will breathe. It will posses life. What they do at the point is without life for it does not comply with the world that surrounds it. Still…it is cute.

The carpenters have finished laying the floor boards and roofing boards. The two Englishmen begin to weave strips of bark between the studs. They manipulate the natural material until it is no longer natural. They string the flexible sticks in and out through vertical rods until the entire space between the studs is filled in—except for a window opening and for a doorway.

In the meadow, the women move with gentle fingers, with gentle arms, with gentle strides. They make their *ahakan* with hands that are careful and precise. Some make quick glances at the point to see if their admirers are watching.

The women prepare to add skin to their skeleton. Reed mats are laid out all along the perimeter of the frame. Each mat is the width of an arm span and twice that in length. Female chatter fills the meadow as mats are hung and tied

POWHATAN:
THE STORY OF A PEOPLE

all along the bottom rung of the structure. The next rung is covered with the ends dropping over the bottom mats. They bind the top ends to the horizontal poles from the inside. Winganusk alone hangs the decorative mats across the inner walls.

The Dutchmen no longer see the women inside. They get back to work. All five men slap and smooth white mud into the latticework. It takes hold with a solidity of soft stone.

Adam and Francis complete their work by laying the shingles atop the roof. Methodically, each works their way upward along either side until meeting at the crest.

Winganusk mulls about her work site. Yes, she has proven her point. But how could it have been a competition? Only she sees it in that light. The strangers have only looked with lustful eyes at those under her direction. The maidens have behaved no better with their titillating mannerisms. In truth, the prize has been the shared amour between the two genders.

Snow drifts wistfully in the open meadow at the point. Two men examine the new structure. The style looks familiar to John Smith. Wahunsenakok is getting to be well-versed with such designs. He has learned many new things, including his guest's recent movements in the region.

The President has been quite active these past days. He has been on another of his grand tours. This time, he traveled during the dead season of *Popano*, when no one in their right mind would roam.

The President has taken both a *kekwiyos* and the little *musawusuk* they call, Discovery. On this occasion, John has brought almost thirty men with him.

But they did not come immediately. Their first stop was at Wayaskoyak where they met a warm reception. They decided to take full advantage of the hospitality, as they haven't had much lately. They even gave the *weyowanz* a young man. A simple *weyowanz* of a small tribe was thus bestowed the same homage as the *mamanatowik*. President Smith then talked the tribe into guiding some of them southward to seek out the Chowanok.

John then crossed the river to Kekotan. The snow and winds and icy rains had grown fierce. The abundant meals of *kaway* and the exorbitant helpings of *apon* in the warm Kekotan homes were too much to give up. They stayed long enough to celebrate the birth of their *manitow* before traveling on.

Finally, they came to Weyowakomako. They blew in with the cold winds. The ice has spread far into the river from both banks, narrowing its width to that of a minor channel.

The English come with expectant hands stretched out. Wahunsenakok expressed that they could not stay long. He asserted that only beggars, desperate to survive *Popano*, traveled to Weyowakomako at this time of year.

Wahunsenakok offered, "Forty baskets. I can give forty for as many of your metal *monahak*."

"Perhaps *matasun*."

"You can not eat my *poketawas* for *matasun*."

President Smith was determined. He did not plead for his people. Instead, he spilled out a litany of false sacrifices he had made for his host.

The *mamanatowik* let his quest speak, amazed at the shear gall of the little man. The wind Children did not even send any tribute during *Takwitok*. Johnsmith had only excuses and arguments of soundless reasoning to explain why they should receive food on credit.

Wahunsenakok interrupted his guest, "Many have told me you come to attack me."

John had thought no one at the fort had listened to his ideas. In that quick moment, he found that someone had indeed been listening after all.

Wahunsenakok elaborated, "Your purpose here is not for trade, but to take my country. You come on the rivers armed to the teeth, placing scorn upon any who refuse your demands. Recently, you have forced the Nansemund, the Chikahominy, even the Apamatuk to give you what they could not. You made enemies of them on your own. You are a *cham*. Put your weapons away and show your friendship. Trust is the best form of proving your love."

Yesterday ended with a promise to give the Wind Children what could be spared—but nothing more. There were more children's mouths to fill before the *mamanatowik* could consider the empty bellies of grown men. Today, the tension between the two is as sharp as the icy air that strikes their faces. Everyone retires to the new *ahakan* that Winganusk built.

A small amount of *poketawas* is offered for a *matasun* kettle. John wants so much more. He tries another angle, "I thank you for this little trade. However, this is not an exchange rate that can stand. I can accept that you managed to harvest much less this year. But this trade must be completed with more from you as soon as it is possible. How else can you expect us to protect you from your *maskapow* if I am not granted proper compensation?"

POWHATAN:
THE STORY OF A PEOPLE

Wahunsenakok is silent for a moment. Then, "I have seen my family die three times. I am the last of those previous generations. I have learned the difference between peace and war better then any. Now, I am old and will die soon enough. My three brothers and then my two sisters will succeed me. I wish their leadership to be well-lived and your love for them no less. I know your people are to remain an integral part of this world.

"The talk of taking my country by force puts fear into hearts. No longer are you seen with soft eyes. Why? Why?

"What can you achieve by taking forcefully that which you may gain through love? Why threaten to destroy those who provide you food, of which you should be able to grow and hunt on your own? How do you expect to make war with us when we can retreat to the safety of the wilderness? By wronging your friends, you will starve. Can you see? We do not carry our weapons. We still wish to care for you. We are willing to provide a piece of our labors. What labors have your people offered? You are their leader. What example are you to them?

"Do you think I do not understand that it is better to eat good meat, lay with good women, and sleep in peace with my family…laugh and be happy with my neighbors? I prefer to enjoy your gifts rather than to be forced from my own home and hide in the cold woods to feed upon the roots and waste of the trees. I wish not to be ever watchful of a breaking twig or hear someone cry out, 'Here comes Johnsmith!'

"Let this be known. Every year, as we promised each other, we will trade during the appropriate season in freedom of fear. And I will furnish you *poketawas* only if you are without your weapons."

The President argues, "We are a people that can be known for our deeds. Some of your people have refused us food. We will seek revenge from their ingratitude. We will always protect ourselves from any rumor of your ill intent. Surely, you know of my travels among your most feared *maskapow*. With our superiority, we could crush you, if we wished. Your people come to Jamestown with weapons as part of their apparel. We do the same.

"We have no need for war with you. Your treasures are of no worth to us. Run. Hide. We can manage on our own better then you think. We entertain your generosity. But need it, we do not. Our way of life is beyond your comprehension."

Wahunsenakok picks up the debate, "Johnsmith, I never treat any *weyowanz* as kindly as I have you. From you, I receive the least kindness. Your father, Newport, came to me. He gave me metal weapons and tools. He gave me *matasun*, clothing, a bed. He accepted what I wanted to give him. He would send his weapons away at a mention. No one denies to prostrate at my feet or refuse my wishes! None, but you. Of you, I can not ask anything. But, to you, I must grant all?

"You call Newport your father. So should you call me. You are a child with no respect for your elders. You cry for me to show you love and then demand it with your weapons."

There it is. That look. John reveals his intention without a word. Wahunsenakok glances at his chief sentinel.

The *kekwiyos* ventures closer to load the food supply. A few armed men sneak onto shore. The bowmen maneuver. The old man retires toward the back chamber for a moment. Three of his women entertain their guest until John realizes that too much time has passed. He rises. He searches. All he can find is an empty city with forty bowmen along the outskirts to delay his soldiers. As soon as John can assemble his fighters, the bowmen vanish into the wilderness.

The great city of Menapukunt is quiet. The air is tainted with an uneasy expectation. Johnsmith has been sighted passing the fork of the Pamunkey River. The small *kekwiyos* makes landfall right in front of the royal complex that stands open atop the little knoll. President Smith and his armed guard make the two hundred strides to the entrance where an old cripple sits. He is wrapped in a heavy *amonsokwat* skin. A boy rustles nearby. No one else can be seen anywhere in town. The cripple does not utter a word. He only stares at the trespassers with conflicting expressions of fear and interest.

The intruders search the buildings for food. They find nothing.

Opechankano appears from the wooded edge with his warriors. The two groups join in front of the great council lodge. The opposing leaders exchange a few pleasantries and then a few other words not so pleasant.

"I seek your brother," John announces. "He has cheated me and ran."

"He has cheated you of his blood," Opechankano retorts. "You shall never have that. You are not worthy of such honor."

John steps closer. "There are no people here. You also have hidden away your food. You have abandoned your seat of power. How can your people be so honorable when they act so cowardly?"

Opechankano looks down. "We are above such worry of material things. We need no place to define who we are. We are great, because we are."

POWHATAN:
THE STORY OF A PEOPLE

John quickly scans his surroundings. They have changed during his battle of words. He finds his small company surrounded by a larger group of warriors.

Opechankano has his long lock freely hanging down his left arm. John grabs it tight. He turns the old warrior around and presses his pistol against the long chest.

Anxiety seizes all. Bows are dropped. Arms gyrate in pleading. The warriors are useless against this threat to the life of their beloved *weyowanz*.

John pulls his hostage toward the bank. His own soldiers gather around the two. Food appears. Desperate men run back and forth through the vacant city to appease the Wind Children. Neither the land nor the food define who the Pamunkey are. But Opechankano—nothing is more precious than him.

The Discovery returns to Fort James. Master Winne is the only councilman to greet the weary travelers. Masters Scrivener and Waldo died a few days previous. They led a small group down the icy Powhatan River in search of food. The treacherous river turned over their *kekwiyos*. Freezing water swallowed the entire crew.

John finds the news bitter, yet sweet. He has only one councilman to deal with. What's more, he is still new and still obedient.

John proceeds to the storehouse with his spoils. As the door swings open, he is taken aback. The interior appears almost empty. "What of the tools, the weapons? There be few here."

"Oh, sir," Master Winne reminds, "I followed ye command."

"Command?" John is puzzled.

Master Winne elaborates, "Aye...The Dutchmen...Adam and Francis? They came to fetch fifty swords, eight pike heads, eight pieces shot powder...three hundred hatchets. They came not long ago, stating thy wish to take for to truck. They had in company not a small number of the naturals to suffer the load. Were they not received?"

John has no answer. What can he say? That old man has acquired what he covets after all.

Chapter 14

Two boys busy themselves near the glass foundry. One collects sand at the riverbank as the other pounds a collection of *tsekoma* shells into a fine lime powder. Their youthful hands operate in the cold, moist air of early morning. Inside, two older workers are shoveling out the ash from yesterday's fire in the main furnace that is built of round river stones and clay. Slowly, they scrape the floor clean of combustible dust. A third man rustles through the wood pile to collect fuel for a new day's production.

A reddish glow radiates from the domed interior through the long tube-like fuel chamber and from each of the four round openings near the top. Each is the diameter of a woman's face. The master glass maker peeks through one to examine the condition of the four containers inside. The pots are short and wide, with flat bottoms. Their roundness is severely warped by the intense heat. They will soon need replacing. He picks up an iron ladle by its long wooden handle. He skims the soupy foam from the top. The mixture of lime, sand, ash, and old glass slowly melts into molten form.

At one end of the long finishing oven, the second worker collects yesterday's product. There is a light chime from the viridian glass as the pieces jiggle against each other. Another kiln is at the opposite end. A third worker ignites the fire channel to fuse the recipe for tomorrow's supply.

The second worker walks around the furnace. The contents in the other two pots are ready. He collects a blob of glowing amber on the end of a hollow iron rod. He takes it to a smooth stone on the floor. Twirling it against the surface, he condenses the material until it is the proper density and size and shape. He reheats it in an opening of the furnace, and then positions the hollow tube next to his cheek. After a deep breath, he puts his mouth at the end. Slowly, he blows while twirling the rod. The material expands.

POWHATAN:
THE STORY OF A PEOPLE

After another reheating, the master attaches a shorter rod to the opposite end of the article to snap it clear from the blowing rod. He rolls it along an arm of the chair-like work table, making sure the thickness of the glass is uniform and the overall shape is symmetrical.

President Smith walks to the little factory, carrying a couple of used glass bottles for the pile. The glasshouse is nothing more than a thatched roof topping a skeleton of massive beams. Wide boards loosely cover the two sides of the building that face the river winds. The other two are completely open to help ventilate the interior. And yet, the Poles are already sweating profusely. They will work in the vapors throughout the day.

The workers have little time for John. He has no real interest in them. At least he feels confident that they will not betray him as the Dutchmen. Those three are still with Wahunsenakok. His hideout lies somewhere deep in the thick wilderness. John has to find it—even if he has to cut down every tree in Pamasawu.

He makes a quick glance at the woods nearby. Slight movement. An enemy is in the underbrush. John quickly sends one of the boys to fetch a company of musketeers from Fort James. Turning back, he sees nothing. He takes a moment to be sure before he leaves.

Just within ear-shot of the glasshouse is a shallow marsh. From it comes Wowinchopunk. John braces for the impact. What he sees is a large body, entirely painted black. Atop the head are two short *wushakwun* antlers to identify his clan.

The *weyowanz* is alone by choice. He has led his people against all the trespass and transgression of the strangers. He has come to recognize the whole of his problem embodied in the man before him.

The two struggle. The *monahak* slips out of hand. The sound of running men intensifies. Captain Smith grabs hold. Wowinchopunk can not break loose. Two of the Poles grab him. The combatants fall into the bog. Exhausted, Wowinchopunk is dragged to the fort.

Wowinchopunk sits on the dirt floor. He is in complete isolation. Only the clank of his shackles taunts the ears. Rust chafes his skin. Particles sift into the open soars. The brig is nothing more than a small hut of wood bones and mud flesh. It is hollow inside. Bound straw blocks out the sky. He stays far from the fireplace. That is the decrepit lung that can suck out breath and fill the room with smoke.

A little voice chirps at the window across from where he sits. He hears a husky exhale from a woman just on the other side. A small hand flutters about the wooden bars that cover the opening. Wowinchopunk twirls himself up. His smile broadens with each shuffling step toward the window.

On the other side of the wall is a small face with big searching eyes. Behind his son, Wowinchopunk can make out parts of his wife's face—twisted somewhat from the strain of holding her growing boy. To be sure, she is not as strong as she was when the child was smaller. Slowly, the naked boy slides down from the window. The daughter sits on the ground. She wears only moss to cover her female trait. A thin strand of shell beads decorates her shoulder-length hair.

His wife declares, "Your son wanted to see you today. They let us inside. We can give you this food." She shoves the bundle through the bars. "They can't feed themselves, so they don't mind us feeding you."

She quickly glares at the guard, just to see if he might understand her. He sniffs back at her with disinterest. She continues, "The children helped me with it. We all miss you. We all want you back."

Wowinchopunk says nothing. He loses himself in her face. He reaches one hand outward. She instinctively guides it with her own to her chin. "You don't look good at all. Don't they know how to treat a *weyowanz*? One of those hateful beasts said they will never let you out. I think he just wanted to see me cry."

Wowinchopunk chuckles, "They don't have to let me out. Don't worry about me, little ones. Just take care of your mother until I get home. It won't be much longer." He studies her eyes. "I promise. I'll be back soon." The guard fidgets. He swings one arm out to push her along.

The bench is nothing more than a split log held up with four choice sticks of kindling. It is not even level. But as long as the time of use is not extensive, the curved surface does make for a comfortable fit. The table is a compilation of clapboard slapped together in a crude square. The top is a bit rough in texture, but generally flat. President Smith sits here. His mind dives into a maelstrom of worry. He knows the hounds are closing in. Dreadful news has arrived in the guise of Captain Samuel Argall.

Although at twenty nine years of age, the mariner is a proven achiever. Causes and effects are not part of Samuel's mindset when given a task. Only the clear focus on a goal becomes his drive. His most recent achievement is finding a more direct wind route to Virginia. He has found it far north from the dangerous Spanish fleets in the Caribbean. Such a discovery is sure to bring promotion. There is already talk of him taking over Captain Newport's position as the colony pilot.

One would think such news would elate the President. But John knows the full story. He knows that Newport has not been ousted, but promoted. Now, John will have to address the man as, Admiral. But this is not John's main concern. The Virginia enterprise is changing. The presidency is being discarded. John's office is soon to end. Royal hands are snatching control from the company. Soon, a Governor will rule the colony. And that Governor will not be John Smith.

Light creeps into the room from an un-boarded window. John sits with his writing book at the ready. He knows that he must defend himself. But how can he begin another letter? His last correspondence has evidently been cast aside. Attention is upon other viewpoints back in England. But who is this contradicting messenger who convinced the company that John has wielded his power too harshly on both his neighbors and his constituents? The most damning evidence is the pitiable export of goods form the colony while under his watch. They seemed to have ignored his explanations entirely. But why? How? He thought his last letter was both forceful and direct. It should have persuaded someone.

John stares at the blank page before him. Attention is blurred into none-seeing. He thinks back on the news. He remembers the name, Thomas West. Yes, the Baron Delaware himself. He is coming to Virginia as the new Governor. The little world that John has worked so tirelessly to create is on its death bed. Its last breaths are numbered to what days are left before the knight arrives.

A dreadful epiphany arrests him. He remembers Francis West. John sent him upriver to forage. He is a brother to Lord Delaware.

John is all alone. Even Councilman Winne is dead. What does the company expect when he must run everything alone? In a hostile environment, priorities call for defenses to be established before any commerce can begin. The natives have become so hostile. The fort needed to be improved. A more efficient social system needed to be implemented. There has simply not been enough time to make product. There is just so much to do, and fewer are staying around to do it. Some of those whom he sent to billet with the naturals refuse to return. Others have abandoned their comrades entirely. The Dutchmen are dangerous fugitives. The general laziness of the lot forced him to implement his "No Work, No Food" dictate.

The company must understand that conditions are not yet acceptable for civilian commerce.

At first, the words are scribed tentatively. The flood gates of composed expression eventually open up. Concentration drowns in the flow of ink. Sentences form on their own. A feverish release of thought builds momentum until the mind can no longer direct its outpour.

Captain Argall's vessel moors at the high banks near James Fort. He oversees the flow of trade between his mariners and the colonists. There are so many items that remind them of the life they have missed while at sea. The settlers can taste England again, and handle it close to their bosoms.

Captain Argall must soon depart. The colony has nothing to fill his vessel. He must get to the bay and pack its hold with *kupowatowan* before their spawning season ends. But most importantly, he must get back to claim his discovered route and deliver news of the colony.

He will also carry his own impressions. Memories have filled his mind. The first is of Kekotan where a score of men have been sent to fish for the colony. George Percy commands the place. The President saw fit to give this gentleman the rank of, Lieutenant. George is not well. He suffers greatly from a recent gunpowder wound and has not been able to perform his duties to the utmost. His group has managed to keep only themselves well-fed.

Another group of three score are camped just upriver from the bay. They were also sent away to find their own means. They eat well on *kaway*, but also fail to collect extra food for those at James Fort.

Near them is the abandoned works of an emergency retreat that the president had planned. It is half completed—as most endeavors are in the colony. Luckily, the colonists have not found a need for the small mud fort; a type of temporary redoubt more suited for European campaign.

At the great bend of the river, just before James Fort, is a marshy island where the colony's livestock have been sent. The residing population of pigs and chickens there have actually thrived much better then the humans. A wooden block house towers near the water's edge to keep watch down river. Another blockhouse is at the entrance to James Island across from the glass factory that stands on the mainland.

There is a constant shortage of provisions. Rat infestation ruins any food that can be stored. The neighbors are not presently hostile. The growing crops keep them busy. There is a general rule not to associate with the islanders. But there are the usual rule breakers who come to the fort anyway.

POWHATAN:
THE STORY OF A PEOPLE

Some even like the president. He is a hero, after all. A Chikahominy youth had been captured for stealing a pistol. John locked him away with some food and firewood. It was hoped that his brother would return the pistol before the convict would be hanged. The brother did return, only to find his sibling asphyxiated from a poorly-ventilated fireplace. The victim was given up for dead. But John helped to revive him. He is now considered a great healer.

People mull about the fort. Neighbors explore the goings-on. Some even participate in the routine activities. The natives help plant a few crops and hunt *masanek, moninag,* and *wushakwun* for the strangers. They help to gather *pitukwu* roots for bread and draw water from the new well. It has been dug at just the proper depth so that it can be used throughout the year.

President Smith was holding Wowinchopunk to exchange for the Dutchmen. But the Paspaheg *weyowanz* got away. In an effort to get him back, Captain Winne and Lieutenant Percy went to Paspaheg Town for a night assault. The battle did not begin until the next morning. A few shots were fired. A few arrows were released. A building or two were burnt. And some native watercrafts were even seized.

John feared such a poor display would hint of weakness. He personally led another campaign into enemy territory to wipe out the Paspaheg all together. He managed to kill more, capture more, and seize more spoils. That was good enough.

The Swiss, William Volday, offered to go and retrieve Wowinchopunk himself. He never returned. Now, there are four men in exile.

The only one John could get back was young Tom Savage who managed to return with a message from the *mamanatowik*. John had sent demands to hand over all fugitives. Wahunsenakok's reply was that he would not disallow anyone to live how and where they pleased.

The two expeditions to the southern lands have also returned. Neither found any remnants of Sir Walter Raleigh's lost colony, but they did find plenty of *wikiyopis,* along with a possible venue for fur trade.

Yes, gentle reader, Captain Argall has amassed a plethora of interesting stories. But he knows the Virginia Company will not care for any of them. Make no mistake. The bottom line is all of which businessmen can consider.

CHAPTER 15

Two *kekwiyos* carefully maneuver through the *kaway* shoals down the Powhatan River. George Percy stands at the bow of the lead vessel. He smells the sent of various blooms that waft from the banks. The warmth of the air is not entirely comfortable. Humidity is just over an acceptable level. Time is about to give way to the steamy season of *Nepino*. George can feel the discomfort in his body and can detect the edginess of his thoughts.

The effects of his wound are subsiding. Although he is doing better, George looks forward to the day of departure. The president has granted him leave. He will go as soon as the fleet is repaired. While he waits, George has decided to stay with Captain Martin's group. The situation at Jamestown is far from pleasant.

The travelers move into the mouth of the Nansemund River. Their plan is to set the foundation for a great city here. Admiral Newport wanted it to be so. Perhaps they may designate the site in his memory.

George was at Jamestown when the seven tattered vessels came in. Every available space along the dock and along the steep banks surrounding it was filled. Battered hulls bobbed beside one another like a flock of birds huddling on the same fragile tree limb. Sails were torn. Yardarms were broken. All suffered lost rigging and water-damaged cargo. Crews were depleted by sickness and death. The tempest that hit the fleet has brought about much misery. Most importantly, was the loss of the flagship, Sea Venture. Its commander was good Admiral Newport. Its distinguished passengers included Lt. Governor Gates and his second, Sir George Somers. The documents for the new commission were also on board.

George studies Captain Martin. He has a face that is slightly red from the sun, and slightly from his hot temper. He is a man of little desire for command, but plenty of drive when it is self-serving. A bit testy and aloof, he is wise enough to endure.

Captains Radcliff and Archer have also returned. George will never forget the sight of the three men debarking. John Smith nearly jumped out of his boots. Blood boiled upon the first words between them. But President Smith still holds the trump card. The transition to the company's new business structure can not take effect because the official documents and the new leaders did not survive the trip. Word has it that Master Winne was designated to govern if such circumstances came about. But poor Peter Winne recently died. The trio of original councilmen refused to take any responsibility without proper authority, especially now that royals pull the strings. And so, that vain-glorious little tyrant maneuvered himself into preserving his post until new authority can come from England.

The travelers find Nansemund lacking in human activity. The *kekwiyos* grounds on a sandy bank and all climb off. Most of the men have gone overland with help from the Wayaskoyak. There is no sign of them up the main trail that skirts the south bank of the Powhatan. The few locals that George meets have no knowledge of such a group.

George offers to take a small company up the path to see if he can run across the overdue column. Captain Martin rolls his shoulders. George takes that as permission granted.

As night descends, so does a heavy downpour. The small party slush on. Finally, George finds the main column safe and dry in their camp.

The new day finds the land of Nansemund freshly bathed by the storm. Clouds hover above. Grey daylight spreads evenly across the landscape. George returns with everyone to the river. Captain Martin's men climb out of their floating cradles to join them.

Across the river is an island. It is a piece of Tara firma that juts from the east bank. Certainly, it is not a true island. But for the English, its feel is that of a body of land separated from the rest. It holds a place of prominence at this point of the river. All agree, it is a good location to plant themselves. The main city of the Nansemund is just down-river from where the English now stand. Two messengers are selected to go there and negotiate a price for the island. The rest get comfortable and wait for their return.

The day slips by. There is no sign of the two negotiators. George speaks with his superior, "I fear them lost, good sir."

Captain Martin grows impatient. "By chance, ye be right. Go thither with thirty shot to the island. Claim it, and drive out any who haunt that plot of ground."

Oars slice into the water. Slowly, the craft gains movement. Flint cords alight. Long barrels are propped along the gunwale. Eyes look forward and at each flank.

There, in the distance. A small *akwintan* cuts through the quiet waters to intercept them. It is difficult to see clearly, but two passengers look familiar.

The *akwintan* stops. The front man pushes his paddle while his partner in the back pulls his own. The craft swings around to begin a quick retreat from where it came. George can only watch. He can not order a volley, as their own may be hit. He can not order a chase, as it may be a ploy to distract the *kekwiyos* from its intended mission. Lt. Percy calms his men and proceeds to the island.

Barks from young *masanek* pierce the air. A few shadows move erratically beyond a thicket as the invaders come aground. The vessel empties quickly. The soldiers spread out to either side until a long line is formed. Wide hat brims shade their faces grey to match their composure. Right hands ready at the leavers while left hands steady their barrel stands in the soft ground. Scouts step cautiously toward the foliage.

Lt. Percy walks ahead of the line. He looks through any available opening in the foliage to determine the positions of the inhabitants. There are only a few bowmen among the distraught innocents. The lieutenant draws his pistol. He calls his men forward. The wave crashes through the little community. A crack of powder resounds. Defenders scatter. Young and old, male and female, all splash into the river and trudge through the murk to reach safety on the mainland.

Captain Martin watches Percy's company melt into the trees. He hears the crack of powder and sees the puffs of smoke. Another call sounds behind him. Alarm sweeps through his command. A high-pitched wail from the trees smacks him in the face. He turns to see a few of his men already aiming at the direction of the sound. Painted bodies recoil at the volley. Arrows whiz back. Captain Martin quickly pushes the huddled troops into a line of defense as their attackers crawl back and forth through the underbrush on all fours.

Captain Martin studies the enemy. One man catches his attention. The man is more decorated then the others. The captain grabs four men and throws them forward. "Bestir ye lads! Fall on the one so bedecked!" He cries out a general order to the rest, "All forward! Into the bush!"

POWHATAN:
THE STORY OF A PEOPLE

George directs his men on the island. They tare apart every garden and burn every structure. One is larger then the rest. Important pearls, important jewelry, and precious metals are snatched up. Important funerary items are taken. The corpses of past leaders are dragged out. Cries of outrage and despair echo from across the river.

Captain Martin's contingent make their way to the island. In toẅ is a warrior and a son to the local *weyowanz*. Both are bound tight. The tormentors gather around their prisoners. A boy is egged on. He playfully takes pretend shots at the son of the *weyowanz* with a navy pistol. His eyes quickly turn from amusement to surprise when the weapon mistakenly discharges.

As the smoke clears and the outcry dims, the boy can see a red chest before him. The wounded man plops into the water. Somehow, he is able to make it to the opposite shore where friendly hands collect him.

"So what are they up to now?" murmurs Pawahunt. He watches the English fort. It sits just within sight from his vantage point high on the hill. It sits right in the bottoms where poor water and dangerous insects abound. "These people choose the worst places to settle."

Both groups watch each other. The restless mingle about. From time to time, some venture down the hill and into camp to see what news and what prizes they can run off with. It is dangerous, but quite exhilarating sport.

Today brings more strangers. John Smith comes to nose about. Too many have run away from this site and found their way back to Jamestown to tell of the endless raids upon the camp. Pawahunt motions to his spies. They report, "The red *amonsokwat* is unhappy with the camp's location. Their leader, West, is gone to get them supplies. Johnsmith is making decisions for them while he is away. They are not listening to him, though."

President Smith sends a messenger up the hill. Pawahunt steps out to meet him. The messenger waists no time, "Johnsmith wants this town for his people. He says you are brothers, since your fathers are brothers. He sends you this boy, Henry, as a gift."

Pawahunt considers aloud, "How dose he believe we will give up this town for him. There is no room to host more than a hundred helpless men."

The messenger adds, "He says we must move."

"What?" Pawahunt exhales.

The messenger elaborates, "For a portion of *matasun*, he wants everything handed to him. He will also give each family a palm of *matasun* for some *poketawas*. He says his men will protect us from the Monakan."

"He is insane!" spits Pawahunt. "We provide them food and shelter—our own food and our own shelter—and they will protect us? And if I refuse, he has threatened to burn this town so that neither will have it."

The messenger nods, "...Yes."

The boy comes up. The deal is made. But the settlement down the hill stays put. They wait for their true leader, Francis West, to return before they do anything. John Smith quietly leaves the scene.

Pawahunt receives another report. The president has attacked a *kekwiyos* and seized all the supplies for the camp. Word has it that the settlers are running out of the black powder and Johnsmith is not letting them have any more. Pawahunt smiles. Such has not been on his face since much younger days.

As night comes, a large contingent of warriors descend the steep slope of Powhatan Hill. Darkness is disturbed by occasional flashes of *pakusak* and gliding arcs of flaming arrows. High yelps and wails of distress pierce the night air.

The sun rises and the fight is still in progress. Powhatan and Awohatek warriors ring the settlement. When tired, some stagger up the great hill to rest in Powhatan. They refresh and re-supply themselves before heading back to the excitement. They are only half the number of the strangers. It is just too much work to wear down the besieged.

Pawahunt finally reaches a decision. He addresses his people, "We can not stay. We must live our lives. We will abandon this place. We are simply too few to continue this. We will move with the Awohatek to safer ground. Leave nothing but hollow buildings. Take everything of real value. As soon as these people grow tired of their isolation and return to their own, we will return to our beloved town."

John feels restful. He looks about. It is as if he is able to see the landscape for the first time. His men in the *kekwiyos* are also happy. They sing. They smoke from their clay pipes. They also admire the scenery around them. The deck is full with supplies of black powder and provisions intended for the camp at Powhatan Town.

A man beside John scrapes his flint. A spark creates a small flare on the end of a stick. The two men glance at one another in camaraderie. The

POWHATAN:
THE STORY OF A PEOPLE

tobacco takes the flame. The man sucks the smoke in, and then releases it back into the clay bowl. The weed burns slowly. Contemplation takes the face. Lips hug the tube once more. A spark escapes the bowl. John turns to see it drop beside him. He does not even think about it until the powder bag against his leg explodes. Instinctively, he looks away. A dreadful sensation engulfs his senses. He looks at the thigh. He can smell charred flesh. It is his flesh. He flips into the river. John nearly drowns before he is fished out by the crew.

Many creatures settle into hibernation between the seasons of Takwitok and Popano. Manibuzo is no different. He fills a great pipe in his abode behind the eastern horizon. Clouds of his fragrant smoke descend upon Pamasawu to cover the land in a warm, dreamy haze.

The brief respite from cold days rejuvenates those at Kekotan. Pokinz is content. His people are happy. They are well cared for. But they are not alone. There is a new structure on the hunting island at the mouth of the Powhatan River. It is a fort comprising of three triangular palisades holding large *pakusak*. The triangles are connected by three walls, forming a small compound for barracks. The island is no longer part of Kekotan. With each passing day, Pokinz understands exactly how Wowinchopunk feels.

The little fort is the responsibility of Captain Ratcliff. He was sent by the new leader of the colony to establish a permanent presence at this strategic site overlooking both the main river and the great bay. Dear George Percy is still in the colony. Instead of departing with the fleet, he was persuaded to stay on to lead the five hundred colonists. At least he is comforted in the fact that his family line has returned to prominence.

President Percy knows there is a dark cloud hanging over his little kingdom. Food is still the daunting issue. Rationing will make what is available last only a little longer. Neighbors are growing more hostile as news of what happened to the Nansemund spread throughout Tsenakomako. Reactions have been violent. Fearing for himself, Captain Martin left his settlement at the Nansemund island. It had been under constant attack since the first day. Conditions were so bad it caused one third of his men to run away. The last time they were seen was when they slipped past Fort Algernon into the cove near Kekotan. Others were found dead. Their bodies were stripped of clothes and their mouths were stuffed with *apon*. The rest finally abandoned the place for the shelter of Jamestown. Captain West also found it necessary to return. Over fifty huts now crowd the old Paspaheg hunting island.

Captain Ratcliff inspects the cargo being loaded upon his old vessel, the Discovery. His orders are to journey up the Pamunkey River in search of Wahunsenakok. The colonists know they must come to terms with him if they are to survive. The old man must understand that John Smith is no longer here. That man has been sent home with letters of condemnation. He is as good as dead. The fleet is gone home to England. Only the *mamanatowik* can help all those left behind.

Ratcliff fills the Discovery with plenty of trade goods. Twenty five men are making this important journey with him. They leave little Fort Algernon and head far up the wide Pamunkey to the point where the river forks.

The Discovery anchors before the city of Sinkwotek. Visitors venture out to the little *musawusuk*. Among them are Pokahantas and her brother, Nakakwawis. They delight in their stay, re-establishing contacts with those on board whom they have met once or twice before. The travelers send their messages to the *mamanatowik* and eventually receive a reply. It is in the form of instructions to his people to come away from the strangers and an invitation to Captain Ratcliff to push on to Menapukunt.

Captain Ratcliff is not confident to take the Discovery up the Yugtamund, especially at this time of year when rivers are generally more shallow and full of debris from the interior. Instead, he loads the escorting *kekwiyos* with sixteen men and various commodities and sets out around the great bend to the Pamunkey capital that hides in the trees on the other side. Wahunsenakok arrives from Owapax. Both agree to rest and begin trade on the next day.

The two parties meet at the food storehouse. Henry Spelman is present. He has been given to Wahunsenakok. Now, the old man has three boys of the winds. Tom Savage is also back in his care. Young Samuel is alone. His two elder companions tried to join Volday's plan to return with the fleet. When the English killed the Swiss, the two Dutchmen ran back to Wahunsenakok. They promised him they would not try to run away again. The old man refused to believe them. As he forced their heads on the execution rock, he lectured that those who could betray their own people so quickly could not be trusted to be loyal to him. He disposed of them both with quick blows to their heads. That was Henry's first experience of the old man's stern disposition.

Henry relays the captain's usual salutations to the *mamanatowik*. Ratcliff lays out his inventory of *matasun* and blue beads. Wahunsenakok nods in

POWHATAN:
THE STORY OF A PEOPLE

acceptance. He summons a number of baskets to be filled with *poketawas*. The two parties enter the storehouse.

Inside are large bark containers full from the last harvest. A native shovels a gourd into one while another holds a basket made of *wikiyopis*. Witnesses look on in patient silence. Captain Ratcliff makes a dreadful observation. He realizes that the man holding the basket has one hand underneath it. He is pushing the bottom up. This is short changing Ratcliff of a truly full basket! Is this being done on purpose?

The captain starts. He retracts. He goes though with the complaint. Tom tries to tell Wahunsenakok politely, but Captain Ratcliff does not wait for diplomatic wrangling. He advances to the one holding the basket. He points at the arm underneath the container. He pulls the man's arm away to demonstrate.

Tom stops interpreting. Samuel looks carefully at the old man. Henry watches everyone. Wahunsenakok mutters, "Have them fill the baskets as he desires. I am done with this." He motions to his wives and guides both Samuel and Henry outside by the shoulder.

Henry looks back to see the hasty departure of Captain Ratcliff and fourteen of his men. Each steps lively with a basket filling his arms. They trot down the path toward the *kekwiyos*. Loaded bows rise up in the *poketawas* field as they pass. The arrows hit their marks. More warriors rush from nearby trees. Blood mixes with spilled kernels on the ground. The cries dissipate into silence as the targets are rubbed out one after the other.

The victory is not complete. Two strangers have slipped out the back of the granary and into the wilderness. Ratcliff lies among his fallen men. He is in a little pain, but it is nothing that could keep him for another ceremony.

Women strip him of his clothes. He is bound against a *pakohikowo* tree. Constantly whimpering, he does not make for a brave captive. This will only drag out the suffering for him. Captain Ratcliff shudders in the cold, scolding himself for returning to this world.

The drums beat for the earth mother. A fire rages before the tree. Women select the pieces of *tsekoma* shells with the sharpest edges. Slowly, they gather around the ghost-skinned man. Each female presses their blade into the quivering skin. Red liquid wells in the gash. It is a burning pain. He cries out.

A pattern emerges in the cuts. Female fingers slip into the gashes. They peal the flesh from the body. Wrathful glee consumes them. They taunt by dangling his flesh before him, then dropping it into the flames. The victim is tied too securely. He can only twist his neck in wild reaction and cry out as only a human can do when in its most primitive mindset.

The power of the departing spirit bathes the crowd. The victim's face is stripped off. The human is no more. The creature that is left is a grotesque embodiment of pain. Eyes are beveled with blood. The last thing it sees is the torch. A healer thrusts it against the head. Flames seep into the core of the skull, consuming all within its chamber.

Ice falls as if rain. It collects on the naked branches, creating a thick crystalline lacquer. Weak limbs snap off. They fall to the ground to be lost among the natural waste.

George Percy stands within Fort James. Frozen air cuts through his skin. His hat blows off—his head is too small for it now. Thinned hair is disheveled. Skin is tightly stretched around his sunken eyes, collapsing the cheeks. He looks around the shambled confines. He can see the shadowy woods through a hole in the palisade. Pine needles are everywhere. It is a layer of rusted brown amidst the carpets of white snow. The ground moves. Colors transform into a solid body as a native dog emerges from its camouflaged invisibility. It sniffs and trots through the frozen underbrush for sustenance. The ground is too hard to dig into any more. George remembers how he saw one of these animals dig into the earth. This was not long ago. It created a small hole, just the size of its long, pointed snout. The snout fit perfectly into the cavity. The creature chomped away at the nutrients that were gathering in the soil for the return of warmer days. George reflects on this practice. Perhaps that is what his people should have done.

The dog probably belongs to someone who may be hidden deeper in the woods with bow in hand. George steps away from the opening. He follows two men who make their way for the house of Master Collins and his wife. All three of the men are no more than skin draped over bones. The skin itself is a yellow parchment.

Food is what any can find. Hog Island has been emptied. There are no more cats or dogs to be found. No more horses are left. Even the ship rats are depleted. Some resort to digging up what roots they discover. Boots and other leather goods are boiled. Fresh blood is licked from the skin as hosts look on in weak consternation. Those that run off become sport for the neighbors.

Captain Archer is no more. Captain Martin is seldom seen. Francis West has abandoned them. He was sent with a crew of thirty six to Patawomik in hopes to renew their friendship. But Captain West found that Wahunsenakok

POWHATAN:
THE STORY OF A PEOPLE

had regained his influence there. The Patawomik refused to sell anything to the strangers. In anger, the captain forcefully took what he could to fill the hold. He killed two men, removing every extremity from their torsos. The vessel he commanded was fully manned and fitted. His crew easily convinced him that the best course was to set sail for England.

The three men reach their destination. It is rumored that Master Collins is hiding food. Such can not stand.

The door is simply propped up, unhinged. Someone is humming a melancholy tune within. George raps against the door. The humming stops. Another man bangs on the door. It sways with every blow but does not fall inward. A rustling sound from inside is the only reply. The third man kicks in the door. They can see Master Collins in the dim interior, sitting at his table. The three men enter.

A Dutch oven sits in a nest of red ash by the fire. The aroma of some kind of meat wisps through the room. George brushes some ash away and lifts the lid. He sees a few straws of grass and herbal roughage floating on the surface.

"How?" George looks at the reluctant host. "What have ye for the stew, sir?"

"I have but some roots and mere snow water." rebukes Master Collins.

Another man sniffs. "I smell the stench of flesh. Sir, what hide ye?"

"Tis not a thing," Master Collins denies.

George reviews the possibilities. Did the man manage to sneak out and catch something? If it was something large, he may still have some of it left to share. George pursues him. "I admit flesh is a forlorn scent. Aye, my memory does confirm it to be so."

Master Collins pleads, "No, no flesh, sirs. Kind gentlemen, pray you, leave me be."

"To what? What have you, sir?" George does not let it go, but the man makes his plea once more, "Pray, I desire but me privacy."

A scent beckons George to the salt box at the far wall. "No! Sirs, leave that." Master Collins rises.

The two men take hold of the arms and force him back down. George raises the lid. It is full of freshly-butchered meat. "Why keep this from us? What, with us all a'starved!"

Master Collins protests, "Sirs, we all make due with what we can. What be the punishment for that? Tis mine! I took. I dressed it. It belongs to me, alone."

George does not hear. Curiosity takes hold of his concentration entirely. "What be this?" He grabs a hunk out of the box. It is an oblong piece that fits well in his hand. One end is frayed with five slender strands. He turns it over in his palm. Toenails are at each tip.

"Oh, dear Collins. Oh, dear man. What hath thee done?" George does not expect a quick reply.

Three gaunt forms work in the dark room. They hoist up the defendant by his thumbs. Defiance sets in until it is replaced with anger. Finally, "Please, sirs," Master Collins pleads, "it all seemed not me. Even as I slit my poor woman's throat. Even as I pulled out her babe from the womb and threw it in the river, and hacked her up for the salting bin…Twas not me…but the devil within! Show mercy. I beg, show mercy! She took all I had. Most victuals I did give to her. She needed to recompense."

George leans closer. "And what mercy had you your family? All suffer this misery, but keep our heads. Those who may steal, I punish. Those who may forget themselves, I must renounce. You, sir, shall burn at the stake. And may the flames take ye swift, and may God take thy soul."

Chapter 16

Although the ruins are silent, silence does not pervade Jamestown Island. There are people everywhere. They laugh. They play. They celebrate. The Paspaheg finally have their hunting island back.

Children play among the strange ovens on the mainland. The very small manage to slip through the long tube opening to chatter and share little clumps of glass with one another inside. Those who are tall enough, poke their funny faces through the four openings from outside. Trauma occurs when a child gets stuck in the tube of a smaller oven. Others cut themselves on the sharp crystal pieces and leave with teary eyes.

More fill the emptied spaces. Playing dangerously, after all, is the most fun. Men beat out the plank walls for use in their own *ahakan*. Women select glass shards for jewelry.

Down the trail, past the blockhouse, is where most of the Paspaheg can be found. Children play in the vacated ruins. Old people do a little jig and sing out a short tune. Wowinchopunk escorts his wife around the gutted fort.

She sighs, "I don't see how any of those people made it through *Popano*. Only one from ten survived. That field, on the east side of the fort, it is sown with their dead."

Wowinchopunk draws her near. "At least they learned how to plant something. This is good news. They should never want to see this place again. We have won."

She mentions, "When the new ones arrived, the survivors all came out singing in their weak voices, 'We are starved, we are starved…'"

"Word has it that those in the little fort next to Kekotan fared much better. They filled up on *tutaskuk*; those big ones, with the big green backs and the long blue legs and those strong, red pincers…" She enacts this with her fingers on his forearms that encircle her neck.

Wowinchopunk feels the frisky pinches. He giggles, "Yes, one only has to sit on the beach and they rush up begging to be boiled."

"All four of those *musawusuk* should be in the Great Blue, by now," she sighs once more. "It is good that Newport is still alive. He is a good man. He will be the one we miss. He can come back. Tell me again what you heard about him."

Her husband relates the most-accepted rumor, "He managed to run aground his broken *musawusuk* on an island far south of here. From it, he built two smaller ones. He saved almost all of his people."

The couple look about. Their people go through the wreckage, looting anything they consider of worth. They take back items that were once theirs. They salvage through what did not fully burn upon the trespasser's departure.

Wowinchopunk whispers, "We did it, my love."

She enjoys the warmth of the body that cloaks her. She feels his heartbeat against the node of her spine. The pleasure is over far too soon.

A messenger steps nervously toward his *weyowanz*. "They stopped short of the bay. Three more *musawusuk* have come. They are big ones, full of people. They are not leaving."

People slowly move up the trail. Some of the bravest loiter about the ruins until they see the canvas wings on the river. The largest vessel is called the Delaware. It is named for the new leader who is on board. Sir Thomas West has come to resettle the colony and start anew. Everything will be different now.

There is a funny man, with lively steps, whistling a happy tune through his flute and taping a steady beat on a tiny drum. Children rush to gather their families and head out to the beach. The happy man works his two hands simultaneously in different actions. A number of strangers stand with *osawas* hats that gleam in the sunlight. They hold long lances and flags of bright colors. How they flutter in the breeze. The merry little clown dances and plays his instrument. Everyone form Kekotan draws near.

Pokinz allows his people to gather some items for trade. How can he stop them? The English are here to stay. That little fort they have at the point is now a permanent fixture.

The new fleet has resettled on the Paspaheg island. They are erecting a large, triangular fort. All three sides are equal in length, this time. It is obvious to everyone that there are many more to take the places of those who died.

POWHATAN:
THE STORY OF A PEOPLE

Namontak was right. He said there is a never-ending supply of them. How can such a stream be dammed?

The clown is so lively. He is too irresistible. The Kekotan gather close to watch the show.

The merry man stops in mid-dance. He runs back behind his people. Musketeers step out from the rank. They point their *pakusak* at the crowd. A few, a very few, are able to react physically before the discharge. A cloud envelops the line of soldiers. Burning streaks of orange tear through the crowd. The strangers charge forward with their pikes. Five in the crowd feel long metal blades go through their bodies. One runs with holes in his body. Blood and internal things escape. He manages to get far into the woods before weakness takes him.

No one enters the walled town. There is only one entrance, one exit. The enemy pursues too closely. All that they have is left within the walls for the invaders to tear up and burn down. People scatter into the wilderness with what they wear. Families are further separated by the trees. Groups join and fragment throughout the exodus. They follow the day westward. Most journey to Chiskiyak. Others continue on as far as Pamunkey. And Pokinz; he goes to Owapax to tell his father that he has lost.

Wahunsenakok languishes in private council with his brothers.

Kekwatog mentions, "They built two more forts next to Kekotan, naming them for their king's two sons. They have taken over the place."

Wahunsenakok deliberates, "Do they think they are so important to name things after themselves? Does this man, Delaware, think he can send me an ultimatum? He is no better than Johnsmith. We are not dogs to be kicked about at their whim, or toil for their pleasure."

Opechankano admits, "There is nothing to do about Kekotan. Their conquest...it is permanent."

The *mamanatowik* dispatches his messenger. "Tell Delaware I have seen his country's trash dumped here. I know how they treat each other in their own world. We will not be treated as such. They can clean up their world another way. They may keep their people in this world if they must—but only on the hunting island. I will not allow them to spread along our rivers. I can kill them all, if they push me to it."

But Wahunsenakok knows that such blustering is no defense. After a moment's meditation, he admits to his brothers, "A new power has risen in the east. Those to the west are still our *maskapow*. We have few friends to the south. We must look northward. We can not lose that connection. The northern lands may be our last hope."

A sultry evening breeze carries the raspy songs of insects. The constant haze of *Nepino* covers Paspaheg Town. Sprightly beetles with lucent tails hover in the darkness. Glimmers of yellow and flashes of bright green fill the air. Everyone settles down for the night. Families gather in their homes for a quick dinner. The air is finally cool enough for individuals to work on a simple task or laze about with one another.

Dogs react to a strange movement at the edge of town. They pace. They howl in quick succession. Rustling in the underbrush intensifies. People pause.

Seventy phantoms hasten from the forest. Metal tubes flash in the moonlight. The battle line spreads along the outskirts of town. Lord Delaware's nephew, William, shoots his pistol into the sky.

The inhabitants stir. Families peer out of their homes. Thunder claps. A long, dark cloud from the *pakusak* materializes. The children scream. To their eyes, the raiders are ghosts, come to collect souls. People scatter. Families split in the confusion. The line moves through town. People flee to evade the deadly smoke and the long metal blades. They finally reach the safety of distance in the black wilderness.

Wowinchopunk rounds up his people. He moves through the broken families. None are his own.

Back at the town, George Percy orders the drummer to beat the rally call. Soldiers pile into the town center. All seventy are present for the grand hurrah. His second brings in the greatest prize of all. A torch light bathes her face. George recognizes her. "This one be the Paspaheg Queen."

She clinches to her children. Both bury their faces in her *matahay*. Her breasts heave steadily. They are bare of jewelry. Such has been ripped from her. William West presents another captive. George studies him, but does not have any recollection. "And why are these not also put to the sword? We are to spare not a one this night."

"I felt, what with who she be…"

George considers, "Well, dispose of the rogue and bring this place to the torch."

The male captive is forced to the ground and his neck sliced through. His remains are thrown into the flames of the dieing town.

POWHATAN:
THE STORY OF A PEOPLE

One *kekwiyos* heads back downriver. The weeping children can not be comforted. Their mother tries to quiet them, but their whining voices continue to aggravate the strangers. A discussion rises between Lt. Percy and his crew. The prisoners do not understand the words, but they know it pertains to them.

She tries to secure her children. They push her apart from both of them. The little ones squeal in fear. Each is hurled overboard. The girl tries to grab hold of the side. One man holds her off with the heel of his boot as another points his weapon at the little head and pulls the trigger. Two more level their *pakusak* at the boy.

The mother can do nothing. Her voice grows hoarse from violent outbursts of agony. Still bodies float away from the vessel. At least the river has them now.

George presents his prize to Governor West who shows little interest. "Why hath this wench been spared? I have no need of her."

"But, me lord," George tries to explain, "I am witness to enough slaughter this night. No more blood I wish on my hands. I have my revenge. I wiped Paspaheg clean form the earth. Captain Davies did also put torch to a nearby Chikahominy town. Even did he put their pagan temple to the flames of hell."

James Davies suggests, "Might we burn the witch at the stake?"

George redirects, "I see it better to grant the poor thing a quicker dispatch."

The Governor consents. Captain Davies takes two soldiers from the Delaware and escorts the distraught queen to land. She realizes their intensions. She squirms in their tight grasp. She wonders why this is to be. Is this how it must be?

One kicks her just behind the knees. As she falls to the ground, each arm is pulled outward to keep her still. Captain Davies grabs the long, silky hair to draw back her head. The cold blade runs along her soft throat. A final tear dissolves in the blood.

Travel is slow going. Some of the crew paddle to help the sails push their little *kekwiyos* against the current. The mouth of the Apamatuk is near. The Powhatan River is very wide at this point. It takes on the appearance of a lake. The travelers have far to go before reaching the *pakwachonk*.

Human forms are spotted on the far bank. The crew does not see them clearly, but they can recognize bright *pokun* on the bodies. The colors move along the distant shoreline. A voice flies on the wind, "Wingapow! Wingapow!"

What minerals that may exist upriver can wait. The crew agrees that a respite in Apamatuk should be taken. It should be safe enough. This tribe has never cared for the Paspaheg—or the Chikahominy, for that matter.

Three greeters point toward a good place to debark. A crewman holds up a container of fresh water with a beggar's gesture. The hosts nod and beckon to follow them up the bank into town.

The small parade snakes through a silent crowd to the main council house. Inside, Oposumokwonusk sits waiting for them with mats laid before her. Full plates are held by the maidens. The men fix their eyes upon both.

Oposumokwonusk observes her guests as they eat. Saffron flashes from the fire reflect off her skin of oiled sepia. She is distant, yet all-commanding. The guests shower her with smiles of gratitude.

One in the audience is brought to her attention by a sentinel. He whispers, "That one, with the bag. Inside are a flute and a small drum. He is the one who lured the Kekotan into ambush."

Oposumokwonusk fakes a smile. The sentinel withdraws behind her as the guests continue their feast. She glances at another sentinel near the entrance. She sneaks a slight gesture to him. The strangers still realize nothing. They continue with their own conversations until a company of warriors rush in.

Guardians step up to either side of their *weyowanskwa*. Oposumokwonusk watches calmly as the visitors are rubbed out. John Dowse manages to slip outside. A chase ensues all the way to the *kekwiyos*. The taborer sheds his bag. He sheds anything that may hinder his speed. He manages to break away from the mob that chases him.

John lunges into the *kekwiyos*. The force of his coming aboard frees the craft from the beach. He picks up an oar and slaps the water uncontrollably for movement.

The launch is slow. Those chasing are fast. Their arrows are even more so. John stops for a moment. He thinks. He reaches for the rudder. Arrows hit the wood with swollen force. The taborer balls up behind the rudder until he can shield himself entirely behind it. With his free hand, he works the oar until gaining an effective motion. He loses the motion. He finds it again. The rudder pushes against him with every arrow that hits the mark. His ears ring from the wails of hatred at the bank. The *kekwiyos* finally gets out of range.

POWHATAN:
THE STORY OF A PEOPLE

John returns the rudder to its proper place. He steers the empty vessel out into the main river, allowing the current to carry him safely to Jamestown.

Seasons pass as days. Cool weather turns cold. The English have secured their settlements. They have learned how to fend for themselves. For the first time, food is in surplus. All are fully engaged in their duties.

Sir Thomas West led a new expedition to the *pakwachonk*. He oversaw the building of Fort Delaware. He supervised the mining nearby. He buried his nephew, William. Fighting with the Powhatan and the Awohatek became a regular occurrence. The two tribes withdrew deep into the backwoods so they could not be attacked like their neighbors.

Time is not good to the Governor. The agony of gout increases with every sunrise. As soon as the first warm winds blow, the Delaware sets sail. Once in the open sea, the winds carry it home to England.

The Powhatan have also been active during the passing of seasons. An important alliance is firmed in the north. Wahunsenakok sends a gift of love. It is his favorite daughter, Pokahantas. The young woman carries out the ultimate act of diplomacy by forming an everlasting union with Kokum, a dutiful nephew to the *weyowanz* of Patawomik.

At the engagement celebration, Wahunsenakok accepts the bridal price that is offered without question. Gifts are exchanged between the two families. The groom's family builds and furnishes a new *ahakan* for the couple.

Upon the next day, marriage declarations are exchanged between the two. The celebration is filled with all the color of food and dance. Wahunsenakok escorts his daughter to her new family. He places the couple's hands together. Kokum's father, Iyopasus, holds up a long string of *peak*. He breaks off an arm's length and wraps it around the joined hands.

Thus begins a new stage in both their lives. Two lives merge into one. A new woman and a new man come into being. Both rise to adulthood in their society. With her new status, the young woman acquires her new name, Matowaka.

CHAPTER 17

Breath—the one true essential—is growing harder to achieve. Every step on the uneven ground is a harsh blow to the nervous system. The feet experience sharp pains from surfaced roots, loose rocks, and prickly cones. Henry Spelman must try to keep going. If they catch him, his breath may be taken away for good.

He can think of nothing but Samuel. How quickly a familiar person became a dull and unfamiliar thing. Samuel's eyes, his eyes where like a candle extinguished of its flame. His inner voice churns uncontrollably, "Why did they do it? Why are they chasing me? Just keep going. Just keep moving."

Henry can hear the sharp squawks from behind. Those chasing him are fit; the best in Tsenakomako. The old man sent them. It was only a short while after his friend, Tom Savage, made an excuse and turned back. The inner voice speaks to him, "Tom knew something. He told on us! He knows the old man longer then any. He's not a friend at all."

The three youths met up at Yugtamund. Wahunsenakok had lost interest in them. But they left him without permission. That was the wrong thing to do.

The inner voice speaks up, "We were with the Patawomik. They did nothing when the Powhatan came up. They did nothing when they followed us and caught poor Samuel and smashed his head in."

That sight. Samuel was on his knees, helpless. That expression. That expression of shock and hopelessness. He realized his own end. It happened so quickly. Then, the face looked so empty. Samuel was gone. The body was no longer familiar.

After his daughter's marriage, Wahunsenakok hosted the Patawomik *weyowanz*. They stayed together a long time. The Patawomik didn't need

POWHATAN:
THE STORY OF A PEOPLE

anything more from his generous host. He should not have tried to steal away the three boys.

Henry stops. His hands slap the felled tree before him. His breath is heavy. His lungs ache. Sweat rolls down his heated body. All of this feels too good to loose. But how is he going to continue?

There are new voices echoing in the forest. Different shouts come from behind those chasing him. The Patawomik are doing something after all. Henry can hear them calling back the Powhatan, encouraging them to stop their pursuit. He crawls over the fallen tree and finds a good pace once again. It is not as fast; not as desperate as before.

"I dare not go back," the inner voice confirms. "What influence do the Patawomik really have? The greed of their *weyowanz* is what created this disaster. His desire to collect all three boys for his own was more then the old man could take. Tom knew. That's why he ran back. He wanted to prove his loyalty. That's why Samuel is no more. I'll have to keep going, until I reach Patawomik on my own. Find Matowaka. She'll save me. She'll help me find a way back to my own people. The old man still has Tom. I'm not much of a loss to him. I have no skills, like Samuel. I'm just a harmless stray."

It is dark tonight. The crisp air of early *Katapewuk* lies still on the land. But it is not quiet. Shouts and taunts ring from the woods beyond the blockhouse that stands at the end of Jamestown Island. George Percy shifts in his bed. He is now a deputy governor. Lord Delaware granted him that title and its responsibilities before he left to improve his health in the open sea. George is once again the king of the colony until valid leadership returns. George is not among the most imaginative rulers. He is more of a reactionary than a proactive thinker. Yet, he is steady. He is reliable. He will do nothing drastic.

George tries to sleep. Howls from the mainland echo throughout the fort. It sounds like a hundred or more warriors are lurking in the dark forest, testing the patience of the blockhouse guard. George has already sent reinforcements to double their number, along with orders to stay put until morning when the threat can be seen in better light.

George dozes out of consciousness. He has seen more dangerous situations then a couple hundred naturals skulking about in the woods. It was not too long ago when Wowinchopunk appeared from the grey forest with his remaining warriors. They were no more than a handful. They crossed the isthmus and loitered in front of the blockhouse. They were either unafraid or uncaring of any danger that could befall them.

The incident occurred when *Popano* was waning. Wowinchopunk did not even see Nathaniel Powell's company of soldiers come out of Fort James. Their orders where to swing around the blockhouse and capture the Paspaheg leader. Cumbersome matchlocks were not carried. The combatants fought brutishly with hand-held weapons. It was John Waller who found Wowinchopunk near the bank. He grabbed firm and called for help. Once more, the Paspaheg *weyowanz* was held by force. Warriors appeared from the woods on the mainland and sent arrows into the mob.

Ensign Waller began to lose his grip. Captain Powell came up and punched his sword two quick times into the captive's torso. The combatants separated. The English headed for the blockhouse while the Paspaheg carried their *weyowanz* away on a crude litter. Wowinchopunk was still breathing, but he had died long before.

George awakens by the same noise of the night before. He steps out into the early morning. Sunlight is burning off the night frost. The sun has not yet fully appeared in the sky.

Fifty men assemble in the fort. Lt. Abbott leads them out. The little army heads to the blockhouse that stands silent near the island's edge. Two men venture inside, only to find it empty.

Howls from the mainland are tempting. The fifty men cross the narrow isthmus and make their way past the old glass house. The sounds intensify. Shadows move in the trees. The soldiers form for battle. Slowly, they advance up the main trail. Figures are spotted all around. There are many yelps and sing-song calls—perhaps three or four hundred strong.

Other figures lie on the trail in a small clearing. The morning sun is enough to see that it is Lt. Puttock and his unit. Arrows cover them all. The entire ground is covered with arrow shafts. Some time during the night, Lt. Puttock must have allowed his impatience to get the better of him. He had tasted blood during the fight with Wowinchopunk. Undoubtedly, he craved for more. Only this time, the blood was his own and of those who blindly followed him into this ambush.

Lt. Abbott forms his little army into a defensive line that almost encircles their fallen comrades. A few shots ring out. The surrounding woods are buzzing with the enemy. There must be five hundred of them. Solid figures are not visible. Only phantoms dart among the trees. The air resounds with, "Paspaheg! Paspaheg!"

POWHATAN:
THE STORY OF A PEOPLE

All the dead are collected. The little army maneuvers back to Jamestown. They can do nothing else in the face of what could only be a hidden force of six hundred, or more.

Another *kohatayo* comes to Pamasawu. A fleet of five *kekwiyos* enters the Nansemund River. One hundred soldiers fill the watercraft. Captain Martin guides them, as he knows the way best. George Percy is not with him, this time. He has finally left Virginia. Francis West, on the other hand, has returned. Of course he has suffered no punishment for leaving Virginia as he did. His brother is the Governor General, after all. He stands beside Captain Martin in the point vessel.

Another man leads this campaign. His name is Thomas Dale. He is also newly arrived, along with many more settlers. Tall and angular, every inch of him is lean strength. Everything about him is long and hard: his legs, his torso, his ears and face. The face is further lengthened by a sharp, straight beard. In contrast to this vertical composition are the shoulders that are perfectly horizontal. Eyebrows and even his thin mustache are straight, horizontal lines. Thin lips express only a grim façade. There is no glint in the eyes, rather a stone-hard stare. He is a military man—a knight to be accurate—fresh from service in the Netherlands where he was Captain of Infantry. In the colony, he holds the rank of, Marshal. He is a man of intense military and civic ethics. He possesses a severity of character that has resulted in no friendships to speak of, nor any care for such trivial things. A true aristocrat, Sir Dale's priority of social order is above any luxury of social wellness for himself, or for those around him.

The duty at hand is to flush out any belligerents that stand in the way of the colony. He starts with the Nansemund.

Warriors appear along the beach head to stop the flotilla from landing. Their arrows do nothing. Dull grey *osawas* protect the invaders. A few *pakusak* bursts scare the defenders into the trees. As the invaders come aground, arrows fly once more. This time, they yield better results. Captain West suffers an arrow to his thigh. Captain Martin suffers one in the arm. Marshal Dale nearly suffers a head wound as an arrow knocks against the brim of his helmet.

Muskets roar at the wooded bank. Many feel the hot lead go deep into their bodies. The Nansemund city lies vulnerable just behind them. They can not halt the methodical advance of the English.

Knowing a *pakusak* uses fire, the seers join the battle on the outskirts of the city. They remember from the last time how their temple had been so desecrated. They know these demons threaten the physical existence of Nansemund. Higher forces must join this fight. One seer comes to the fray with a rattle made from a *tuwupen* shell. The wooden handle is wrapped in leather. Long strips dangle from the end, weighted by shell beads sewn to the tips. Tiny *matasun* beads pattern the grip area. The shell is an artful design in its own right. It is covered with squares of plating in varying shades of green that are framed with thin yellow stripes. They appear as if painted with a small round brush. It is the armor of the mystics, for it is alive with the mysteries of the unrecognized world that surrounds reality.

The seer throws fire into the air as if from his hand. He cries out in the language of the Ancients so that the gods can hear his plea. With voice, with arms, with body, he reiterates his entreaty. Defenders join him with gyrating exertions.

Their efforts bear fruit. Thunder rumbles in the distance. A flash is detected in one direction. It is coming. The sky darkens a pale indigo from where the clouds blow in. Rain begins to pour far off in the distance. But will it continue to the place of this battle?

"Oh great Okius," the chief seer pleads, "come quickly! Roll across the sky to this place!"

Defenders cheer in their high-pitched wails. They wait for the coming rain. The English do not wait. Musketeers wear their wide-brimmed hats specifically to shelter the slow-burning wicks of their firearms. The weapons are leveled toward the seer. They produce their own thunder. Distraught defenders run from the field of battle. The rains do not come. The *manitow* show no interest. Okius would rather drink the blood of the Nansemund this day.

Metal men with long pikes drive forward. They cause demoralizing grief. The city burns. Crops are cut up. Lives are snubbed out. Marshal Dale does not stop. The campaign moves deep into Nansemund territory. Even the lords of the Southern Peninsula can not stop the Wind Children.

Deep in the woods, nestled within the rolling hills that buttress the curls of the Yugtamund River, is an assembly of old men. An *akwintan* rests below the cliff of Utamusak. The three minor temples are quite. Bowmen hold silent vigil around the perimeter. A ray from the setting sun impregnates the great

POWHATAN:
THE STORY OF A PEOPLE

pokowanz stone. There is a faint luminosity from within the quartz that weakens with every fleeting moment.

Inside the great temple, Wahunsenakok holds council with the seven high priests. They join him in a circle around the perpetual flame, sharing important thoughts with one another through simple verbal exchange.

Orange flames blend with the red and black body paint on the priests. Their half-god is fully oiled in yellow *pokun*. He wears a simple *machkow* of *wushakwun* skin, embroidered with purple *wowanok* beads. The skin itself is freshly tanned. It reflects the light of the flames in a subtle off-white glow. In contrast, each priest wears an old *machkow* of *wikutis* pelts. The skins are naked of fir in some spots. Even the stitching that once bound the pelts tightly together has loosened in places. Generally, they appear chewed up by time.

Wahunsenakok addresses the little assembly, "The strangers have run the Nansemund south to the great swamp. The Paspaheg are no more. Even the Wayaskoyak were attacked. They have always been the most cordial to the strangers…even to Johnsmith. All their crops were cut down and wasted. Everything they had was burnt to the ground…every *akwintan* broken up. That is all the Wind Children do. This new man, Dale, plans to push our people away and plant his own on top our towns. The prophecy, we thought to have avoided…It has come after all."

A priest speaks up, "We can not fight them off any longer. We must yield when needed and retreat when it is best. If they want the Powhatan River, let them have it. We can go elsewhere—farther up our rivers, deeper into the land. Tsenakomako is where ever our people are."

Another priest interjects, "Our pursuit is for survival. It is no longer a location, but a condition. The Wind Children are now our reality. We must submit…"

"We must not submit!" roars Wahunsenakok. "If we do, we will lose ourselves. How can we exist if we forsake who we are? In the burial chamber, behind me, lie my ancestors. My ancestors! What will become of them?"

Another priest calms the debate, "Once, long ago, the Monakan were faced with a dark fate. They adapted. They changed much. But they flourished anew. They evolved. Yet, after all this time, they are still the Aligewi. We must emulate their pursuit for survival. We will not conform, but we must sacrifice. Perhaps we can not aggressively confront the strangers. But we should still be able to inflict pain on them from time to time. Our people can feast during those times…and fast in between. We must hold on to that which makes us who we are and nurture it until the day comes when that part of us can once again go of its own."

The priest across the fire from Wahunsenakok advises, "We can not allow fear nor anger to slow us down. No matter how often we may stumble, we must keep up with the herd. If our people become stranded from Time, then Destiny will prey upon us with no remorse."

Wahunsenakok interrupts, "But we will lose so much of who we are."

"Yes," the priest admits. "But we will at least continue to be. Our core, our essence must remain, no matter how often we shed our skin."

Wahunsenakok contemplates. He thinks of his people. He thinks of the Monakan. He comes to an understanding—no, an appreciation for those he has hated for so long.

The head priest concludes, "What we do in the future will be dictated by circumstances. Patience and fortitude will aide us. The present dilemma is of a spiritual challenge. We are children of the Great Light, Manibuzo—the one who lives in the sunrise. They are children of the winds, for the wind is white. You can see it in the clouds, the mist, the dusting of snow, the vapors of warm air. Their power is an evil mystery. Only we, the enlightened, can successfully fight them. First, we must stop them from spreading throughout our land."

Chapter 18

Along the south bank, just below the rushing waters of the Powhatan River, is a little family settlement. The Wind Children came to the site once before, when Captain Newport first ventured upstream. Thomas Dale has made himself at home. The place is a little worn down, but it still exerts a presence from recent habitation. The tall stalks of a *poketawas* field almost surround the little cluster of buildings.

Wahunsenakok warned Sir Dale not to come to the falls. But the new Dept. Governor does not take the old man seriously anymore. It has been many tough campaigns of late. Prisoners are being taken by both sides. Too many lives have been lost. There is much destruction and misery for all.

The gentlemen in the group enjoy quiet relaxation in an abandoned *ahakan*. It is dark outside. The common sort lounge around a fire behind a low trench they have dug for their bivouac. All huddle in light repose to rest up for tomorrow's continued journey upriver.

The fire pops and crackles with excited zest. Eyes fixate on the dancing flames. A few tales of mirth tickle the ears. It is a while before they realize the strange chanting in the darkness beyond. The noise comes from one direction, then another. Eyes fixate on the stalks. Heads scan for something, anything. Grunting, wailing chants sound from unfixed positions. Everyone is motionless, silent—as if waiting for a storm to roll over.

The sounds fade away in the blackness. The stocks rustle. The noise intensifies once more. It lessens. It stops.

Moments pass. The *poketawas* field appears empty. The seven high priests crouch among the stalks just out of eyesight. The head priest waits. The right moment is near. He turns to his left. His partner there slowly rises and begins to slide through the stalks. He picks up speed as he nears the edge of the field. Sound cannot keep up with him. He glides across the open patch.

He leaps over the trench. He hops right over the fire, dropping a small bundle into the flames. There is a quick snap. The flames change from orange to blood-violet. The running man re-enters the *poketawas* field before they even realize what he is.

Powhatan warriors appear beside every defender. The English grab their adversaries. Thus begins a bestial melee.

Those in the little *ahakan* fumble for their weapons. The fog of confusion overwhelms them. Firearms are held the wrong way. Understanding of their use is lost to them. Sir Dale grabs hold of something solid and makes determined steps toward the exit.

The fight outside grows desperate. They glare at the crazed faces with whom they are locked in battle. It is a primitive brawl by men drunk with fear-driven rage.

The painted faces melt as if wax. Underneath are the bloodied and muddied countenances of fellow Englishmen.

The men seek to mend the wounds they have caused one another. Sir Dale searches the night for the enemy combatants who never where. Reality finds a pathetic scene of men who have turned upon each other like made dogs. Sir Dale concludes that this conflict must end. No one can withstand such constant fighting.

"How wonderfully strange!" exclaims Pawpawisk. "People actually live on that thing. It is a man-made island!" Matowaka nods in agreement to her mother-in-law. Both females wear the simple *machkow* of a married woman. Iyopasus is pensive, paying their chatter no mind. His *matahay* is more decorative than his wife's. A longboat makes its way to shore. He recognizes Captain Argall among the crew.

It was not long ago that the two first met. Iyopasus handed young Henry Spelman over to the captain when he last stopped in Patawomik on the Discovery before returning to England. The Discovery had been in Pamasawu since the beginning. It had been utilized so much by so many different men. Captain Argall has returned in the new company vessel called, Treasurer.

The first reunion between the two men occurred just the day before. But that was a business encounter. Today, the visit is much more genial in tone. Captain Argall gives Iyopasus a small kettle made of solid *matasun*. Pawpawisk also receives a small chest filled with pretty things that women like. The captain is introduced to Matowaka who greets him warmly.

POWHATAN:
THE STORY OF A PEOPLE

Pawpawisk grows excited. "Please, may I go with you and see your floating village?"

"Such nonsense!" Iyopasus snaps. "Don't embarrass me. You can not invite yourself and go unescorted. You know better."

"But I want to see!" Now the tears fall.

Matowaka comforts her, "No. Maybe it's not a good time. It's late. They aren't prepared for gusts. I know. They are very protective of their privacy."

Argall intercedes with a gesture to come aboard for dinner.

"Well, if you come with us, Matowaka..." Iyopasus gives in.

The longboat pushes into the water. Two oarsmen begin the smooth, coordinated strokes. Matowaka studies the watercraft. It looks like a *patawok* carcass, cut open at the belly and turned over to expose its flat ribs and spine.

They glide closer to the *musawusuk*. Three sturdy polls—like tree trunks—rise skyward from its body. Strait branches span each one at measured intervals. Rope is strung like spider webs all over. They are all for the simple purpose of moving the branches side to side and the cloth up and down. Everything on the vessel is made of wood and metal by talented hands and creative minds. It is a house turned over so that the top is bottom and the entrance is downward. Only one from the opposite side of the world could think this way.

It is easy enough to learn how to climb up the mesh-like ratlines to the roof. The guests walk carefully along the deck. Their eyes can not take in all the different parts of this machine. Everything has a shape of its own. It is all solid as it is beautiful in design and form and color.

The delegation goes inside through a miniature doorway. As if entering a cave, they bow low and readjust their eyes to the dark interior. Space is used efficiently. Nothing is larger than need be. The wood creeks and echoes. They can hear the men above and below them. The guests enter Captain Argall's private quarters. Windows fill three sides of the room with semi-transparent sheets of solidified liquid. The host sits his guests around a low table that has been pre-set with metal plates and drinking vessels. The food soon follows them in.

The meat is of those hogs that the strangers like so much. The flavor is strong in salt and very smoky. Matowaka does not try the flat, square cakes. They are so hard, she fears she will break a tooth on them. The big yellow fruit is a good desert. It has such thick, prickly skin. Such is brought up from the southern islands for trade with the colonists who can afford the asking price.

With dinner complete, the host offers a place to rest in the Gunners Room. The three quests go down to the deck just below where they had dinner. Well fed, they soon drift into slumber.

Matowaka awakens. It is a quick and rude departure from sleep. Her body is on edge because of it. Something seems wrong. She is alone in the room. She tries the door, but finds it to be unmovable. She beats it. She pulls at the metal handle. She screams. Both forearms press against her head in a fit of confusion. There is a rattling of the handle. She straitens to face the opening door. Captain Argall throws himself in and shuts the door behind.

"A good nap, I trust," the captain hums.

Matowaka tries her English, "Where be Iyopasus and Pawpawisk. What is now...afoot?"

"Calm now, maiden. Pray, sit. Already, your companions go to shore with a message to your good father."

"Wh, what is this?" she stammers.

The captain explains, "There are eight of my people, and not a few weapons and tools, recently taken from us. Me dear will be kept for exchange for said people and material and, per chance, some meal. Once this business is resolved, you shall be restored. No, shriek not. Upon my word, I shall use you most courteously. That, I have sworn. You are well liked by our people. You shall be used with all fair and gentle handling."

Matowaka remains anxious. She looks about the room with quick, fearful turns of the head. Her arms fold tightly below her bosom as she sits on the bunk from which she had arisen into this nightmare.

Leaning close to her with calm tones, Captain Argall tries again, "Kind madam. Suffer me your trust. Soon, we will repair with all speed to Jamestown. Remember the place?"

Morning peaks through the open windows of the church. Matowaka wakes up in the gallery. It is her favorite spot to sleep. She likes the main hall; its openness, the height of the raftered ceiling, the general spaciousness. It takes her back to her father's great council lodge in Weyowakomako. She straightens her *machkow*. The English clothes are fun to wear during the day, but she does not find them at all comfortable for bed-time use.

Mumbled sounds of Reverend Whitaker departing from his slumber echo from the old church building next door. Mrs. Sizemore is at her morning housekeeping duties. The old church is now used as the parsonage. But Governor Dale has promised the reverend that he shall have a better one with

POWHATAN:
THE STORY OF A PEOPLE

its own land. Matowaka shuffles to a window to welcome the sun. One hand rubs the eyes clear as the other sways listlessly along with her movement.

She looks at the buildings that line three streets. Each has a room half in the ground. The English call such a thing a raised basement. Brick walls rise above the ground where wood walls stand atop. The frame is covered with a skin of long boards, horizontally fixed. The roof is shingled with much shorter strips, laid vertically. They are all made this way; every store, workshop, and house.

The population of Henrico is still predominantly male. The inhabitants mutter under their breaths that this is more a penal colony, due to the way Governor Dale rules it. His law is very stern. Thievery is punishable by death. Those caught trying to run away are executed by various methods.

Soldiers live in the five block houses that anchor each corner of the palisade surrounding the city. Their primary task is to defend the city from outside dangers. Most often, however, they seem to keep watch over the inmates.

Matowaka is the only real prisoner here, yet she enjoys the most freedom. All Sir Dale asks of her is to master his language and understand his religion. Both he and the reverend pay much attention toward their pupil who enjoys the chore of learning. She already possesses a good foundation of knowledge that she gained from Tom Savage and Henry Spelman. Now, she is immersed in all the complexities of a new culture.

Her own culture seems but a memory. Circumstances have changed little. Seven of the English prisoners have been released. But as soon as a chance reveals itself, more run back into captivity. Three *pakusak* have been returned—the broken ones. Useful tools for tree cutting were also returned, along with an *akwintan* full of *poketawas*. Wahunsenakok has sent a request for Sir Dale to treat his daughter well and to visit him in person for the rest of what was demanded.

The people of the great Powhatan River have relocated far away. Poor Oposumokwonusk was attacked. Her people were driven up the Apamatuk in the cold of the last *popano*. The Weyanok soon followed them. Now, the large settlement of Bermuda Hundred stands just down river from the great *moninag* island. English houses line the southern bank of the Powhatan at this place. In back of the buildings are fields to grow food. Behind that is a long, tall palisade.

The strangers control the Powhatan River from its mouth to the falls. Their capital is now Henrico. The Chiskiyak relocated to the vacant city of

Weyowakomako. The only tribe left on the Lower Peninsula is the Chikahominy. They will never leave the river to which they belong. They have always defied Wahunsenakok. They defied the Spanish. Even if pushed away, they would surely return to their river. This is not a boast, rather a simple truth.

Matowaka listens to the cries far off in the woods. Her mother's people have also fled deep into the mainland. But the Awohatek are still close enough to menace the residents of Henrico. They send arrows over the walls and taunt those in the block houses. Munetut has led the harassment throughout construction of this settlement. He is a big talker and a flashy fighter. Always, he adorns himself with feathers trapped in his body oil and a short *kawasow* of *wopusok* wings that covers his shoulders. The Wind Children call him, "Jack of the Feathers" (among other things).

Henrico is a virtual island as it is environed on three sides by the Powhatan River. It is a small arm of high ground, buffeted by a basin of marsh. The arm extends into the mainland, creating a great pasture for the livestock. It is walled off from the point at which the river begins to curl to where the curl is completed. Block houses dot the length of this straight wall. Across the entire front is a wide moat. Sir Dale learned such military engineering from his service with the Dutch Army.

Just north is lower ground, environed by another curl of the river. More fortified settlements are there. This area, called Coxendale, is a large expanse of pasture, dotted with five separate fortified settlements. The settlement that Matowaka visits most often is Mount Malado, where the sick and the lame reside. She shares a few home remedies with the resident healer and enjoys the company of the patients. Henrico is nothing like Jamestown. It is so much cleaner and well tended, with more secure buildings and food supplies that are stored properly.

The inmates go about their morning routines. Matowaka will soon begin hers. She sees John Rolfe strolling up the street, cradling a gourd full of dirt. She knows he is coming to see her. What a darling man. And only ten years her senior.

Master Rolfe traveled to the new world to establish himself, as he is not the first-born son of his prominent English family. He and his wife hopped on board the Sea Venture. The journey changed for the worse when they blew into a tempestuous ocean storm. The vessel crashed onto a tiny island, far from their promised land. His wife survived the shipwreck, only to be taken ill on the island. She exhausted her last energy in an effort to bring her baby into the world.

The newborn was christened, Bermuda, for the island on which she was born. But the little girl did not stay long in this world before she went to keep her lost mother company. John continued alone, reaching Virginia with the rest of the survivors.

Life was a void for John Rolfe. He saw only his experiments, unaware of all the life that flourished around him. Such an awareness emerged one day upon moving to Henrico, where he noticed a young native woman. He sensed an energy; an excitement from her presence. To John, she is a person of beauty, a woman. She has also become fond to him.

Matowaka knows the reverend will be a while with his morning routines. She answers John's request to steal away with him for a little while. He is not yet confident in his understanding of her language and she is still coping with the intricacies of his. Never the less, both rely on the basics of communication between a man and a woman. She concentrates on his adorable mouth as he explains himself slowly, being mindful to use the most simple, direct sentences, "My hope is to grow tobacco."

"*Upook*," she corrects him.

"Yes," he nods, "*upook*. Much *upook*...for my people."

She nods eagerly. He continues with a responsive smile, "I did collect various seeds, some here, more from the Caribbean."

She smiles understandingly. He realizes she is ahead of him. And so, he comes right to the matter, "Know ye the horticulture of tobac...*upook*?"

She is confused. "How you grow good tobacco?"

"Yes. My exact purpose," John affirms.

Matowaka questions further, "How doth thee now do it?"

He begins to explain, "Thusly, do I splice and join the seeds from the two lands and drop them in the dirt..."

She waves her hands against each other. "The seed is but a gift of God, to plant with...tender care...with a prayer, and a goodly thought."

She puts the gourd on her lap and begins to knead the soil contained within. He follows her lead. Hands touch.

Matowaka holds out her palm. "Now, the seeds."

John hands them over. She murmurs a few prayers. John watches her. He listens to her voice rather than the words she utters. He concentrates on the lips from where the soothing tones come.

She realizes his attention and playfully kisses the seed. Glancing back at him, "Now, cover it careful."

Matowaka attempts to explain in her language. "Earth Mother is the garden of this world. Ahon nourishes this garden. Okius is the one to weed the garden. Both make the garden strong."

John can just make out what she says. He continues the conversation, "Do ye believe in the true God?"

"God is God. Yours is mine too. All gods answer to the one that is everything." She continues the debate in his language, "Your good book sayeth God is separate from us. But in act-u-a-li-ty, God is of us all. We are God, thee and me."

John questions, "How be ye certain of this?"

Matowaka answers in her language with a story, "When I was a child, I went to the temple with the other children. The seer told us all to sit before the mat partition at the back of the hall. He then went into the dark space behind it. Soon after, the mat rolled up. We all sat eye to eye with Okius. He sat there with a pipe full of *upook* in his mouth. He was smoking it! I not only saw Okius, but felt his chilling presence come into me. I put my arm under a ray of sunlight that shot down from the smoke hole. I could feel the warmth of Ahon enter me. The two communed with me. Your god holds a distant connection with those devoted to him. He has taken all bad things from himself and embodied them into a shunned *manitow*. Together, they are part of the one that makes all possible. Good and evil, life and death, love and hate…they are not opposites, but co-existing aspects of the whole."

"I know not wherewith I agree," John retorts. "Tis in our sacred book that the two are truly separate."

"Well, we know better," she exclaims in unquestionable triumph.

His face is blank. He is confronted with an unfamiliar concept. "Me faith beseeches not to allow such words to turn the heart."

He looks at the gourd. "Teach me of your world."

She explains, "Tis but the same world. Do we not want the same thing…to live at most ease with another? As with these seeds, conjoint bliss should result."

John considers fully. Yes. All people have the purpose to live. In Matowaka, he finds the desire to live again.

Chapter 19

Winds of *Katapewuk* blow down the Pamunkey River valley. The surface of the water is choppy. The current is strong. Pushing against the water is the hull of the Treasurer with three *kekwiyos* in tow. Sir Dale moves upriver with one hundred fifty men and one woman.

Matowaka was taken from her people on this vessel. Now, it brings her back to them. The young woman stands atop the forecastle, trying her best not to be in the way of the mariners. She can hear the incoherent shouts from those on the far off banks. Fleeting glimpses reveal painted human faces or the heads and tails of *nantam* pelts moving through the changing veil of tree branches. Her mind's eye has to fill in the gaps to comprehend what is really there.

John Rolfe stands beside her. He has recently professed his love. It is a love unlike that promised by her husband. She has not seen Kokum for over a year. He hasn't even tried to seek her. The memory of their marriage is lost in the shadows of the northern woodlands.

Slowly, the Treasurer maneuvers through the deepest parts of the channel. Sometimes it comes near a bank where the words of those ashore can be understood. They are the expected questions and blusterings:

"What are you doing here?"

"You are alone here!"

"You will not leave from here alive!"

Tom Savage shouts back an answer to no particular person, "We have Matowaka! We are here to exchange her! We have not heard anything to our demands for almost a year! We come to get that answer or burn your towns! We are ready to have peace or war with you!"

Tom focuses on one of the responses. "What do you want from us?"

He offers, "Bring us the rest of our stolen weapons and tools! Bring us *poketawas* for the trouble of having to make this journey! Bring us those Englishmen who are still with you! Give us audience with Wahunsenakok!"

"You want too much!" they laugh back. "We can give you death!"

Another reply warns, "We will keep our food for our own! We are not the Paspaheg! You will get the same as those with Ratcliffe!"

This insult riles everyone on board. It is shameful enough for the naturals to harm their fragile pride by keeping their material as trophies. Why must they be reminded of Captain Ratcliffe? Not just one of the soldiers raises his right hand to form the gesture of two upright fingers.

The Wind Children make their way to the southern fork of the river. The channel narrows with a thickening of marshes as they reach Sinkwotek. All non-essential travelers go below deck. A cloud of arrows blow in from the northern shore. There is a heavy thud of rock that pounds thick wood. There is a snap of splintered wood. One sound is different. It is the crack of stone entering into a human skull. The mariner panics. He can see the long shaft protruding just above his eyes. He faints as others rush to him. They carry the victim below to their surgeon who extracts the object and stops the bleeding in time. Never will he be the same, but at least his life will go on.

Armed men fill the *kekwiyos*. Sir Dale sends the order over the rail. Slowly, the three vessels make their way to shore. Those on the deck of the Treasurer watch their progress. They see the line of battle form along the beach. Some defenders mass along the raised bank among the trees. A barrage of arrows is released. Claps of black powder resound. The battle line scales the embankment and disappears within the tree line. Screams are heard from within the city. Forty plums of smoke billow into the clear sky. The victors set a defensive encampment in the light of the smoldering ruins.

Matowaka listens to the reports coming in. Her uncle, Kekwatog, lives in Sinkwotek. She worries about him. Daybreak brings her word that he is unharmed.

The sun moves into the sky as the flotilla moves up the river toward Menapukunt. More defenders are spotted in the marshes. The shouting resumes.

"You are strong and many. But you are not invincible!"

"You will be remembered well in our victory songs!"

"Can you die as bravely as you talk, or as cowardly as you kill?"

Another city appears along the bow of the river. It is the new settlement of Machut, comprised mostly of refugees from the Lower Peninsula.

POWHATAN:
THE STORY OF A PEOPLE

A longboat is lowered from the Treasurer. Matowaka joins the landing party. She takes a seat next to John Rolfe.

A growing number of painted forms appear along a ridge above the landing site. There must be at least four hundred of them. And still, it is but a fraction of what Wahunsenakok can bring together if he chooses. All have a scalp comb of spiked hair, stiffened by red *pokun*. Other trophies from past warfare decorate the knot of their long black manes that hang closely down the left side of their bodies. Geometric symbols stain their shoulders and arms. These are the best in Tsenakomako. Concern for their fragile mortality is non-existent. Only the will of their *mamanatowik* rests within their minds.

The warriors allow an easy landing. They quietly wander down from the ridge and mix with their guests. Their movements are certain. No fight is offered as they wait for negotiations to play out.

One moves through the crowd. "Where is your *weyowanz*? Who is to speak for you?"

Tom explains, "He is on the *musawusuk*. I will speak for him."

"You?" Tom senses a baiting tone in the other's voice. "No one but a *weyowanz* may have audience with Wahunsenakok. Opechankano can speak for him. You may speak with Opechankano. But what do you wish to say? How will you explain your actions of yesterday?"

Tom answers, "We seek peace. We come in that light. But we stand firmly, ready for battle. If given reason, we can also fight you today. Another city can burn. We want our things back and we want our men returned. For them, we will return Matowaka to you."

The warrior delays, "Well now...Such colorful hair I see on you all. They would make wonderful scalps. A decision to what you ask could be here tomorrow. Then, we will know if such colorful scalps will be ours.

"Your people run to us fearing for their lives. Why should you be allowed to claim them? Some have died before you can kill them...One is with the Tapahanok. We will send word to him, to see if he wants to return to you. Do you wish to wait or fight?"

"We can wait," Tom assures. "But if we decide to fight, we shall give you warning with our drums and flutes."

The warrior nods, "Then we shall give you word from Wahunsenakok as soon as we receive it. And then, we will give you a moment to decide what you will want to do." His eyes rest on Matowaka. "What do you say about this? Do these people now speak for you?"

Matowaka has no answer. She just knows that she is weary of being nothing more then a prize. There are so many conflicting points of view swarming in her mind to make sense of it all. To the English, she is worth a few replaceable objects and a couple of scared fugitives. But her own father will not even part with them for her. She can understand the refusal of food. Food can be grown by anyone. Her people should not be expected to feed the Wind Children forever.

The English have been kind to her. Captivity has been comfortable—even somewhat enjoyable. But a husband does wait for her in Patawomik. What is her duty to her people? What charity should she give the strangers? Current circumstances focus only on two choices. Matowaka quietly formulates another solution.

Two familiar faces appear in the crowd. Nakakwawis and Namontak embrace their little sister warmly. The siblings talk of family matters and she introduces John Rolfe to them.

The evening sky blushes in pink and purple. The brothers tell their little sister they will go back to the *musawusuk* with her if two Englishmen could stay behind.

"I will stay." John grasps her shoulders. "I shall speak to thy father directly. It will prove him my desire for you to be real."

Matowaka studies his face, unsure if she will see it again. The three siblings climb into the longboat. Her eyes do not leave John until distance and darkness dissolves her view.

Two bells sound from the church steeple. Curiosity gets the better of a few townspeople. They move toward the little church that stands just east of James Fort. The current church is of framed timber. It even has windows with glass-filled casements and real hinges. As it should be, the entrance is through the bell tower at the west end. The structure has been standing atop the old burial ground for four years. Today, it is a place of life beginning anew. The whole town is invited. People stream up the two main streets. The town has also grown outside of the fort with permanent wood-frame buildings like those at Henrico. It may no longer be the center of the colony, but it is still the most significant place of this little England.

People shuffle through the entrance to find an interior completely garnished. All the casements are swung open. Light rays seep through them, thick with morning haze. Fresh wildflowers bloom in the warm glow. Reverend Richard Bucke presides at the alter. His friend, John Rolfe, stands with Governor Dale by his side. Other men of importance already fill the front benches on the groom's side.

Standing on the other side of the hall are three wildly decorated men. It is somewhat alarming to see them in such a place as this. Their arms and shoulders gleam with yellow *pokun*. Each midsection is covered at the front with a fringed *matahay*. It is hard to determine if there are more beads on their *mokasin* than wrapped in their long locks that drape half their bodies. The trio stands quietly and calmly. They observe the proceedings of an Anglican wedding. Other naturals sit quietly on the bride's side. Most have slipped in from their peddling at the fort to witness this important occasion.

In the center of it all stands the whimsical young woman whom everyone knows. Matowaka stands ready for union with Master Rolfe. Recently baptized, she now goes by her Christian name of, Rebecca. Soon, she will own a sir name as well.

Except for a new pair of *mokasin*, Rebecca is not dressed like her maternal uncle, Opachisko, or her two brothers, Nakakwawis and Namontak. The ladies of Jamestown lent the bride more proper attire. From the varied trunks of British femininity has come an ensemble of the best the middling class has to offer. The long chain of pearls that was used in her first wedding to bind two people together is now thrice wound around her neck. This time, it will bind two cultures together. She becomes a grain of sand to develop into an English pearl. A long, white veil with blue ribbons covers her face. At the proper time, the groom raises it to press the Indigeny's lips with his own.

Reverend Bucke announces the marriage complete. There are various levels of happiness among all those present. Perhaps happiest of all is Sir Dale. The governor is proud of Rebecca. She memorized the Book of Prayers. She was inspiring at her baptism. She accomplished everything she was asked with great ease. He looks on her now as a father might. It has been easy for him to keep his promise to Wahunsenakok to treat her as his own. No one could have a better daughter. There is so much pride in his heart. But it is mixed with a touch of envy.

Rebecca's real father provides the newly-weds with a plot of land that lies just downriver from Awohatek. It is the same land given to her mother. John names the place, Varina, after the strain of *upook* that he has perfected. He hopes to market his product soon. The new couple builds a small cottage near the river's edge.

Shadows glide along the wooded trail. They move to the edge of the forest. Sunlight finds bright colors that enliven sparse foliage. The grand procession descends the steep cliff. Members of the Kwiyokohanok come to the bank of the Powhatan River. They come not from the town of Chawopo, but from deeper in their territory. A long time ago, Pepiskunima fled with the stolen wife of Opechankano for the safety of a small wilderness village. Since then, the same woman began a tradition of visiting Jamestown three of four times each year to trade.

Her *akwintan* is not a large one. It fills quickly with furs and food. The distinguished passenger climbs in. Her guards push off.

The water is high today. Shoulders burn with the hard push of the paddle. She sits quietly, assured they can do their job. Though not quite the best of Powhatan beauty, she has the self-assurance to carry herself in such a light. Her mother-in-law, Ohalas, has taught her well. She dresses in a pure-white *matahay*. A corral frontal both invites and detracts attention to the features of her upper body. Bird-claw earrings and a long chain of matasun around her neck draw the most attention to her refined countenance. Her sable hair is further enriched with a variety of small feathers and wild flowers. Most eye-catching is her deep purple *kawasow*. Dozens of *mowakus* feathers are thickly sewn together, creating a sleek, glossy appearance and a soft, almost liquid feel.

She does not carry as much as she would like, but the season has been dry and the yield has not been good. Pepiskunima asked his chief seer to plead for rain, but the land experienced a drought all the same. He is sure that the spirits are still mad at him for stealing away the girl. But that is the role every dashing young hero must play. He will never admit wrong-doing for such a youthful act, no matter what the gods do about it.

Since there were no children involved, divorce was acceptable. Never the less, it was a divorce. What helps is the fact that the girl was young and it was her first marriage. She feels it has been the right decision. The resulting spurn of the Powhatan ruling family has enabled Pepiskunima to move securely into the graces of the strangers. Though just a puppet, he has not seen his followers pushed off their homelands as all the neighbors have been. As for his wife, she has replaced Oposumokwonusk as the goddess of the river.

The *akwintan* floats by the pier at Jamestown. It passes a few *kekwiyos* that slowly bounce on the water's crust. Her own vessel runs aground on the small beach nearby.

POWHATAN:
THE STORY OF A PEOPLE

The strangers point in the direction of a cleared site near the landing. The old fort is the only similar sight before her. The little city looks much more robust then anything built here before. Everything looks much more permanent.

The two assistants carry their *weyowanskwa* to the five mats stacked upon the ground. Not one part of her body touches the earth. Such purity must not stain the ground. She sits in patient silence. The tribute is laid out before her and a sentinel stands on either side. The traditional announcement of arrival is sent into town. Within a few moments, members of the colony leadership make their way down to the landing. The usual ceremony plays out for another season.

Chapter 20

Another step follows the last. A breath is taken. A breath is given back to the crisp night air. Four men make their way along the trail. The moon is about half way through its nocturnal journey. Their destination is near. Two Apamatuk men comprise half of this group. Tom Savage makes up one quarter. His master, Ralph Hamor, is the final member and the core reason for their travels.

Even though he is young, Ralph is a seasoned adventurer. He survived the shipwreck in Bermuda and has proven to be a faithful servant to the colony's leadership. Although of average frame and regular health, his inner candle burns brightly.

It has been step after step all the past day and throughout the day before. Legs ache from fatigue. Calves and feet grow numb. The pace is steady, but not fast enough to keep up with the mind that has gone ahead along the trail of meditation. The pain in the legs, the sweat on the skin, and the general discomfort of the body will not be remembered. Only the visual impressions that color the mind's eye and the voiced thoughts that echo in the consciousness will be preserved.

Shoulders ache, reminding them of the packs they carry. Each is filled with gifts from Sir Dale to the one who still rules this land. Tom speculates the future. How will the old man receive him after such a long time away? Ralph looks upon the future as an opportunity. It is a chance to meet the *mamanatowik* of whom so many have spoken. He is known by many as the omnipotent leader whom Sir Dale has come to admire, as well as the monster about whom the Chikahominy have warned.

It was not long after the marriage of Matowaka that two Chikahominy ambassadors appeared at Jamestown with an offer of submission. Ralph can still remember the two lavishly garbed men and the two large *wushakwun*

POWHATAN:
THE STORY OF A PEOPLE

they gifted. They proclaimed the sincere willingness of their people to be called not Powhatan, but English. The tribe was willing to look upon King James as their only *weyowanz*.

Phantoms play among the shadows that haunt the surrounding darkness. Unknown sounds are thick in the black air that presses against the illuminated space along a narrow path. The mind is lost in erratic excitement. Agitation nips at Ralph's intellect. There are too many stories, both good and bad, concerning the one he is to meet.

It was a positive event when peace was formally sealed with the Chikahominy. Governor Dale personally took a *kekwiyos* to meet them. The Treasurer followed him deep into the river's mouth. As a new morning broke, the Chikahominy heartland galvanized with festive activity.

As Sir Dale watched from the *kekwiyos*, Captain Argall conferred with the eight members of the *kawkawas*. Tom interpreted for the two sides. The first thing they accepted was the oath of allegiance to King James and the proclamation of unquestionable faith in Governor Dale. Since they would now be an English community, they would help keep their English friends from mortal harm and all their property from physical injury. In return for military support against outside enemies (namely the Spanish), the Wind Children would help protect their native brothers against any belligerent neighbors (namely Wahunsenakok). It was also agreed to look upon the Lower Peninsula outside the Chikahominy River as English domain—to be traversed only with good intentions and only along designated trails. Naturally, an agreement was established for the Chikahominy to deliver food at every harvest until Infinity itself terminated. To keep their river, the *kawkawas* pledged to see that this treaty would never collapse. They all consented with great enthusiasm to every aspect of the agreement. Each received a *matasun* medallion with the image of their new father etched onto the surface. A strong cord was provided to hang them from their necks.

The chief *kawkawas* rose to conclude the affair. His cadence and choice of words were appropriate for everyone. Even the English delegation fell prey to the auspicious fervor of its tone.

But Captain Argall did not stop. With right hand held high, he promised each *kawkawas* a thin slab of *matasun* to adorn their heads and a *tomahak* to fill their hand upon every passing year. Beads, bowls, and good tools would also flow from the Wind Children for the cross current of furs, baskets, and *upook*. Such trade between the two cultures would be continuous and substantial. Neither side would have to trade with anyone else ever again.

The Pamunkey River is near. The four travelers quicken their steps. They reach the winding bank just across from the western skyline of Machut.

The two guides make their presence known with a pair of high-pitched caws. They hear a question come from the opposite bend and yell back an answer with a question of their own. The reply comes in the form of an *akwintan*.

One by one, small torches light up the landing site as if stars emerging in a twilight sky. The *akwintan* comes aground. Wahunsenakok is among the greeters, slightly bent at the shoulders. He speaks in a voice hoarse from weakness, "I recognize you." The old man's eyes gleam at Tom. "Yes, you have returned to me at last. Why have you stayed away for so long? You are my child. Do you remember, how Newport gave you to me, and I gave him my son, Namontak?"

His attention turns to Ralph Hamor. Tom replies, "I have brought you this man from your brother, Dale."

The old man steps up to his guest. "Hum, I don't see it. Perhaps my eyes fail me." Wahunsenakok glides his hands about the man's neck. "Strange. There are no pearls on you. I gave my brother a pearl necklace for his messengers to wear. Are you really here on his sending, or are you another runaway?"

As the translation is made, Ralph thinks of a good explanation. Tom answers, "He says that Dale thought the necklace should be used in times of urgency, when the messenger would come without guides. This is a humble visit, in good will, with guides."

"Good enough." Wahunsenakok turns away. "I will receive you. Come. We can talk further after a good meal."

The town emits a melancholy amenity. Very few are up at this time of night. It is a short walk to the council lodge.

Wahunsenakok lounges on his raised platform near the back of the lodge. A woman sits down at each flank. Both of the girls are very lovely; fresh and congenial. The rest of his women and a few councilors relax among the visitors on the mat flooring. Ralph can hear the personal guard assemble outside, but decides not to worry. His host imbibes the smoke from his pipe, and then offers it to the messenger. Ralph draws in the flavored mist and returns it casually.

Time drifts away with the smoke. Wahunsenakok speaks, "How are my daughter and her son that I have yet to see?"

POWHATAN:
THE STORY OF A PEOPLE

The answer comes through Tom, "The boy is also named Thomas. He is healthy and happy. Your daughter is happy too. She has no desire to return to you."

Wahunsenakok breaks into laughter, "I am very glad of it." He turns serious. "Now, state the cause of your unexpected arrival."

Tom receives instructions from his superior. He turns back. "Our message is private...to be delivered to you alone."

The hall empties except for the chief councilor and the two females. Master Hamor keeps his interpreter and one guide with him.

"Now, speak to me."

Ralph mumbles in his language at Tom who refines it into the correct speech, "Dale, your brother, sends you greetings of love and peace. He sends you gifts: two large pieces of *matasun*, five strings of white and blue beads, five wooden combs, ten fishhooks, and a couple knives. There is also a large grinding stone for you, when you are able to send some men out to get it."

Wahunsenakok nods pleasingly. Tom continues, "Your youngest daughter is well known for her perfect beauty. Master Hamor comes to ask you to give her to Dale in brotherly friendship. Her sister, Matowaka, needs her help. And if the girl is as wonderful as she is known to be, Dale would gladly make her his...companion?"

The two young women turn sour. Wahunsenakok tries to intercede, but the stranger pleads to be heard fully.

Tom elaborates, "The reason for this request is that Matowaka's union has strongly bound our two nations. Dale feels that a bond between you and him would be even better for everyone. Dale wants to live here forever. She would be with him for as long as he lives. Therefore, the friendship between you and Dale would be permanent through her."

Wahunsenakok answers, "I gladly accept your leader's words of love and peace. While I live, I shall, and my people shall maintain friendship with you. I thank him for these gifts, even if they are not many. I know Dale to be a greater man then Newport who showed me more appreciation through his words and gifts.

"As for my daughter, she is already promised to a great man who lives three days from here. He gave me two great baskets of *wowanok*. She has already gone to him."

The debate continues, "You are the greatest man in Pamasawu. Certainly, you could negate the marriage in light of your loving brother's needs. Dale can give you the same amount of *wowanok*. Since she is not yet twelve, she could not be...ready for marriage. Dale offers a way to confirm our peace. Dale would gladly triple the amount with beads, *matasun*, and many other useful items."

The old man purses his lips, crinkling the wiry strands of his thin mustache. He replies, "I love my daughter. She is as precious as my own life. It is true, my children are many. But none bring me more joy than she. If I could not see her often, I would cease to live. If she lived with you, I know I would never see her.

"Be sure that Dale understands that I need no more assurances of his friendship. Your people will always have the gift of my daughter, Matowaka. The love between us will prosper for as long as she lives. That should be enough. When she dies, if it is still desired, your people may have another of my children. I do not think my brother would want me to be without two of my children at one time.

"Let Dale understand that if he had no pledge at all, he should not feel threatened by me or any of my people. We both have lost too much. While I live, there shall be no more death. I want to end my days in peace. If you would threaten me, the land is large enough to move far away. You must be tired from you journey. I am ready for sleep."

The old man motions for the food to be served. "I am sorry this is all I can offer. I was not expecting you. I have already eaten for the night. These leftovers are all I can offer."

Two wooden bowls full of round *apon* cakes are placed before the guest. Wahunsenakok motions to one of his females. She goes to a storage space nearby and pulls out the green rectangular bottle of sack. Only a small portion has been used. Wahunsenakok utters, "I have kept this with utmost care all this time. It was given me by my *cham*, Newport. It is an important thing to me."

He fills a *kaway* shell with the burning liquid to share with Master Hamor. The two drink attentively. The guests are then escorted to their lodge for the night.

After his morning bath, Wahunsenakok comes to the visitor's lodge. There is no one inside. Instead, he finds them under a broad *powamink* tree. During the night, they had brought their sleeping mats outside to get away from menacing insects that infested their *ahakan*. He leads them to an open area for the morning meal. They feast from a great wooden bowl of *misikwatash* and fresh *apon*. The second course is boiled fish and *tutaskuk*, along with roasted *tsekoma*. Ralph notices the hunters returning with their

POWHATAN:
THE STORY OF A PEOPLE

fresh kill of *wushakwun* and *moninag*. They begin dressing the meat to have later in the day.

A man comes to them. At first, he appears to be just another native. Ralph soon realizes that it is William Parker. He has been kept from his people for over three years.

Ralph addresses him, "Why, Master Parker. We thought you dead!"

William smiles pleadingly, "Kindly sir, might thee deliver me from this place?"

Ralph immediately seeks out his host through Tom, "We request this man return with us. If Dale learns about him, he will only send Master Hamor back again."

"Well..." Wahunsenakok steams, "if you must have him, then go...but without guides. And if any harm befalls you, then thank yourselves for it."

The reply is a little cutting, but understandable. "Master Hamor would rather go alone if not with the man. He knows the way well enough and is capable to assure his own safety. However, if anything would happen to one who is traveling in peace and entitled to your care, revenge would be sought. Dale would lose trust in you if he were to return without guides."

The old man leaves with no more words. Ralph does not see him again until the night meal. Wahunsenakok expresses a mature, gracious façade. He does not even mention the morning. Ralph retires for the night, but is awoken by his host not long after.

"You three English may take one of your guides and one of my own with you in the morning. Tom, tell him to send my greetings to my good *cham* and ask him to send me ten pieces of *matasun*, a shaving knife, one of those tools that slices thin wood, and a grinding stone...but not a big one. Also, I would rather have two combs made of bone, like those Newport once gave me. My own people can make wooden combs. I also want a hundred metal fishhooks...or, if he could spare a fishing seine, that would suffice. And also a dog...and a cat. If my brother, Dale, would furnish these, I will give him fine skins to keep him warm. I do not have any, right now. But I'll collect some for him. Can you remember everything?"

Ralph assures him, but Wahunsenakok is not convinced. "Repeat it to me, so that I can be sure."

The list is echoed in full with a little impatient coaching from the listener. Still, this is not good enough. "No. You are not people who can remember well...unless you put it in your talking leaves, like the one I have."

Ralph reaches for it, but Wahunsenakok refuses him. "This one is important to me. I like to show it to my company. I don't want to ruin it."

With a slight chuckle, Ralph pulls out his own tablet and writes everything down. Satisfied, the old man leaves them to sleep.

Before departing, the travelers fill themselves on a breakfast of boiled *moninag*. They even get another whole bird and three baskets of *apon* for the trail. Ralph is presented a new buckskin. Two similar skins are packed to send to Matowaka and her husband. Wahunsenakok asks Ralph to repeat the list once more from the tablet.

The old man seems contented. "Very good. I hope my answer pleases him. If not, I will go three days from you and never see any of your kind again. But I will always welcome messengers whenever he wishes to communicate with me."

Utamatomakin studies the long staff propped beside him. He is to use it to count the English for Wahunsenakok when he arrives on their island home. A light spray of sea water slaps his face. The Great Blue is everywhere. The Treasurer floats upon this liquid desert between two worlds. Utamatomakin is accustomed to this. He is an experienced mystic.

Sitting on the quarter deck, he observes the little community on board. To break the monotony, some of the Indigeny passengers help the sailors. Two of the young women interact with a group of flirtatious crewmen. It is hard to tell if they are the subject or the audience. In such plays of affection, one can be both.

On the forecastle is the wind father with his earth son. Little Thomas flaps his arms and giggles while the father points at the sails that billow in front of them. Utamatomakin squeezes a pouch of *upook* that Master Rolfe gave him. John is carrying much of his own blend in the hold to sell in England. The seer does not care for that idea. It is taking something sacred and cheapening it for mere social delight.

Wind ruffles the *wikutis* down on his garment. Some of the fur separates. He tries to grab what he can. A disgruntled whisper escapes his lips. "How much longer?"

The vessel cuts through the uneven water toward England. Utamatomakin wonders if this is the same course that the ancient ones took when they rode on the great *tukupewuk*, skirting the icy land before it melted into the waters. In the old stories, those people came from the abode of Manibuzo in the east. The *tukupewuk* are so important to his people. Even neighboring nations,

POWHATAN:
THE STORY OF A PEOPLE

with the same beginnings, revere this animal over all others. Did they really ride on the backs of those creatures, or follow them? The story is so old. Only condensed verses of that history remain. Each simple strand is a trace of the story that has been memorized and studied by generations of mystics before him.

Rebecca sits just outside the steerage, watching Captain Argall and Governor Dale survey their sea charts. They seem different. Both men are comfortably within their proper context. For her, it is all so new. She opens herself wide to take in everything she possibly can. The journey has been a blur, too quick in passing. She has grown used to life on the *musawusuk*. The grime, the infestation, the wetness, the confining closeness, the clammy haze of the decks below. She has been consumed by it all. The void ocean no longer seems so overwhelming.

Rebecca had spent time as a prisoner in the gunner's room of this vessel. Now, she shares it with John and Thomas, along with Matachana and her husband, Utamatomakin. The rest of her entourage has taken over the forecastle. Rebecca can tell they are weary of the voyage. It is a grueling test of patience, where resistance brings agitation and surrender brings impassivity of consciousness. But soon, their feet will touch the earth again. And for Rebecca, an exiting adventure will begin.

Chapter 21

The Treasurer arrives in the harbor of Plymouth. Anticipation runs rampant in the crowd. Anxiety rises in the members of the Virginia Company who have made their own journeys to this port city. All their remaining funds have been spent for this publicity scheme. The company has advertised their new lottery far and wide. Both the government and the clergy have been contacted. Even the royal family has been seduced. A decade has almost passed, yet nothing has come from Virginia. There has been no gold (the Spanish have secured that treasure), no major supply of furs (the French have monopolized that market), no trade goods of any significance (the Dutch have a better merchant fleet). England's only claim is virgin land along the coast of a broad continent. And thus far, the company has only managed to mismanage the project.

Human activity grows thick at the docks. Officials mix with the interested and the bored. Sponsors worry how this delegation from Virginia will be received. The group of natives from the New England region was a fiasco. The public only saw a pathetic collection of dirty, scared heathens.

There is a prospective cash crop on board the Treasurer. John Rolfe is promising that his tobacco will rival any the Spanish colonies have produced. Such a commodity does not sit well with King James. He has despised the nasty habit from the start. But any efforts to quell it will prove fruitless. There is no question that the sweet Virginia weed will find its way onto the trading tables of every coffee shop and on the selves of every grocer's store in England.

The sponsors are counting on Rolfe's wife to win over the royal family. She is not a mere savage. But will she come across as a freak? The answer lies with Sir Dale. Any failure from this tour will rest on him. However, if he has planned well, the company should at last enjoy success.

POWHATAN:
THE STORY OF A PEOPLE

Cannon boom as the vessel maneuvers to the designated pier. Songs and shouts ring in response. Some of the socialites in the crowd had the opportunity to see the last Powhatan visitor, Namontak. They look forward to meeting some of his siblings.

"See them?" The spectators grow anxious.

"I spy a feather. There! That must be one. Know ye how they bedeck themselves all over with feathers."

A glimpse. A mirage. Fleeting moments of clear sight.

"That one must be her!"

"I see not a thing!"

"When shall they come ashore?"

The Vice Admiral of Devon, Sir Lewis Stukley, leads the gaggle of dignitaries to the landing plank.

Sir Dale cries out, "Good people, may I present the Lady Rebecca, of Virginia!" The crowd explodes into applause. John escorts his wife to the plank. The audience blooms.

The lady wears a beautiful dress of English make, decorated with tiny shell beadwork around the neckline and shirtsleeves. Her tattooed limbs are hidden by the cloth. A pearl necklace hangs loosely around the throat in double strands.

Rebecca beams. This is her moment. She is a *weyowanskwa*. She grants her barbarian subjects to ogle at her to their heart's content. So many people. So much noise from voices and from musical instruments. So much stone—natural and man-made. These people do not carve out a world from the land. They produce a world entirely of its own. The buildings are tall. Church towers pierce the clouds.

Her entourage slowly follows. The four young men are in full regalia. Dazzling designs are painted upon arms and legs and backs. Lavishly decorated breechcloths are all that cover them below. Their long hair is decorated with scalp locks and bird claws and other paraphernalia that hold personal meaning to each owner. The four young women step ashore. Their faces are splattered with tattoos. Their bodies are hidden by larger-then-usual *machkow*.

Most noticeable is Utamatomakin. Painted in the customary black and red, he is adorned in the *wikutis* uniform of his position. He makes one last mark on the counting stick before tossing it away in disgruntled resignation. The seer escorts his wife who carries her nephew/son, Thomas, to his mother. The little darling captures the adoration of many a woman in the crowd.

As Sir Stukley bows to his guests, the lady curtsies in response. The crowd is captivated. Company members eye one another with relieved exuberance.

While the men break out into ceremonious dance, the women greet their hosts with smiles and gifts. The crowd admires these representatives of a truly wild lavishness. They are true throwbacks to the antiquity of human civilization. They are sure minded, relaxed. They are Powhatan. It is clear that Rebecca is the daughter of royalty, as any in Ireland or Scotland or Brittany could produce. Life in Virginia seems endless with possibilities. Many in the crowd begin to dream of their lives in a land on the other side of the world.

The Treasurer sets sail. It moves eastward through the Strait of Dover, skirting the tall white cliffs before rounding the southeastern point to enter the mouth of the Themes. Gentle winds race through the river valley. The emerald landscape sparkles under a cool sun. The river narrows mildly until reaching Gravesend. Passengers debark once more.

The hithe is right on the river's edge at the center of town. From here, quiet buildings spread into the land toward the little hill where the main church stands. The town looks so alien to the visitors. And yet, it possesses the familiar character of kinship and brotherhood, as any in Tsenakomako.

They stay for the night in the Flushing Inn. The Belgian host delights in his special guests. He provides them a private room. Servants diligently kindle the fire for a warm sleep.

Upon the next day, the passengers board a small barge that can swiftly maneuver up the narrowing channel. It is a long ride, but the final destination does come.

Rounding the bend, they spot an ominous structure. It presents itself out of nowhere—a solid block of silvery Portland stones with simple openings. It has stood there through five centuries, and various owners. Indeed, possession of this island has changed hands several times. The original inhabitants are long forgotten. Rebecca hears the name, "London" from her smiling husband. Sir Dale had told her much about this fortified city that was first built by those who suckled from a great *nantam*. Most buildings are cramped inside the old walls. Each room is stacked atop another and pushed tightly against each other. Most have shops on the ground floors. Above them are storage areas and quarters for the owners and servants. Boats, small and large, criss-cross before and behind them. They enter into a swarming urban hive.

POWHATAN:
THE STORY OF A PEOPLE

Utamatomakin is not in a light mood. He looks about with a heavy sigh. Ahead he sees a big wall of buildings stretched across the river. He counts nineteen pointy arches rising upward between walls that were pounded into the riverbed. Small oval islands of piled stones hold the walls secure. People are everywhere along the bridge. Some look out their windows of the tall, slim buildings that line the span. The noise of activity increases until the barge travels under an arch. Now comes a deafening, hollow echo. The light and the noise and the smells slap him hard as the watercraft reaches the other side of the bridge.

Rebecca looks back at a group of urchins watching the river traffic. She waves at them with a straining, "O'ye there!" Two make for the safety of home, leaving their mates frozen in wonderment of the strange woman. Only one reacts by waving back. She giggles and grasps her own boy's shoulders.

The vessel turns right. It makes for the heart of the city. Tall steeples and sharp roofs form an uneven skyline. More members of the Virginia Company are at the landing. Rebecca looks through the group. There are familiar faces from the settlement, along with a few new ones to match names she has heard. Pleasantries are exchanged. Governor Delaware is here with his wife and daughters. Rebecca reshapes her opinion of the man. Perhaps he is not the mad brute after all. As long as he stays in England, he is a charming fellow indeed. His wife, Lady Shirley, comes near with searching eyes. "My, what a wondrous little creature ye be," she exclaims. "I am to help madam in proper instruction for the Stuart Court. Would ye like to meet the queen?"

Rebecca replies, "I would like that not a little, m'lady."

Looking back to her husband, "Well then, let us get them gone. Upon the morrow, we shall begin the dainty schooling."

The eight native youths are separated here. It is already arranged for them to be quartered elsewhere to begin their own schooling. Rebecca's family climbs into a flat vehicle. It makes its way up the ruff street, through a maze of buildings, until stopping before the old inn that is called the Belle Savage. This place was built even before Rebecca's grandfather was alive. Company members make their embarrassed apologies of not having the funds for better living arrangements. Rebecca assures them that she is quite pleased with everything.

Once inside their room, everyone plops down where they can find a comfortable spot. Rebecca looks at her companions. "We are here," she rejoices. "We are actually here!" She stays awake at length, watching her people as they drift off to sleep. She gazes out the window, observing the unfamiliar scene of life outside. She turns to see the pleasant faces of her loved ones lost in dreaming. Her hands clinch together to control her excitement. She knows this is but the beginning.

With some of her daughters to assist her, Lady Shirley continues her instruction. Others who have returned from the colony come to visit. Rebecca remembers some of them. Others are not as clear to her. With each visitor, she hones her skills in social pleasantries.

One day, a carriage stops in front of the inn. Rebecca ventures outside. The passenger is an older man of distinguished appearance. He has an attractive face that possesses a softer, more quiet allure. But it is one that can still skip the heart of a woman.

The gentleman steps closer. With captivating grace, he bows with a wave of his hat and a flex of his hosed calf. "M'lady, I, Sir Walter Raleigh, seek the honorable Lady Rolfe. Might thee be her?"

"That I am, Sir."

"Ah." He leans forward to take her hand for a peck. "And a woman of high beauty, if I may be so bold."

"That you may, Sir."

His laugh is the example of pleasant joviality. The demeanor is warm and sincere, proving he is a man who truly loves the presence of women.

"I have heard much of you, my dear," Sir Raleigh chirps.

"Sir, would thee please me in sitting to tea?" she offers.

His face turns serious. "I should think myself honored."

"This way." Rebecca guides him to a private dining chamber. A servant girl comes with the tray. The gentleman catches a quick look at the wench's physical attributes as the girl asks, "Take ye tea in saucer?"

His answer is simple. The girl understands its hidden implications. She has heard it all before, but never with such flare and sophistication. Rebecca may be knowledgeable with the language, but she is not versed in its communicative complexities. She remains oblivious to her guest's lewd innuendo with the wench.

Sir Raleigh returns his attention to the lady. "Ah, the sweet sent of freedom. I am newly released from the Tower."

Rebecca directs the conversation, "Poor thing, in that monstrous tower for so many years."

"Ah, not once, but twice."

"Twice?"

POWHATAN:
THE STORY OF A PEOPLE

Sir Raleigh bends over his tea in reflective meditation. "Aye, the first for loving a woman other then the former queen. Thus, did I lose the love from said queen. As for the second…well, the present king hath found no love for me at all."

He looks up. "I do hear, tis in the works that ye shall soon visit the Royal Family?"

Rebecca replies, "I do hope he shall like me, else I may find me self in that wretched tower."

Sir Raleigh sits up. "Oh, nay m'lady. Only upon gilded pedestal should ye go. I feel we be of the same cloth. People see our kind with softened thoughts only."

"Are we the beautiful people, sir?"

Walter sits back. "Aye, that."

Rebecca fuels the conversation, "And what of this freedom newly found?"

"Ah, I am but the adventurer, my dear," the gentleman trumpets. "Preparations are under way as we speak. Soon, shall I journey back to the new world."

"Truly exiting," the lady encourages.

"Aye, and dangerous. Truly, tis a dangerous adventure to go into Spanish claimed lands and seize gold for our own. Alas, am I but an old sea dog and know no other life."

"As Captain Newport?" Her eyes dance.

"Ah, a gallant man, to be sure. Twas the Caribbean he did go to privateer and lose his arm in assailing two Spanish treasure ships near Cuba." Memories pour in. "Ah, those days of high living, what? May I only hope to rekindle that spirit once more. The Tower hath bled me much. Tis a cruel place, m'lady, filled with dark agonies and excessive despair. I left a dear friend in the Tower, Sir Percy."

Rebecca sits up. "Percy, George Percy?"

"Why, his eldest brother, Henry. The very head of the family."

She thinks back on the cruel treatment George Percy suffered while in the colony, as well as what he meted out. "That family is the name of anguish."

"Ah, quite. A family so close to rule this land. That Scotsman, James, came and took it away. Percy and like-minded fellows did devise a plot to dispose of king and council to start anew. They acquired a cellar next to the governing council chamber in Sir Percy's name. Twas their first mistake. Nearly a year did they dig a tunnel to the cellar of Parliament and filled it with gunpowder to wait upon the day both king and council would convene. Then, with a great explosion, they would have hurled every one into glorious oblivion. Alas, did the second and most damning mistake occur when the plotters let the secret out to certain councilors they did like, warning not to attend that day. Tongues wagged. Thus, poor Henry sits in his castle, ruler but himself.

"And I, once the proud owner of the eastern coast of Northern America…That Scotsman King did take from me. I am reduced to take from the Spanish a treasure to purchase my freedom. Sir Henry and I doth share a common enemy in King James."

Rebecca lightens the moment, "I wish friendship with all."

"That you have, m'lady." The complement is taken quite well. He attempts, "On the topic of friends, I did loose many near your lands. Twas a time before your birth. However, might ye know of their fate? Tis rumored some may have gone to Chowanok."

The lady turns cool. "We care not for the Chowanok."

Sir Raleigh studies her. "Lovely earrings. If by chance, Master George and I might secure a visit to the Tower, I will have poor Henry lay them in silver. He much revels in such hobbies. It shall be a present from us all. But fear not the Tower. Tis a wondrous place with great cats and other strange wildlife from across the globe, and halls of great majesty with crown jewels from William the Conqueror, himself. Twas he that built that castle, and nine like others. It abounds in imperial mysteries and other such. Ah, but those ravens be the property's true owners. They have taken up residence there before any can remember."

The gentleman's gaze is lost in thought. "Me queen's own father did use that fortress for many an exploit, none pretty. Truly, a severe man was he."

Rebecca sits back with a prideful gleam. "Well, sir, he be no match for me father."

Sir Raleigh straightens. A vision of his Elizabeth clouds the eyes. "Well, doth that strike a familiar tone, and one, I wager, of no less truth."

"Sir, I would be wrong if not, as well, to gift thee." Rebecca takes up a leather pouch, decorated with beadwork that she did herself. "Twas to be for the King. Alas, I do hear he cares not for tobacco. Might thee, sir, enjoy me husband's brand?"

"I would! Admittedly, my addiction to this glorious weed is strong. To think I possess what the King has missed. I am truly honored and sincerely thankful for this generosity."

POWHATAN:
THE STORY OF A PEOPLE

At an old refectory table sit Samuel Purchus and two other clergy members. On one end of the table is Henry Spelman. On the floor in front of the table sits Utamatomakin, who is in the middle of a story. "He was a thief and accepted his punishment. I knew my duty was to send him from this world. Thieves are not for this world."

Some of the speech is omitted. Some is changed around so that the listeners can keep up with it. This has become a familiar scene for both the reverend and the seer. The two men have met several times in various churches around London.

Utamatomakin continues, "Your people came to us knowing the one who had robbed them. We were able to find him. The thief has no longer a name. He is long dead. I will not say it. But I will say his expression was that of acceptance when he descended to his knees and laid his head upon the stone. If I could not strike him clean, I should place my head upon the same rock. This is a serous matter. As I raised the *monahak,* I entered his eye. With all the strength in me, I came down hard and to the mark. Your people were satisfied with this execution."

Utamatomakin looks up at his audience. Focusing upon Reverend Purchus, "Do you perform executions?"

The reverend mumbles a few words to the interpreter. In turn, Henry gives this:

"It is not ours to take a life. They are brought before judgment in the hereafter. We do tend to give the last rights to the condemned."

Reverend Purchus voices a question. The seer answers, "No, no sacrifices. We teach. That is the purpose of Huskina…to transplant a soul of ignorance with one of understanding. They are chosen for their strength. Only the weak die. The strong live and grow. That is natural."

Utamatomakin ponders the next question, "Our healers provide care for the body. Seers tend to the *netshetsun.* We keep the knowledge of the Ancients. We tend the sacred sites, the temples, the images of the *manitow.*"

The translation is made. A charge come back, "You should not worship idols."

Utamatomakin explains, "But all things are of the Spirit Force. It is in me. It is in the rock, the tree, the flowing water, the drifting cloud. The image of Okius is an empty vessel, made for that being to concentrate within so that he can commune with mortals. Through the natural senses, everyone, from the simple minded to the one most enlightened, can recognize the spirit world…like that man hanging on his tree, on the wall behind you."

He waits for a reaction that does not come. Utamatomakin dismisses the silence. The Wind Children simply do not know their beliefs well enough. After all, John Rolfe once told him that Christianity is not their original dogma. These are exploring people. They consume so many things without fully comprehending it all.

Utamatomakin continues, "We preserve the Knowledge in our hymns and in our symbol books. We keep it alive through recitation. We communicate with the spirit world by means that the ancient ones discovered. We..."

A question interrupts him, "Do you talk to Okius?"

Utamatomakin pauses. He cannot understand their fascination with the giver of suffering. "Of course. Okius is the power of the universe, that which is dangerous. Okius has many names. He is the lightning. He is the dried river. He is the disease and the hunger. He is the force of the natural world. We must answer to him, or we will not exist. We appease him to keep ourselves safe."

The seer gets an idea. "Let me show you how to communicate with Okius."

They nod in reluctant interest.

Utamatomakin stands up. "The temple is occupied by four seers, and I am one. We start with a song of welcome." He steps lively about the room in a circular pattern, singing a verse in the ancient language that Henry does not know.

Utamatomakin considers. What if Okius comes? He leaves out a few stanzas to be safe.

"Now, eight others enter to help. Okius makes himself known by consolidating into a human form. He has a face of *matasun*, a white chest and spotted thighs, and a long black lock of hair that reaches down to his toes."

The holy men grimace. They know the hairstyle well. The single long lock that dangles down the side of the face has been popular among the fashionable in England since Namontak's visit. That cursed "Love Lock" has created such a fad to the discontent of all the clergy. Fashion is such evil to those who do not participate.

The seer continues, "Okius gives a demand or an insight, or a prophecy. We guide our people from it."

"Ah ha!" the reverend rejoices. Utamatomakin is happy to have touched the man so.

Henry relays an urgent query, "So you listen to what he says?"

"Yes," the seer responds. "Okius is right. While on the long journey to this land, Okius told me that my return to him would be longer then Captain

POWHATAN:
THE STORY OF A PEOPLE

Argall had told me. We have been told recently that our return home will, in fact, be delayed. Okius does not lie. Only your people do that."

Another question follows, "Do you give your *netshetsun* to Okius when you die, since you live for him?"

Utamatomakin is taken aback. "Okius is not one to live for, but to answer to. Life is individual…to be lived as part of the cosmic order, not for any part of it. I was granted life in this world. I am thankful to live on my mother.

"I have been told that you love and fear your god. How can you do both? Do you speak with your god to find answers? Do you listen to the words of the spirits?"

A reply is made, "We trust God's will and do not question his plan. We surely do not speak with the evil one, whom you call, Okius. We follow Jesus Christ."

Utamatomakin chides, "Jesus? The *manitow* that became a mortal, or is it the mortal who became a *manitow*? I am still confused over that. It is better to seek the light then submit to blind faith. There are mortals, immortals, and that which gives life to all. Do you not see that mortality is part of immortality? Do you know the other side? I hear you dismiss those who visit the spirits as witches, and you run from the spirits you call ghosts. How can you call yourselves seers if you always look away?"

Utamatomakin sits back down. He tries to work out the strange thoughts in his mind. These people are not comfortable with their spirituality. All they seem to do is defend it. If it were Truth, they would not need to be so defensive. Why do they think they are the only ones who are right? Their priests do not search the other side. Their study is too selective. They never listen to anything. They do not even try to listen to the meaning of their own words. All those rules to follow, why? Truth should bring a feeling of freedom. These two worlds are simply too opposite. They will never come together.

Another subject arises, "And what happens when you die?"

Utamatomakin replies, "We travel on the road to the afterworld, to Monshakwatu or Popogusu.

"We climb the tallest tree of the cloud forests. We climb to its very top. There, one finds a path that is very easy to travel. On either side grows rare fruits and herbs. Midway, one comes to an *ahakan*. The first woman is there to see all her children. Her place is always bustling with them. She cares for everyone. She always has plenty of food. Once refreshed, one runs further down the path with a strong guide through a great wilderness, until reaching a fork in the road. A flash of lightning separates the good from the bad. The good continue on a level path at right.

"Monshakwatu is a great meadow where everything is always in bloom. There is abundance of food sprouting up from the land and running upon the land. Gardens are full and game big and meaty, but gentle. The sky only darkens with clouds of birds. All the ancestors are there to dance and sing with you. All are youthful. All the women are charming, wanting only to please. They never speak a scolding word. Sickness is never present. No one grows old. But when one's time in Monshakwatu has ended, they become born into the mortal world again. That is how we see an uncle in a grandson. That is why we recognize a sister in a nephew's daughter.

"To get in, one must pass the venerable old man who sits on a mat. He examines all seekers. He determines how long one's stay will be and where one's family can be found within.

"But if you have done bad in mortal life, the lightning will scare you down the rocky, uneven path to the left. At the end of this path is a dreadful old woman sitting on a giant mushroom. Her head is covered with *ketasku*. She has gloomy white eyes that strike unspeakable terror into all that casts their view upon her. She pronounces one's sentence. The condemned is thrown to scavenging birds that carry them to the place of greatest torment.

"Popogusu is dark, dismal country where only Popano is the season. Snow covers the ground permanently. Only ice cycles hang from the trees. All are constantly hungry and sick. Everyone is old and decrepit. The women are old and ugly, with *utakaway* claws for hands. They scratch. They talk too much. Their voices are shrilled and hurt the ears.

"And in the middle of it all is the filthy, stinky lake that is constantly in flames, yet yields no heat. People are thrown into it. As they swim back to shore, they are thrown in again.

"The condemned suffer their time here to purge their badness. Then, they are allowed another chance through mortal birth."

Utamatomakin relaxes. He can see that these are people who enjoy story telling as much as any. They do possess imagination, and can be easily inspired. Perhaps they are not so hopeless after all. Although the two peoples are opposites, they are still from the same bag. The connection between these cultures must lie in the beginnings of both, when all were one.

Chapter 22

Nestled deep within the labyrinth of White Hall Palace are the private apartments of Queen Anne. Although usually active in giddy play with her maids, Anne has retired to her little haven of solitude. Lounging in her tester bed of lavish Jacobean design—its gaudiness equaling the rest of the exorbitant furnishings in the room—she peruses the latest reports of the goings on in London.

With concentrated care, the Danish queen opens her vile of arsenic. She adds just a pinch under the tongue to help preserve her porcelain-like skin. Appearance is still at the front of importance for her—especially now that the king's interest in her is waning. From clothes to cosmetics, her middle-aged majesty does everything to keep her wasp figure and boyish face.

At the top of the pile is the latest report of Rebecca Rolfe. It is of her last attendance to a reception held at Lameth Palace by the Lord Bishop of London, John King. The guest of honor was none other then Lady Rolfe. All accounts confirm the young woman was a standard of royalty. All the talk is of her regal countenance, the flawless way she carried herself, and the admiration she drew from the other guests. It was, to most witnesses, an effortless performance. Surely, this young creature of the wilds is a proven example of aristocracy.

The girl has been quite active all over town. She has attended every ball and every theatrical event on the municipality's social calendar. As for the local landmarks, Rebecca has visited just about every one. Moreover, every one who is someone has visited her.

The queen glances over the letter of introduction the Virginia Company sent. John Smith offered to write it. He has written much to promote the Virginia adventure. Although a bit self-serving, the information hits the mark on some key incidents that capture the queen's interest. She is fascinated with all the miraculous deeds of the girl whom the letter mentions. It is heroism beyond belief. A little girl, not more then a baker's dozen in years, saved Captain Smith from her own brutish father. The Captain's good brains would surely have been beaten out if not for the girl's defiant challenge.

Another episode mentioned is just as courageous. In one night's journey, this little girl traveled from two days away, just to let Captain Smith know of a deadly plot her people were planning against him. At the risk of her own death, she saved him and the good people of the colony time after time. But most important is her conversion to a Christian life. What a child! She is the embodiment of true self-sacrifice and utmost civility.

The queen almost salivates at the idea of making Rebecca a lady in waiting. To have such a celebrated young woman under one thumb would definatly place so many more under the other. She must meet this heroine from pen's birth. Anne hops out of bed. She saunters out to fetch a messenger who will officially summon Lady Rebecca to White Hall.

Days with the Queen are full of delightful merriment. Rebecca plays all the games with the other maids. She even has a few games of her own to teach them. She becomes an expert at cards. They are similar to the rush cards with which she and Matachana used to wile away a childhood afternoon or two. Rebecca finds that English cards can be used for many games. She tries to master every one.

Today, the young maid is not attending the Queen. She has been granted time alone to explore the meandering arrangement of White Hall. There she is, in a forgotten chamber that is lost amidst the innumerable corridors.

Her mind soaks up every thing it can. But her body cannot keep up. Fatigue sets in. Invisible demons infiltrate her lungs. This synthetic atmosphere is slowly paralyzing her from within.

The city is an unhealthy place for those not accustomed to it. Word has come that some of the other students that made the journey with Rebecca are dead from similar ailments. Utamatomakin says they must leave this tainted air, or it will kill her too.

Rebecca tours the row of portraits along the wall. They are of people who once stepped through these same rooms. Their presence, though weakened by time, can still be felt. She opens her inner senses to realize them.

She remembers the artist for whom she sat. He was a young man from the Netherlands, close to her age. It took such a long time to sit for him. All physical movement was disallowed while he diligently scratched away on his paper. The man just sat there, staring at her, studying her, objectifying her. His work was haphazard. He seemed unsure in his markings. It was obvious that his technique was freshly learned. There were too many facial details that hid the form and features of her personality. The portrait looks more like an old man than a young woman. She does not look Powhatan at all. The face possesses too many features of those in the artist's own country.

Another engraver will soften the image until it becomes that of an English woman. A painter will give his version color. With the addition of color, the portrait will lose accuracy and detail. Nevertheless, it will inspire yet more renditions of the same young life long after the model in gone. Such is the case with the portraits surrounding her. Though the person is long dead, their likeness has become immortal.

Rebecca thinks of her son. She thinks of the children of her people. Upon returning to Virginia, she will take on a role as a creator-mother for the children. She has gone through her own *huskina*. She can make the same transformation easier for them. The two cultures can connect through her efforts. She is, after all, a woman of exalted nature; one who possesses that quality of true leadership that is present in only the few and recognized by the many.

Rebecca does not often see her own son. At times, he is allowed into the palace to amuse the queen and enthrall the maids. John is not invited at all. He is merely a commoner. But Queen Anne does not hold in against Rebecca for marrying down. She simply ignores the fact that the girl is married at all.

Rebecca distinguishes one portrait from another. She has seen so many of their faces that she can recognize their varied features. Visions of those she knew haunt the recesses of her memory. She reviews the fragments of recollection. Some, she thinks of often, like poor Thomas Dale and the woman he had married just before coming to Virginia. Neither Rebecca nor Matachana could keep their dismay in check when they first learned of the wife's existence. They were apart for five years. No wonder the poor woman became ill. Sir Dale's social health is also failing. He has found that friends are close to non-existent when one's own wealth is deficient. What will become of him? Already, he speaks of following Christopher Newport to Asia. Both their remaining careers lie with the East India Company—perhaps even their remaining lives. And what of George Percy? He visits often, but expresses no desire to return with her. His eyes are now on the European continent where his career began.

Rebecca comes to a large mirror. A woman she can almost recognize pears back with curious attention. She runs her hand lightly along the soft silk of the red jacket. She lowers her long hands to her waist, watching the way the light plays with the gossamer white cuffs that cover half her forearms. Thin fingers glide along the thick embroidered braids on the under jacket of gold brocade. The materials feel so different. They are made to be enjoyed by touch and sight. The earrings are large teardrop pearls that stand out against the glossy richness of ebony hair that, in turn, stands out against a wide lace collar of pure white. Atop is a tall crowned hat of white *pokiyu* skin, with a gold band and a dark feathery hair ornament on one side. The girl is completely altered. The overbite is not as prominent as in her youth. But the eyes—those black pearls that move back and forth in little pools of cream—they are still her. The clothes are borrowed from Cecily West. The Lady Shirley was overjoyed to sponsor her at court. She even enjoyed her role of escort, until the position proved unneeded.

The eyes fixate on the jewelry that dangles from each ear. Her mind recalls the trip to London's Tower. A slight smile appears as Rebecca recalls her guide. What an utterly charming, utterly flirtatious man, that Raleigh. He constantly found excuses to touch her hand or stroke her hair. Such behavior must have been what captured his queen's affection—and lost it.

The visit with Henry Percy was interesting. He has grown mad from the confinement of his body and from unprepared explorations by the mind. But he was a pleasant man.

It has all been a fascinating adventure. But how will the young woman be accepted by those she left behind? Will she be shunned as Sir Henry Percy? Can she really join the two worlds? She is but one young woman, yearning to learn so much more. Her competence must be strong. Her wisdom must be sound. But is she wise? Has she learned what both worlds are really about? Can she embrace what they need to become? Time will bring the future to her. Rebecca is heartened by the fact that time is what makes a life full. There is so much more living to do. Most importantly, she knows that life is circular, which makes opposites depend on each other.

The round face of a clock down the hall disturbs her meditation. Rebecca feels so tired, but she stays with the company of her thoughts for just a little longer.

It is the Twelfth Night—the most important of a long celebratory remembrance of Jesus. This momentous occasion, when his likeness was born into the mortal world, is an event that has been cherished for over a century and a half.

The building that stands most prominent within the complex of White Hall is the great banquet hall. It is an enormous rectangular treasure box, slightly larger than the church at Henrico. The construction is mainly of stone, replacing a temporary structure set in the same place by the former monarch, Elizabeth. Large wooden doors are at the entrance to a lavishly decorated interior. All the moldings and other wall décor are gilded with silver and gold leaf. Along both lengths of the hall are not one set of benches, but stepped rows for the seating of multitudes. Three massive chandeliers hang from above, filling the space in a warm, yellow effulgence. At one end is a stage, hidden by a large drape. At the other end is the high platform for the royal spectators to sit. Between both is a long, wide carpet that is green in color and soft of texture.

The king mingles with the usual admiring subjects and visitors. He has the typical long legs of a Scotsman, as well the slight huskiness of one enjoying a pampered lifestyle. His face is at first a visage of tired boredom with soft, fleshy features. And yet, upon further study of his eyes, an onlooker may see an impatient demeanor and stern will.

Tonight's Christmas masque is similar in concept but different in the composition of the audience. Only the most important have invitations. The Spanish ambassador was not invited. When he protested, good King James disallowed many other foreign diplomats as well. Only the princess from Virginia will sit with him tonight.

The king takes his place front and center on the platform. His wife gets comfortably seated on his immediate left. At her left is their only son—at least the only one still living. Charles is feeling well tonight. He was recently appointed the Prince of Wales. The title was given him just a month ago upon his sixteenth birthday. He is now officially in line for the throne and loving his proud father even more.

King James is flanked on the right by another woman. Lady Rebecca sits in high fashion tonight in a royal gown lent her by the queen. It is an elegant costume of a fresh silver with streams of blue as light as a clear afternoon sky. Anne's daughter, Elizabeth, could not attend tonight's gala. And so, the good queen has filled the garment with her newly appointed child. To Rebecca's right is her chief escort and protector, Utamatomakin. His native dress is naturally the most colorful in the room.

The king basks in the bows and curtsies of his admiring subjects. Everyone takes special notice of the exotic young woman who matches in dignity and grace any they have seen from the Eastern of Middle Eastern kingdoms. King James takes a subtle glance toward his guest of honor. That smile of hers. It has a hypnotic affect on all the onlookers. Let Spain writhe in jealousy. Allow France to boil in envious exception. May those of Savoy, and Venice, and all the others wince in begrudging hurt. The king relaxes in his chair.

Rebecca's eyes blur from the overwhelming amount of people and décor in the hall. Her ears buzz from the verbal outpour of the audience who wait in excited anticipation for the start of the show.

The host leans toward his guest. "Me court architect, Indigo Jones, hath designed both stage and hall."

"Truly, a fine display, Your Majesty," Rebecca responds. "Quiet dazzling."

"Hum, quiet indeed." The king exhales a haughty boast, "I refused not one expense for this night."

The queen leans over with her fan to hide the two female faces. "The play is called, 'The Vision of Delight.' Understand ye a pageant, dear one?"

"Aye, Your Majesty. Alas, none have I seen shall be as wonderful as this. Tis sure to take my breath." They share a brief giggle before the man between them motions with an irritated flutter of hands.

Finally, the author of the production steps along the green carpet toward the center of the hall. Ben Johnson voices the usual introductory remarks. The audience listens with half interest, then makes the usual applause as he retraces his steps. All eyes follow him to the stage where a large painted curtain veils the contents within. The moment wears on the collective anticipation. The curtain drops.

A city in miniature is revealed. Depth is created with simple illusion by crowding the concave stage with strategically painted facades. It is not much, but it is enough to aid the imagination and visualize insignificant details that clutter reality. Like magicians, stagehands carefully swing aside their backdrops to create yet another scene. Players sing their lines and dramatize their movements in a careful orchestration. They are not people, but personified representations of aspects. Delight comes to the fore with Love and Laughter close behind. Grace and Harmony step up to their marks while Revel and Sport assume their roles. A chariot, covered with stars, somehow levitates high in the invisible depths of air—Night has risen.

POWHATAN:
THE STORY OF A PEOPLE

The earth is left for a setting among the clouds. Strange people and fascinating birds scatter about the stage. Spring explodes with legged blooms and vines. The musicians play their instruments with growing vigor as the lead dancer prances toward the center stage.

Utamatomakin watches the dancer. He sees a man of very strong physique. The body shows through his form-fitting clothes. Apparently, the Wind Children frown on public nudity. But nothing is said against sheathing their true form within revealing cloth. The dancer has arms of a swimmer and a back of an oarsman. He has sleek running legs. But why does he hop about like a little girl?

Utamatomakin observes the crowd. Everyone appears accepting of such behavior. It is graceful. He is in complete control of the movement. The seer observes the king's reaction. There is a special interest in the eyes. It is a spark of admiration, or pride, or something.

Utamatomakin whispers to Rebecca, "These Englishmen have a greater fondness for each other then they have for their women. I will never understand these people."

Rebecca does not even hear him. She is too enthralled. Time cannot be halted, but she hopes with all her might that it can at least slow down for her to cherish this evening as much as possible. The audience joins in with the players in a grand dance on the green carpet. Rebecca looks for her husband whose seat is beside the musicians. But it is not her time for dancing. She must stay put and admire the guests. Rebecca allows an uncontrolled smile. Her eyes moisten with the emergence of bittersweet joy. It is an understandable display of emotion. The king pays it no mind. The musicians play on in this hall of dreams.

Chapter 23

To improve her health, Rebecca and her family relocate farther upriver to Brentford. They find lodgings on the grounds of Sir Henry Percy's property. His brother, George, arranges everything. In her chambers, Rebecca finds the earrings that she lent Sir Henry. The thin double shells are now surrounded with delicate strands of silver. She admires the fine job. It is a good combination of two precious materials from two precious worlds. The jewelry is now perfect.

Her health improves a little with the change to better air and less hectic surroundings. She stays quiet most of the time. Visitors come less often. Some days are good, but breathing grows more difficult. Utamatomakin warns that she must return to her own world if she is ever to recuperate.

The young woman sits in a chair, overlooking the landscaped garden, enjoying her hot tea, watching little Thomas romp on the lawn. The garden is designed as if it naturally grew this way. It is how the English do it.

New visitors are escorted to her. The group's leader is a short, husky man with a big red beard. He slows his pace as she rises to greet him. The good hostess smiles as her husband makes the announcement. Rebecca does not catch the name. "…your old friend."

He takes off his hat in customary etiquette. She studies the naked head. The face is familiar. This…this is him!

Rebecca says nothing. She can only turn away. Her face twists with an agonized reaction that no one else sees. The one who was thought to be dead stands behind her. He is of the past that should be forgotten. She had long accepted his end. Now, she is confronted with the reality that John Smith still breaths.

POWHATAN:
THE STORY OF A PEOPLE

Rebecca calms her thoughts. She is a woman now, and must act her age. With gracious pleasantries, the lady turns to rejoin her former acquaintance who is in the middle of a conversation with Utamatomakin.

The seer blurts out, "I have still not met with your king."

It has been eight years, but John Smith remembers enough of the Powhatan language to understand what is said. Mr. Rolfe tries to guide the recollection. Utamatomakin thinks back on the memory in question. "Oh yes...That was him? Not impressive." He looks back at Captain Smith. "You once gave my *mamanatowik* a white dog. He fed it well, and took good care of it. Your king gave me nothing. I am better than that dog."

Memories are shared. Lighter episodes are recalled. Utamatomakin holds his usual dismissive look while the Captain develops a somewhat envious gaze at Mr. Rolfe. Rebecca trains her eyes on them all.

During the conversation, Rebecca calls her visitor, "Father," which surprises him. She does not understand his refusal to be called so. She explains, "You promised my father that what was yours shall be his. From him the same was to be for you. You called him, 'Father.' You were a stranger in his land. For the same reason, I call you, 'Father,' as I should."

The retort comes, "Dear lady, you are here a princess, as from a principality do ye come. One among the royal class should fear not to belittle an old commoner as me. Though might I forever think you a beloved daughter, I must salute a dear lady."

Rebecca does not agree. "You shall call me, 'Child.' And I will always be your friend. We two people are now one. Were you not afraid to come into my father's land? I fear you in your land. I should see you as a father." Her tone is not that of a request, but a decision. Her feminine will gives no room for any further discussion. Smith nods in delighted obedience. "And why such fear m'lady?"

"Everyone told us you were dead. That is what I knew, until I came to Plymouth. But I did not accept the new story.

"My father commanded Utamatomakin to find out the truth of your mortality, because your people tend to lie so often."

The conversation continues for a while longer. Two languages weave pieces of memory and points of view throughout the verbal intercourse. It seems so far in the past when this connection between the two was formed. With his parting, John Smith can not help but wonder if such ties will at last be severed.

A season of renewal is fast approaching. Blooms are sprouting from every stem. Warm showers feed them. The air is replenished with the sensation of new beginnings. The time to set sail is near. Three vessels: the Neptune, the George, and the Treasurer, are fitted. Crews are hired. The new colonists sign up. Samuel Argall commands the fleet. Not only is he an admiral, but also the new Deputy Governor. Once again, his ambition has rewarded him.

The lottery has been a success, thanks mostly to Lady Rebecca. She completely won over London society. She even won over the royals. Her name also spread to rural England with a trip to her husband's ancestral home in Heacham.

Admittedly, the five-day journey over the rough roads had been difficult. Rebecca loved the countryside with its small villages and peaceful landscapes. She saw every shade of green she could imagine, as well as some she never knew existed. The Rolfes instantly accepted her upon their first meeting. This was a great relief for John. He found the family manor as he had left it; a simple Tudor home of two stories with a few dormers and three chimneys. Rebecca knew that it was not a home without a *muskiminz* tree to shade it. Before leaving, she planted one in the formal garden.

The tour of England by this child of the wilderness nears its end. The barge carrying the celebrated family reaches Gravesend where the George awaits. Henry Spelman is with them. He looks forward to the journey back to Virginia. Everyone will look up to the young man, now that he is an official interpreter.

But all expectations must be put on hold. Henry assists his childhood friend who has slipped further into the illness that has nagged her since she first arrived. Matachana and little Thomas are also feeling the effects of a whooping cough. Rebecca is carried to the Christopher Inn that stands near the hithe. They manage to get a private room on the second floor of the three-story building. Utamatomakin frantically searches for the herbal ingredients he needs. He still has a good supply of bloodroot and goldenseal. He recognizes the horehound and lobelia in some of the private gardens and apothecary jars. He even accepts other plants that are highly recommended by the locals. The compound he devises helps his wife and nephew. They continue to chew on *winak* to help them along.

Utamatomakin is not a healer. He hasn't enough knowledge to mix the medicine, nor the expertise to perform the appropriate ceremonial operation on his patients. But he does know what sounds wrong. He does not allow his family to be bled. He does allow for a syrup of mallows and peach blossoms to purge them. He gathers fruits and vegetables, along with good cider, to help them regain their strength.

Rebecca's illness is too far advanced. Nothing slows her deterioration. Her lungs are too inflamed. Her fever refuses to break. She is too weak to fight it any longer.

Other guests at the inn grow apprehensive that her condition may be contagious. They grow uneasy of the grief-stricken wailing from her sister and the strange chanting from her brother-in-law. The innkeeper arranges their transfer to a friend's property at the end of a nearby street. It is a private little cottage overlooking the three vessels that wait at the hithe.

Rebecca is in a good bed with plenty of covers. Utamatomakin leans over her with a handful of burning sage. He slowly spreads the smoke over the body with his feather fan. A few gentle shakes of his gourd rattle and a few subtle words in the language of the ancients soothe her. Utamatomakin knows that death is the only cure.

Reverend Nicholas Frankwell stands near the bed to offer his aid. Matachana softly touches the small shoulder of the boy. "It is time, little darling. Let us go so that your mother may prepare for her journey."

Thomas does not move. "Let me come with you."

Mother smiles, "No, little sir. Your journey is on the water. Mine is in the sky. But I will be with you, always. I promise."

Matachana grasps the other shoulder. Thomas continues to look upon his mother's smiling eyes as he is guided from the room.

John takes his son's place at the bedside. Breath becomes more difficult. She tries not to move, but she does explore the faces of those around her. She alleviates their sorrow with her accepting smile. Faces in the room and in her memory fill her sight—all of them are so precious to have known.

The reverend bends down to whisper, "Wouldst thou call me now to give the last rights?"

She looks at Utamatomakin and nods, "Both of you."

Two hymns fill the room. English speech and Powhatan song blend into one. Each holy man touches her forehead in blessing.

John's face glistens. "I wish not to loose ye, also."

She responds, "All must die...Tis enough the child liveth."

The body slackens. The eyes darken. A happy little sprite skips along the path above the clouds.

The old parish church of St. George stands atop a gentle slope that overlooks the Themes. It is a simple rectangular building of dark masonry. A square bell tower rises above the entrance at one end. Light-colored stonework surrounds the openings. Stone quoins and a belt course are the only decoration left outside. The interior is very discreet. No longer do Catholic statutes occupy their places. Though built long ago by Saxon hands, it is now used by Anglican hearts which need only a simple cross on which to focus their devotion.

A black robe glides to the entrance gate. Reverend Frankwell watches the small procession slowly ascend Chapel Lane. The dark procession consists of a good number of colonists that are bound for Virginia and a few of the town's folk who were touched by the one, now lost. Their number is enough to fill the pews for the service. All entwine into the cortege of shared sadness as they file up the little street.

"Welcome, my children." The reverend shows them the way. "I bid thee welcome, my brother," he motions to Utamatomakin.

The world is left at the door upon entering. Candles burn in the hall. The light of day filters in through the windows to help illuminate the dim interior. The men make their seating choices on the left, while the women find suitable places on the right. The coffin is gently placed beside the hole in the stone floor. Hollow echoes of quiet attendance fill the air.

John sits with little Thomas. On the lady's side is Matachana, surrounded by a host of strangers whom she recognizes only through the connection of the human spirit. She is very quiet today. She is too weak from to properly grieve for her sister. The tears that glide down her blackened cheeks will be her only expression. Her husband places his red hand on the box. His black hand steadies the body from behind as he descends to the floor. He sprinkles a few bits of *upook* atop the box.

Holding firm the rattle, he waits patiently for the reverend who takes his position at the podium. "Now, shall I read from our sacred book of prayer." Reverend Frankwell sheds a slight smile to his counterpart. "Twas a favorite read, I hear, of our dearly departed." The suitable prayers are recited.

Matachana takes her mind through a parade of memories of when her sister was with her. The two shared so many wonderful occasions as they matured together. She can not fix on any particular one. They all seem equally special to her now.

POWHATAN:
THE STORY OF A PEOPLE

On the other side of the aisle sits Henry Spelman, quietly recalling his own childhood memories of the one who was like a sister to him. Returning to Virginia does not seem as exciting anymore.

John thinks of the present reality he endures. He must make a decision on what to do with little Thomas. Everyone tells him that the boy must remain. The journey may be too much for his weakened state. John must allow the boy to grow in the arms of the father's family, rather than the mother's.

Admiral Argall's thoughts wander through the church interior. His eyes fix on the light beyond the window. His mind roams into the future; to the mission that he shall soon begin. He is certain there are great opportunities ahead.

The ceremony ends. Church attendants carefully lower the box into the vault. Utamatomakin shakes his gourd rattle to an appropriate melody and sings the proper farewell to his lost relation. The crowd slowly disperses.

Reverend Frankwell wishes good departure to those who return to the hithe. Two tolls from the bell tower resound, followed by twenty one more.

The new addition is placed among the silent community of the entombed. Stone masons replace the slab in the floor. A pair of alter boys extinguish the wicks before closing up the building. The minister takes one last look down the hillside before closing the gate and retiring to his private chambers.

Sitting at his desk, Reverend Frankwell pulls open the leather cover of the old church register. He gently flips through the parchments, perusing the ancient markings made through the years. He admires the text. It is a vehicle for the eternal community to yet speak with the living through the ever growing barrier of time.

With pen dipped and the tip angled forty five degrees, he scratches the introduction for the silent community's newest member. He notices the waning sun through the window beside his desk. It is time to retire for the evening.

Chapter 24

The incision slowly opens along the back. Skin peels off so that the organs and muscle tissue can be taken from the bones. Everything is carefully packed into baskets. The seven high priests work on the dead. Each knows the steps to be taken to prepare their lost *mamanatowik* for his final journey. The progression of days takes only a moment to realize. The priests croon long stanzas of ancient poetry to guide them through every task.

They rub oil into the skin and generously apply gum all over to keep it supple and moist. They lay the skeleton upon a scaffold to dry until it is pure white. Only the sinews that attach one bone to another are left on the frame.

The clean skeleton is returned into the skin. White sand fills the mass. A few favorite trinkets and a number of choice articles are stuffed into the body. The four-sided bottle that Captain Newport gave him finds a place within the rib cage. Hands raise and lower as the skin is sewn up tight. Fingers flurry as bracelets, anklets, necklaces, and other decorative chains are tied on at every joint.

Freshly tanned skins are wrapped around the body. The priests roll up all of this in decorative mats and lay it with the others upon the racks in the ossuary of the great temple. Images of personal spirits are set up to guard his material self that remains here in reality. The special fire is tended to by the head priest. Baskets filled with riches sparkle from the light of the flames. Other containers filled with charred bones of captives crowd the space before the ossuary.

Like the flame, a life leaves this world. Everyday moments pass into memory. The memories of a life lived long or short will dissipate in the depths of time. Such occurrences are nothing more then flashpoints in the collective mind that ever focuses on tomorrow.

POWHATAN:
THE STORY OF A PEOPLE

Perched on the old *muskiminz* tree outside is the little bird with a large repertoire of beautiful songs to serenade the rising moon. It is a long, narrow bird of a tawny-grey color. A patch of white flashes as it stretches each wing. It captures the attention of the priests by chirping, "Pokowanz. Pokowanz. Pokowanz. Pokowanz."

The little bird carries the *netshetsun* of Wahunsenakok into the sky. He will climb a tall tree to a bridge that leads far beyond the mountains and the setting sun. He will remain there, a full deity, with head painted in brilliant *pokun* and shoulders draped with a fine *kawasow*. The best jewelry will adorn him. He will sit on a high bed of *upook*. He will sing with his predecessors until the time is right once again for a mortal birth.

Henry Spelman sits alone in the crowded church. He is alone because he is the accused. Governor Yeardley leads those who will pass judgment. Henry finds this a bit unfair because it is Sir Yeardley who is making the accusation. It is a simple charge. The Governor claims that Henry has sided with the naturals.

Henry shakes his head, knowing he has done nothing wrong. He has weathered worse times then this. One would say he is growing into his own. Henry has become lean and tall. His face has lost all baby fat. It is now smooth and cut, with a clear jaw line and sharp eyes.

Henry knows Governor Yeardley is just trying to establish his authority. Thus far, it has been a great struggle. The blame lies fully on Samuel Argall. He is the cause of all the disorder. That man is nothing more then a simple pirate.

Corrupting the colony was not enough. Isolating it from its neighbors was not enough. Governor Argall had to scorn the Chikahominy as well. The very man who confirmed the treaty with them was the one to cast it aside as if it were something insignificant. It is doubtful that they will ever trust the English again.

Naturally, the pirate absconded before he could be arrested. Some are destined to avoid the consequences of their wrong doings. Henry knows many such men. One sold him to the Indigenies, after all.

Henry notices Francis West in the crowd. His elder brother, Thomas, was lost earlier in the year. Along with a number of others on board, poor Lord Delaware succumbed to sickness before the vessel could reach Virginia. Francis is now alone to protect his family's interests in the colony. It is more then one man can handle. Fortunately, he can now rely on the help of his younger brother, John.

Henry looks back at Governor Yeardley. He is a man of usual stature, with soft facial features. The eyes are not very large, not very fearless, and not all together tireless in their gaze. But when an opportunity arises, they can blaze challengingly enough. Sir Yeardley has worked hard in returning order to the colony but has done nothing to fix things with the naturals.

Virginia is changing at a rapid pace. So many new people have come this year alone. Henry thinks back on the Tiger's arrival. He was among the bright-eyed young men who witnessed those wonderful passengers debark. They were all women! They all were agreeable and healthy and ready to make a family.

Then, the others arrived. They came in a Dutch man-of-war. The Treasure was escorting it to Jamestown when the two vessels were separated at sea. They met up in the Caribbean and captured a Spanish frigate together. What they found on board was neither gold nor silver. Instead, the cargo consisted of Africans, bound for slave labor in the Spanish colonies.

Henry can not imagine such an existence. He tries not to. Their journey was far more difficult than any of the colonists had endured. One hundred people were chained in place within the dank bowels of the hold for days on end. They were preserved for the duration with the most meager of rations. They could not share meals or enjoy social interaction. There was no privacy or sanitation. All the simplest luxuries that define humanity were unobtainable throughout their long journey. Prisons are known to be like this. Henry does not want to be in one of those either. He would rather be wild and free, then reduced to animalistic confinement.

The Dutch vessel carried only twenty or so who had survived. Henry was at the pier when they came ashore. He can still picture them. Both the men and the women expressed the same mix of relief from the past, fear of the present, and hope for the future. All where happy to see the sun; to feel the earth under their feet.

Governor Yeardley accepted most of them to work off indentures on his lands. They were quite happy about it. Finally, their humanity had been restored. The lesser sort in the colony where happy too. Finally, there would be a class of people around that they could consider lower then themselves.

The trial is not long for it is not a real trial, but a civic condemnation. The first general assembly of the colony's leadership is winding up their business.

POWHATAN:
THE STORY OF A PEOPLE

It is a form of representative government, not unlike that of the Chikahominy. Finally, the colony will be governed like a real society.

The censure continues without Henry's attention. Why should he participate? They have already made up their minds about him. Sir Yeardley lectures on at the podium as the delegates sneer from the choir. Once the sinner has been fully chastised, they take away his position as Colony Interpreter.

Henry glances at Tom Savage who has done nothing to defend him. Tom has abandoned him as he did once before in the wilderness. But that is alright. Henry knows these people will eventually turn on him, as well. Then, Tom will also find himself an outcaste.

Opechankano turns the key. The metal box clicks shut. He turns it again. It opens once more. The result never disappoints him. He pushes the door open. He pulls the door shut for another try. A toothy grin spreads across his wrinkled face. George Thorpe stands nearby in proud observance.

It is a quaint little cottage of English design, not too dissimilar to that which now lies in ruins at old Weyowakomako. The new house is for Opechankano. It stands in the peaceful forest near Menapukunt. Reverend Thorp had it built for the old warrior king. Governor Yeardley's hard-handed ways has gotten nowhere with the naturals. George knows that a gentle approach works best. All that is required is sweet dialog and the Lord's grace.

George uses this tactic often. When his converts are mistreated, he punishes the aggressors. This only wins him more converts. Once, he even killed some dogs when they scared the timid naturals. Opichapan is their new leader. But the English know Opechankano better. He is more available. He is more influential. Reverend Thorpe is grateful for the old man's cooperation in recruiting native children for his school—if only George can find a way to retain them. At least he is close to converting Opechankano. Their conversations have grown more intimate. The old heathen has even admitted, in so many words, that none of his gods are as good as the one true God. George smiles uncontrollably.

Opechankano plays with the window shutters, swinging them together and flipping the metal hook to fasten them shut. With the same authority, he flips the hook away and swings them back open. He can never get enough enjoyment out of the wonderful gadgets the Wind Children can make. It is their only good quality. There are so many of them now—as many as the Pamunkey. Unlike everybody else, they do not settle in one place. English communities have rooted all along the major rivers throughout the core of Tsenakomako, pushing his own people further inland. All the fish, all the crop land, all the riches that could be used for trade has been taken away. No one has enough to eat.

Okius only made things worse. The *manitow* brought a drought on the land, a plague on the *wushakwun* population, and sickness to the people. The demise of Wahunsenakok was truly befitting a half-god. Relations with the English are so strained since his death. The Wind Children only use the peace to serve their own advances. They care nothing about mutual responsibilities. Everything seems so different. Opechankano feels out of place in this world.

Opechankano observes Reverend Thorpe as he tours the interior. The two are alone. Neither understands the other's language. They simply do without talking today. George has a good-natured quality about him. Along with the college lands, he oversees Berkeley Hundred. Governor Yeardley planted this settlement in the middle of the West Family lands. Francis complained to no avail. The plantation was established by thirty five men under the leadership of Captain Woodleefe, who later proved unworthy. According to their charter, the Berkeley group's first activity was a salute of thanksgiving for delivering them to this world. It is a good observance that Reverend Thorpe has continued as an annual event—the first of its kind in all of Virginia.

Opechankano is not impressed with these Christian things. He feels the strangers worry too much about the propagation of their religion when they should just focus on the enrichment of the spirit. However, George is a seer, and thus deserving of respect. There seems to be no harm in humoring the man.

Old Kekwatog peers out into the evening. Snow covers everything. The cold wind dusts powder from tree limbs to rest upon the ground. The air is icy, but it feels refreshing on his face. He ventures out, taking a moment to escape the confines of the family lodge.

Both hands grasp a small gourd filled with *pikuw*. He hurls large drops of the syrup into the freezing air. The crystals harden before they sprinkle onto the ground. Kekwatog wonders if he will ever see warmer times again.

Attention draws to the little holes in the snow. Slowly, he bends down and pulls out a brown crystal from each pock. Kekwatog jiggles them about in his hand. The glimmer dances in his eyes. His hand is gnarled from age. The skin is tough and cracked.

POWHATAN:
THE STORY OF A PEOPLE

Kekwatog turns back to the entrance of the lodge. He pulls the flap aside. The heat from within almost burns him. The light almost blinds him. The chatter of familial voices lightens his heart. Mothers are busy with the children at the cooking pit where *pawkawn* and *opominz* roast above the flames. Everyone's attention is fixated on the last remaining explosions of *poketawas* that simmer in the gourd dangling over the pit. Upon entering, the old man catches their attention with a whistle as he holds out the little brown jewels. Joyous screams burst from young throats as small hands stretch out to receive their share.

Kekwatog stations himself at his spot in the family circle. A little one cries out, "Tell us a story!"

The old man shyly lets go a grin as he scoops up some popped kernels from the gourd. Another little voice echoes, "Please? It's so cold and dark out. We won't be sleepy for a long time."

"What story should I give you tonight?" Kekwatog muses. "A tale of heroes or *manitow?*"

Tonight's reply is, "Heroes!"

"Alright, I will tell you about a hero…but not of one from long ago." All eyes from the very young to the young at heart widen as the circle draws close around the fire. His audience ready, the old man begins this story:

"Munetut was a great man; a fierce defender of Tsenakomako. He was aggressive against the Monakan. He always challenged the English. He was flamboyant. He was brave. He was a real leader.

"This youthful hero adorned his strong shoulders with a short *kawasow* of the largest white feathers. He always had a quiver full of arrows. He was successful in every raid carried out against the intruders from the great wilderness in the west, and those from the Great Blue in the east.

"Once, the long peace between the Powhatan and the English was threatened when they returned to stealing our land. Did the two tired old brothers do anything? No. Trespassing went unchecked until Munetut raided the intruders and stole many of their weapons. As every hero will do, he gave final insult to his *maskapow* by showing up amongst them, demanding they fix the broken weapons he had stolen.

"Munetut was not afraid of the *pakusak*. He was immune to their flying lead. Such things could not hurt him, because he could move faster.

"Once, Tsenakomako was attacked by Monakan warriors. They killed our women! To retaliate, the two tired brothers brought up the old idea of a combined strike on Machimko. They chose Munetut to deliver the message to the leader called, Yeardley. Naturally, the English liked the idea of joining the raid and filling their watercraft with food and their school with captured children. Naturally, the English did not go beyond dreaming. Munetut asked for just sixteen soldiers with their thunder weapons to join him. He was willing to settle for just twelve of such men. The English did not even send one. And so, Munetut went on a raid with only his warriors. And he was victorious.

"The children of the Mother rallied behind their hero. His influence spread. Constantly, Munetut terrorized the countryside. Everywhere, the English would scream, 'Here comes Jack of the Feather! Run! Run away before he catches you!'

"It was a beautiful day when Munetut coaxed a man, named Morgan, from his settlement to go hunting. But this was a trick. Morgan became the trophy. Then, our hero forgot to think. Munetut placed the hat of his victim upon his own head and pranced back into the settlement to show off. The English do not understand this form of teasing. They see a challenge in such acts, worthy of retaliation. They would rather further violence then accept the insult and patiently wait for the next game of revenge to be played.

"Two men recognized the hat. Munetut soon realized he was in danger. He put air under his feet. But his flight of foot was too slow. The thunder of *pakusak* sounded behind him. The bullets rushed closer. Munetut knew that he had to go faster. The feathers of his cloak suddenly spread down his arms. His legs shrunk. Munetut grew into a *wopusok* and flew away. That is the story of Munetut, the one who was master of the land and the sky."

The children are happy. The mothers are content. Kekwatog does not bother admitting that the bullets actually caught their hero. And as he lay prostrate on the ground, he begged his foe to bury him in their graveyard, so that his people might not learn the truth.

Chapter 25

Good Friday arrives one cold morning. At Berkeley Hundred, George Thorpe watches his good people. Wives flurry about their fenced yards while husbands toil over their food and cash crops in the fields. A few make products to sell while some create furnishings for the home. Others are at the distillery to begin the day's production of the plantation's original brand of squeezed corn spirits.

Master Thorp comes to the edge of the field nearest the river road. A young servant is at his side. The air is crisp. The sun rustles behind its blankets of cloud cover.

Taking a breath from his pipe, George bends down and gathers loose dirt between his fingers. He thinks of John Rolfe. The sad news is all over the colony. Poor Master Rolfe recently passed away, due to an acute illness. If it were not for his success with tobacco, the colony might not have prospered.

The servant spots incoming visitors. They appear to be Weyanok men. Knowing he is well loved by these children of the wilds, Master Thorp steps forward to greet them. Field workers call out warnings. George motions back in disapproval. He will surely punish them later. He turns back to the group of visitors who come closer. They are in festive colors, perhaps in respect this holy day.

George is startled when the boy at his side makes a quick retreat. Such rude behavior! There is nothing that can be done about it now. The host welcomes his guests, "Ah, good children, what news from my friend, Apichankanu?"

One picks up a scythe abandoned in the field. George reaches out to receive it. Only when the blade is thrust through his chest does poor George Thorpe realize this is not a peaceful visit after all. The warriors dance around the wide-eyed corpse. They take turns in striking it, cutting it open, tearing it apart in order to harm the very soul within. This is definitely the worst thing one human can do to another.

It is only a piece of glass, half-buried in the ground. The green glint catches his eye as he walks along the path. Plucking it from the earth, he rolls the thick shard carefully in his hand. It is just a small chunk from a bottle, but it transports his thoughts back to earlier days when he was a glassmaker's apprentice. Once a naive youth from Poland, he has grown into an experienced tenant farmer at West and Shirley Hundred. Hopes no longer rest on mastering a craft, but on acquiring land of his own Perhaps he can even become a family man. Just across the river at Bermuda Hundred is a woman who has expressed interest in sharing these dreams.

He descends the depression in the bank toward the boat landing. At the sandy beach are a couple of men who ready some products to be sent out. A small flotilla suddenly comes into view. Each craft is filled with distraught people. His fiancée is one of them. None have much to say. They can only cry out, "Apamatuk! Apamatuk!"

The group streams up the landing slope. As they near the small cluster of buildings, they notice the painful sight across the river. The south bank is nothing but a wall of smoke. A sharp clap of flames echo against the trees and buildings around them.

The overseer, Isaac Madison, seizes control of the situation. He arms the men with every available weapon and any sharp tool that can be found. The defenders take positions behind the low fences and at the windows of buildings around the periphery.

Weyanok warriors come along the edge of the forest. Once, they lived here. Their principal town was on this very spot. Memories of that time still haunt the area. Their homecoming is discouraged by the current residents. Slowly, the Weyanok fade away into the wilderness.

Survivors from Berkeley Hundred eventually reach the plantation. A few from Henrico manage to float downriver with news of the western settlements. The Powhatan and the Awohatek have also joined this uprising.

Step back for a moment. This day must start anew in order to understand these actions more fully. Go back to the beginning of the day, before the sunrise, to discover what unfolds elsewhere.

Winds jostle the surface of the Powhatan River. Richard Pace struggles to reach Jamestown Island. He has to start well upriver to maneuver his small craft to the opposite side. He carries only the information he received from a native boy whose older brother tried to convince him to kill Master Pace. The boy could not do it. He thinks of the man as a second father. Instead, he told Richard everything.

The sun has not yet risen, and neither has anyone on the island. Richard walks up the silent street to wake up Governor Wyatt. The two race back down the street toward the fort.

It is not long before the alarm bells toll from the church. People race to the old fortifications. Mayhem takes hold. The older and younger sort are hurled into carts and pushed along. Babes squeal in their mothers' tight grip. Men file through the arsenal before taking their places along the walls.

The wait is excruciatingly long. The landscape is too peaceful. Could they be mistaken? Some point to black clouds hovering low in the distant sky. False sightings stir the torrent of emotion. Powder is wasted on phantom targets.

Some movement is detected in the trees. Arrows, with flaming tips, soar toward the fortifications. Some houses at the farthest end of town are set ablaze. A few more shots ring out in response. Nothing else can be done at Jamestown. Reluctantly, the Chikahominy return to the mainland.

Word travels back across the river, reaching Flowerdieu hundred. The windmill at the point does not churn. The warehouses are silent. The tobacco barns stand vacant. The usual clang does not resonate from the workshop or the forge. There is no attention focused on George Yeardley's pristine manor house. Women draw water from the well in the wooden fort that stretches along the western edge of this little neck of land. Their movements are hurried as they fill several buckets. Artillerymen prepare their ordinance within its earthen rampart. The militia assembles along the worm fence that stretches across the southern edge of the settlement. Young and old, black and white gather together along the fence.

A contingent of warriors make their presence known with a volley of arrows. It is answered with a volley of shot. Both varieties of projectiles are sporadically exchanged throughout the morning. Warriors sneak through the swampy eastern edge of the little peninsula. Some manage to get around to the rear of the militia. Six defenders die before the attackers can be pushed back into the wilderness. The difficult fight eventually ends in the peace of the afternoon.

In his home near the mouth of the Powhatan River sits Master Thomas Hamor, bent over his writing table. Slowly, he descends into deep concentration to where the words staining the page is his entire world. He is disturbed by a group of Wayaskoyak men who bring a message from their *weyowanz*. The tribe is very small now. It was never strong. They live much farther inland—long displaced by English settlements.

The visitors announce an invitation to join their leader in a hunt. Thomas sends a message to see if his brother, Ralph, could join them. He returns to his writing, leaving the naturals to wait alone outside.

The Wayaskoyak loiter impatiently. Some watch the half dozen workers in the field nearby.

Thomas is again disturbed by the naturals who warn him of a tobacco barn on fire. He jumps to the window and calls the workmen to go and put out the blaze. It is a simple thing that needs not his personal involvement.

The workmen rush toward the smoke with the naturals following close behind. One by one, a man's back feels the sharp pain of an arrow head burrowing deep into the body. Soon, all six men lie on the ground, helplessly waiting for a *monahak* to crush their brittle skulls.

The victors look about to see if anyone noticed them. Gingerly, they step back toward the main house.

Thomas signs his letter. He rises from the table and ventures outside to see if word from his brother has come. He sees empty fields. No one has returned from the barn. A spire of smoke rises above the trees down the lane. His steps are few in number before Thomas also feels a sharp pain in the back. His legs give way for only a moment. Fear carries him back to the house where he slams the doors shut.

Thomas calls out for anyone who can hear him. He has no time for his wound. The arrow has to stay where it is. The table is not heavy, but it does take some time to push and pull the cumbersome thing against the door. Some women and children rush in through the back entrance. They follow his lead by blocking the windows with other household items.

Frightful screeches flood the interior. It swells to unbearable intensity after someone smells smoke coming from the roof. Flames ripple in through every crack and crevice. Thomas can not stand it any longer. Weakness brings him down into the arms of two women who try to look after to his wound. Pain spreads through the nerves. Thomas can not see much around him, but he does notice a boy raising the musket barrel. The piece is already loaded. The boy levels it at no particular thing and unleashes the dreadful thunder.

The interior is consumed by silence. Someone moves. Another does also. Barricades are swept aside. Coughing, staggering, everyone breaks out into the open. They prepare for strong hands to grab them, but they find no one around.

The invitation reaches Captain Hamor at his house near the James River. He accepts the offer and assembles his helpers.

On the trail, he notices strange movements by solid shadows in the forest. They creep and crawl through the brush. They dart from one trunk to another. Ralph leaves the trail and begins to mimic this maneuvering. One group moves. The other matches it. One chases. The other chases. Ralph backtracks until he comes to the site of his new house, still halfway completed. The men search the construction sight for spades, axes, and even brickbats to use as weapons.

Arrows fly. Warriors infiltrate the defenses. They are beaten back. The hand-to-hand fighting drags on until six musketeers come up from a vessel in the river.

Captain Hamor ventures into the interior, collecting more muskets and fighters as he goes. Finally, he finds Thomas and his group at the Baldwin settlement. Stories are shared. Fears are comforted. The decision is made to remove everyone to safety at Jamestown.

Look elsewhere. What has happened to others during this day? A craving grows from each killing. All the rage that has lain dormant in the children of this land explodes against the colony. A rite of passage, from victim to aggressor, is celebrated with an unrestrained outpouring of impassioned hatred. The frenzy builds until none are in control of their actions. Vengeance rules the minds of all.

Nathanial Powell finds himself surrounded by three men who nurse boyhood memories of what he did to Wowinchopunk. They separate him from his pregnant wife. Her body is torn apart while he watches. Captain Powell unsheathes the blade that had twice pierced the Paspaheg leader. He pivots about as the three men surround him. Nathanial's reflexes are not as sharp as in earlier days. The weapon is easily taken from him. Within no time, the captain finds himself flat on the ground with one man sitting upon his chest, holding down his arms with strong legs. The blade pushes into the throat. Nathanial can do nothing about it. Slowly, the head breaks free from its trunk.

He can not concentrate. Who is he? Where is he? This is not England. This is a strange situation, far from the world he once understood. Alone, amidst the ruins of Martin's Hundred, he peers out the hole in the back wall of what appears to be his home. It is nothing more then a broken shell—the roof is burnt away and the walls are shattered. The world outside is covered by smoke. There are ruins everywhere. Holding a butcher's knife close to the chest, he cautiously steps outside. Part of the church near the bank of the river is standing, unblemished by the flames. He can see another structure that is also intact. Carcasses are strewn throughout the yard. Some are animal and some are human. He can not distinguish what others may be. The remains of his best friend are nearby. There are no arms, nor legs, nor head. All that is left is the charred torso which is fused to a post in the ground.

A pop resounds from the fort behind him. Somehow, he has to join the rest of the survivors there. He listens. He looks about. He takes a few steps along the back of the house. He nears the end. All that he needs to do now is turn the corner and run as fast as possible to reach the fort. He listens carefully. He takes one last look at his surroundings before turning the corner.

The point of a hoe comes down beside his nose, just above the right eye. He falls. The assailant props up the body so that the shoulders rest against his knees. A reed blade slices into the left side of the upper forehead until it scrapes the skull.

Hot blood spits out. This one is still alive. The warrior works fast, pulling the blade across and ripping the scalp off. The man slumps forward. He almost regains his senses before the death blow goes deep into the back of the head.

On the outer reaches of the settlement, near the water's edge, is a woman crawling on the ground. She is naked, except for the hair wire that is entangled in her thick red locks on the right side of her head. She still has her scalp. There is a deep cut in the small of her back. She is sure it is her fault. Why did she have to resist them so?

Her man is no where to be seen—neither is the child. Perhaps she should look for them. The bodies of two other women lie nearby. One has the key to the trunk in her pocket. She needs that. The tin cookie cutters are in the trunk. Her boy will be upset if she looses them. She needs to get over to her friends and get the key. The three women have been together since boarding the Tiger

POWHATAN:
THE STORY OF A PEOPLE

and traveling across the treacherous waters. They thought it was an opportunity; a new life. She buries her head in the earth. Why did she have to act on such foolish dreams?

She crawls toward a ravine. No one takes notice of her. Just on the other side of the thicket is the main settlement. A pop sounds from the fort. Others are still alive. There is a sound of men behind her. The underbrush looks dense. She rolls into a hidden gully within.

As she curls up on her right side, the world behind her fades away. It is so cold. Darkness thickens around her. She closes her eyes, leaving everything behind.

Chapter 26

Captain Spelman stands at the bow of his small watercraft, the Elizabeth, as it pushes up the Patawomik River. He managed to pass through the land of the Piskataway without incident. It will not be much longer before entering the Anakostan territory. Henry watches the banks carefully. The river is quiet. It is well into *Katapewuk*. The tribe should be back together by now. There is no sign of anyone on the land.

Water churns against the prow. Henry thinks back on the turbulent year. The attack of the first day alone took a quarter of the colony. Starvation has run rampant throughout the land. Instead of tending crops, the two sides fought each other throughout the warm seasons.

The colony is counting on this trade mission. Henry is confident. He should achieve the same success as he had last year with the people of Wikokomiko. It was rumored the tribe had sided with the Powhatan. Henry went to change their minds. That was easy. He reminded them of their love for John Smith while he passed out glittering tools and jewelry. Henry shakes his head. A soft grumble escapes, "They should have sent me to Patawomik."

A couple of the men take notice. They soon realize the conversation their leader is having is for no one but himself. Half of it is in English, the other half is in that garble the naturals regurgitate. Henry understands himself just fine. "Raleigh Crashaw didn't know the Patawomik. That's why he failed. They're too independent…too strong."

While Opechankano demanded they kill Captain Crashaw, the Englishman kept pressuring them to abandon the Powhatan. The Patawomik did what Henry expected. After two days of deliberation, they decided to say no to both demands.

POWHATAN:
THE STORY OF A PEOPLE

"And that Poole...he's no interpreter. Nothing more then a rumormonger. He's the reason the North Country is in such a mess. They should never have replaced me with him."

The crew discover a *muz* along the riverbank. Its broad antlers have not yet grown for the year, but it should happen soon. It is easy to understand why the Indigenies see a resemblance between this animal and a horse. Both have long faces. Both are about the same size. However, the *muz* stands on much longer legs, and the hairy beast is much less to look at. It is so big. Everything is so much bigger in the northern reaches of the bay region. Henry tries to remember what the locals call the larger breed of *wushakwun* that is so prevalent in this area. The name escapes him for the moment.

The little vessel moves along at a good speed. The problems at Patawomik return to Henry's concentration. The main issue was that Raleigh Crashaw was untrusting, and his main go-between was untrustworthy. Instead of opening his arms, the captain isolated himself from his hosts.

Henry releases a long sigh. The crew look around to see if he has spotted something. Their curiosity is not strong. They pay him no more attention. Henry is too deep within his thoughts to pay any attention to them.

He remembers the raid. It was Ralph Hamor's idea. He felt that a joint venture would be good to strengthen relations. Volunteers from both cultures went upriver against the Piscataway. The allies pillaged a bounty of food for both their hungry peoples.

Isaac Madison came toward the end of the year to help protect the Patawomik harvest. "Ah, Captain Madison...even worse for matters." Henry shuffles his feet in irritation.

As the reinforcements settled down at Patawomik, a message from Mrs. Boyce found its way to them. It spoke of the score of English still held by the Powhatan. Captain Crashaw felt he needed to personally deliver the information to Jamestown and help plan the captives' retrieval. This left Captain Madison among people he didn't understand. "At least Crashaw was patient. At least he was, in a way, optimistic." Henry shakes his head.

The vessel turns quickly to avoid a log floating downstream. Henry almost loses his balance. He remembers the day when the Patawomik *weyowanz*, his two chief councilors, and his son were brought to Jamestown in irons. "Oh, what was Madison thinking? Trying to suppress a tribe already willing to be peaceful with us...at least wiser heads prevailed and the prisoners where soon sent free. How on earth can anyone like us when they get such mixed behavior?"

A slight smile stretches across Henry's face. He knows that stopping at Patawomik helped return relations back to normal. But it was not enough. The Patawomik still had no food to offer—not even to him.

Henry refused to participate in another raid against the Piskataway. He knows that, if the colony is to have any chance, the northern lands must live in peaceful co-existence. His gaze rests on the river. "John Smith did it. And that man didn't even like these people. I'm sure I can do better."

The vessel turns into the confluence of the Anakostan River. The tribe's principle town should be just up the southeastern bank. Henry looks for the landing site he knows is near.

There is no sound or sight of human activity anywhere. Henry gives the order to drop anchor near a sand bar. The path that bends up into the woods shows recent wear. Henry whispers, "Someone must be in the town."

Captain Spelman instructs the men to take the trade goods ashore. He leads all twenty-one members of his company up the trail, leaving the five mariners in the *kekwiyos*. The walk is not rushed. Henry is content. He is home.

The crew finish a few tasks before settling down. The river is very peaceful here. Water ripples freely around them as thin clouds swirl in the sky above.

A heavy knock sounds along one side of the hull. Hands slap the gunwale. Painted men leap onto the deck. Bodies collide against one another. The melee grows in desperation. A sailor fires his weapon wildly. The assailants leap overboard as quickly as they came. They swim to shore, abandoning their *akwintan* all together.

The shipmates check on each other to find none seriously hurt. They watch the shore. They wait. A long, lowly wail comes from the dark tree line along the bank. Something round—something familiar but out of context—catches their attention. It rolls down the bank and into the water. Spelman's head bobs on the surface for only a moment before sinking into the cold depths. Thin ripples spread out toward them, gently kissing the hull before dissolving away.

Opechankano waits for his visitors to arrive. He sits with his old friend, Otahotin. The Chiskiyak *weyowanz* stays near him quite often these days. Most in Tsenakomako have huddled closer together for mutual support. Everyone is tired of this constant fighting. The Nansemund were hit hard

POWHATAN:
THE STORY OF A PEOPLE

again. Yeardley lead a campaign against them that was reminiscent of Sir Dale. The harvest on the south side of the Powhatan River is ruined.

Opechankano looks over the scene to be sure everything is set. The last time the English came, he had to orchestrate a delaying action of words so that his people could get what little food they had out of town. Warriors then burned their own *ahakan* to deprive the English of the satisfaction. The soldiers followed them into the woods where they were ambushed and finally run off.

Captain William Tucker arrives with his associates. Opechankano greets them, "*Wingapow, Wingapow*! Come in welcome."

Otahotin rises and points to the row of empty mats. The visitors take their designated places. Women step out with the food. It is not as much as once was offered, but it is more than what can be given.

When the meal is complete, *upook* is passed around and speeches commence. Otahotin goes first. A few others follow. Opechankano sums up everything, "You have heard our stories. We both have suffered this past year. If we continue to fight each other, neither will survive. We must live together. Now, we can leave everything behind us. I have the hostages. You may take them with you, if you have the ransom."

Captain Tucker nods in the affirmative. He motions one of his men to lay out the payment goods. Everything seems to be here. Opechankano turns slightly around and waives an arm. The hostages are escorted out. Some bolt toward their people with uncontrolled joy. Others take their time. The rest express the full range of emotion between these extremes.

The freed English go to the river while Captain Tucker pulls out two bottles of sack. His interpreter mentions, "We can celebrate this new peace with a toast." Opechankano agrees. Glasses are passed around and the fiery liquid is poured. After the captain voices a few words, the glasses are turned up.

Opechankano rises. "This is how it should be. We should respect each other. It is how civilized people act…"

Otahotin moans uncontrollably. Opechankano glares back at him. "Your poor digestion is ruining this." He tries to continue. "I have seen many of you. I have known you all since you first came into my land. But this land is not really mine. It is not yours. We should be able to share it…"

There are more sounds of discomfort. "Well, I…"

The pain is too much to resist. Opechankano doubles over. Vision is indistinct, but he can tell the English are rising. He focuses on the shinny object lying before him. It is the glass that he used. He remembers now. The English poured their drink from a different bottle.

A thunder rumbles in his head. The atmosphere darkens with grey smoke. Bodies rush all around him. Everything becomes a blur. Opechankano falls into a sea of colors and lights. He cannot hold himself together within the whirlwind that has engulfed his being. There is nothing to hold on to. There is nothing to hold with. The mind is separated from the body to swirl in a maelstrom of ether until the calm of unconsciousness finally takes him.

Opichapan sits high on his carrier, surveying the field of battle. The sun pours its harmful rays upon the dry meadow. Only a few trees dot the outer edges to provide relieving shade. Hundreds gather around him. Every available fighting man in Pamunkey has honored the call.

The *maskapow* are seen gathering near the riverfront. *Poketawas* stand tall in nearby fields. More grows here then ever before. The large production is to make up for all the lost crops in Tsenakomako. The Pamunkey have promised to provide for all their people. But first, they must protect the food from those sworn to find and destroy it.

Opichapan adjusts the feather crown atop his head. It is the same that his eldest brother wore. The band is browned and the edges of the *moninag* feathers have frayed. The fit is loose, but with constant adjustment, it stays on.

Upon the stand beside him sits the idol of Okius. Warriors rally around it before taking position for the fight.

The enemy moves into the field. It is an impressive show of *osawas* chests and colorful shields; of drums and flutes and flags; of *pakusak* and long pikes. They are only sixty in number. But with such weapons, they can fight as if they were many more. The Pamunkey have *pakusak* of their own, with a few extra flasks of black powder. Opichapan commands, "Take the *pakusak* out first! Shield the arches! Get close and let fly your arrows!"

Eight separate groups move forward. They move toward the English from different angles, converging as they near their foe. The English dig into the ground, throwing up low mounds of dirt to hide behind.

Pakusak roar. The English do not run. Arrows bounce off their shields. The Powhatan archers step closer to increase the force of their impact. As they come near enough, the English fire back. Lines are shattered. A few stand their ground, unsure whether to rush forward or run back.

POWHATAN:
THE STORY OF A PEOPLE

The heat of the day is multiplied by the fighting. Exhausted warriors continue to attack the defenses. Heroes gather their followers. Back and forth they go. They leapfrog toward the opposing battle line. They release their arrows. They crawl backwards. They advance again. The English send out their men with the pikes to scatter every advance.

The English bring larger *pakusak* from their vessel and position them along their battle line. All hope of getting close to the enemy is lost. The tattered Powhatan ranks withdraw out of range.

The sun sets. The humid night finally grows cool enough for sleep. A morning haze finds the English have not left. Both sides continue the battle in a defensive stance.

Opichapan takes his place atop the carrier. He smears an ointment across his limbs. It soon causes extra sweating to free his sluggish body from excess water. It is a common mixture of *amonsokwat* grease and charcoal powder from swamp plumb. Reports of the fighting are few today. Both sides appear to be waiting for the other to do something.

A messenger runs up. "They are in the *poketawas* fields! They have hacked down much of it already!"

"What is this?" Opichapan tries to understand.

The messenger continues, "There are twenty of them in our fields. They must have snuck away from the main force during the night."

Opichapan sways about on his platform. "Well, get them out! Someone go and get them out!"

The crops lie off to the side of the battlefield. The English are closer to them then the Powhatan. Each time the warriors move toward the fields, the large *pakusak* scare them back. It is suicidal to fight like this. Life is too important to waist it this way. A group of warriors swing around a grove of trees to reach the far side of the *poketawas* fields. As they make their way through the stocks, the English set them aflame. The wall of fire spreads, chasing the warriors out.

Opichapan watches helplessly. He cannot do a thing about it. He cries out, "How can we be defeated? How can the Pamunkey see this and do nothing? Even we are helpless. We have lost. We are surely lost!"

Chapter 27

The vessel has weathered a long journey. She makes her way up the main river. With growing fondness, Sir William Berkeley takes in the quiet scenery. He observes the variety of lush vegetation. He spots the earth and rock of the southern cliffs and the gentle rise of the northern bank.

The new governor is thirty seven. He is old enough to enjoy respect, but young enough to retain a youthful gaze of the world around him. He possesses a comfort of presence along with the quiet unease of expectant aging. His visage is handsome, with a dignified stance. Under heavy brows are dark eyes that can dazzle any lady and can put any gentleman at ease. He is definitely one of polished arrogance. In all, he is the form of impregnable grace and the aura of unmatched intelligence.

The vessel passes the eastern end of the river island. Through the trees, William can see hints of crop fields bathed in sunshine. Coming around the island, he spots activity among the cleared areas near the shoreline. He sees a little child, then two. Women carry ceramic containers along a small rustic street that parallels the river. A small crowd of merchants and patrons intermingle on the market grounds.

A mariner quietly disturbs him, "There she be, gov'na Barkley. That there is your James City."

The place is well-used. There is an array of clapboard structures the Virginians are known to build. Property lines are established with shallow ditches and worm fences. Brick chimneys tower against gabled ends with wisps of smoke rising peacefully into the clean sky. Steep roofs are covered with shingles, tiles, or slates, according to the owner's personal wealth and ability. Some of the better sort have dormers. Even here in this wilderness colony, the levels of class are discernable. It is a social phenomenon that exists in any group of animals or humans.

POWHATAN:
THE STORY OF A PEOPLE

Beyond the old tar swamp is another row of houses aligning the north bank of the mainland. To the west are the ruins of the old glass foundry that has twice failed. Even the Italians that were brought over could not revive the business.

There are orchards and pastures dotting the whole area. Both genders and all ages toil about. People gather around the well and in front of the shops for commerce and conversation. Such activity is so droll in its constant repetition. William can see that this is a well-settled area, not unlike some English villages that have witnessed the monotony of simple existence for ages. It is the kind of place where generations change just a bit to show progression, but not enough to break from the quietude of life that is slow and delightfully boring. Here, one can daydream with comfort and sleep in peace.

The longboat maneuvers the vessel to pier-side. The port is neither solidly built nor kept in good care. Barrels full of pressed tobacco and packed commodities clutter the place. A new statute forces everyone in the colony to send their products through James City, reestablishing it as the most important place in Virginia.

William notices two faces in the crowd that are much darker then any of the others. Anthony Johnson, from Akomak, stands in the crowd with his wife, Mary. He arrived two decades ago where he was sold into a couple years of indenture. He worked off his freedom and quickly began amassing his own property. But he has not yet reached his goal of establishing a plantation of his own and settling it with people like himself. And so, he bides his time well and holds tight to his dreams. Opportunities in this new world is unending. Everyone has the wide eyes of expectation. It almost frightens Sir Berkeley. There are over eight thousand spirited people to govern. With civil unrest boiling in England, many more will soon be on the way.

Governor Berkeley greets his subjects. Edward Hill stands with John West. William Claiborne and Abraham Wood are also present. They are part of the new elite in the colony. Their stories have just begun in this land.

William follows his hosts through the earthen redoubt where the fort used to stand. He gives a brief inspection of the ordinance and of the militia who assemble in parade formation.

Governor Berkeley is escorted into the church for a formal welcoming ceremony. It is a rectangular structure of brick with a gable roof between decorative parapet ends. Along each length are three leaded casements amid plain buttresses. The west entrance is modest. There is no bell tower as yet, but plans are spoken of. This church stands on the same ground where the last two were located. It is the same place where the first General Assembly convened, where John Rolfe married his Powhatan wife, and where victims of the Starving Time were buried. It is hoped that the current church will outlast its usefulness so that no more will have to be built. So quickly does a structure of wood decay in this humid climate.

The welcoming party swells as word of the new governor's arrival spreads through the city. The surveyor, William Claiborne, shows off his town plan. He leads them through the old quarter and heads eastward to the dozen buildings of the new town. There are three lanes that connect the main street with the back street. They reach the farthest end between the two streets where the city's only brick house stands. It was first the home of old Governor Wyatt. He recently sold it to be remodeled into the state house. It is a large rectangle, comprising of two stories atop a raised basement. The facade is along the main street. Like a shy child, a duplicate house in miniature is fused behind the larger. Each has its own roof. In England, such a place would be considered a middling family residence. But in Virginia, this is the grandest house in the land.

William examines the collection of people arrayed before him. There are a few black faces among the white ones. There is even a sprinkling of tawny faces in the mass. Male and female, large and small; the variety is considerable. Very few are wrinkled, but most show the ravages of the pox that has become an expected ailment for those newly-arrived.

On the mainland, just north of James City, is Sir Berkeley's new plantation. His workers have recently moved in to work the land that lies along a peaceful green spring.

William inspects the site where his country mansion will stand. The foundation is complete. The walls take shape with each course of brick the masons lay. It promises to be the first jewel of domestic architecture in the colony. It is certain to be better then staying on that filthy little island. William does not have the heart to relocate the capital, even though that is what London has called for. The locals love the place too much. He has thus removed only himself.

Thomas Rolfe stands with the governor. He has been in the colony for seven years and has establishing himself well with his English countrymen. Tensions have lessened between the two cultures. He yearns to see his granduncle that still lives and be with the aunt who was once his second mother long ago. He can not recall her name. But she looked like the famous Egyptian queen of old. At least that is the image he uses to remember her.

POWHATAN:
THE STORY OF A PEOPLE

There is a lull in the conversation. William breaks the silence, "And you are well settled with your father, his widow and family?"

Thomas affirms, "Aye, sir. She did speak much of father's final years here, whilst I was raised in England."

Sir William considers a new subject, "What chance have you in reaching the savage relatives with life intact? Rarely do we seek them out these days. And only for to beg do they come 'round us."

Thomas answers, "Aye, sir. They oft come to me for employ. By them I did learn that my mother, her family desires me to visit. It is with their help do I plan to reach my maternal relatives. It may be my last opportunity."

The governor ponders, "I would not wish to deprive any of their blood. Might you also carry to him official introduction? Your grand uncle does at present speak for the natives. If we shall ever keep the peace, I need to establish communication with him."

Thomas assures, "I am at your pleasure, sir."

Sir William concludes, "Then go. Find Cleopatra. You may yet rediscover your mother through her."

And so, young Thomas Rolfe makes for the wilderness. With guides and gifts, he seeks out his other family. The visit is a private affair and can not be mentioned. But one can get an idea of how it shall go by thinking of visits with relatives; of travels to a grandmother's house or the residence of a distant cousin; of all the informal gatherings with those who share one's familial heritage. It will be as those.

Although it is quiet at Utamusak, the atmosphere is not peaceful. The heart of Tsenakomako beats in a cadence of distress. Opechankano walks alone on the sand-covered path toward the main temple. He caresses the sacred stone on the *pokowanz*. His fingers are knotted from extreme age with calluses that can no longer heal.

The priests go about their daily responsibilities. Their movements are methodical. Their expressions are vacant. Their minds are far away from the present.

One of the priests welcomes Opechankano into the great hall through the main entrance at the east end. The eternal flame claps in the hollow interior. Black effigies of his fathers from countless generations stare down the long hall toward the ossuary. It is a long walk for a man with ancient legs, but it is where Opechankano must go.

At the eternal flame, he descends to the floor and rests. "None of you are here. I can't feel any of you." The effigies remain silent. Opechankano struggles to rise. He shuffles toward the mat partition at the end of the hall. He can not find the opening. Rolling up the mat is too tedious. Instead, he rips it down. Light falls upon the mummies within. All are facing west toward the afterworld.

Opechankano searches the racks. The oldest remains are distinguished by the extent of wear and discoloration of the mats that bind them. He recognizes the body of his great grand uncle. He remembers the stories of the man's life that his father told him. All the achievements and heroics live again, if only for a fleeting moment in a solitary mind. On the rack immediately to his right is another whose stories have always guided his own life decisions.

Opechankano tries to retrace the line of decent with the help of the symbols painted on the burial wraps. One catches his attention. "There you are, my brother." Opechankano leans over the burial wrap. After a cautious glance toward the great hall, he pulls out a ceremonial knife from under his *machkow*. He cuts through the mat covering and the wrap of *wushakwun* skin. "Yes. Still with that unreachable look on your face. Death hasn't changed you a bit."

Weak hands grasp the rack for support as he kneels down. Leaning close to the head of the mummy, "If you could've seen how we lashed out at the Wind Children…But that was twenty years ago. They've grown strong, but we haven't. We just hide."

He turns his gaze into space. "I remember when I could walk the land and find people everywhere. Now, I look and I look, and I find only a handful, far apart from each other."

His gaze returns to the mummy. "I have failed you. I was faithful to what I am. And still, I failed. How could this happen? Where did I go wrong? Guide me, brother. Guide me! Tsenakomako flourished when you lived. It has withered away since you left us. I will follow you, still. You must lead me, somehow. I can't do this alone any more. Speak to me! Please tell me what to do. We could have rivaled the Masawomik. Now, I doubt I could gather a thousand warriors to defend us."

Opechankano leans closer. He tries to expel tears, but neither the low wailing nor the jerking motion of the shoulders produces any. "Brother, I'm used up."

Thoughts stream through the mind. "I've been threatened. I've been manhandled. I've been abandoned…even poisoned. But I'm still here. Why? Why am I the one left with all this?

POWHATAN:
THE STORY OF A PEOPLE

"They're everywhere. The land east of the Chikahominy River is swarming with them. They've spread onto the south side of the Powhatan River and to the eastern shores of the great bay. They've even begun to wander into the middle peninsula where they promised they wouldn't."

Opechankano rests against the scaffolding. "They've never wanted to live with us. Now, we can't even live with them. If we had the rivers back, we wouldn't have to depend on them so much. We could live strong, as we always did. Our boys don't hunt for their own families any more. They'd rather fill the strangers' bellies and hoard any riches they gain for themselves. We've grown helpless and hungry. We're strangers in our own world; dependents of people who refuse to acknowledge us. We are Powhatan! Oh, brother, what has happened to us?

"I was always there for you. I knew your dreams best. Opichapan didn't understand what you left him. But I did. I fought him at every turn when he strayed from your vision. Kekwatog never showed any interest. He distanced himself from us all. Our sisters...they understood. They were on my side. Everyone was on my side because they knew I was following your will."

More thoughts resurface. "Patience was your greatest power. But I am too old to wait. We grow weaker every day. We must do something soon, or we'll loose our chance to do anything at all. I am a defender of the people. I've always been that. I can only lead them as such. The people want me to lead them. They have no one else. They yearn for a hero. They yearn for you. Return to us. You can return to us, through me. I'll always follow you. Guide me. Guide me now."

Opechankano stares at the remains, searching for a sign or some fragment of wisdom to materialize. He waits. He waits. He turns away. "All this comes from that prophecy. Our people want to strike at their *maskapow*. But how can we when it will only continue the prophecy? They don't know what they ask. But there's no other choice. It has to be done. But how? How, brother? How can I fight a prophecy?

"The Chesapeak...it wasn't them. The Wind Children are those from the East. Oh, how could we have been so wrong?

"They've been nothing but a disease among us. We must deal with them or we'll never be cured of our sickness. You sent me to rub out the Chesapeak. I think I remember. We'll do it that way. Even if we fail, the strangers will have to notice us again. Maybe we will be important, again."

Chapter 28

It is a small collection of men. All are heavily styled with rich *pokun* and beaded garb. The procession is ringed with more men who are armed with either a bow or a *pakusak*. There is a seer in the lead. He guides those who carry the litter. Two healers follow at the rear. Surrounding the litter is an assortment of chief strategists who straighten their *kawasow* or adjust their necklaces of *matasun* and pearls. Messengers rush to and from them, reciting reports and memorizing commands. Sitting cross-legged atop the litter is Opechankano. There is a bright saffron glimmer from where the sun hits a *matasun* plate fitting the right side of his skull. A long lock of hair on the left side gently hangs down to tickle his right toes. These wiry strands are a dull white. The lost color is reproduced with an array of dangling black feathers. Black skin oil covers his body, except for the chest and thighs which are coated with a white paste. The pendant that hangs at his chest is an oblong *tsekoma* with an impression of a human face etched into its surface. Suspended from his slouching neck is a thin strand of *wikiyopis* that runs out of one nose hole and into the other to hold the pendant straight. The entire necklace is strung with tiny beads of *tsekoma* and *matasun*.

Four members of his personal guard carry Opechankano into a meadow. It is a location along the spine of the Lower Peninsula, east of the Chikahominy River. The view from here stretches far and wide. The immensity of the sky can be seen all around. The rain has stopped. The air is warm. Every bud is coming into bloom. But Opechankano can not see any of this. He no longer has the strength to raise his own eyelids.

The litter is brought to a knoll near the middle of the clearing. The four attendants set their load down as softly as possible. All the same, there is a heavy thud upon touchdown. The two healers come up to stand on either side. Everyone begins to discuss the billows of smoke that rise above the trees in the distance. They debate over the name of the settlement that is freshly aflame.

A runner comes into view. "We are fully engaged at James City! Every house along the north bank that faces the island is on fire!"

Opechankano twists about. "Let me see. Someone help me. What is happening?"

The healer on his right climbs upon the litter and crouches down from behind. Slowly, he spreads his fingers that rest on the eyelids. Sunlight floods the irises. Opechankano tries to focus. Everything is a bright green, a bright blue, a bright brown. Even the distant smoke seems a violet instead of a deep grey. Thick streams rise to a dark worm cloud hovering above the horizon.

The eyes loose their moisture. "*Taws,*" Opechankano motions. He returns to the darkness within himself.

Another runner arrives from the Southern Peninsula. Opechankano listens to the account, picturing what is hears with the mind's eye. The Nansemund have attacked everywhere east of the old hog island. The Weyanok and the Apamatuk have struck everything west of there, all the way to the rapids of the *pakwachonk*.

A third runner comes up. More internal images form. The Matapaniyund have rushed through the small settlements of the Middle Peninsula with ease. Only a few trespassers have settled there.

Reports from the fight along the Lower Peninsula are no different. With the Powhatan supporting them, the Chikahominy have attacked every settlement lying west of their river. To the east, the Pamunkey have moved all the way to old Kekotan. The Chiskiyak have supported them. Everywhere, the grim tide has pushed to the banks of the Powhatan and Pamunkey rivers. And yet, as waves break upon solid beaches, the grand assault dissolves on the shoreline of resistance. No one has admitted it, but Opechankano can sense that his intent will end unfulfilled of its objective.

The seer spits, "After today, we shall be rid of more than five hundred of those people."

Opechankano shakes his head. "Then we have failed. That is not nearly enough. This should have been the last day for all of them. You should now count the days we have left. Take me home. I am tired of this."

Seven forms move about the sacred grounds of Utamusak. A sound like crisp rain echoes within one of the secondary temples. The head priest exits through the front as thick bands of orange light curl out from the smoke holes. It is not long until the body of the structure if fully wrapped in the fire.

The English have lashed back hard. Foot soldiers first marched into the heart of Chikahominy and burned Mamanahunt to ashes. Then, they wiped Menapukunt from the earth. The Pamunkey are on the move upriver to a swamp-encircled island near the mouth of Mankwin Creek. The holy men must join this bitter exodus.

The head priest checks with his subordinate inside the next temple. Together, they finish preparing the structure to be ignited. Once the flame secures momentum, the two men go to help yet another of their members in the third temple. Before entering, they stop for a moment to watch the last of Opechankano's personal guard carry away the material wealth of Tsenakomako.

Everyone is relocating. The Matapaniyund have fled far up their river. The Chiskiyak have joined them. The Chikahominy have gone to hide in the swamps beyond Owapax with the Powhatan. Even the Apamatuk and the Nansemund have withdrawn deep into their lands.

The Weyanok have forsaken their old allies completely. They have fled south, past the Yapiya River. This did not sit well with Opechankano. He sent eighty Pamunkey warriors to bring the tribe back into the fold. He lost all eighty of them.

A few words in the language of the ancients are shared between the three priests before they fuel the flame. They walk up the sand-covered path to the main temple. One lifts the sacred crystal from the *pokowanz*.

Four statues quietly hold their position at each corner of the empty structure. The head priest knows that the statues will soon be empty as well. That is why he feels an apprehension emanating from them now. The three join their partners inside. All of the effigies of past leaders and hanging spirit vessels have been removed. They lie under dirt and brush in a hidden gully.

There are too many bark tablets to carry away. It has been decided to use them to kindle the perpetual flame. The seven form a ring around the pit. They pepper the flames with herbs as a final song flows from their lips. The head priest takes a piece of burning kindling and transfers the flame to a torch. The fire grows. Pictograms wash away as each strip of bark curls and blackens.

Six of the priests move to the landing where three long *akwintan* await. Each is full with the great skins that hold the annual counts. Bundled inside them are the mummies of the ancestors. The priests pair up and climb into each vessel for the long journey. The head priest does not go with them.

POWHATAN:
THE STORY OF A PEOPLE

Instead, he places the *pokowanz* crystal in a small *akwintan* and secures the torch at the front. Once he is across the river, the old man pulls his load over his back and grabs the light firm before he starts down the darkening path toward the *pakwachonk*.

Upon the next day, the old mystic arrives at the site of Powhatan Town. There is not much left of it anymore. A few upright posts stand in the ground. A few pieces of pottery and a few fragments of mats lay in the undergrowth. He descends the hill. The riverside trail leads him into the deep chasm of Shako Creek. From here, it is just a little farther to go along a foot path that runs beside the gurgling water.

He stops at a large rock. It is a stone like any other cluttering the creek bed. But this one is different because of what is imprinted into its surface. He knows them to be the vary foot prints of Okius. There is a story about this, but the traveler is weary and cannot recall it now. It is enough to exhale a few stanzas of homage. And so, this legend will stay hidden within the silent recesses of his mind. Slowly, the torch is lowered into the water.

The old priest stumbles through the area. Once he finds the right spot, he carefully gives the *pokowanz* crystal back to the Mother.

The young governor can be found at a writing table in a cozy little chamber of the State House. The afternoon sun flows through a casement window, providing ample light by which to work on his literary project. Thoughts race haphazardly through William Berkeley's mind as he meditates on the fresh page. What he writes will be a significant proclamation. How he crafts this document is of utmost importance.

A slender bird appears on the window sill outside. Its general color is tawny-grey, with white patches on dark wings. After pecking at the glass harshly, the bird beats its chest against the window three times before calming down. William notices the little creature through the distorting glass.

William leans toward the window pane. "Tis a most blissful morn. That wretched beast hath been snared. Even now doth he sit under guard…me blind, feeble captive."

Opechankano is the one who sits in the Gael downtown. Some of the more privileged are allowed entrance into the confines so that they may gawk at the one who for so many years caused them so much grief.

"He doth complain of this," William croons. "He said I would have been served with utmost respect and honor if, by chance, I would have found myself his prisoner. I should expect to be so loved with humane charity."

The young governor ponders, "What example of instruction to his subjects might be demonstrated with his imprisonment?"

Last year's campaigns against the Nansemund and the Apamatuk were successful. Neither tribe has any fight left in them. But the cost has been too much. No financial or military aid can be expected from England. The last reports do not fair well for poor King Charles. His realm is falling apart, and allies have disappeared with the changing of the winds.

Governor Berkeley fairs much better in defending his domain. Tsenakomako no longer exists. The western island in the bay is now full of Powhatan men captured from the fighting. Others have been sold into servitude and sent far away. A defensive palisade stretches across the western boundary of the Lower Peninsula and a quartet of forts are strategically placed in the frontier. The most northern outpost stands in a horseshoe bend of the upper Yugtamund River. It is called Fort Royal. Capt. Roger Marshall commands the garrison there. Fort James is located just west of the old Chikahominy borough of Moysonek. In charge is Lt. Thomas Rolfe. Capt. Thomas Harris and his garrison are stationed at Fort Charles which stands high atop a hill overlooking the western bluffs of the Shako Creek Valley. And, of course, Capt. Abraham Wood commands his unit at Fort Henry beside the falls of the Apamatuk River. Neither the Chinese nor the Romans could have constructed a better defense.

The bird whistles a praising tune. Images form on the blank page lying on the writing table. "It took much to find the savage king, his camp. Through the winter, the poor naturals do make themselves vulnerable, as they separate onto private lands in the smallest of numbers and at great distance from one another. Tis their number but few in all.

"I did commission sixty volunteers, five with horse, as I. The horse did put such great terror in their hearts.

"Truly, I was to negotiate a peace. But when the old man showed resistance, there was but one course left me.

"Twas a removal in great haste, back to James City with him. Now is the poor wretch under lock and key, the changing of the guard be the single difference in his day."

William glances at the clock. "The coming of a new guard should be presently. He is lost to his people. He is their inspiration, their link to all that was…their single hope for its return. He must be sent from this land so that those devoted to his treachery shall be firmly broken of spirit. I must secure his delivery to England. It is the best conclusion."

POWHATAN:
THE STORY OF A PEOPLE

The bird hops twice, repositioning itself to face the window. Its little head jerks upward to get a better view of the moving mouth inside.

William focuses on his dilemma, "A dead prize will do His Majesty no good. Who can I entrust with this most difficult task? What vessel is right for a smooth voyage for one in such wretched physical condition?"

The bird's visual attention sets on something outside, but it keeps its ear turned toward the glass. William is still unable to reach for his quill. "Planning, there is the key…and simplification. All complexity must be cleared. I must think clearly. What testament is to be made? The subject would be myself. The object would be the prisoner. Therefore, the custody of said prisoner is the topic. Although…Nay. His capture is not the end. An ending is but an introduction to another beginning. Oh, I do go on so."

Once more, William leans toward the window. He waves his finger at his little muse. "Me dear fellow, this should be but a simple thing. Are you not…"

A strange echo comes up the street. William stills himself. The bird turns its back to the window. Words resonate against the glass, "It can not be."

The bird rotates its little head back toward the one within. It flexes its wings only once before jumping from the window sill. William watches helplessly as the form disappears.

Sir Berkeley rises from his chair and walks without emotion from the building. The light of day hits him, jolting every nerve. He steps onto the main street. People begin to stir. All heads turn westward toward the old quarter where the Gael stands.

The governor makes his way downtown. Spectators grow in number to witness the one-man parade. Agony builds with every step. Steps quicken. William pushes people aside to make his way through the entrance.

Sir Berkeley notices the worried look on the Gaelkeeper's face. In the cell are two other men. One holds the guard who wears a grin of blissful satisfaction. There, in the cage, is the slumped body that was once Opechankano. His eyes have opened on their own from the shock that befell him.

The murderer cackles. It was a simple act of walking up to the cage, pointing the barrel at the back, and pulling the trigger. After two years, his family can finally seek rest in the afterworld.

Governor Berkeley sighs heavily. Every measurable portion of stress condensates in the chilled air. Just like that, all the future problems are settled. All that the old man had lived through has ended in a fleeting instant. So swiftly has the link been severed. It is such an abrupt end to everything.

His clothes are usual for his high rank. And yet, somehow, his appearance is simply grey. The luster of yesterday has been washed away with forgetfulness. His eyes are greyer still. Life has apparently retired deep into the body.

Nekotowanz is left to speak for his people. All four brothers are dead and both sisters have past. And so, the eldest son of the eldest sister now leads the dieing people.

The peacemakers move to the assemblage in the field. Their strides are slow. Anguish increases with every step toward the lackluster stage set before them. The young governor gives a salutation that the Indigenies recognize. He even interlocks index fingers with the tired speaker. Bright flags hang on their poles. Matchlocks rest on the arms—their fuses are not lit. This ceremony is a simple matter of protocol; a meager event within the events to which it is strung.

The English have their talking leaves to mark on. It helps them to tangibly allow one people to lose gracefully and the other to justly accept the spoils of their win. Nekotowanz carries his thoughts within him. He will free them orally so that the words will be forever in the air. That is his way to reach the same conclusion. The English will be polite during the monologue. But they will not be able to understand the meaning of the man's words as no interpreter is present. It is the one thing forgotten during the planning of these proceedings.

His words still mingle in the winds of time. Fragmented. Perhaps in parts. Parts mixed together and apart. But still, the speech can be heard in a form that still holds the meaning of its creation. Listen carefully. Draw your attention to the breeze around you. It will come. The oration will be something along these lines:

"We flourished before your interruption. Wahunsenakok was loved by the *manitow*. His boon was prosperity for all who followed him. He was our heart that beat strong through all the difficult and the gentle times. We were the stronger in the face of our neighbors for we were not set in our ways. We dominated those around us for they were stale. We embraced change. We embraced the future. Now, we do nothing but sift through our lost past. We stopped on the path forward. For that, the spirits have grown tired of us. Our ancestors are ashamed of their children who have held on to old dreams and have not awoken to create new ones.

"Our two cultures must bond. But the bliss of that marriage must be strong. We must work equally to see it succeed. When one side grows too strong, the other becomes weak and sickly. And it perishes. That is how her marriage was. Our hopes died with her.

"Think of your children. They will not worship your memory. I can die secure in knowing my memory will be cherished by those not yet born. The same love I have for the Mother will spread to them. We have always lived in the Mother's care. You ignore her. We have always lived according to what the natural world demands. You try to shut everything out. Do not be so foolish. The *wushakwun* have been run off. The planted fields have been rendered barren. But none of this matters. The land is all. I fear not for the earth I stand upon. You can only harm the surface. Time will heal all, including we who live on this land. I can wait for that moment. We will flourish again. In which generation will we return, I know not. But we will continue in our children.

"I will mark your paper so that you feel my honesty is genuine. But what will you do? Yes, I will agree to be your king's subject. And when it is time, you may tell us who we will have as our *weyowanz*. Be confident. We will never miss an annual payment of twenty *pokiyu*. When you see the leaves drop, look for us. We will come. But be sincere in your promise to protect us. Be there to shelter us with just as much commitment.

"Yes, we will stay away from your settlements. The lower peninsula, from the falls of the rivers you call York and James, all the way to its eastern tip will forever be yours. And all that lies east of the Yapiya River and Machimko will be free from our trespass. We will also allow you to settle along the southern shore of the middle peninsula, eastward from where the York River forks, as long as you let us know of your coming. Whatever you do outside of these bounds, you will have to negotiate with the tribes of the Upper Peninsula and the Eastern Shore. I can no longer speak for them.

"Kill any you wish who do not abide to these boundaries. You may have those children of ours who are not yet twelve and wish to stay with you. That is an expectation of conquerors that is well understood by us. We will bring in all of your people, white and black, that we now hold.

"If unfortunate circumstances bring any or yours to our lands, they will not be harmed. Cut the trees you need from our land. Collect your stray animals in assured safety. We will be a part of you. And we will stay apart from you.

"We will also commune with you under the rules you lay out. Be sure your forts have enough silver pendants and striped mantles to wear. We will come often with warm desires to talk and trade with you in your new dominion. Assure our safety in your land. We will forever make the north side of your Fort Royal our gateway for communication and trade with you. Fort Henry will be our southern entrance to your world. All this is promised. We will always keep our promise as long as we exist.

"A pearl forms in the darkness, forgotten in the depths of a *kaway* bed. Its uniqueness disappears in the masses. But our pearl is unique. It is special. It deserves a chance to sparkle in an open eye. Do not forget we are here. We now wait for the one to open the shell and allow us to live again under the sun's warming light. Patience will drive this desire. It must! How else can Truth rein? Hope is what will shape our desire. We will be submissive. We will be patient. We will wait. Do not forget us! Do not…forget."

And now, this speech, this world, this dream has come to

THE END

VOCABULARY

ahakan	home; a house
akwintan	canoe
amonsokwat	bear
apetapon	fry bread
apon	corn bread
aposum	opossum
ashowut	cardinal bird
asiminz	walnut
askutaskwash	squash [Narragansett]
asunomink	walnut tree
awakun	raccoon
ayosapanik	flying squirrel
cham	chum
chikikwaminz	chinquapin nut
hwow	wow; amen
kask	ten
Katapewuk	Cool Spring
kawasow	feather cloak
kaway	oyster
kawkawas	caucus member
kekata	nine
kekwiyos	boat
ketasku	snake
Kohatayo	Warm Spring
komoting	six
koyakwus	seagull
kunsenakwus	stone hatchet
kupotun	sturgeon
machkow	buckskin tunic
machkwon	silver ore

makak	pumpkin
manitow	a god
masanek	squirrel
maskapow	bitter enemy
matahay	apron
matasun	copper
misikwatash	succotash [Narragansett]
mokasin	shoe
monahak	wooden sword
monahamsha	piping plover
monawateyug	shad fish [Narragansett]
moninag	turkey
mowakus	purple martin
mowok	cedar tree
muz	moose
musawusuk	ship
muskeskiminz	strawberry
muskiminz	mulberry
nantam	wolf
nekut	one
Nepino	Summer
nesakan	fishing weir
netshetsun	soul
ning	two
nus	three
nuswasto	eight
opominz	chestnut
osawas	any robust metal
pakohikowo	hickory
pakusak	gun
pakwachonk	fall line
patawok	porpoise
pawan	five
pawkawn	pecan
pekatas	bean
peak	thick-shell money
picheminz	persimmon
pikuw	gum of the Virginia Maple

POWHATAN:
THE STORY OF A PEOPLE

pitukwu	tuckahoe
poketawas	corn
pokiyu	beaver
pokowanz	alter; mineral stone
pokun	an herbal dye
Popano	Winter
powamink	oak tree
takahowapon	tuckahoe root bread
Takwitok	Autumn
tatamoho	garfish
taws	no more; enough
tomahak	metal hatchet
topawos	seven
tsekoma	mussel
tukupewuk	sea turtle
tutaskuk	crab
tuwupen	turtle
tsehaho	flax
upook	tobacco
utakaway	panther
weyowanskwa	female chieftain
weyowanz	male chieftain
wikiyopis	hemp
wikutis	rabbit
winak	sassafras root
wingapow	good friend
wisokan	an herbal drug
wokohomin	hominy
wopusok	swan
wowanok	thin-shell money
wushakwun	deer
yog	four

Printed in the United States
55879LVS00004B/82-120